FROM **DEATH** TO **VALHALLA**

The Last Einherjar *Book One*

Odin is an asshole.

FROM DEATH TO VALHALLA

The Last Einherjar *Book One*

RANDALL P. FITZGERALD

ISBN-10: 1543284604
ISBN-13: 978-1543284607

First Edition: February 2017
10 9 8 7 6 5 4 3 2 1

To My Inability To Take Dedications Seriously

CHAPTER ONE

"**R**ISE." ERIK GROANED IN HIS BED, ROLLING OVER AND doing his best to ignore what was an unnecessarily loud and strangely accented voice. A deep thud sounded on the floor and the voice boomed again, louder than before.

"Haki Erik Styrsson! Rise! You are chosen!"

He rolled his head around without opening his eyes. No way he was getting back to sleep now.

"Look, I don't know if—"

He opened his eyes and saw a tall, muscular blonde woman standing at the end of his bed dressed in gold-trimmed leather from head to toe and holding what looked like a spear. She looked to be in her mid-twenties at the most

1

and stared at him wordlessly with ice-blue eyes.

Unable to contain an annoyed sigh, he rolled to the edge of the bed and put his feet on the ground. He eyed the clock and saw it was nearly two in the afternoon. Ignoring the massive girl at the end of his bed, he called out through the apartment.

"Guys, this is hilarious, okay? Very elaborate." There was no answer. He put his head in his hands. "Great, so they just left her..." He turned to the girl. "Look, this is really funny, honestly. I've got Icelandic parents, you're in valkyrie dress-up. I get it. So, I mean, I don't know if they paid you or what but you can go home." He stood up from the bed, suddenly aware that he was wearing only underwear in front of a strange girl. "Right. Right. Sorry, just, uh, don't look below my waist for a few minutes."

She looked immediately.

"I said... I'm sorry. Jesus. This doesn't count as... I mean you aren't why it..." He gave up trying to muster a defense. "Probably shouldn't have drawn attention to it. I'm going to take a shower. Don't worry about locking the door on the way out."

The bathroom was an awkward, careful walk across the room but he was happy to have the privacy. The door was locked and he turned on the shower. It heated up quickly enough but he hadn't heard the front door open and shut when he got in. He normally could. Maybe she was waiting in the living room for Derek or Chris to get home and pay her. It wasn't the first time they'd done this sort of thing. It was a subtle one, by comparison. Not that he was free of guilt. He'd hired a clown to run into Derek's room at three in the morning once with a chainsaw. Fair enough response for giving up the embarrassing knowledge that a 24-year-old is scared of clowns. The clown had taken a kick to the gut and that had been when they'd put a moratorium on that specific brand of friendly torture. This one was new by Erik's estimation though. It wasn't frightening or particularly strange. No zombies at the table for breakfast, no fake burglary.

He turned the shower off after a halfhearted once-over with soap and pulled the curtain aside.

"Fuck!"

He nearly lost his footing, barely slapping a hand against the plastic wall of the shower. The girl was standing right in front of the curtain, eyes fixed on him. He reached out and whipped his towel off the rack.

"Jesus fucking Christ, how much are they paying you? This hasn't turned into some weird... you know, thing? Right?" He stared at her waiting but she said nothing. "How did you even get in here? I locked the door. Did you..."

He looked past her and saw that the door knob had been broken. It was dented, even. How had he not heard her hammering on it? Looking at her, she was definitely capable of the feat.

"You can't just... you know, I have to pay for that out of my security deposit. Do you rent? It's not just my door. I don't own the door." Nothing. He sighed, trying to keep his anger in check. "Can you move at least? I'd love to get dressed and go ask whichever one of my asshole roommates set this up what the magic word to get rid of you is."

She backed away, indicating that she at least understood more English than whatever she'd said when he was still barely awake.

He pushed past her into the bedroom and walked to his dresser. The girl followed him, keeping only a few feet between them at any given time. He sighed again, the edges of his patience really starting to fray.

"You're going to see my dick, okay? Is that part of the job? Look at my dick?" Her silence annoyed him all the more, so he dropped his towel. "There you go!" This was definitely a crime. "Happy?"

She didn't bother looking down, which somehow dinged his pride. The wounded ego was enough to trigger a sane thought about exactly what it was he was doing. Time to get dressed. Quickly. He kept shooting looks her way and at no point did she stop staring at him. It was, frankly, starting to get a bit weird and the thought entered his mind that this was just some crazy arts and crafts woman who'd escaped a house full of cats. When he was dressed, he decided that her lack of response wasn't something he could live with.

He turned to her, looking as stern as he could manage. "Who are you, and why are you here? What's your name?"

"I am Göll. You are one of Odin's chosen and I will guide you to Valhalla."

Erik rubbed his temples and shook his head. "Great. So we'll go see Chris then. Is that okay?"

She said nothing.

Erik walked around her and went to the living room. Really, it was one big room with the kitchen at the far end containing the door out of the apartment. They kept their shoes there to at least pretend they weren't slobs. He put his shoes on and opened the door, holding it open as Göll stood on the other side watching.

"Well?"

She walked out and stood beside him in the hallway while he closed and locked the door. There was no one to see them until they came out into the main parking area. A few people from the complex were there. They stared, pointing and laughing. It wasn't so much embarrassing for him, but he wondered how Göll felt about it. Clearly she owned the armor, so presumably she'd worn it in public before.

As soon as they were outside, Göll paid much more attention to their surroundings, watching the sky and the paths ahead of and behind them.

They'd covered half a block when Erik got tired of the awkward silence. "So, how did they find you? Your accent is sort of Icelandic sounding. My parents were from there. I spent summers there."

More silence.

"We can talk, right? The whole joke is over now." He paused, but she showed no sign that she was going to talk. "No? I'm not hitting on you or whatever. I just... small talk? What do you do?"

She looked at him with a serious expression. "I have come to guide you to Valhalla."

"Right, stupid question. Þar sem þú ert valkyrja."

His Icelandic was terrible and rusty, but he thought it would at least trick her into speaking or giving *some* reaction. A failed plan. She only looked around the sky and again to the sidewalk ahead of them.

The failure was enough to convince him to stop bothering with any attempt to make friendly chatter and so they walked on toward the burger place. Mercifully, there weren't a lot of people on the street, though there must have been two dozen pictures taken of the pair of them by people in cars and standing at crosswalks. A few asked for permission to take pictures. Göll ignored them and to keep things from getting weird, Erik said it was fine and that she was in character, explaining the gag to a particularly curious set of girls at a stop light that seemed to last a month.

They made the last turn and Bosko's Burgers was only a half block away. It was owned by this excitable Polish couple who were never there. Chris worked the place alone most days. Really, he ran the entire operation at this point with only a pair of high school aged kids for the busy times.

As soon as Erik walked in the door, Chris came walking out of the back of the empty restaurant, laughing and clapping.

"Oh, this is fucking fantastic, man." He walked over to Erik and Göll, looking her over. "You finally lose it? How much are you paying her? This is a fetish, right? You're the viking warrior and she's come to send you to heaven? I dig it." Chris slapped a hand onto Erik's shoulder.

"Oh yeah, it's hilarious. She broke the bathroom door."

Chris laughed even harder. "Oh god, dude. I was just

5

joking. You're paying her to dress up like this?"

Erik rolled his eyes. "Jesus, so you're not even in on this? I don't even know who this girl is. And she just keeps saying she's here to guide me to Valhalla."

Göll scanned the windows, ignoring that they were talking about her.

"Holy shit, man, really?" Chris breathed a lazy laugh and pulled himself together. "Derek didn't tell me shit. It's the clown shit, isn't it?"

"Yep."

Chris threw his hands up in the air. "Great, so I'm next. Going to get followed around by a mariachi band or some shit." He turned to Göll. "How much did he pay you?" She looked at Chris and said nothing, then scanned the windows again.

"Yeah, she's dedicated. It's ridiculous." Erik looked at Göll. "Hey, Göll—"

"Weird name. That part of her act?"

"Probably. She's got an Icelandic accent. Listen. Göll, what am I? What have you come for? Tell Chris."

She looked at Erik, dead in the eyes. "You are one of Odin's chosen. I have come to guide you to Valhalla."

Erik started laughing, and looked at Chris. "See?"

There was a confused expression on Chris's face. "What'd she say? I didn't understand it. Is that Icelandic or some shit?"

Erik shook his head. "No man, it's English. You serious?" He looked at Göll again. "He didn't understand you. Why are you here?"

"I have come to guide you to Valhalla."

The words were plenty clear. Erik turned his face back to Chris, smiling expectantly.

Chris had stopped smiling, he shook his head. "There wasn't a word of English in that sentence, man."

Erik's smile faded. "You're not fucking with me, right?"

"No, man. Like I said, I'm not in on this. You understand

her?"

Erik turned to Göll. "One more time, say why you're here."

"I have come to take you, Haki Erik Styrsson, to Valhalla."

A shiver ran through his body and he looked back at Chris who shook his head solemnly. "You need to go see Derek, man. Figure out what this whole thing is."

Erik nodded. "Yeah. Derek's..." He shook his head, not sure why he'd bought the whole thing. Chris was in on it. "Yeah, I'll go see him."

Chris gave a nervous chuckle and patted Erik on the arm. "Alright man. Keep an eye on her. She's starting to weird me out, yeah?" He paused a second. "Oh, almost forgot." He ran to the back and came back with a bag full of food.

"Yeah, thanks."

"Hey, I figured that's what you came for." Chris kept shooting glances at Göll. "How are you going to get to Derek's work?"

"Bus."

Chris looked at Göll and raised an eyebrow.

Erik sighed. "Göll, do you have a bus pass?" She ignored the question. "Money?" Same response. "Super. So I guess we're walking." He started toward the door and Göll followed. "Thanks for the food."

The walk to Derek's job was probably only the better part of a mile, but it was a straight shot by bus. There almost definitely weren't any pockets on the ridiculous leather costume Göll was wearing and she wasn't likely to break character at this point just to make his life easier.

The walk wasn't so bad. A decent burger and a bag full of fries made the time pass more or less without him having to over think the whole thing. He'd get to Derek's job, he'd get laughed at, he'd tell Derek to guess who was paying for door repair. The burger also made a fantastic prop for all the people who wanted pictures of the two of them. A few asked to take a picture with her, but she always stepped away any time they got within a few feet. This led to Erik apologizing for something that had nothing to do with him, but it was fair enough. As much as she was obnoxious in her dedication to her gig, she wasn't a prop.

It was nearing four when they came up outside of a standard beige shipping warehouse. The lot guard had seen Erik come past the booth often enough that all he got was a nod and a bit of an awkward look at Göll. He laughed and shrugged, going back to his cameras.

Erik walked in through one of the open bay doors to the warehouse. He could hear laughing in the distance. Word would probably get to Derek before he could find him, but he found the warehouse boss anyway. Tom was a stern old guy who had a pretty limited pool of patience for the sort of shit their group of friends tended to bring to the warehouse.

The already present frown on Tom's mustached face deepened when he saw Erik walking up with Göll in tow.

"What sort of game are you two playing now? I told you about a million times this is a place of business."

Erik raised his hands. "You can't put this on me. Derek hired her and she won't stop following me."

Tom shook his head, his mouth turning in disappointment. "Buncha goddamn children around here."

"Hey, I'm with you, Tom. We're on the same side here. So if you could just tell me where—"

"He's with a pull team over on C8, prepping an order. A big one, understand? I expect your ass out of my warehouse before I feel a need to make sure you're gone."

"Wouldn't dream of making you walk anywhere, Tom." Erik turned and started walking away quickly, immediately regretting his sarcasm.

"Alright, smartass!" Tom called after. Erik could hear Tom's face reddening. "Tell your little boyfriend that this rendezvous counts as his break!"

Tom mumbled something under his breath, but Erik was out of earshot by then. He kept his brisk pace, though, just in case Tom decided to stay upset.

The aisle Derek was on was a short walk. Erik could hear the crew moving things. He came around the corner and found six workers largely standing around as the one with a forklift did all the work. Derek's back was to him, so one of his co-workers was the first to laugh and point. Derek followed their pointing fingers around and his lips immediately curled as he tried to hold back a laugh.

"Holy hell, that's amazing." Derek came walking over, shaking his head and his face covered with amused disbelief.

"Yeah, it's hilarious." Erik shoved him as he came close. "Tell her to go home."

Derek stumbled back a few steps holding up his hands, laughing. "Why would I tell her to do that? Oh, man. This is fantastic. Where'd you find her?"

"No, no. That game's not going to work. I already talked to Chris."

Derek's laugh faded in his confusion at the statement. "Talked to Chris? Oh, did he do this? This is classic though. I get it. You're like a viking guy. From Norway or whatever. I thought valkyries had wings and shit though. Big metal helmets. I mean the leather's cool, but—"

"Look, I know Chris was in on it. The game's up. How long's she going to follow me around?"

"Don't know what to tell you. I've never seen this chick in my life. Maybe she's a long-lost cousin." He laughed.

"Just tell her to go home."

Derek shrugged. "Sure. Not sure what that'll do, but fine." He looked at Göll. "Go home, uh..." He shifted his eyes to Erik. "What's her name?"

"Göll."

"No way I'm pronouncing that properly on the first try." Derek shook his head and looked back at Göll. "Go home, Garrl."

She stood there, looking blankly at Derek for a moment

before looking toward the exits.

Derek seemed slightly confused by the lack of a reaction. "Does she talk or what? Is she deaf?"

"You should know."

For the first time, Derek's smile disappeared. "Why should I know? I don't have any idea who the fuck this chick is. I thought you were fucking with me. So she doesn't talk?"

"She can. I mean..." He waved a hand in front of Göll and she looked down at him. "Why are you here?"

Her eyes narrowed and her face showed just the slightest hint of annoyance. "I have come to guide you to Valhalla."

Erik immediately looked back to Derek. His friend was not wearing the expression he'd hoped. It was blank, like Chris's had been.

"What'd she say? What language was that? Some Scandinavian shit?"

Erik felt a flush of panic. "This isn't funny anymore, man. She busted up my door, she's been saying weird shit."

"You can understand her?"

"Look, I know you and Chris worked this out."

Tom came walking up, half shouting. "Alright. Break's over. Back to work."

Derek forgot about Göll, having heard that this was his break. "The fuck you mean, Tom. That wasn't my break! And it's barely been five minutes."

Erik turned around. "Tom, listen." He turned to Göll. "Tell them why you are here."

She did not look away, only at Erik. "I have come to guide you to Valhalla."

He felt the bottom fall out of his stomach and he looked at Tom, desperate.

"What? She from Europe or something? I barely know English, so if that was supposed to be impressive, it ain't working. Five minutes, then I want you and your mail order bride out. And you," he pointed to Derek, "back to work the second he's gone."

Derek came around in front of Erik and looked at his face. "Holy shit, man, you're serious. Where'd she come from?"

Erik's eyes moved slowly from Derek to Göll and back. "I don't know."

"Work!" Tom was shouting from the far end of the aisle.

"Look," Derek said, his voice steady and sober, "Take her home. I'm off at seven, okay? She hasn't done anything weird, right?"

"Weird like fucking following me around all day? Shouting me awake? Watching me shower?"

"Look, she hasn't tried to hurt you, right?"

"Yeah, I mean..."

"It's fine. If she was going to stab you, she'd have done it while you were asleep."

Erik spun, throwing his arms up. "Fuck me, that's your way of comforting me?"

"Well? I'm not wrong. It's not like you can just attack her. And what would you even tell the cops? She says you forced her to dress up like that and you're done."

Erik shook his head. "Fucking... fine. Fine. But don't fuck around after you're off shift, alright?"

Derek nodded and went back to work. There was nothing Erik could do but grudgingly leave the warehouse and walk back to the apartment.

There were no pictures this time, at least not posed ones. Just shots of Erik walking as fast as he could manage with Göll following behind him. The apartment complex was a welcome sight. He nearly sprinted upstairs to the door, unlocking it. He was half tempted to leave Göll outside, but thought better of it, considering the bathroom door.

He locked the doors once she was in and dragged himself to the couch. She stood oppressively close, silently looking down at him.

"Do you have to do that?"

"I do."

He looked up sharply. "So you can do more than tell me that you're here to guide me to Valhalla?"

She nodded.

"Then why are you really here?"

"I have come to guide you to Valhalla. You are one of—"

"Odin's chosen, I get it." He gritted his teeth. "That's not..." He took a calming breath, letting it out slowly. "That's not funny anymore."

"It was never said in jest."

His heart sank and fear crept over him. "Then how will I—"

Göll's head whipped toward the window. A half second later, the building shuddered and the sound of metal being crushed reached his ears. Göll adjusted her grip on the spear she'd been carrying and it began to glow with an intense heat.

"They've come."

CHAPTER TWO

THE SOUND OF RAPID FOOTFALLS IN THE HALLWAY CAME only a few seconds after Erik had managed to drag himself up from the couch. Göll watched the windows intently, not moving from her place near him. The steps stopped at the door and the doorjamb buckled and splintered as the first kick landed.

"We cannot stay here."

Erik turned, alarmed. "Who is it?"

Before Göll could manage an answer, the second kick pushed the door into the far wall revealing a girl with light brown hair standing in the hall. She was dressed in a t-shirt and jeans, nothing like what Göll had on. In her hand was a short sword that was glowing white hot.

The floor cracked where the new valkyrie kicked off. There was a sharp hissing noise as she flew toward him. It was fast, too fast. The sword was aimed dead at his chest and all he could do was close his eyes and wait for it to hit.

He felt a wave of heat and pressure push against his chest just after a dull metal clang rang in his ears. The edge of the sword that had been aimed at his chest ran across the front of his arm, effortlessly digging a wound and burning it shut in the same instant. At the far side of the room, something impacted the wall, crumbling it.

He felt a hand on his arm and his eyes opened. It was Göll.

"This is not how you are meant to die."

The spear she'd held was now a warhammer, glowing with a dull intensity that was markedly different from the blade's.

"The other will be here soon."

"Other?"

She didn't dignify the question, dragging him toward the door to his room. She pushed it shut. It seemed like a useless thing to put between them, but Erik was in no place to complain. He stared at the door while Göll moved to the window and inspected it. She raised her foot and struck the frame of the window. It swung out, taking chunks of the wall as it went, hanging for a moment before it fell to the ground below.

"Haki."

"Erik."

She gave an annoyed look. "Erik, we are leaving."

He walked over to the window and looked out of it, hesitant to jump. The door to his room splintered. As he turned to look, he felt an arm around his waist. Göll had grabbed him and was pulling him off the ground.

"Hey, hey, whoa. Don't you jump."

She jumped. He was tucked under her arm like a half-drowned cat, and not securely at that. They landed heavy and he slipped from her arms, bouncing off the grass on the far side of the sidewalk with a thud and a wheeze. She moved to him quickly, dragging him up as Erik tried to catch his breath.

"I am sorry. I had thought that... you are heavier than your form suggests."

"Let's just..."

Göll turned her eyes up to the window. The valkyries looked out of the hole in the wall. Without wasting a breath, Göll spun her hammer and slammed it to the ground. The earth rippled away from the strike, shifting the building. Stucco and glass broke away as it swayed. There were terrified screams from all three floors.

"Run. Now."

There was no room in his mind for an argument. He wasn't more than a hundred yards away when the building began to collapse. Dust and chunks of concrete flew past him but none hit him directly. He could hear the debris slapping heavily against Göll's armor until they were out of range.

They made it to the street before Erik looked back. Two buildings had gone down under the power of the hammer. He stared at the destruction, not sure how to feel.

"What is this? What's happening?"

"I have come—"

"Ah! No! Okay." He shook his head clear. "Are they dead?"

Göll shook her head. "We cannot die. It will take them some time to dig out from the rubble."

"So, we shouldn't be here when they get out?"

"We should not."

Erik nodded intently, collecting his thoughts. "Right. Okay. Maybe the bus." He patted his pockets, happy that at least his wallet was still there. "Let's go."

He started walking, deciding that trying to board a bus near the ruins of an apartment building didn't look great. Checking his front pockets, he found that he didn't have his keys and that his phone was smashed.

"Why are they doing that? Why are they attacking me?"

Göll seemed almost confused. "What do you mean?"

Erik narrowed his eyes, confused by the response. "Valkyries take great warriors to Valhalla, right?"

She shook her head, but then scanned the skies around them rather than expounding.

"Okay, so what do they do?"

"We guide great warriors to Valhalla."

He clenched his teeth and took a deep breath. "I feel like that's what I said."

"They are not the same."

There was a bus at the stop so he let the frustration of the conversation be replaced with a panicked run to flag the driver down. He went to the rear door of the bus, hoping that the driver would ignore them. He entered without much fuss, in spite of the slowly dripping blood coming from his arm. If anything, it made sure he got less attention than he otherwise would have. Göll entered the bus to a completely different reaction. There was immediate chatter and phones were pointed at her straight away. Sitting at the rear of the bus did little to help.

Still, in defiance of every dire expectation running through his head, the bus started moving. He let out a relieved sigh, thankful that bus drivers weren't paid well enough to bother with what was obviously a shit situation. Erik settled down for a second, figuring if they just rode silently, they would be left alone.

The growing noise of the chatter from the seats ahead of him killed that dream before it could find a comfortable place in his mind. Göll was doing little to help draw attention away from herself. She stood in front of him, staring down at him. He'd been dealing with it all day so it had almost slipped his mind how insane it must look.

Erik stood, his voice as quiet as he could manage over the noise of the bus. "Can you do something about your...

armor or whatever it is?"

"Why?" Göll was not a whisperer.

He nodded over her shoulder. "You're attracting a lot of attention. Too much."

She looked back at the people on the bus who had no intention of pretending not to be gawking at the scene.

"I can change them if you want."

"Change them? I mean, aren't you wearing anything underneath?"

She ignored the question and a silver shimmer started at her head. It ran down to her feet, replacing the leather armor with jeans, a shirt, and a thick jacket. Aside from being unseasonably warm clothing, she had just magicked herself into new clothes in front of a bus full of people.

The noise ahead of them could no longer be called chatter. They were in open awe of what they'd seen. More phones came out, this time to make phone calls. He immediately leaned over and pulled the wire to stop the bus. The driver pulled over dutifully and opened the doors.

"Go. Get off. We can't stay on here."

She turned and walked down the steps and Erik kept himself close behind her, stopping at the bottom step to jog back up.

"If any of you follow us, I'll fucking cut your throats!" He stuck his tongue out and made the weirdest noise he could think of before running back down the stairs. The bus took off at speed before anyone could even stand up.

He walked over to a pitiful wooden fence near where they'd been dropped off and leaned against it, letting out a ragged sigh.

"Where can we go? How do we get to Valhalla?" She ignored the questions and Erik felt his temper begin to fall apart. "I just watched you fucking murder a few buildings worth of people, can I have some answers?"

"No."

He spun and punched the fence. The pain radiated

through his hand and that was enough to calm him down. Göll turned at the sound and looked at his hand.

"And what if I don't want to go?"

Her attention went back to the sky. "You must go."

"Why?" he shouted. "Why must I go? Huh? Explain it! Any of it!"

"You have been chosen."

He groaned in frustration and shook his head. "Fine. What about those other two? Who are they? Why are they after me?"

"They are Hild and Thrúd. Since they have failed to stop you in their first attempt, they will seek anyone who might aid you in reaching Valhalla."

"Seek them and do what?"

She didn't even bother to look back when she said it. "Kill them."

Erik pushed himself away from the fence, looking down the streets to orient himself. They were only three or four blocks from the restaurant. He started running toward it, Göll coming up beside him.

"There is likely no hope for your friends. They would have aided you."

He ignored her, running as fast as he could. His legs were burning when he first saw the smoke. "No, no." He forced himself to move faster. "Come on." He watched the smoke rise above buildings that cruelly blocked his view.

He put his head down as he came to the edge of the last building, rounding the corner on the street where Bosko's sat. Everything in his mind told him not to look up, but he did.

The building was in flames, the roof half collapsed. Erik started toward it, running directly at the fire. Göll passed him and tripped him. His body hit the concrete and slid. He flew to his feet and swung at her, his fist striking her shoulder squarely. She barely shifted and the pain was horrible, like punching a slab of concrete.

18

Erik immediately bent over, clutching his hand and swearing. "Why? He might still be in there."

"This is not how you are meant to die."

"But I am meant to die, right? Just like Chris?"

She nodded. "There is no other way to Valhalla."

"Why would I want to go there?!"

"Very few do." The voice was new and came from behind him. Erik spun on his heels and Göll moved in front of him, her hammer shifting back to a spear.

She looked barely eighteen, thin and short. She had black hair and eyes to match that contrasted against pale skin.

Erik stood up, still holding his fist to keep the pain as dull as he could manage. "What do you mean?" He walked to Göll's side and she gave him an annoyed glance.

The girl looked at Göll before speaking. Her voice was flat and hoarse. "It was stupid of you to come here. She knows that." The girl nodded at Göll. "You've been given a poor bargain, Haki Erik Styrsson." She paused, looking at the flames, her face never giving away the slightest hint of emotion. "But Hel wishes to meet with you, and offer her assistance."

Göll flew into a rage and stomped her foot, splitting the sidewalk. "Never! There can be no gain in a deal with that creature."

Erik looked at Göll. She was seething, focused intently on the girl across from them. "Who are you?"

"I am called Vár. Surely even the modern people know Hel?"

Erik knew the name. "Loki's daughter? She rules the realm of the dead."

Vár raised an eyebrow. "Near enough." She turned her eyes to the sky around them. "There is a place not far from here where you can sleep without worry. She has prepared it for you and the valkyrie."

There was very little to consider. There was no safety

elsewhere and he had no reason to trust Göll any more than Vár.

"Take me there."

Göll looked at him with angry eyes. "It is not safe to trust this girl or her master."

Erik started walking and Vár turned to lead them. "She hasn't tried to kill me yet, at least. And where else would I sleep?"

Göll scoffed but offered nothing in the way of an argument. Vár moved along at a leisurely pace, casually checking the air from time to time, her loosely braided hair shifting whenever she did.

They had walked nearly a mile when Vár came to a stop in front of a dingy motel that Erik had passed only a few times before. It hadn't been updated in decades and he'd never seen more than a car or two in the parking lot.

"You will be safe here. Two rooms have been afforded by Hel's kindness so that you might both sleep in comfort."

Her voice hadn't given any hint of it but Erik couldn't help but think there was some sarcasm there. As they came close to the motel, the air changed, warming the slightest bit and growing still.

Vár produced a key and opened the door to room 19. "For Odin's chosen."

Again, his instincts told him there was mockery somewhere in her words but he walked into the room anyway. Göll followed him in with Vár behind.

"The rooms are modest, for which Hel apologizes."

"And when do we meet her?"

"Not until the morning."

Erik took in a deep breath, letting it out as a tired sigh. "Fine. Not much else I can do."

Göll ignored their conversation and stood in front of the window, watching through the blinds.

"Is there anything else you desire?" Vár asked Erik the question, but her eyes kept finding their way to Göll.

"No. I just want to sleep. Or... sit. Quietly. I don't know."

Vár nodded and walked to the door. "Should I show you a room, valkyrie?"

Göll didn't look at the dark-haired girl. "Do not talk to me."

"Then, I will look forward to the morning."

CHAPTER THREE

WHAT LITTLE SLEEP ERIK WAS PRETENDING TO GET WAS abruptly cut short when a loud knocking sound came from the bathroom, followed by a few bumps and the muffled sound of an argument. Göll's weapon began to glow as she turned toward the noises. It was only a moment later when Vár stepped out, brushing the plum-colored dress she was wearing to smooth it out. She moved to the corner of the tiny alcove without a word and motioned away from the bathroom door.

A woman came out. She was no older than thirty, dressed in tight jeans and short, bright red heels. There was a loose off-the-shoulder t-shirt under a leather jacket and curled stark-white hair at the top of her head. Erik looked at her, hopelessly confused.

She walked to the end of the bed before looking over at Vár. "This is him? I'm not convinced." She looked back at Erik and pointed at Göll with a thumb. "And with her track record..." She sighed. "Hi. I'm Hel. You go by Erik, right? Not Haki?"

He nodded slowly.

"Well, he can hear anyway." She looked around the room. "Isn't there a chair in this dump?"

Vár ran to the door and left when the question was asked.

"You're Hel?" Erik was slightly annoyed at not having a better question to ask, but it was as good a starting place as any.

"I am. Do I not seem like her? Is it the shoes? I wanted taller ones, but really I get enough of being tall at home."

"You don't... seem..."

"Seem... stuffy? I don't talk like I got shit out of a medieval courtyard?" She curled her arms and did a mocking dance. "Oi blimey, ye have offended..." She stood up shaking her head. "No thanks. People like Vár and your little murderous friend—" She turned to Göll, "I can see you staring at me," and then back to Erik. "They don't really keep up with the times. You'll get used to it."

Vár re-entered with a disused chair. Hel looked at it, unimpressed. Without Hel saying anything Vár apologized.

"It was the best they had, I could not..."

Hel patted Vár on the head and sat in the chair. "So, Erik. I assume you're fully confused and the ogre by the window won't tell you anything."

Göll took a step forward at the insult but Vár moved to Hel's side and faced the valkyrie.

Erik looked from Göll back to Hel. "That's about right. I mean, not knowing anything. Göll's not so bad. I assume there are reasons she can't tell me things."

"Oh, there are very definite reasons she's choosing not to

tell you. And, well, I'm not opposed to the odd secret, so I'll just let you two sort most of that out. But we at least need to establish a baseline, agreed?"

"That would be... something. Maybe not nice, but, yeah. Something."

"Horribly put. So!" Hel patted her pockets, but found nothing. She turned her head to Vár. "Hm. Did we leave those at home, Vár? The dolls I made? Doesn't matter." She returned her attention to Erik. "I made visual aids. It doesn't matter. You've been chosen by the great and powerful Odin." Definitely sarcastic. "Göll is actually the one who chose you. The process goes something like this: A valkyrie chooses a person eligible by deed or ancestry to enter Valhalla. Then, the other valkyries try their best to make sure that special little flower never, ever blooms."

"They... don't want me to get Valhalla?"

"Sure, why would they? Either way, once Göll showed up, you were going to die. That's already set. But let's not get bogged down in the minute to minute stuff. You humans are so worried about dying. Vár used to be that way." Hel nudged Vár with her elbow. "I'm here to make a simple offer of assistance."

Göll took another heavy step forward. "And why should he trust you to do anything, Hel? Vile giantess."

Hel smiled broadly, but her voice was sharper than it had been. "*You*, ale-bearer, should not trust me." She tilted her head toward Erik. "He should." She went back to ignoring Göll. "Now, you won't understand what exactly you need my assistance with, maybe even when you get to my lovely home. But I recommend you come."

Erik sighed. "More half explanations. I'm really getting sick of it, you know?"

Hel laughed. "Oh, it's precious. You've hardly even started yet." She wrapped her arms around Vár's waist and pressed her head against the girl's back. "Remember how you used to be Vár? It makes me so nostalgic. Let's get ice cream before we go home."

"So you're just here to mock me? Maybe I should be listening to Göll."

"Oh, boo." Hel pushed her lip out, feigning a pout. "If you're going to ruin my fun then I'll just come out and say it. Even for me, saying too much could cause headaches that I don't have a cure for." She chuckled. "And it's more fun the less you know." Her chuckle became a full laugh. "Ah, I made fun of your valkyrie for that just a minute ago, didn't I?" She stood up abruptly. "Okay. I've said my piece. Keep my offer in mind. I'll be leaving Vár here in Midgard to look after you."

As she started to walk back to the bathroom, Erik spoke up. "What should I do? How do I..."

Hel stopped and looked at him. "Die well. And then come see me." She smiled and went back into the bathroom.

There was no noise, but Vár went to make sure she had gone and closed the door again when she'd confirmed. She walked to the chair, lifting it up, and spoke in Erik's direction.

"I will be outside if you have need of me."

She walked off with the chair, leaving Erik alone in the room with Göll. She turned back toward the window.

"So, I have to die?"

Göll did not turn back toward him. "All humans must die eventually. It is a necessary part of the cycle."

"Then what should I do? How do I die well?"

She turned from the window. "You must fight. You have muscles, but they are not a fighter's."

"Okay, ow. Tough but fair. I don't know how to fight."

"Then I will teach you. We will need an open field."

"Right, there's a lot not too far from here that's empty. It's at the back side of a business park so I doubt anyone will notice us."

"Then we will begin tomorrow morning."

Erik was nervous, knowing he wouldn't be able to sleep, but he didn't have the will to try to make conversation with Göll beyond what she'd already offered. There was an amount of excitement in her voice or at least approval. He wasn't sure which, having said so little to her. The duty-bound nature of every single sentence she'd let out made it hard to try to talk to her. Training was something, at least. When his arm had been cut, he'd only been able to stand there. Wishing it would all go away wasn't going to work, and the next time it might be his chest that got split open.

The motel room offered nothing to do. The television was broken, there was no clock radio, no mini-fridge. It was just sitting in silence, staring at the wall until the sun came up. Erik would have strongly preferred not having to be alone in the quiet with his thoughts, but it was more bearable than he thought it would be.

It was barely light out when Göll turned from the window. "The sun has risen. We should go and train you."

Erik headed to the door first, opening it. Vár was beside the door sitting in the chair that Hel had been in earlier. She opened her eyes and looked up at Erik.

"She's decided that you should be able to leave?"

"We're going to train."

"Worth a laugh, maybe."

Vár stood up and stretched, Erik moving away from the door to let Göll out. Göll had shifted her clothes to something less conspicuous. Even though neither of them knew where the lot was Göll insisted that Vár walk in front.

"She thinks I mean to kill you." Vár chuckled at the thought and then yawned. "Rich coming from a valkyrie."

Neither of his attendants offered any conversation and they didn't exactly get along swimmingly, so the prospect of trying to start one up seemed stupid. There was less foot traffic in the part of town they were moving through, so Göll's spear drew less attention. It still garnered a few stares, but it wasn't nearly the issue that her outfit had been.

They made it to the lot around the time the sun had burnt away a thin morning haze. The lot itself was overgrown at the edges and filled with cracked concrete through the middle. It was surrounded on two sides by the window-less backs of buildings and another by a tangle of brush and a few trees that must have been not worth removing. The re-maining side of the lot pointed toward a highway on-ramp. It occurred to Erik that this wasn't necessarily an ideal place to do anything if the people who meant to kill him could fly as high into the air as his minders' regular checks suggested.

He walked to the center of the lot, with Göll following behind him. Vár waited casually at the far edge.

"Do I need a sword or something?"

He saw Vár move out of the corner of his eye. He turned his head in time to see a short sword land on the concrete and slide toward him. It was dinged up and scuffed.

He looked at Vár and called to her. "Where did this come from?"

She only smiled. It made him hesitant to pick up the sword, but there weren't likely to be any others around, or if there were, they were likely just as suspect in origin. He grabbed the blade. It was lighter than he'd imagined swords to be. A few idle practice swings drew a scoff from Göll.

"Really? Just from that?"

"It embarrasses me to watch."

Erik rolled his entire neck from one side to the other. "I mean, I know... you... could you be nice? Tact? You picked me, remember?"

"Ready your sword."

"Oh, I can't swing it, but I know how to do that."

Göll rolled her eyes, the biggest hint of any sort of hu-man emotion he'd seen. Her spear formed down to a sword the same size as his. She placed both hands around the grip and assumed a stance that Erik copied as best he could. She seemed satisfied and her weapon shifted back to the spear it normally was.

"Near enough." She backed a few steps away. "You must be ready. Push the blade away, do not try to stop it."

"Got it. Ready."

She charged at him, the spear glowing, and Erik's muscles tensed, freezing him in place. She slapped the sword out of his hands with the blade of her spear and pointed the tip at his face.

Erik stood bolt upright, backing away. "Okay, clearly wasn't ready. That's fine. I'm new. Right?"

He could hear Vár laughing from the side of the lot. Whatever pretense of respect she'd been operating under on the first day was gone now that he'd met Hel. The mockery only made him feel more determined to shut her up, so he went to retrieve the sword and took his stance again.

"Okay! Definitely ready this time."

She charged again to the same result. The sword clattered on the concrete and Vár had to turn away to catch her breath. When she'd finally settled herself, Vár managed to mock him between fits.

"She's... so slow. Ahaha! And you, you... and you... still you cannot even move." She slapped her leg.

Erik retrieved the sword, annoyed. She wasn't wrong, but the enthusiasm of her insults wasn't heartening.

"Ignore her." Göll's voice was softer than it had been. "You must learn. You must move."

Erik nodded. He concentrated on watching her feet, rather than the blade. It made him nervous, but if he could just mimic her movement, it might be alright. She charged again, and it went worse than before. He moved a foot back, stumbling over the other and falling to the ground before she even got to him. Vár started up again in the distance. Erik rose quickly this time, dusting himself off.

"Again. Let's go."

She charged again and again and the result was the same each time. Göll was unwilling to pretend there was improvement and chided him for expecting it so soon. She was readying for another charge when she stopped and looked toward the overpass. Hild and Thrúd stood on the edge of it, silently watching.

"Why aren't they coming after me?"

Göll considered them for a moment and then looked at Vár. "Most likely because she is here. It leaves them no open side."

"They always fight in pairs?"

"Most."

Göll went back to her position and readied herself. She charged and slapped the sword again. He'd managed to keep the sword in his hands about half of the past dozen or so times. It had become his goal to both move and hold the sword. She charged and slapped. He held, taking a few steps back, readying himself again. His wrist had begun to hurt, but he couldn't allow himself to worry about it, not with the valkyries watching. He wanted to seem at least more capable of mounting a defense than a toddler.

Eric tensed as Göll charged again, but only for the tiniest spec of a second. He managed to push himself backward, away from her blade, but one of his hands came from the grip of the sword. In a panic, he balled it just as Göll's spearhead made contact with the metal of the sword. For no reason he could express, his brain told him to swing. And so he did. His fist hit the staff of the spear and a sharp sting ran from his knuckles up his forearm, followed almost immediately by a blinding heat and the sound of sizzling. He hardly felt it in that second as Göll's spear rocketed away from his blade and into the ground.

The pain came back all at once and Erik dropped the sword, gripping his bright red knuckles. Göll was quick to pull the tip of the spear out of the concrete. She stared at him, face drastic with alarm and confusion. As if she'd just remembered they were there, she scanned the overpass for the valkyries. Erik followed her gaze. They were gone.

"Sorry," Erik finally managed. "I didn't mean to touch it." He took a deep breath, wincing as the pain slowly started to wane. "I'm glad you pulled it away so fast. Did the concrete mess it up?"

Göll snapped out of her haze and looked at the blade. "There is no damage. These blades are not meant for human hands, you... you should be careful." She paused. "It's enough for today. In truth, you've made more progress than I thought possible."

"I'll take it as a compliment." Erik strained the words out. "I was hungry anyway."

The walk back was painful but involved food, so there was only so much to complain about. Vár wiped some sort of salve onto his knuckles when they returned to the motel and told him to sleep. He had no reason to argue.

CHAPTER FOUR

HE'D MANAGED TO GET SOMETHING APPROXIMATING SLEEP. It came in fits and starts, mostly. The noise of Göll shifting her weight in her armor woke him up as reliably as any alarm clock had ever managed. It was dark out when he decided he couldn't manage it anymore. Erik hadn't noticed that his hand was almost entirely numb until he reached for the lamp beside the ratty mattress. He chuckled at the meaty slapping noise that resulted from plopping it onto the bedside table over and over.

"Is that all it takes to amuse you?"

Göll was speaking without being spoken to. Erik considered this a welcome change of pace and it brightened his spirits even more than the noises had.

"I'm easy to please. Is that so wrong?" She didn't respond, not willing to play along. "Come on, you smiled didn't you?"

"Why would I smile?" She sounded almost defensive.

Erik chuckled. "Are you not allowed to smile either? What about ice cream? They let you eat ice cream?"

"I can eat whatever I wish." She turned in a huff. "You... what manner of questions are these?"

"You just seem so serious about everything. And I don't intend on dying anytime soon, so I figure we should at least be on speaking terms."

She sighed, not quite relaxing her posture, but her expression softened. "I must be serious. My sisters will be, and so must I."

"Right," Erik nodded at the cliché. "Only a moment's lapse in diligence and I'll be felled by their unforgiving blades."

"So you understand, at least."

He rolled his eyes. "I was fucking around."

Her lips curled into a disappointed frown and she turned back to the window.

"Ah, come on! Don't be like that. I've got a cut on my arm already. I know it's serious. But Vár's around. Like a canary in the coal mine or something. A horrible, mocking canary. That pulls... You know, nevermind." He stood up and walked over to the window. "She put it somewhere on the walk back here and I didn't see her do it." He eyed Göll looking for any hint of a reaction, sighing when he got nothing. "Okay, let's go train. I slept. My hand's fine."

Göll nodded and they went outside when Erik had gotten dressed.

Vár looked annoyed to see them. "If it's more punishment for your wrist you're after, the privy's less of a burden."

"Privy?"

She scoffed and turned away from him, starting toward the road. The walk went by quickly, it being the middle of the night. Mercifully, no cops came by. As fun and quirky as a spear might seem in the daylight, it was less likely to be seen that way in the dark. Erik found himself thankful for the portability of meat and vegetables wrapped up in things since Göll refused to sit in a restaurant. She kept a wide berth around people other than him. As unwilling to supply him with any interesting information as she was, it seemed like a waste of time to ask. But then, having burned his hand as badly as he did, there were reasons that Erik could imagine without being told.

The lot wasn't lit, but there were no clouds in the sky and the moon was mostly full. It got the job done when mixed with the horrible orange glow of the sodium lamps from the overpass. Vár produced the sword again when he wasn't looking and handed it to him with an unnecessarily wide smile on her face.

"I don't like what's happening here."

She just nodded, still smiling, and watched him as he walked away.

He pointed the sword back at her as he walked toward Göll. "She's got a real problem."

Göll ignored his concerns. "The night will make you slower to react, less accurate. Ready your sword."

He did and Göll charged, the same speed as in the day. He stepped back, tilting the sword away from Göll's as she'd showed him in the morning. It was shallow and Göll stopped her spear just short of his arm.

The glow drained from the blade and she slapped it against his arm. Erik winced waiting for the pain, but it didn't come. At least, no more pain than a flat piece of metal slapping against his arm would be expected to create.

"That would be gone."

Erik gave a serious nod. "Let's go again."

Göll returned to her position and charged again. The sword dropped this time, Erik cursing his lack of ability. There was no consistency to the next dozen charges. Sometimes he would barely clear the spear and others his sword would be on the ground. His feet weren't any better. He would trip or try to move some new way and fail entirely.

Vár had been watching their training the whole time, yawning. Just after a successful defense, she stood, shouting.

"What do you hope to give the boy? A sense of accomplishment?" She started toward them, Göll turning to face her. "How long is it you imagine they will sit idle? Do you imagine I'm some valkyrie repellent?"

"Training is slow work. I won't hear criticism of how I perform it from one of Hel's animals."

Vár was unimpressed by the comparison. She didn't seem likely to start a fight outright, but Erik didn't want to wait to find out how far they were willing to go.

"What do you mean?" He looked over to Göll. "What does she mean?"

"I'd gladly show you."

"No." Göll's protest was immediate. "No, I won't have you laying a finger on him."

Vár snarled. "When did it become your say, valkyrie?"

"And if you kill him?"

"It'd be far worse for me than him if I was fool enough to do it."

They'd largely forgotten about him until he interjected. "Fine. I might as well learn to fight someone human. Or, was human."

Vár smiled. "Near enough." She looked at Göll. "Happy with that?"

Göll relented with gritted teeth and walked maybe a dozen paces away before turning back to them. The glow of her spear was more than enough of a message that she didn't trust Vár. Trust wasn't really something Erik felt like considering at the moment. There was a vast ocean of questionable motive between him and either of the two in the empty lot with him.

"Pick up your sword if you want." Vár was stretching her

arms, backing away from him.

He did and readied himself. "Okay. Show me what it is I'm missing."

Vár smiled.

There was a pale blur across his vision and he felt his stomach compress. All at once Vár appeared in front of him, her fist buried in his stomach. His feet left the ground as the image reached his brain, but the center of the punch was low in his gut and that traveled out behind him faster than his face. He could see the rough concrete of the lot rushing past below him. His arms hit first, dragging the rest of his body down. He slid sideways and rolled, finally coming to a stop thirty feet from where he'd stood with a feeling like his intestines had exploded.

Göll rushed over to him, kneeling down at his side and pulling his hands away from his stomach. He realized he was screaming sometime after Göll put her hands on his gut, pressing to see that everything was intact. She stood, turning to Vár to yell at her. Erik could hear none of what they were saying over the sound of blood rushing through his ears. He could hardly see through the water pooling in his eyes.

The food he had eaten exiting his mouth at speed was enough to draw their attention. Vár came over and squatted by him.

"That is what you are missing. Her softness will make you a victim. Understand that."

Göll came up, shouting, telling Vár to leave him be and she went back to kneeling beside him.

"You'll be fine." She put a hand on his arm. "This is not how you are meant to die."

He spent hours lying on the pavement, motionless except for the occasional involuntary spasm. It was sunup when he managed to move again, even then it was only to sit up. Göll stood beside him the entire time, watching. Vár had returned to her spot at the edge of the yard. It was mid-morning when he finally stood himself up.

"You must not rush these things, Erik."

He smiled, almost laughing before he felt the pain in his stomach. "No, I asked for it. Very literally."

The walk back to the motel was slow and excruciating. Even small steps up an incline were enough to weaken his knees to the point of collapsing. Then it was another ten minutes dragging himself up. He'd refused any help, trying his best to save some measure of dignity. He regretted it as he rolled on the lumpy bed.

Vár came in a few minutes after he'd gotten himself onto the bed and rubbed her strange medicine onto his stomach and the places the skin had been removed from his arms. It burned fairly horribly for a minute but subsided. There must have been a decent amount of guilt in her somewhere since she quietly insisted on handling lunch before leaving the room.

Göll stood beside the bed rather than near the window, but she still kept her attention focused toward the outside.

"She was wrong to do that. No living human could stand against a valkyrie."

He wanted to ask why she was bothering to teach him then, but the only outcome he imagined was her returning to cold and silent.

"She is a child, unable to understand the difference between teaching and training. I had not sought to teach you what it is to fight a valkyrie."

She was quiet after that for the better part of a half hour. The salve was beginning to numb the damage done to his stomach. Moving was not outside the realm of possibility, it felt like. He sat himself up in the bed and Göll turned to look at him.

"You'll only irritate your wounds that way."

"Ehh." He waved a dismissive hand at her. "This stuff is pretty magical. Maybe actually magical. I mean, my hand is healed up and that was pretty severe." He tried to take a deep breath but ended up coughing. The pain broke through the numbness when he did and he grabbed at his stomach. "Learning experience," he croaked.

Erik rolled his head back against the wall behind him, waiting for the pain to calm. When it did he adjusted himself on the thin pillows that were beneath his back.

"So, you can't tell me how I die?" He received the quiet he expected when the question formed in his head. "Why not? Oh! Do you not really know?"

He was disappointed. After his grievous wound, Erik was convinced she'd offer up a little more than normal. He'd underestimated her devotion to the job title. Or maybe overestimated her kindness. Both were possible.

"What do you think Vár's going to bring us to eat?"

"Poison."

It was so unfair of her. She stone-faced him for two days and then dropped a joke after his stomach had been destroyed. Erik couldn't hold back the laughter. The salve had only half-numbed his stomach but the pain was enough to stop him.

"Why? Why would you do it to me, Göll?" He sucked in a deep breath. "Oh maaan. Ugh."

She hadn't even turned around to look at the damage she'd brought on.

"Tell me you at least smiled at my suffering."

"I'll tell you nothing of the sort."

Erik smiled.

Göll ran to the window before Erik heard a familiar hiss. It was louder than it had been in his apartment. The sound of concrete shattering came next and he could see the room shake as the wave rippled under them. Göll ran to the door and whipped it open, a hissing sound like the others coming from her back as she left the room.

The salve had done its job and, though Erik hardly trusted it, he found his feet underneath him without much in the way of pain. He ran to the door, looking out. Hild and Thrúd stood in a small crater in the parking lot. They wore armor now, matching Göll's. He heard Göll speak to the blonde. She was taller with sharper features than her brown-haired partner.

"Hild, this is fight without honor. He is meant to have a month. Why is it always this way when I have chosen?"

Hild ignored her. Erik saw her mouth move, but couldn't hear her from where they were. A pair of blurred lines flew in opposite directions. The line that had been Hild crashed against Göll and flew up into the sky. Thrúd had continued on toward the far side of the lot, chasing Vár who wouldn't meet her head on as the other two had done.

Hild came back down, readying another charge, but her eyes found Erik standing by the doorway. She flew at him and on pure instinct he flattened himself against the ground. She plunged through the wall behind him, sliding on her feet into the bed in the next room. It barely seemed to slow her, crumpling and flipping away from the force of her body. He remembered how his fist had felt running into Göll. It hadn't been the armor he realized.

Göll appeared in front of him, throwing him to the side just as Hild flew headlong at him. He saw a glowing short sword in her hand before a wave of heat and pressure forced him to close his eyes. Göll caught Hild at full force and slid back, dragging deep lines through the concrete as she went.

Hild fled, keeping herself outside of a sweep of Göll's weapon. As her opponent landed a dozen yards away on the open parking lot, Göll's weapon shifted to a hammer on a medium staff and Hild's did the same.

Without looking at him, Göll shouted, "Get to the covering. Go!"

There was a small outcrop from the building for cars to park under while they checked in. Erik spun himself over and ran for it as fast as he could. He'd made it just under the edge when Vár landed beside him, sliding on bare feet.

"Fun, isn't it? Exciting, even! Ha!" She was manic, voice

higher and faster. A blur was coming from the far side of the covering. "Die well!"

Vár smiled as she said it and leapt back, forcing Thrúd to give chase up and over the covering. A half second later, the valkyrie came crashing down through the covering, staring at Erik. She'd remembered her quarry was not one of the girl she'd been chasing.

"Look, I get how this is supposed to go, but—"

Vár appeared behind him as Thrúd charged. She spun him to the side, out of harm's way. Thrúd wasted no time stopping and doubling back, sending chunks of the driveway up into the side of the motel. Vár pushed the back of his knees and leaned him back. She frowned down at him. Thrúd turned but did not charge again. She'd missed twice and there was plain exasperation on her face.

"It seems they want you more than me." Vár yanked him up to his feet. "I'll help. Try not to move too much on your own."

He could hear the sounds of fighting across the parking lot as Thrúd charged at him. Vár pulled him out of the way, but only barely.

"What use is my effort if you won't even try to strike one?"

Erik was in a panic. "How the hell and I supposed to punch that?"

Vár let out an annoyed sigh and moved herself in front of him. "A different method, then. Clench your fist and raise your elbow."

Thrúd was wary. She shifted her weapon to a short sword and paced back and forth a few times.

"Ha! Look, Erik. The valkyrie is scared of a few humans."

Vár's barb had been enough. Thrúd charged them at speed, screaming in a rage. The sword she'd aimed at his chest did not connect, but he felt a hand push the elbow he had cocked and ready. His fist came around, pulling his shoulder along behind it, and planted squarely into the side of Thrúd's face. He felt the bones collapse as a pain rolled up his arm. He saw the skin compress behind the force.

Thrúd stomped the ground, stopping herself. She stood upright, letting her sword arm fall as her other hand came up to her lip. Erik saw Göll and Hild stop and stare from their places across the parking lot. A shimmering trickle of red came up and over Thrúd's lip, silver flakes in a pool of rose blood.

"Oh my." Vár had moved behind him. "That will do very, very nicely."

He heard Göll scream something as he felt a prick in the center of his back. The pain came as the dark grey, immaculate blade pushed its way through his chest. Erik tried to exhale and the lung she'd pierced collapsed. His body spasmed as it realized something had gone horribly wrong. The spasm wrenched him to the side and the blade moved effortlessly sideways, pulling more of his insides apart. Vár pulled the blade out of him. Blood rushed out of the hole and down the front of his body. He dropped to his knees and slumped over, all his strength gone.

"No! Not like this!" Göll shrieked the words, but she was behind him and he couldn't see her face. He felt his heart shudder and stop and as the world became a blur, he saw Vár flee into the night.

CHAPTER FIVE

Erik shot up to his knees, sucking in a breath as fast as his lungs could manage. He slapped at his chest, front and back, frantically feeling for blood, but there was nothing wet or even odd feeling about the area where he knew he remembered a blade going through.

He noticed the ground below him was covered in grass and decided that it might be worth looking at his surroundings. He came to his feet, and aside from a stiffness in his chest there was no pain. He looked around idly, finding himself next to a very old looking well in a thin forest of oak and spruce trees. Erik looked down at his shirt. There was a hole through it, but no blood that he could see. Checking his pants, he saw the same. His shoes, somehow, had gone missing. A cursory look around showed that they weren't in the area. Looking back to his clothes, Erik lifted his shirt, checking his chest for wounds. There wasn't so much as a scratch where the blade had gone through him. The bruises on his stomach were gone as well. The only blemish at all was a small scar on his side where a piece of fencing had cut him as a child. He rubbed his hand over it, not quite sure what to make of the situation he now found himself in. It wasn't Valhalla. At least, he didn't think so. Valkyries were nothing like what he'd been sold in stories, so maybe Valhalla was just a stupid forest with a well where he waited for something to come and kill him. There were no weapons around and so, though the air was warm, he decided that it was best to go somewhere else.

He took his socks off, not entirely comfortable walking around with them on but no shoes. The grass under his feet was pleasant. Soft, and on loamy soil that felt more like walking on a cushion than ground. There was a trail nearby that he headed for, reasoning that trails usually led somewhere. The trail seemed clean and smooth but dirt paths weren't exactly in Erik's wheelhouse so that could have meant just about anything. He flipped a mental coin to decide which way to go and, not liking the outcome, decided to go left instead.

The trail wasn't unpleasant to walk. Only a few small rocks pressed into the bottom of his feet from time to time. The worst part of it all was the quiet. There was nothing except the sound of his feet falling and the occasional sound of hooting from the forest.

He'd been walking for what felt like a mile at least when it struck him that Göll had not been near him when he woke up. Something must have gone wrong. Or maybe it hadn't. He vaguely remembered her screaming when Vár stabbed him. Maybe he hadn't died as he was supposed to. If he could find other people, they might know. And they might have food.

In spite of apparently having died, he was starving. Somehow, noticing that he was hungry made it all the worse. Another hour had gone by when the trees thinned and the babbling of water could be heard somewhere off the trail. He could see the moon for the first time. It looked different, somehow. A ball of light that he couldn't really see features in, even squinting. The clearing went on for ages, but at least the moon was bright enough to show him the shapes of buildings in the distance. He was so happy that there were signs of human existence that he almost broke into a run. As soon as he jogged his first step, it occurred to him that a strange man running into a small village at night was probably not received well, regardless of the level of advancement of the people living there.

He kept his pace steady, nerves building the closer he got. Making it to the edge of town without being attacked by anything with a sword or bow and arrow was something Erik was willing to consider a success, considering how he'd ended up in the woods to begin with. Remembering the fight in the parking lot sent a shiver down his spine.

There was more noise in the small town than there had been in the woods. He could hear people talking behind the walls of wooden buildings. He'd spent a few summers in Iceland as a child where his parents forced him to stay in one of the earthen walled long houses that the vikings lived in and these were decidedly not those. They looked more like things built later. Stave churches, only they were simple houses rather than anything meant to revere gods. There were dim, flickering lights from behind some of the shutters and some of the buildings had two storeys to them. There were signs on those, but not enough light for him to be able to read them easily. He wandered through the town, sticking to the main road, such as it was. It wasn't paved, but it was level with the smaller roads leading off to the sides. They were wide enough to walk but they didn't seem like the sort of place he'd like to be found.

There was no strong center to the town, but he heard the noise of people as he came close to a small cluster of buildings that looked more like they were for business than for people to live in. He passed a small stable and an open stall holding a forge and anvil before entering into a small square, where the buildings all faced the center. There was some stone paving, but no fountains or trees or stalls or anything he might have expected. One building was well-lit from the inside and had shutters opened to the square. Inside were maybe two dozen men and women, drinking and enjoying themselves. Erik stood in the square, watching them, not sure if he should enter or what their reaction would be. They wore loose woolen clothing nothing like what he had on. A large man with a deep brown beard came from behind the bar and served drinks in large clay mugs to people near the open window. His eyes crossed the square and stopped on Erik.

Erik took a step back and the man leaned his head out the window.

"Hey! You there!"

Erik started to turn, fully intending to run.

"Stop! Hey! You've only just come, haven't you? May as well have some drink!" The man was gone from the window in the next instant and the door opened, spilling light across the square. He turned behind to the patrons who were all suddenly deeply interested and waved a hand at them. "Don't all make a fuss, you'll terrify the boy."

Erik walked hesitantly toward the open door. "I, uh, this will sound a bit odd, but I don't know where this is."

The man came out of the building to meet him, offering a hand. "Not strange at all. I'm called Gerhard and this is my alehouse in the town of Kvernes in Helheim."

Erik extended his hand and Gerhard clapped his own around Erik's forearm. The grip was strong and as much as he might've wanted to match its firmness, he knew he'd just embarrass himself.

"Erik."

"A good name." Gerhard nodded, smiling wide under thick bristles. "Come. Let's get you out of those odd clothes and feed you."

As much gut as he had, there was muscle under it all. Erik found himself entirely thankful that Gerhard seemed to be a kind man. Although, maybe when he was in the ale-house, they'd kill and eat him. Erik was troubled that he couldn't bring himself to entirely dismiss the thought.

"Go on! Stop starin'!"

Gerhard waved his hands, prompting the gathered on-lookers at the door to head back to their seats. The building was warm inside and there was the smell of food and thick drinks. There was conversation about him that no one made any particular effort to keep secret. Most of the chatter was about his clothes. It was definitely not the thin wool that they wore and they seemed to have never seen its like. The denim was especially curious to them. Gerhard pointed at a place at one of the long benches between a pair of women who looked to be in their 50s.

Erik sat down and hands were immediately on his body, pinching at various places and squeezing others. They rubbed the fabric between their fingers.

"So soft! Oh, it's been ages since we've had someone new."

He smiled politely, not sure what to say. The women were hardly talking to him, and more to each other and the people around.

Across the table questions began to come at him.

"So what were you, boy. A farmer?" one man asked.

Another spoke up, "Nah, look at his arms. Scrawny. He's a jarl's son for sure."

They didn't wait for answers and quickly devolved into spirited debate about what he was and where he'd come from.

"Shut up, the lot of you!" A younger looking woman in

the corner shouted. "Ask him, not yourselves!" The room quieted and she looked at Erik. "Where've you come from? What's your name? No sense in only Gerhard knowing!"

"My name's Erik. I lived in America."

Everyone looked at him without a hint of understanding on their faces. The mumbling began.

"Some new country?" "Things change so much back in Midgard."

They forgot about him for a moment, long enough for Gerhard to come back through the door to the kitchen area holding a mug and a dish that was somewhere between a plate and a bowl. He placed them both down in front of Erik along with a wood-handled knife and a metal spoon that flattened at the end something like a shovel. The bowl was filled with simple food, boiled turnips and carrots and a fatty cut of boiled lamb that looked as though it had at least some herbs on it from the liquid it was cooked in. Gerhard ran off two of the men sitting opposite Erik at the table and sat in their place.

"This is for me?"

Gerhard laughed as did a few others. "Of course. Can't expect you to arrive in such a place with a full stomach."

"I can't pay."

Gerhard nodded. "No need for that yet, boy."

Erik started eating, stopping after the first bite. "Thank you. I should have said it before. For the food. I'm grateful. It's delicious."

It wasn't, really. It was fairly bland, but he was hungry enough that his stomach seemed not to care.

"Fulla prepared it." Gerhard turned his shoulders, pointing to a woman behind them. She looked young and blushed to be pointed out. "She's got skill in cooking."

Erik smiled at her and Fulla hid her face to the amusement of the entire alehouse.

"You've not been here long, is that true?" The room went quiet as Gerhard spoke.

Erik shook his head between bites. "No. I just... I woke up near a well."

There were murmurs of knowing agreement with the statement.

"And you walked here?"

"Yeah. I came, uh, there was a path near the well and I just decided to go left."

Gerhard nodded. "Well, it's good you did. The other direction would have led you into the woods. Not so many folk out there. Kvernes is easily the better place to find yourself."

"Ey!" The patrons all raised their mugs and shouted in unison.

Erik hurried to do the same, taking a drink as the others did. The light golden liquid inside was thick and warm and heavy with alcohol. He coughed, nearly spitting the drink all over his food. They laughed.

"You'll get used to it, boy!" An old bald man encouraged him from the back of the room and others did the same in response.

Erik spoke up when the shouting died. "Kvernes isn't a word I know. And this building isn't like the longhouses. I don't mean to be rude, it's just strange to me."

"You live, still, in longhouses in America?" Another man shouted the question in disbelief.

Erik spoke up. "No, I just... I've never seen a building like this."

Gerhard put a hand up at the chatter. "This is how things were made in my home, Kvernes, when I died. I came to Helheim as all men do and was unsatisfied with what I saw, so I came to this field and built what I knew. More came and for ages we've lived as we please here."

"When did you die?" He blurted the question without thinking and was thankful when Gerhard laughed.

"I can hardly remember now. They'd remind us every winter. Thirteen and something. Always the year of their lord."

The patrons booed and then broke into laughter.

The food had disappeared from Erik's plate and he was in no hurry to take another drink. He had questions, but most of them he didn't want to ask. There was no way of knowing how people would react if he mentioned how he'd died. "Is all of Helheim like this?"

Gerhard leaned back, crossing his arms. "No. But there's little reason to travel. There are other cities, but they are harsh or full with criminals."

"Is there any way someone could find me here? If they were looking?"

Gerhard chuckled. "Who would look for you, boy? Were you married so young?"

"No, there's... A girl. Her name is Göll and..."

The faces of the people around him changed at the mention of the name and Gerhard stood up. He walked around the table briskly and grabbed Erik by the shirt, dragging him toward the kitchen. He was pushed through the door and Gerhard came in behind him. There was a low din from the main room. Erik looked around frantic, there was a door behind him.

"I don't mean to hurt you, boy, but you've just said something that it'll be hard for folk to forget."

Erik shook his head. "Look, I can just go. It's fine."

Gerhard's face was stern. "I will ask for a clear answer from you. Göll, the one you believe will come and find you, she is a valkyrie?"

"Y-yes. Yes. She is supposed to guide me to Valhalla she said."

The large man in front of him softened, heaving a weary sigh. He pointed to a door at the side of the kitchen. "Go upstairs. And keep yourself quiet for a while." Gerhard rubbed at his temples, shaking his head. "They'll be badgering me all night."

He prepared a handful of mugs and went back into the main hall, people shouting questions at him immediately.

Erik decided it was best to get upstairs before anyone came to look for him, so he did as quietly as the stairs would allow.

The room at the top of the stairs was simple, furs and a small table with roughly hewn chairs. An oil lamp hung from the ceiling lit things well enough. Erik sat at one of them, listening to the sounds of the hall before. The shouting died and turned to laughter as they forgot whatever had made them angry about Erik's presence.

Hours passed and the noise died until it was just the sound of mugs being cleared away. Gerhard came up the stairs and into the room, grumbling about having had to serve so much drink.

Erik stood as soon as Gerhard entered. "I didn't mean to cause trouble. I didn't know."

A dismissive hand was waved. "How could you? They forget that. Sit." Gerhard moved to a chair and sat. Erik did the same. "You may not have seen it before you ended up here, but valkyries are not gentle creatures."

The look on Erik's face must have told Gerhard enough since he left the explanation there.

He continued, "I can't promise you much, but you'd do well to make yourself a welcome addition. I can find you work come the morning."

"Shouldn't I try to find Göll?"

Gerhard gave him a pitying look. "You're welcome to do as you like. But valkyries sometimes leave their chosen, forsake them. I hear it's some sort of game for them. A way to seek Odin's favor. And with you ending up out here... I can say you're a rarity. We haven't had a new face through here in hundreds of years, such as they are in Helheim."

With what Vár had done to him, Erik could imagine that explained most of the situation he found himself in. His mind wanted to jump to conclusions but the only reasonable thing to do was wait and see.

"I'd like to pay you back, if I can. So I'd like to work."

Gerhard smiled. "Good man. Fulla's said she has some

clothes she thinks might fit you." He chuckled. "She'll bring them when the sun's up, give you something to wear that isn't full of holes and bad memories."

Erik looked down at his shirt. "I'm grateful for that. For all of this. I hope I can pay it back."

Gerhard stood, and moved to a small closet, pulling some furs. "Keep up like that and I'll really believe you were chosen."

CHAPTER SIX

GERHARD SLEPT HEAVY AND LOUD AND THAT MEANT ERIK spent the rest of the night sitting in the corner staring at nothing. What little moonlight made it through the shutters landed on Gerhard's bed and that scenery had become boring fairly quickly.

The sun seemed to take forever to crawl into the sky. Gerhard woke up before when the room was still dim orange and rolled himself out of bed. He looked at Erik and jumped back, having forgotten he was there.

"Oh, right. Apologies boy." He slapped his naked stomach and exhaled heavily. "I forget the world when I sleep."

Erik stood up, looking at the window. "It's fine, really.

You think there's any work for me? I just want to do... something."

Gerhard walked toward a bucket, pulling it up from the ground. "This early? Won't be much." He stopped by the door, turning around. "Maybe Ósk and her husband, Raggi. They own a bakery and Raggi is as lazy as I've met." He laughed. "They might need something this early. They're back the way you came. You'll be able to smell the bread."

Erik followed Gerhard down the stairs. "They won't be angry with me?"

Gerhard turned as they entered the kitchen, unlatching the back door. "They haven't a reason to be. Wary, might be. Not your fault. The valkyries choose who they choose." He yawned looking over Erik's clothes. "No sense going out in that. Best you wait in the front hall for Fulla. I'm going to wash and fetch water for the cleaning."

He left without anything else, leaving Erik alone in the hall. It was quiet again, something he wasn't entirely accustomed to. Erik walked out to the front hall and sat at one of the benches. The hall was fairly large, with ceilings higher than he would have expected. Last night, when it was full of people drinking and shouting, it had seemed so much smaller and all the more terrifying. The feeling wasn't helped by their reaction to him saying the name Göll. He walked around the hall, looking at the tables and benches. They were made of boards at least, unlike the rough chairs in Gerhard's room above. They were smooth to the touch and felt as if they'd been sealed with something. They definitely weren't bare wood. They may have even been shiny at some point. There were divots worn into every single seat and the edge of every table where people had sat. There were knife marks among the chips and stains. He ran his fingers across them in the silence, forcing himself to accept where he was. Everyone in the hall had accepted it.

A light knock at the door to the alehouse startled him.

"Fuck. Just..." He straightened himself up. "Coming. Hold

on."

He ran to the door, looking at the latch. A metal spike through a pair of loops and a metal handle that operated an iron bar to hold it shut. He pulled the spike and opened the door. It was the girl from the night before. She seemed surprised to see him.

"Oh, cock." She flushed, eyes opening in surprise. "No! I didn't mean to... not you. I just... I hadn't expected you would be here." She looked down at his ripped shirt and held out the clothes she'd brought. "I'm not married." She shook her head, panicking. "No, I mean. The clothes. I..." Her hands opened and she let out a squeak. The garments landed on the stone by her feet and she turned and ran off.

Erik reached a hand out. "Wait!" She kept running. "Thanks!" He yelled it after her and the girl stumbled.

He winced through a smile, not wanting to laugh at her. Erik really wished he could thank her properly. She'd made him feel more normal than anything else. He bent down and picked up the clothes, shutting and securing the door. There were shoes as well, something he was thankful for even though they looked strange. Leather with wood on the bottom. All of it was used but it seemed clean enough. He pulled his clothes off and laid them on the table, dressing himself in the things Fulla had brought. The clothes were rough but comfortable enough. As much as his brain screamed to keep his old clothes, he figured that was a bandage best ripped off now. He'd be used to the wool before long.

Erik opened the door and stepped out into Kvernes again, this time in the light. The dim orange had changed color, but a fog was hanging over the town. It wasn't terribly thick, but it kept the morning light reasonable. He was thankful for that, really, never having been a morning person.

The path was much easier to see in the early morning light, as were most of the shops of the square. Some part of his brain told him that the words on the signs were in runes, something he'd never learned to read, but he could understand them. They were all simple signs bearing the name of the owner and what the shop was for. "Smithy" on the top line of the blacksmith's sign and "Halfdan of Kvernes" on the bottom.

It was quiet, generally, along the main street. A few people standing by their doors and talking. They waved at Erik as he went by and he returned the gesture. He wondered about the magic that made him able to understand everyone and even read the signs. It was useful, either way, and in the face of shape-shifting weapons, it seemed almost a given.

The smell of bread surrounded him all at once, reminding him of why he was walking down the main path in the first place. He looked around, noticing a single-floor wooden house that took up more space than most of the ones around it. There was no sign hanging near the door, but rather one on the ground. "Bakery."

Erik guessed there weren't likely to be multiple bakeries in a town of maybe a hundred or so people and he knocked at the door. He heard bickering from inside and then the locks being seen to.

The door swung open to show a middle-aged woman who looked him up and down. "What're you after?" A wave of realization swept over her. "Oh, you're that one. Want work, I'll bet?"

He chuckled, not sure what to make of her but nervous either way. "I think I'm that one, yeah. Are you Ósk? I'm Erik. I'd love to help out."

"Expecting pay too, I bet."

"No, I mean—"

"Fool enough to work for no pay, is it?"

"I don't—"

She threw a bag at him which Erik caught. It was warm, full of soft loaves of bread. "Work pays two coins. Don't eat it. If there's red wood hung outside, they want bread. Knock. That's it."

She slammed the door and Erik stood in the street, not

entirely sure which way he should walk or what he was supposed to say. He looked around, seeing no red wood on any of the doors around. What he did see were small black hooks to the side of some doors and in the center of others. He went for the side streets, deciding that would be the best place to start and quickly found the first house.

He walked up, standing awkwardly in front of the door for a minute, listening for the sounds of people inside. He heard the creaking of wood and decided he'd be alright. He knocked and immediately heard footsteps coming toward the door. It opened just the slightest, a man peered out, his grey-streaked beard pressing through the crack.

"What? Bread?" He opened the door. "Alright, let's have it."

Erik opened the bag and reached into it, pulling out a loaf. The man looked at it and then at Erik.

"You're new." He reached into the bag on his own and pulled out a loaf, then pulled the red wood block off the peg beside the door. "Don't touch the bread."

The door shut and Erik stood there holding the bread in his hand and feeling like most of an idiot. He told himself there was no way he could know. The man wasn't even particularly clean looking, really, so it made no sense he'd be upset at someone touching his bread. Erik smelled the bread in his hand, figuring it couldn't do any harm. He'd had barley bread a few times and it smelled like that. Not something he really enjoyed immensely. He put the loaf back in the bag and moved to the next house with a red block on the peg.

He knocked and an old woman answered in a loose gown that looked like it was for sleeping. He smiled.

"You wanted bread?" He held the sack out, opening it.

"You intend for me to bend over'n reach down into that bag?"

She did, holding her back with her other hand, shaking her head when she'd retrieved her loaf of bread. She didn't say anything else, only pulled the wooden block and gave

Erik a disapproving look.

When the door closed, Erik closed the bag, gripping it tightly in his hands, and stomped around in the dirt outside the old woman's door. Somehow, he didn't scream.

The next houses went smoothly enough, with Erik offering to grab it for them if they wanted. They declined and didn't seem to suggest that he was disgusting or in some way mentally deficient. As he worked his way back toward the square, he began to see white and yellow blocks on the pegs as well. He stopped a man who was walking toward the square.

"Hey, sorry. Are these... do I have to do anything about the white and yellow blocks?"

The man looked down at his hands, seeing the bag. "Bread? No. Those mean they'll have milk and eggs as well."

Erik thanked him and the man continued on. The houses were a bit farther apart in this part of town and as he neared the end of one row, he noticed there were no more red blocks. Deciding he was being clever, Erik decided to cut between a pair of houses. He was halfway down the way when the houses came closer together than he'd expected and he had to turn sideways. As he did, he looked behind and saw the silhouette of a head looking at him. He froze, watching it for a minute.

"Hello?"

There was no response and it didn't move.

"Hey! Why are you staring at me?"

He saw the head look to the side and then back to him, but the sun had become too strong to see any features. Erik started shuffling sideways between the houses as fast as he could, the head still watching him. He started to panic even though he was only a few feet from the back of the houses. He stopped looking behind, worried there might be an accomplice at the other end waiting for him.

"Shit, shit, shit."

He popped out into the small side street, stumbling and

whipping his head back and forth. The street was empty except for a few women talking to each other a few houses down. One turned to look at him but quickly lost interest and returned to her conversation.

It was nearly impossible for Erik to relax as he finished handing out the bread he'd been given but even when he decided to randomly spin around and walk a different direction he didn't catch anyone following him. There was an amount of whispering, though. It wasn't the best way to make a decent impression.

He returned to the bread shop, not looking forward to another interaction with Ósk. He could hear arguing through the door before he knocked and Ósk's annoyed voice came closer. Erik put on his best smile when she opened the door.

"What's wrong with your face, boy?" She stuck her head out the door and looked up at the sky. "Took you long enough." She grabbed the bag from him. "I'll get your coin." She closed the door for a moment and then came back. He held his hand out and she pressed two coins into it. "There. Deal's done."

She started to close the door and, against his better judgment Erik spoke.

"Sorry, wait! Please!"

She stopped closing the door but didn't speak.

"Do you have a bathroom?"

She opened the door. "You want a bath?"

"No, it's not... Jesus. A... restroom?" Her face was souring with every passing second. "Toilet?"

She rolled her eyes, finally understanding him. She turned around, leaving the door open. "Raggi! Take this boy to have a shit."

A rotund man, wearing patchy stubble, came walking up to the door. He waved Erik in.

"Yer the new one, eh? Heard some stories. Well, reckon you shit like the rest of us." He laughed. "S'out back."

Those words did not fill Erik with a sense of confidence.

It occurred to him that none of the doors in Gerhard's ale-house seemed to go to a bathroom. And that there was already liquid in the bucket he was heading to the river with.

He walked through the main room of the house. It was a wide kitchen with three ovens at the edge of the house farthest from the other rooms. Ósk was already back to work, rolling what looked like much more normal bread. It wasn't nearly as dark, with white flour.

Raggi opened the rear door and led him out into a small yard in the back. There was an outhouse standing in it, along with some parts that looked to be for ovens.

Erik looked at the wooden rectangle, despondent. "So, there's no plumbing?"

"Hm?" Raggi looked at him, eyebrows raised, and then at the outhouse. "Oh. Hah! Fancy man, aren't you? You'll get used to it." He pushed him toward the outhouse and turned to head back toward the bakery.

Being in no rush to find out how bad the smell would be, Erik dragged his feet toward the suspect building. He opened the door and saw a small box of dirty sheep's wool sitting beside the hole that had been cut into a wooden bench. He whimpered looking at it, but went inside, expecting to vomit from the smell. Instead he was greeted by a quiet babbling. Against his better judgment, Erik looked down the hole and could just barely make out rushing water. Looking at the side of the small reservoir, he could see pipes made from hollowed rocks. They'd redirected the nearby river to run through pipes.

Erik had no idea he was capable of feeling such relief and he quickly undid the rope around his new pants and pulled them down, sitting on the seat. The water was very relaxing, it turned out, and he felt stress falling away as he sat on the borrowed wooden bench. He tensed again, hearing footsteps outside. Raggi must have been coming to check on him. Wanting to avoid a conversation he decided to speak first.

"I'm doing fine, thanks!" He gave a half-chuckle. "I thought it was going to be awful in here."

There was no answer and the footsteps moved to the side of the outhouse and then around the back. He heard a sound like someone jumping and landing.

"Hello? Raggi?"

The footsteps sped up, moving to the far side. There were vents toward the top of the outhouse that Erik had just noticed. He had no way of closing them. He heard jumping again, this time on the side. The sound of a door creaking open sent the footsteps running away from the outhouse and as Erik was looking frantically around, he heard Raggi's voice coming closer.

"Not so bad, is it?" There was pride in the statement. "Took years to get those damnable things working right. Worth it though, eh?"

"Yeah, it's... it's really amazing. Listen, did you see someone around the outhouse just now?"

There was a brief pause. "No, no one out here but you. I've heard you're called Erik, is that right?"

"Yeah?"

"They say you're from some new land in Midgard, what's it like? Been stuck here with the missus— and I love her, mind you— but I used to dream of adventure."

This was not relaxing. Erik explained that the Italians found it and that there were natives, trying to end the conversation. It failed. Finally, he gave up and just forced as much from his bowels as he could manage considering the situation. There was a second box next to the one full of wool, it was covered unlike the other. Erik grabbed a handful and cleaned up as best he could with what was clearly not prime grade material. He understood thoroughly after opening the closed box why Gerhard used the river.

Erik left, thanking them both on the way through the bakery. Ósk grunted at him, but Raggi seemed to have taken a liking to him.

He headed back to the alehouse. It was mid-morning from the looks of the sun in the sky, and he opened the door to find Gerhard cleaning the tables with a rag. He stood up when Erik came in.

"Good, Fulla saw to some clothes."

Erik looked down at the clothes and then back up at Gerhard. "She's not married."

Gerhard laughed. "Oh, that girl. She's never been good around people. Was there work?"

Erik held up his two coins, moving over to the bench nearest Gerhard as he did.

"Work well done, then. Ósk is usually a stingy one. Must be she likes the look of you."

"Is that what that means?" Erik huffed out something like a laugh. "At least she shows it somehow. What should I pay you for letting me stay here? I don't really—"

Gerhard held up a hand. "Keep what you earn." He wrung out the rag into the bucket of water. "Earn enough to buy some drink and buy it from me. Now, let's eat. There's work for you in the afternoon."

CHAPTER SEVEN

GERHARD FINISHED HIS CLEANING, TOSSED THE RAG INTO the bucket, and then made for the door. Erik stood up, following him, and they both left the alehouse into the late morning sun. It was a warm day, pleasant, if a bit too humid. The haze of the morning had burnt off in the half hour that Gerhard had finished the cleaning and more people were out now with the sun up.

Erik watched people smile at Gerhard and greet him graciously as he passed by the shops. There was an integrity about the man that Erik admired, likely all the more because that integrity meant that he'd been given a place to stay and protected, in a way, from what the people in Kvernes might have thought of him.

"Where are we eating? Is there a restaurant or some-thing?"

Gerhard waved at a group of women who looked to be about his age and they seemed happy with the gesture. "Something, yes."

Gerhard stopped in front of a modest house and knocked on the door. A few minutes later Fulla pulled it open, hold-ing a pair of small pots.

"Gerhard, I..." She stopped talking when she saw Erik was there.

"You?" Gerhard chuckled.

"You hadn't said you were bringing him as well. I have cooking. I have to... take these." She handed the pots to Ger-hard. "The rest'll be done in the afternoon." She looked at Erik and swallowed hard. "Thank you."

Erik raised an eyebrow. "For?"

She blushed and turned around. "I have work!" Fulla closed the door and Erik could hear her walk quickly away from it.

Gerhard handed the pots to Erik and motioned for him to follow. "Seems she likes you."

Erik gave a nervous smile at the statement. "She seems nice."

There was something too normal about it all. There was no way he could say that to Gerhard, at least it didn't feel like he could. And what would he say? Where are all the sword fights? Why haven't any giants attacked? He wasn't even sure what he wanted or expected Helheim to be like, but somehow it wasn't what he imagined. That was some-thing of a running theme since Göll showed up. Gerhard's popularity meant regular stops along the walk back to the alehouse to chat with people. They all welcomed him, no one asked any questions beyond his name and where he'd come from. Gerhard was subtle in interrupting anyone who asked much more, but he did it each time without fail. They were nearly back to the alehouse when Gerhard explained himself, even though Erik hadn't asked.

"They will have plenty of time for questions later," he said, not looking back. "Best you have some time to arrange your thoughts. Us in Kvernes... we've been about a very long time. We forget what it was like."

Gerhard pushed open the door of the alehouse and shut it back behind them. He sat his pot down on a table near the windows and opened the shutters.

"Sit. I'll fetch the drink."

The thought of the syrupy alcohol from the night before made Erik think it might be better to decline the offer, but he didn't, sitting across from where Gerhard had put his food. He came back with a pair of the odd spoons and two mugs. Instead of the golden liquid from the night before, they contained a dark brown liquid that smelled much more like normal beer, if more pungent.

Gerhard took his place across from Erik and pulled the lid from his pot, smelling it and smiling. He noticed Erik eyeing the mug. "Problem?"

Erik looked up, seeing Gerhard had opened his pot and so did the same. "No, no."

"Not used to the drink, are you? Had a few like you through Kvernes before. Ale for lunch and dinner, mead for dessert." Gerhard took a big spoonful of the stew in the pot and shoved it into his mouth. "That is the way we live. In time, you'll wonder how you lived without them."

Erik doubted that. "Is Kvernes the only town?"

"There are others. Are you a restless sort, Erik?"

The stew was well-made, if a bit light on beef. "I don't think so. No one's ever called me restless. I'd just like to know where I am."

Gerhard looked at him, considering the statement for a moment. "There are other towns, if they could be called that. More you'd call them farmers who've banded to one another. Two and three dozen at most. Best that you get your bearings here before venturing too far without some guidance."

Erik didn't know enough to argue with the point, though the city seemed safe and generally happy. He hadn't seen all of it, though. Maybe the world was dangerous. It was strange that he hadn't heard any mention of Hel or of gods or valkyries out of anyone.

When lunch was done, Gerhard grabbed the pot and mug and carried them toward the kitchen, talking as he went.

"There's work for you. Real work." He went into the kitchen, coming back running a dry rag. "At the south edge of town, there's a small farm."

"South?"

"Right. The main path runs east to west, same as the sun crosses the sky."

Erik looked out the window, as if that would confirm something. "Okay."

"The work won't kill you, it's a small plot. Enough to grow some root vegetables we need. House with a green door." Gerhard looked out the window to the street. "Best you get there. Sun won't shine forever."

The streets weren't exactly bustling, but there were enough people to make Kvernes feel larger than it had in the morning. No one talked to him without Gerhard leading him around the city. They stared, though, and a few gave idle waves. Erik wondered if it was simply because he was new or if it was somehow related to the reaction to his mention of Göll the night before.

The farmhouse was easily found just past the south edge of the rows of houses. A field about fifty yards square had been marked out with a fence, though it didn't really look like a farm so much as just a big rectangle of patchy land.

Not sure what he'd be doing, Erik knocked on the door with some hesitation. It was a few minutes before anyone came to answer.

"Had to get dressed, y'see." The woman looked up at him

without issuing any sort of greeting. "My fool arse of a husband broke 'is leg yesterday mornin'. Won't be right again 'til tomorrow. You can hear 'im moanin' if you listen close." She stopped talking, lifting her chin and waiting for the noise. She laughed when a moan came from the main room. "Hah! Slipped on a rock. Anyhow, I got a woman's work needs doin'. Ever pushed a plow?"

"A plow? No. I've—"

She pinched his arm between thin fingers and grimaced. "Didn't figure from the look o' ya. It ain't so hard and you seem a smart one. Stick it in the ground and push it straight. You menfolk ought to understand that well enough." She cackled, pushing past him to come out into the street. She closed the door and pointed absently toward the fence. "Plow's it. It's all you'll need. Do all you can before sundown and we'll call it a day's work."

With that she started northward toward Kvernes, leaving Erik standing in the middle of the street. He looked at the closed door and figured he was expected to just hop the fence, so he did. The house was a part of the fencing itself, with a side door letting out to the main area. He doubted the man inside would welcome his presence. He hadn't even gotten the wife's name so explaining why he was there would be difficult at best.

The ground in the field wasn't nearly as soft as what he'd walked on near the well. He spotted a wood-handled device with a wheel on the front and a maybe foot-wide claw behind it. It was held in place with a large bolt and there was a more spade shaped piece of iron on the ground with roughly the same look. Erik could sort of remember seeing much larger versions of similar tools attached to cows at the old longhouses he'd had to visit. He hadn't been interested enough to watch them do the work, but he could assume the order of them easily enough. One tilled up the dirt, the other made rows for planting.

He groaned as he pulled the plow up, looking at the size

of it compared to the field around him. It seemed so much larger now than it had. As he got to the edge of the field, Erik pushed the edge of the tiller into the dirt, thankful that at least the handles were smooth. He started pushing, surprised that the dirt gave way fairly easily. He had no idea how harsh the winters were, but no one seemed to mention it. Maybe they were mild enough to keep the dirt pliable come the spring. It was a bit of luck he hadn't expected, but it was welcome enough. Even with the weather as pleasant as it was, the work was hard and so he pulled his shirt off, tossing it on the ground beside the plow. In the span of a few hours, he'd managed to till almost half of the field. Wanting a change of pace, and to keep his mind off the lack of ready access to water, he switched the tiller for the plow and curious if it would save time, walked to an untilled bit of dirt. He plunged the plow in and it stuck, not wanting to move. He strained, trying to push it forward, making slow progress.

"Erik!"

He looked to the side and saw a short girl with dirty, light-blonde hair staring at him. She had an annoying grin on her face.

"What?"

"You're meant to till it first."

He rolled his eyes and pulled the plow from the dirt, deciding to ignore her. He walked to the area he'd tilled to start practicing with the plow.

"Erik! Oy!"

He ignored her, starting down the line with the plow hoping she'd go away.

"Why would you pretend not to hear me? I offer good advice and this is how I'm treated?"

He did his best to move down the tilled soil in a straight line, but it was much harder than he'd expected and the row veered a foot out in places. Out of the corner of his eye he saw the girl climbing the fence.

"Hey! You can't be in here."

She ignored him, landing on the dirt at the edge of the field and started walking toward him.

"You can't be in here!"

"Why not?"

He didn't have a good reason. "It's not your land."

"Not yours either," she said, looking around at the tilled soil.

"I was asked to help."

"I've heard the rumors about you. And I followed all morning. Are they true?" She was grinning by the time she'd finished the sentence.

"I have no idea what rumors there are about me. And that was you?"

She pushed his arm playfully, ignoring his annoyance at having been followed. "Don't play the fool. You know. Valkyries."

A small panic rose inside of him, not sure what it meant. The girl's demeanor didn't suggest anything dangerous, but how could he know?

"Oh! Is it a secret?" She snickered. "Horribly kept secret, if it is. I just want to know about them. You're an einherjar, aren't you? One of Odin's chosen?"

He let the plow settle in the earth. "I guess."

"So you've met a valkyrie."

He scoffed. "Met, yeah. Real majestic."

"Are they? I've heard they're fearsome. Horrifying, some say. But it's all stories, I bet." She was almost giddy talking about them. "Why are you here? Why aren't you in Valhalla?"

He shook his head and decided to go back to pushing the plow. "No idea. I woke up next to a well and now I'm here."

"Hm, that's pretty normal. There's wells all over. Spit people from Midgard out. Are you sure you're not just making it up?" She kept a slow stride beside him as he practiced pushing the dirt into straight rows.

He laughed, somewhat indignant at the accusation.

"Why would I make it up?"

She shrugged. "Maybe you want that people should think you're a great warrior. Some folk are that way."

"And that's why I'm pushing a plow in a potato field."

"Carrot."

He reached the end of the row and looked back down the other way. "Look it doesn't matter, I'm not lying."

"Then have you met Odin?" She seemed as hopeful as curious.

"No."

The girl sank. "Have you met anyone? Your valkyrie was the one called Göll, wasn't it? Ah!" Her mouth fell open. "My name! I've not introduced myself. I've Tove."

Erik just nodded.

"Now you say, 'I'm Erik.'"

"But you already know."

"It... of course I know. But we're meant to be introduced."

Erik chuckled. "Right." He held out his hand. "I'm Erik."

She looked at his hand and then back up, grinning. She slapped her hand around his forearm. "Good. We're introduced."

There was nothing to do but shake his head at how odd the girl was.

"I'll help you plow."

Erik raised an eyebrow at the suggestion. "I'm pretty sure this is a one person job. And I should get back to breaking up the stuff."

"Then we can take turns!"

Tove was maybe a bit more than half a foot shorter than Erik and the rig was hard enough for him to push, but he felt like the sight of her pushing it would be worth the lost time. He switched the tools and walked it to the edge of where he'd stopped tilling before, handing it to Tove.

She pushed, trying not to show the effort on her face at first, but eventually giving in as her face reddened. It was slow progress, but she was getting somewhere at least.

"Alright, that's enough of that."

She turned around immediately. "It was working! Do you mean to insult me?"

Erik laughed. "No, I'm trying to get the work done so I can afford to eat."

Tove screwed up her face, turning back to the plow. She pushed it another six inches through the soil before noticing something.

"There are places for straps! For a harness!"

"I'm not going to wear a harness."

She ignored him and ran toward the door to the house, pushing it open without knocking. Erik could hear pained complaints followed by Tove's voice, full of annoyance.

"Shut your gob, old man! I just need the harness!"

He could feel that the likelihood of him getting paid was becoming worse with every minute she was in the house. She came running back outside, holding a leather harness.

"I found it!"

Erik decided to just turn around and start pushing the plow, hoping that maybe she would put it down and leave. It was a hope he knew wasn't going to pan out, but it was worth a try.

Tove ran up beside him. "Ignoring me won't plow the field any faster."

"I'm flatly rejecting that statement."

"What?" She looked at the harness. "This is not sized like I expected it would be. Must be meant for a goat?"

She phrased it as a question as though Erik would have been able to offer any insight into animal harnesses.

"I don't believe you'll fit into this." She said those words with implication that she was joking.

Erik stopped. "Why would I wear a harness?"

"You could pull the plow while I hold onto it."

He rolled his head back for a moment, exasperated. "Well, since it looks like it'd fit you, how about you pop it on?"

She looked at it for a minute, considering the idea. "Sure.

I think it buckles in the back, though."

She started putting the straps over her arms and the leather pushed up her chest, making it noticeable for the first time beneath her loose clothes. Erik wasn't sure whether to feel embarrassed for looking or for the fact that his brain hadn't really registered her as a girl until just now.

"Okay, buckle me up and hook it to the plow."

Erik shook his head, but did as she asked. "This isn't right. This isn't how you're supposed to plow fields."

"It ought to make the work go faster, right? How can you find reason to complain about being done sooner?" She was strapped to the plow and turned around to face him, looking rather pleased with herself. "Alright. You push and I'll pull. It's simple."

She turned around and started walking without giving him any time to complain. Erik barely grabbed the handles before it turned over onto Tove. Left with no other choice, he pushed the plow as she pulled. They were nearly at a jog tilling through the first row and when they hit the end she spun around, hopping in place.

"Didn't I say?" She smiled a wide, genuine smile and Erik couldn't bring himself to be upset.

"You did. I was wrong to ever doubt you."

She nodded, a sly look on her face. "Remember you said that."

They turned the plow around and kept going. A few people passed over the next hour, all of them laughing. Erik felt bad seeing the people pointing at her.

"Maybe we should unhook you and stop this. I can finish it from here."

Tove stopped dead when he finished talking. She turned to him with an intense look on her face, no hint of a smile. "Those people are idiots and fools. You can never let them make you think as they do." Her smile returned. "Besides, my idea is working well. What are a few laughs if we finish our work sooner?"

"Our work?"

"Isn't it?" She started pulling again, dragging the plow through the last row.

"So you're after half my money?"

"I've my own money, thank you."

"Then what are you after?"

"Adventure," she said, huffing as she took heavy steps forward.

At least she was forthright, though Erik had to admit that adventure sounded a bit more fulfilling than the work they'd spent the day doing. He chuckled to himself at the thought that wandering around with a sword might be the easier way to live.

In spite of their combined inability to move in a straight line, they managed to properly make rows just under half of the field when the light started trending toward dark. Erik put his shirt back on and left the plow and Tove walked with him back toward the city.

"That's no kind of beard for a man." She brushed her hand over the stubble that had begun growing in on his chin.

Erik rubbed the area she'd touched. "Yeah, I wasn't allowed to grow one."

"Wasn't allowed?" She laughed. "What sort of world has it become?"

They were watched fairly intently by a pair of men in their late thirties as they got to the edge of town. Tove quieted when she saw them. The two started out into the road as they approached.

Tove sighed in annoyance almost immediately.

"Keep it quiet, you." The man who spoke had a patchy beard and thinning hair. He looked at Erik and then back at Tove. "What're you doin' around this lout anyway? You ought to know he's trouble, talkin' of valkyries and worlds no one's ever heard of."

"My brother sent you two, didn't he?" The men looked at each other. "Of course he would. What business is it of his?

Or yours? I'll keep company with anyone who suits my liking and you can tell Vali I said as much."

They ignored her and turned their attention to Erik. "You'll keep a distance if you know what's right. No one likes you, newcomer."

Without saying more, the two men left, making for a side street. He looked at Tove. Her face was twisted up in anger.

"I'm sorry for making trouble."

She shook her head. "No, it's the same with everyone here. This town..." She started walking. "We should eat something after all that work. And drink."

He kept with her. "I don't know enough to say anything either way." He drew in a steady breath. "I just... I'm hoping things will make sense with some time, maybe."

She stopped, looking up at him. Erik carried on a few steps before he turned back to her.

"I have to go. I'll find you later, understand?"

He narrowed his eyes, slightly amused by the sudden change. "Sure."

She nodded, looking over her shoulder. "Good. Very good." She turned and started jogging toward the side streets. "We're a warband now, okay?"

He laughed. "No we're not."

"We are! We're going adventuring!"

CHAPTER EIGHT

WHEN HE'D WOKEN UP, GERHARD HAD TOLD HIM THERE was a surprise for him. It turned out the surprise was that he'd heard last night that a small group of farms a few miles from Kvernes were harvesting and needed an extra pair of hands. Erik ate a quick breakfast and left the alehouse early. Gerhard had recommended he travel light, saying it was only a few hours walk mostly over a well-trodden path. There was a sign post pointing the way to the farms. They called their village Gandrup.

He was nearing the edge of town when he spotted a familiar dirty-blonde head. Tove was looking the other way and he considered hiding but the odds were that she'd been waiting there for him for a while as it was. She turned her head and when she saw him came trotting over.

"What's with the pack?"

Tove looked toward the pack and then behind them down the streets. "Adventure pack."

Erik nodded as he started walking. "Not sure the walk to Gandrup is that far. How did you know I'd be leaving north?"

She followed along beside him. "Everyone knows everything in Kvernes. I can hardly stand it."

They left the north side of the city, the dirt becoming a bit less packed within a hundred yards of the outer edge.

"So am I tying you to the front of a plow again today?"

She shrugged, laughing lightly. "If it helps." Tove looked behind her after saying it.

"You must be pretty eager to leave Kvernes."

Tove kicked dirt at his feet. "It's easier to leave for some people than others. Whatever else I might imagine I am, I'm small and a girl. And bandits aren't so kind as people like you."

Gerhard had been fairly heavy-handed with the bandit talk to him as well, that morning. Erik hadn't seen a single soul— on the road or off— the whole day before and there seemed to be no one around them now.

He looked down at Tove who was doing her best to kick a rock along as they walked.

"Have you seen any? Bandits, I mean?"

She kept her focus on the rock. "No. Not myself. I've heard stories of people being robbed or people disappearing. That's why I had need of a warband."

"I see, so I'm the leader?"

She tossed her head back and forth. "More or less. You are one of Odin's chosen so there must be some merit in you."

"I'm not sure the process works the way either of us think."

Tove gave the rock a strong kick, sending it off into the woods. "Perhaps it doesn't. But at the very least, I can follow you for a time. It will pass the days."

She went quiet after that and they walked on for the next hour and a half until they came to the sign. It pointed only one way, toward Gandrup. The trail leading there was not nearly as well-kept as the road that led away from Kvernes. Roots had grown up in a few places and it had washed out and become uneven in others. It was nearly another hour along that trail, but Erik felt like they hadn't covered nearly as much ground.

The woods cleared to a set of fields, each about half the size of the one he'd tilled the day before. These were all full of fully grown crops. He knew next to nothing about seasonality but if it was the beginning of spring it didn't make much sense that they would be harvesting anything. A man came walking up to them, looking over Tove and then Erik.

"Welcome. I am Gaddi. You two are from Kvernes?"

"We are. I'm Erik and she is Tove." Wasting no time, he changed the subject before it could be glossed over. "Can I ask something?"

Gaddi nodded. "How is it that you're harvesting at the beginning of spring?"

"Beginning? It is always spring here."

Tove spoke up. "He's just come from Midgard."

Gaddi gave a large, knowing nod. "Ah, I understand. It's rare for us to see new faces here." He turned and started toward the farm. "Most of the tasks today are simple, even if you've not done them."

They moved to a small square where five houses sat around a large fire pit. There were outbuildings holding drying meat and one of the fields had stooks of some kind of grain drying as well.

Gaddi pointed toward one of the buildings. "Tove, you can assist the women until it comes time to cut the grains. They're seeing to the cheeses, I assume you know your way around such things?"

Tove nodded. "Born to it." She smiled.

Gaddi returned the smile. "Glad to hear it."

She left, jogging to the house as best she could with the pack on. Gaddi turned his attention to Erik when she was away.

"We've got turnips and carrots that need digging and grain that needs threshing. Both require a strong back and stamina, though I doubt you're lacking in either."

"I know how to dig, I can say that confidently. I've never threshed grain, so I can't say as I know how to do it."

Gaddi seemed surprised at the news. "Never? I'd gladly show you." Gaddi walked over to a small shed with Erik in tow and produced a long pair of sticks attached by an iron ring.

"This is a flail. You hold the longer end and strike the wheat to thresh it."

"Right, that sounds like something I could ruin, so…"

Gaddi laughed. "Then we'll have you dig."

He was walked to a field where four other men were already at work pulling turnips up from the ground and tossing them into baskets. Gaddi pointed Erik to the baskets and then took his leave. No one spoke to him as he picked a row over from the men who were working and started pulling. There was a knife in the basket which made Erik curious so he watched the men around him. They cut the root and the greens from the turnip, taking the bulb and leaving the rest in the field. He'd avoided being screamed at by people so far and he was intent on keeping it that way for as long as he could manage, so he copied them as best he could. He'd half-filled the first basket with turnips when the idea occurred to him that most of these people had been here for hundreds of years. Tove seemed to be the only person he'd met so far who was bothered by it. He tried to understand why, deciding that maybe it was simple enough. They were farmers, they hadn't known anything more than what he was doing just now and they lived in a place where it was eternally spring. It could be a sort of heaven for them.

He filled baskets at half the speed of the other men, who took to ribbing him when they were done with their rows and he still had half of one left. He'd managed three rows of the ones that were there when he'd arrived. Not an impressive number, but he was happy enough to have helped. His back was less happy about it, but that was just a punishment for spending a lifetime mostly sitting and eating fried foods.

Lunch was served when the turnip field was done. Some of the women must have undone Tove's loose braids as they had done them up into something much more intricate. She brought him a plate of cheese and cubes of boiled meat with turnips. The meat was good enough but Erik was already starting to wish he had better options. Tove stood near him, eating her plate of food as well.

"What's with the hair?"

Tove put her food down and patted at the braids. "For work in the fields they said. There's meant to be a headdress to cover it up as well. Is the cheese to your liking?"

"You make it? It's sour."

Tove made a face. "It's meant to be sour."

"Well, then it's the way it's supposed to be and it's not very good." He picked up a chunk of the cheese and ate it.

"Not good but still you ate it?"

"I doubt I'll be offered anything else. Plus, I'm a guest, right?" He ate the boiled beef and handed the plate back to her. "Thanks."

She smiled and stacked the unevenly made plate as best she could under her own. The others were finishing their food at roughly the same time and Gaddi called the men over to the carrot field. The work there was much the same as it was with the turnips and went by quickly. The men had introduced themselves briefly on the walk to continue their jobs, but that was the end of their interest in him it seemed. He wanted to be sad about it, but he knew he would be heading back to Kvernes at the end of the day and they were likely thinking the same thing.

It was mid-afternoon when the carrots were done and they moved on to the wheat. The women walked ahead of the men with scythes, cutting the wheat. The men were in two rows, one tying the sheaves, and then Erik and his group stacked them. It was nearing dark when the work was done.

As they were preparing to go, Gaddi approached.

"You both did well." He looked at Erik. "Slow, but the work was good." He laughed, relieving Erik's tension at the statement.

Gaddi handed over five coins for each of them for the day's work and sent them on their way with good wishes.

Tove waited until they were out of earshot to start her complaints. "How did you find the work, Erik?"

"Honestly?" He rolled his head back and forth, deciding how much to say. "It was boring. Hard. Hot."

Tove trotted out in front of him, spinning and walking backward. "Isn't it all so boring?" She was smiling again when she spun back to face the trail. "I can't begin to understand how they smile in Kvernes. Or in that sorry little town. None did while I was stuck inside with them, making sour cheeses in silence."

"And you want to leave?"

She slowed, coming back to his side. "I do. I hope to."

"Turnip farming seems like a pretty cozy life, though. Same thing for dinner every night. You might be missing out."

Tove scoffed. "No turnip farmer ever smiled as he died. And he woke here, and went back to all he knew with the same bland face and no family to help." She spit at the ground. "What good are they?"

The mention of it made Erik think of how no one seemed to have much in the way of family with them. Fulla even mentioned marriage. People married young when she died. It was strange.

"Tove, are Ósk and Raggi... how did they meet, do you know? The bakers?"

She looked at him. "A strange thing to ask." She thought about it a moment. "They must've met in Kvernes. It's a town of strangers. Or, they were strangers."

"But you said your brother—"

She made a noise and walked ahead of him. Erik left the thought alone and waited, hoping she would fall back into line or talk to him again, especially as night fell. They rejoined the main road with her still walking ahead of him.

The moonlight was as strong as it had been the night he arrived. It allowed him to see well enough ahead of them to tell that there were three people standing in the middle of the road. Tove froze and Erik came up, putting himself in front of her. He recognized two of the men when they started forward. They were from the day before. He could guess who the third was.

Tove screamed from behind him. "Go home, Vali! You've no business here!"

"Quiet!" Vali's shout caused Tove to shrink.

Erik put a hand out in front of her. "I don't know—"

"I have no intention of listening to your false words, snake! You've come to kidnap my sister and bring ruin down on Kvernes. Puppet of the gods, don't think I don't know about you."

"I'm not planning to kidnap anyone. Now let's just calm down."

Vali motioned to his friends. "Bring her here."

They started forward and Tove turned, rushing from the trail into the woods. The men followed her in and Erik started to go after them but Vali ran at him, pulling a knife. Erik jumped back, taking a few extra steps just to put distance between them.

"Filth like you keeping yourself near my Tove. She doesn't know things. Always talking of leaving. She doesn't know the world beyond our Spring. I do. I've seen it." He ran at Erik screaming. "And you would take her there?!"

Erik dodged backward, keeping his footing. Vali seemed

so slow that it was almost effortless to keep his distance. He had time to think, even.

Vali stopped, seething, and started to circle around. Erik looked to the woods as he circled, half-expecting to see one of the men there, but there was no one. Vali dove at him anyway, hoping to push him into the brush, but Erik moved to the side, dodging the initial thrust and another enraged swing.

Erik had backed along the edge of the road when he heard Tove shout from the woods and then a man's pained scream. It drew his eyes away from Vali and the madman took the opportunity, knocking Erik to the ground.

Vali swung the knife up and slammed it down to the side of Erik's head. The panic was setting in and whatever speed Vali seemed to lack disappeared now that the man was on top of him. Vali pulled the knife down across Erik's shoulder as he pulled it back into the sky. There was no other choice in Erik's mind but to grab at his wrists, so he did.

"Let go! Let me kill you!"

Erik wrenched his torso to the side as best he could, pulling Vali over. It was a valiant try but Vali kept rolling, pulling himself back onto Erik, this time lying flat on him. Erik's eyes searched frantically for where the knife was when he saw the moonlight glint off of it, still in the hands of his attacker. Vali pushed his own knees down onto the ground and rose up. He pulled the knife to the side, aiming it at Erik's ribs. The grin was that of a man lost to the world and he let out an insane, cackling scream as he began his swing.

Erik's eyes were wide open when he saw the flat of a pan connect with the side of Vali's head. Tove had put her shoulder behind it and taken a running dive into her brother's head. The speed of her charge pulled Vali over and onto the ground under the full weight of the girl, pan still pressed firm against his skull. There was a sick crack and the knife fell from Vali's hands into the dirt of the road.

Tove was quick to her feet, dragging Erik up.

"Are you hurt? He didn't?"

"I'm fine."

Tove ran to the knife, kicking the twitching body of her brother before grabbing Erik by the hand and dragging him toward the woods in a frantic run.

"What about your brother? Is he going to be okay?"

Tove shook her head. Her voice was manic, shaking with adrenaline.

"It doesn't matter!"

Chapter Nine

Tove kept ahead of him the entire time they ran. His lungs were burning after the first twenty minutes, but she showed no sign of stopping. It was the best part of an hour when she finally decided that they'd run far enough, looking behind them, breathing hard. Erik collapsed onto the ground as soon as they stopped, wheezing, his shoulder still burning though the bleeding had already stopped.

"Should have spent the day making cheese." She laughed before bending over to catch her breath.

Erik rolled over onto his back. "I don't think they would have let me. Not that I know how to make cheese. Mozzarella maybe."

Tove pulled the pack off, sitting down. "What's that?"

"Huh? Oh, it's just a kind of cheese."

"Is it good?"

"Yeah, it's pretty good. Like the stuff we had today but firmer and not sour." Erik was close enough to being able to breath properly that he sat up. "So which way is Kvernes from here?"

"We can't go back there," Tove said, laughing. "Not now."

"It wasn't really part of my plan. Avoiding it was more what I was thinking." He thought for a moment. "Was it true no one liked me?"

Tove shrugged. "They hate anything they can relate to the gods." She stood up, grabbing her pack. "Anything that would bring some interest to their boring lives. We should find a clearing."

Erik stood and followed her. "You sound kind of bitter."

She looked at the ground. "It's not the first time I've tried leaving. Not nearly the first."

Tove's voice trailed off and he decided to leave it at that. They found a small clearing and Tove dropped her pack. She pulled two light bedrolls from it and threw one toward Erik.

"You seem incredibly well-prepared." There was annoyance in his voice. As much as he'd felt Kvernes was a bit strange, the bedroll served to remind him that he'd nearly been stabbed.

She put her bedroll down and looked at him with a pitiful face. "I meant to ask. I meant to suggest it. I swear I did. I meant to ask as we walked back. But you mentioned my brother... and then he..." She shuddered and turned away.

Erik sighed, wanting to stay mad but unable to find the will. She had her own circumstances, clearly enough. Even if he were angry, there was very little for him to complain about. The weird reluctance to discuss what Helheim was beyond Kvernes and the nearby farms was something he found nearly impossible to ignore. They'd sent him on busy-work and then ignored his questions. It was a train of events he was growing sick of.

"We'll start a fire. You brought food?"

She turned back to him hesitant, but gave a nod.

"Good. Then you'll answer every question I ask."

Tove smiled. "Of course. Everything I know! You're my chief and I'd never keep anything that might help from you."

The woods weren't exactly thick with fallen limbs, the forest floor being clear and easy to navigate for the most part. Still, he managed to find enough for the fire to carry on long enough for a meal at least. Tove started the fire as he had no idea where to even begin. She cut a notch in a dried stick with Vali's knife and split it, lighting some dried leaves. She was impressively quick about it, something Erik decided he shouldn't be impressed by as much as he should be worried he couldn't do.

There were maybe six small metal pots that were sealed inside the pack. She took them out along with a folding iron grate and some utensils. She put the grate over the fire and put the pan on top of it. Erik's failing interest in food was turned around immediately.

"You're not going to boil it?"

Tove made a face. "Gods, no. It's fine enough, but it ruins most things. And there's no sense for flavor most times. Oily water with bones in it."

She opened one of the jars and Erik could see a creamy white substance in it.

"What's that?"

"You've not seen lard before? What sort of world do you come from?"

Erik protested. "Look, I've seen lard, you people just cook with weird... we don't boil meat where I come from so how was I supposed to know that's not seal fat or something?"

She opened another jar and pulled out thick strips of fatty meat. "This is pig belly, to put your mind at ease."

"Yeah, and if I showed you a cheeseburger, you'd have no

idea where to start, so let's not get all judgmental."

The lard melted and the pork went into the pan, sizzling. It was a sound Erik had realized he'd missed after so few days.

"You were going to ask me questions, were you not?"

He stopped staring at the pan and looked over at Tove. "Right. First off, where is Kvernes and what else is there?"

Tove nodded. "We're in the area known as Spring. I've heard from people who lived here that every season has a place in Helheim, but I don't know much more about the others. Lofgrund is the largest of the cities that I know of. I assume you want to make for Valhalla?"

"You know where it is?"

She shook her head. "Only that it is north somewhere. Lofgrund is to the north and the east. I've never been, but I know of a few small towns that exist between here and there—"

"Wait. Valhalla is here?"

She nodded. "Why would it not be?"

"It's Odin's hall. I mean, isn't it?"

"One of them. Have the tales of the gods changed?"

Erik sighed. "They must have. I thought Valhalla was in Asgard."

Tove laughed, almost dropping the piece of pork she was flipping in the pan. "The dead do not go to Asgard. What sort of foolishness do people believe in your time?"

"It doesn't matter. I'm in the right place at least. So Lofgrund? Is it safe there?"

"I've only heard the stories of people near Kvernes. Most never travel more than a few miles from whatever home they built."

"Why don't they leave?"

Tove frowned and shook her head slowly. "I do not know. They never seem to mind so long as their lives carry on as they did the day before. It may be some magic Hel has placed on them."

Erik's brief visit from Hel hadn't told him much about her, but it was a theory he was willing to believe. "And why not you?"

She went quiet for a minute, ignoring the meat even as she stared at it. "My days were not as fulfilling as theirs, I suspect." She snapped out of her daze in a panic. "Oh, the meat!" She turned around grabbing a plate and put a piece of pork onto his, handing it across with a big smile. "But things can always change."

He took the plate and smelled the meat, his mouth nearly flooding. He hadn't realized how hungry he was until the food was so close to him. He took a bite, nearly burning his mouth. It was far too hot but he couldn't convince his brain to stop trying to chew it. Sucking in large mouthfuls of air was all Erik could do to try to cool the meat down. Tove laughed at him, dumping the pan and putting it onto the ground to cool. She opened another pot offering him pickled carrots, then pulled a pair of clay jars from the pack. She handed one to him and he opened it. There was no smell, so Erik put it up to his lips hesitantly and tipped it back. It was water, fresh water. He drank probably too much of it, nearly choking when he ran out of breath.

"It's water!"

"Is that so surprising?"

"All they gave me was ale and mead. There's drinkable water?"

Tove gave a disappointed shake of the head. "All the water is drinkable. Except what's downstream of the toilets. They don't drink it, for superstition or preference for ale."

"Well, I'm glad that we're gone then."

That line was enough to bring a smile to Tove's face and some of the energy she'd had the day before was back. She talked cheerily about the tales she'd heard of Lofgrund. Stone walls and buildings and streets and hundreds of people. Before the fire ran low, Tove packed up the things they'd used and put them neatly back into the pack. They slept next to the dying embers of the cook fire, the woods quiet except for the occasional hoot of an owl.

Erik rose to the sound of a flock of cawing birds passing overhead. Tove had slept through them so he went to her bedroll and poked her with his foot. She groaned but started to sit up as Erik turned his attention to the woods around them. The ground was surprisingly comfortable under the thin coverings they'd slept in. It was a refreshing morning, somehow he felt energized by an odd feeling of freedom. There was no large man in a closed space who was going to send him anywhere to work for coin.

Trying to re-roll his bedding proved to be trickier than Erik had expected and Tove pushed him away from it, finishing the job herself. It was another reminder that he wasn't suited to the world he found himself in and he began to understand the comfort of a place like Kvernes to the ones who'd stayed there. Whatever else it was, it was simple to live in. Still, the thought of returning made him less comfortable than whatever things he couldn't yet do well.

Erik took the pack, insisting that he carry it in spite of Tove's protests that the chief of the warband shouldn't do such work. It was heavier than he'd expected. For Tove to have run with it, her small frame must have been hiding muscle fairly well. If she could handle it then, to Erik's mind, that was all the more reason for him to be the one carrying it. He needed to make himself strong, so much as he could. Away from the numbing ease of Kvernes, he remembered clearly his brief time with Göll and Vár and knew that it was only a beginning.

They worked their way east through the forest steadily. It was well before noon when they came across a road moving north across their path.

"Are we far enough from Kvernes to follow it?"

Tove thought on it a moment, looking south down the road. "We'll move faster on the road."

The road it was. The walk was quiet, with Tove grabbing

bits of dried meat every hour or two. They moved to the woods to move around smaller towns that Tove knew were immediately attached to the road. They were all similar to Gandrup, small farms cut into the land, being worked endlessly by the people who had built them up. They'd passed the third such farm when Tove finally relaxed.

"That was the last of the farms which trades regularly with Kvernes." Her voice was cheerful and she could hardly keep herself still, walking from side to side of the road in front of Erik. "They won't know my face now."

"And I won't have to explain who I am." Erik huffed a laugh, adjusting the pack. "I'm not good at talking like... you guys."

"You're easy enough to understand." Tove kicked a rock off into the woods, holding her pose while she watched it fly. "And dressed the part now too."

Erik looked down at his clothes. They were dirty from working the farms and sweating nearly constantly the previous day. Still, they weren't uncomfortable because of it, but Tove had made him think of them and now he felt a strong need to bathe. "How far to the next town?"

Tove swayed her head in thought as she looked up the road. "Two hours, if I remember it correctly. I've never walked it myself."

It was an easy enough walk, the main road being as well-kept as the others he'd traveled. They chatted idly about what sort of foods they hoped would be in Lofgrund, a conversation that was cut short by the appearance of a person coming down the road in the opposite direction of them. Tove came to Erik's side, walking stiffly.

"Who do you think it might be?" she asked Erik, clearly not realizing how ridiculous expecting an answer from him would be.

He still managed to give one. "Maybe just a trader."

There was a man walking next to a large black horse pulling a cart. Erik couldn't see what the cart held, but the man looked young, maybe just a bit older than he was.

"Hail, friends!" A hand of greeting went up as the man came closer to them. "Strange to see travelers this far west." He brought his horse to a stop and looked them over. "I am Kjalarr."

"Erik." He motioned to Tove who said nothing. "And Tove."

"Good names. I like them both." He turned, reaching over into his cart and Erik could see Tove's arm shift backward toward where she'd stowed the knife she'd taken off of Vali. His arms came back over holding a small basket of fruit, raspberries and cherries. Tove dropped her arm to her side before he looked back toward them. He held it out.

"Oh, we don't... we don't have much coin." Erik held a hand out refusing the fruit.

"Nonsense. A gift. Travelers must eat." Kjalarr pushed the basket into Erik's hand. "Try them!" He smiled a genuine smile.

Erik pulled one from the basket. The berries were plump, fresh, and better than any he'd ever eaten. Tove obviously agreed after her grudging bite of the first one. She plucked four more from the basket and ate them greedily.

"If I might ask, where are you headed? I've often found myself jealous of the folk who live out this far. They live such simple lives. Happy, free of worry and pain."

"We are headed for Lofgrund," Erik said, not wanting to sound as stern or serious as he had.

Kjalarr frowned. "A complicated place full of danger and pain. But you seem sure."

"I am."

Kjalarr gave a sad smile. "Very well, so long as you're sure of your decision. I would only offer this advice: Once simplicity is left behind, even those who yearn to return most often find they cannot."

Erik narrowed his eyes at the man. The trader had looked only at him since stopping. Somehow, even through the calm, kind tone of the words, Erik sensed a challenge.

His body told him to fight. It screamed a demand to swing from every muscle.

"I don't want simplicity." Erik tried as best he could to keep his rising anger from showing on his face.

Kjalarr only kept his calm smile and nodded. "Then, I have work I must be getting back to."

He walked past them, watching Erik until he was no longer within arm's reach. The horse and its minder continued on down the road. Despite his unease at turning his back on the trader, Erik started to walk again.

Tove tossed the berries away when they had walked on a bit. "There was something odd about him, don't you think?"

"Odd is a way to put it." Erik looked over his shoulder, the cart was still drifting into the distance. "The sooner we're in Lofgrund, the better."

CHAPTER TEN

THEY WEREN'T FAR FROM THE NEXT TOWN WHEN TOVE turned to Erik and stared at him for a while. She finally spoke up when he started staring back at her.

"How do you cook things?"

"*You* cook things."

"Not here. Where you come from."

"Ovens. Microwaves. Stove tops."

"I know ovens. They're expensive. We had two of them in the bakery in Kvernes."

"No, not... they still use those kinds of ovens for some things, but most people don't own those. They have smaller ones."

"Small... everyone has an oven?"

"I'm pretty sure everyone has an oven."

"Wow. And what's a microwave?"

"Yeah, I didn't really think of how to explain this before I said it." Erik pulled in a deep breath. "We have this thing called electricity."

She gave him a blank stare.

"Right, most people basically consider it a magic box that makes things hotter without fire."

Tove screwed up her face. "You're mocking me."

He laughed. "I'm not! They're real. How am I supposed to explain that when you don't have toilet paper?"

"I've heard of paper. For writing important stories on. Did you write in the toilet?"

"Oh god, see? There's so much... You'd wipe with it."

She looked shocked. "With paper?!"

Erik threw his hands up. "It's not weird! It's a little weird... but it's way better than sheep's wool. Not that it matters, there's really no way for me to show you."

The sun had just passed the midpoint of the sky when they came across a small town, just smaller than Kvernes. The houses here were a wider mix of styles with longhouses toward the outer edge and less stylistic wooden houses nearer to the center of town where a small stream ran through under a simple bridge.

"Do we need supplies?"

Tove nodded, too busy looking suspiciously at the people around to answer aloud. A rotund woman beckoned them over.

"Come now, you two! Travelers are welcome 'ere. And I expect yer 'ungry."

There were a few benches outside of the door the woman was shouting from. Erik walked over with Tove sticking close behind him.

"Simple stew, but it's cheap." She smiled wide. "Farthing each."

Erik pulled a whole silver coin out of his pocket, having nothing but the five he'd been paid at the farm.

"It's all I've got, whole coins."

"No coin cutter?" She gave him a queer look.

Erik shook his head. "No, I don't..."

She nodded. "Not a problem. Set yourselves down and rest a spell."

With that, the woman went into the house and Erik offloaded the pack. He sat first and Tove sat beside him.

"They seem normal enough," Tove said. "I'll call myself happy that they're not so interested in us as I'd expected."

Erik looked around, seeing the people of the town mostly ignoring them in stark contrast to Kvernes. "Hopefully it stays that way."

The woman returned with two bowls of stew and soft white bread. She handed the bowls to Erik and turned to pop back into the house. She returned much more quickly this time, holding an iron tool that was hinged at the end.

"Let me split them coins for you. It'll make things easier if you mean to buy supplies anyway."

Erik pulled a coin and handed them to the woman with a slight hesitance, but she placed the coin face down into a circular plate on the press and pressed the thin, dull ridge protruding from the other side down onto it. The coin made a small clinking noise as the tool cut in to a cross-line drawn into the back.

"You want 'em in farthings?"

He wasn't entirely sure what that meant but nodded and she turned the circular bit a quarter turn, pressing again, splitting the coin into four. She dumped them into her hand, showing him two before pocketing those and handing the other two back.

"You need any more done? Might do to split 'em now. Some folk ain't so honest and charge. Silly, I says. A smile sells more stew than tricks."

Erik pulled two more coins and had her do the same to

them, figuring that the price must have been fairly common. Tove hadn't complained about the prices or the practice, but she'd never been this far out before and mostly spent the time between bites of stew staring at people rather than paying attention to the business with the coins.

The woman finished the work and smiled wide. "You need anythin' else, just give a knock. And just leave the bowls whenever it is you're done. I'll collect 'em when I can."

She was back inside after that. The stew was good, with potatoes and carrots and peas. They were vegetables he hadn't seen in Kvernes and the bread was like nothing they'd been making at the bakery there.

Tove was more than halfway done with the sizable portion when she first said anything.

"These tiny green bits are delicious. Turnips taste different, though."

"They're potatoes," Erik laughed. "And the green bits are peas. I think we may have been lied to about the world outside of Kvernes."

Tove smiled. "I always knew they were lying. And now I have proof of it." She laughed. "And here I am eating potatoes and, and…"

"Peas."

"Peas!" She held her spoon up. "I can't imagine anything better and we've only just started." She nudged him. "It's only just started, Erik."

They finished the bowls of stew and left them on the bench. Erik asked the men standing around across from them where they could buy supplies. Tove clarified that they needed dried meat, some bread, and anything else that might be helpful.

Everyone selling things was pleasant without any of the odd feeling that Erik had gotten off of the trader before. Part of him wanted to ask if the man was from this town but it might add undue awkwardness to their short time there and that wasn't worth doing. They'd bought two small loaves of fresh bread, one of which Tove couldn't resist pulling a piece off of. The baker noticed and laughed.

"You like it that much, I'll have to throw in another."

He went in and grabbed another, wrapping it up in a piece of cloth like the others, handing it to Tove. She was lost for words.

"I don't think she's ever had anything like it," Erik said, chuckling. "It's very good, I must say."

"You flatter a man, I'll tell you." The baker leaned out the door looking just down the street they were on. "If she finds that a treat, I reckon she's not from 'round here. There's a man just down that way, sells plums. Four doors from here."

"Plums?" Tove was quick to ask.

"Thought she might say that, but you've had 'em, eh boy?"

Erik nodded shaking his pockets. He had five farthings and his two coins left. "I'll go see him. Thanks."

The baker nodded and headed back into his house. They walked down the way he'd shown them and knocked. An old man came to the door.

"What is it you need, stranger?"

"The baker said you sell plums."

"That I do. Four to a farthing."

Erik pulled a farthing out and put it in the man's hand. "There you go."

He disappeared back into the house and Erik looked down at Tove who had returned from pressing the third loaf of bread into the pack.

"Don't guess you packed any coin of your own?"

Tove crossed her arms as the man came back with the plums. "Of course I did. Anyway, we're a warband. It's all the same coin. We share."

The old man chuckled at the word warband and Tove took exception.

"What's funny about that? We are! We're going to—"

Erik put his hand over her face and pushed her back to stop her walking toward the old man. She turned away in a huff. The old man handed over the plums and Erik gave them to Tove to hold, which she did grudgingly.

"How far to Lofgrund from here?"

The old man poked his head out of the doorway and looked up at the sky.

"Day like this? Should make it there just about sundown if you stick to the road."

Erik thanked him and they returned to the main road, headed north-east. After filling their jars with water, Tove handed him a plum and then tried one herself.

She frowned. "Too sweet. I prefer the bread. And we are a warband, you shouldn't have interrupted me. He ought to know."

"We're not likely to be taken seriously with only two."

She waved the plum at him dismissively. "It's early days yet. We'll make Odin take notice by the time we make it to Valhalla. He might even let me in at that rate."

She finished the plum in spite of the complaint and Erik did the same, agreeing with her that it was too sweet. They kept the other two in spite of not being elated with them. The walk wasn't any different than any other part, the roads quiet and the woods empty and easily watched. He thought it would actually be sort of hard to be a raider so long as people were armed in general. They had two knives between them, one packed with the rest of their supplies and the other with Tove. They definitely wouldn't be effective if caught out unless Erik was given time to unpack. But he wasn't any sort of expert with a knife except for generally knowing where to put the sharp parts.

The road wouldn't be the place for him to find out. With the sun setting, Lofgrund came into view at the center of a field that went on for miles in each direction. Even with the city in sight, they had a half hour of walking left before they finally arrived at the gates. It was dark by then and Erik was starting to feel the deep regret of a man who decided to carry a heavy pack all day.

There were a trio of guards standing at the far edge of a drawbridge. They kept close watch on Erik and Tove as they crossed the bridge toward the gate. The construction was definitely not something Erik expected, and Tove had been in stunned silence ever since she'd seen the guards.

One of the guards took a few steps forward as they came across the bridge, holding up a hand.

"What is your purpose in Lofgrund?"

Erik stiffened immediately, hearing the official tone. "Uh, eating. Eating, sleeping, and then continuing on."

"How long will you be in the city?"

"A few nights at most? Maybe only one."

The guard nodded. "Submit your pack for searching." He turned around and walked back as the other two moved to the center of the open gate. Erik walked to them and removed the pack, Tove keeping her distance behind him. The area was lit by torches at the top of and beside the gate arch. It didn't seem to slow the guards who rifled through the bag as though they could see things well enough. The third guard watched over Erik and Tove as the other two did their work. Erik turned to him.

"Are there cheap rooms in the city?"

The guard leaned his head toward the northern part of the city. "Might be some up that way. Can't say as they're nice, but they're rooms and they're cheap. Not too pleasant when it gets late enough, but so long as you're in after dinner, I never heard no one complain."

They finished with the pack, making a catalogue of the things inside of it and sent them on their way. Erik thanked the guard and they went into the city. They hadn't gone fifty feet past the gate into a large, ornate square lit by torches on a stone statue of Odin.

She was open-mouthed and breathless. "It's amazing. The buildings they... they're six storeys. And so much stone. I've never seen so much!" She turned to Erik. "Let's not leave." A horse drawn carriage rode through the far end of the square and Tove ran toward it, pointing. "What was that?! It wasn't a cart."

"It was a carriage. Rich people ride in them. I think."

"I've decided that I'd like to become rich, Erik."

He laughed. "I doubt you're alone in that." He started toward the north, waving for her to follow. "You'll have plenty of time to be amazed after we've eaten and bought a room. Days, even."

She followed him, eyes still locked on the buildings around them. Signs and lit shops, painted colors they simply didn't have anywhere he'd seen in Kvernes. As they approached the north side of the square a young boy came running up with what looked like a table leg with a tar covered piece of sheet over it.

"Need of a linkboy, sir?"

"Linkboy?" He looked at Tove who shook her head and shrugged.

"Ah! New to the idea. No need to feel bashful, sir. For a farthing, I'll show you to where you need to go. Dangerous to be out at night, sir, when you don't know the city. Especially if you're headed north."

"Sounds fair enough. We need an inn, a room. Somewhere near food. You know a place?"

The boy nodded enthusiastically. "That I do, sir."

Erik produced a farthing and handed it to the boy who bit it and then put it into his pocket.

"This way, sir."

He swung by one of the lit torches in the square and lit his own, holding it out in front of him.

Tove was busy sniffing at the air, and making plaintive moans. "What are these smells, Erik? When can we eat? Maybe we should just eat now. No sense walking all the way across the city."

The linkboy spoke up. "Don't recommend it, miss. Food's not so different, I've heard. Fancier plates to look at it sitting on."

"Smaller portions too, I'd bet," Erik complained. "Porcelain and nice chairs sound about right?"

The boy laughed. "Sir understands. Are you from the southern kingdom to know such a thing?"

"No. But I've seen the same game played before."

There was a jewelry store with glass windows, something that most of the other shops around the square didn't have. Tove grabbed Erik by his arm, dragging him over.

"What are these?!"

The linkboy followed them, holding the torch out toward the window as there was no light inside. "She has an eye for fine things, sir."

"It's jewelry and I doubt either of us has enough money for any of it."

"But it's so beautiful. We'll come back for it, after a raid, maybe."

Erik pulled her arm, waving the linkboy to continue on. In spite of Tove's complaints, she eventually contented herself with a promise that they'd go and see things in the morning. Erik couldn't bring himself to be annoyed by it. She had never seen anything like it before. Really, he hadn't either, but he at least knew that sort of thing existed. She made him feel almost guilty for not enjoying the majesty of it all. It was a world he never could have known, enjoying it might not be so bad.

The linkboy came to a stop in front of a sign that was painted white and red, with only the word "Inn" carved into it. He nodded to them and snuffed out the torch in a metal extinguisher on the wall of the inn before running off back to the south. Across from them was a bustling restaurant, labeled "Inga's."

When the linkboy was gone, Tove started toward the restaurant.

"I'm not convinced we needed to pay him a farthing for that work."

Erik shrugged. "Hard for me to argue with you, but we'd

have been all night trying to find this place. It was a one time expense."

They entered the restaurant and a large woman welcomed them with a booming voice.

"Find a seat and drop your pack! Inga will serve you!" She laughed heartily and went into what Erik assumed was the kitchen.

There were individual tables, with chairs instead of benches, except for a long set in the back, where larger groups sat drinking and laughing.

A table with two chairs was next to the door, so Erik went to it and sat, Tove nervously taking the seat across from him.

"What if this table belongs to someone?"

Erik gave a sideways smile. "It's a restaurant. They're for customers."

Tove looked down at the table and then back up to Erik and huffed. "For knowing so little about Kvernes, you sure know plenty about Lofgrund."

Erik looked around. "It's more like where I came from."

The large woman rolled up to their table, smiling. "Travelers? Welcome. Inga will make sure you are fed. Meat and a vegetable for a half coin." She put a meaty hand on Erik's shoulder. "What will you have?"

Tove was confused. "Have?"

Inga pointed to a menu board on the wall behind them. It was a short menu, but they offered beef steak, mashed potatoes, and a half dozen other items.

They ordered and when Inga was gone, Tove leaned across the table. "People live like this?"

Erik couldn't help but laugh at it. "Apparently so."

"Did you eat at restaurants?"

"Pretty much exclusively."

Her eyes widened. "Were you rich?"

He laughed again, leaning back to stretch his tired muscles. "I was not even a little bit rich, no."

She looked out the window. "It's amazing. This was how you lived?"

Erik shook his head. "No, it wasn't like this. There were indoor toilets and... I guess, carts that didn't need horses."

"You're picking fun at me again."

"I am not!" Erik feigned indignance.

The food came before Erik could further defend himself. It was well-cooked, amazing by the standards of everything he'd had since he'd woken up in Helheim.

Tove was nearly weeping after she took the first few bites, having gotten the beef and mashed potatoes.

With her mouth full, she looked at Erik, barely keeping it together. "Ith gaht tho mush budder."

A few men at the tables around them laughed at her and slapped Erik on the back.

Inga shouted at them from the far side of the room. "Inga said, did she not? All who eat here leave satisfied!"

Half the room cheered, and then began shouting orders. Inga yelled at them and they calmed down. She started making rounds, taking orders properly.

They were nearly finished when a middle-aged woman poked her head through the open shutters, looking at Tove, frowning, and then to Erik. She sniffed the air around him and then left, coming through the door and leaning over, rubbing her hands through his hair.

"Excuse me, do I..."

"Quiet..."

She flipped his hand over, and ran a small knife across it. Erik yelped, but her grip was inhumanly firm and he couldn't wriggle his hand free. She licked his palm and breathed in deep, letting his hand go. The woman stood up, rolling her head back. Tove stood up from the table.

"How dare you! Seidr woman!" Tove pulled back to swing at her, but the woman jerked away. Inga came from the back, holding a dozen mugs. She saw the woman and immediately flew into a rage.

"Seidr! Begone from Inga's! You know not to come to this place!"

The woman ignored her, looking down at Erik. "You..." She whispered the word, her eyes swirling with black and green.

Inga put the mugs down and came thundering across the room. The woman ran outside into the street, stopping by the window.

"I know you, Haki! I know!" Inga followed her out the door and the woman fled down the street, laughing wildly.

Inga was quick to return to their table as Tove inspected Erik's hand. It was still bleeding, though not much. It looked almost as though it had already begun to heal.

"Inga cannot... free! Drinks, food! Whatever you wish. No seidr woman should ever come near you in Inga's."

Erik smiled. "Thanks, but it's not—"

"Inga will not hear it! Eat! Drink! I will bring them! No one leaves Inga's unhappy!"

The room cheered again, returning to their revels in short order. Tove sat down, looking with troubled eyes at his hand.

"She called you Haki."

Erik looked at the now-scabbed cut on his hand. "She did..."

CHAPTER ELEVEN

IT WAS BARELY SUNUP WHEN THE SOUND OF KNUCKLES RAP-
ping on the door pulled Erik out of an uncomfortable sleep.
It was the old man who'd rented him the pair of ground-
floor rooms after they'd eaten.

"I'll have you out! Paid for the night, not the day. Want
another day, ye'll pay for it!"

It wasn't a change of attitude from the night before,
when the hunched old man had taken a silver off of him for
the two rooms for the night, "and nothing more." Erik could
hear him continue down the hall shouting the same command at every single door. The bed had been less comfortable than the ground, somehow, and Erik figured he would

103

likely have been better off sleeping in the fields surrounding the city.

He'd slept without clothes since the night was so much warmer in Lofgrund than it had been in Kvernes. He hadn't noticed it while they were walking, but now that it was morning he could feel the heat of the sun coming in through the shuttered window. They must have left Spring at some point during their walk, but Erik would have found it impossible to tell where. The sun had fallen as they walked and cooled the day fairly evenly. The excitement of having made it to Lofgrund made him forget to take notice of how the night had been until he was undressing to sleep.

The old man's voice was farther off down the hall, and Erik didn't want to have to deal with him opening the door, so he pulled on the loose, unclean underwear he'd had since arriving in Kvernes and pulled on his unclean pants and shirt on top of them. The whole ensemble needed a wash, and Erik wouldn't have minded one himself. He held the hand the strange woman had cut the night before up, looking for any sign of the wound but there was nothing, not even a line of red. He had meant to ask what seidr was and what it had all been about, but Inga's fussing over them had been so overwhelming that he'd forgotten until he was in his room at the inn.

He checked his pocket, pushing the thought from his mind, and found the remaining three farthings still there. The money was dwindling, which made him nervous to say the least. He hadn't looked through the pack that Tove had prepared and had only trusted her to mean what she said about having her own money. She'd taken the pack to her room the night before, wanting to organize things and make a catalogue of what they had remaining.

Erik opened the door before the old man had the chance to finish his rounds. He made for the lobby and found a yawning Tove standing there waiting for him.

"Paid for the night." She scoffed the words as soon as she

saw him.

Erik gave a sideways smile. "He's a man who takes his definitions very seriously."

"It's day and I was told I could go see jewelry."

"After breakfast." He slapped at his stomach.

Tove chuckled. "You're starting to talk like a man. And maybe look like one, just the slightest bit."

Erik rubbed at the hair growing in on his chin. It was still barely more than stubble, but he felt strange, having been forced to shave for so long.

The old man made it back to the lobby. "Less yer waitin' to hand me coin, get out. My inn's for sleeping, less you pay proper."

There were higher floors, which Erik assumed the man meant. There hadn't been an explanation the night before when they'd come to pay. He'd told them a fixed price and taken their money. The dirty clothes and rough pack must have made their finances clear enough.

Tove left first with Erik just behind her. The sky was still a purplish blue, but there was already a stream of people making their way all in the same direction. Inga's was still closed so early and had been fairly costly in spite of the extra food they'd enjoyed.

"Maybe we follow them?" Erik motioned at the passing people.

Tove nodded her agreement and they started after the people.

"This must be Summer," Tove said, shifting her shirt away from her body. "I can't say as I enjoy it."

"Never been a big fan myself. You can only take off so much. Makes me miss air conditioning."

Tove gave him a questioning look so he didn't wait for the actual question.

"It cools off rooms and buildings. Sort of an automatic fan that blows air over ice." It wasn't strictly accurate but she might at least not call him a liar.

"I am starting to be jealous of this world you're describing."

"It wasn't too bad, really. All the complaining I did seems a bit silly now that I've wiped my ass with dirty wool."

Tove left the conversation there, more interested in the shops around them than in retreading the conversation about toilet practices. There was a marked difference in the shops in general, but they seemed to be getting nicer as they followed the people southward.

It was a few turns and a ten-minute walk among the grounds before they came into a bustling square with dozens upon dozens of stalls and businesses lining the lower levels around the square. It was nearly impossible to see all of the stalls through the throngs of people doing their morning shopping. At the far edge of the square, Erik could swear he saw a bread shop that looked to be putting out croissants. Tove's eyes were wide, scanning the booths with manic energy.

"You got money? Coin?"

Tove tapped the pocket of the loose pants she wore. "Of course. Warband funds." She smiled. "I'm going to buy dried fish. And fruits. Some of those tiny, red, bumpy ones, like we had from that strange man. These should be fine, right? So long as the vendor's not strange, I mean."

"Raspberries." He pointed down toward the end. "I'm going to look at that bread shop."

"We have plenty of bread."

"We don't have bread like that bread. Trust me. I'll wait there since it's easier to find."

Tove headed off after saying she understood and Erik made his way down the row of businesses. There were a number of small shops between him and the bread. One sold spices and another was selling assorted fabric in a dozen different colors. There was a shop selling jams and preserved fruits right next to the bread shop. It was a shrewd arrangement. Small jars of raspberry jam were a half coin each. The jars were smaller than he would have liked for the cost. The bread shop was, at least, selling croissants. In fact, it was all they were selling. There was a line in front of him, waiting to get them. He looked around, spotting other bread shops along the adjacent row, but they were all selling more traditional looking loaves. In a way, he found having to stand in a line to be fairly refreshing in general. There hadn't been so many people around before and Erik took a strange sort of comfort in the idea that there were towns larger than Kvernes had been. The large stone walls helped the feeling of ease that he felt.

A pair of people had bought their croissants at the front of the line and moved on when the third approached, insisting on haggling over the prices. Erik was watching the argument escalate when he felt a sharp pair of fingers dig into his shoulder and turned him around.

"Haki!" It was the woman from the night before. She had a scar across her cheek in the shape of a cross that he hadn't noticed in the restaurant. Rather than looking at him after calling his name, she looked around frantically. Not seeing whatever she was wary of, the woman turned her attentions back to Erik. "You should come with me, Haki. There is much I could tell you."

"Look, I don't know how you know my name, or whatever is happening, but there's literally no way I'm going anywhere with you."

The woman flinched at nothing, rubbing her hands together nervously. "I know—"

The pit of a cherry thocked against the side of the seidr woman's head. Rage flushed her face and she turned to scream but Tove beat her to it.

"You again! How dare you touch him? I won't have you put your hands on him again, understand me seidr woman?"

She ignored Tove, who walked toward them at speed. "Haki, you need my help. I know the safe ways. You go north, yes? Toward Valhalla. It is a treacherous journey. Seidr is for

107

these things, ask the girl. I can help you avoid the valkyries."

Erik turned to look at Tove whose face showed her annoyance plainly, but she relented. "She speaks the truth. Seidr is used for such things."

The woman reached out, grabbing at Erik's arms but Tove was quick to strike at the woman's wrist.

"Don't lay a hand on him!"

Erik looked at Tove. "Can she be useful?"

Tove stewed on the question for a minute, looking the woman over as she continued to scan the buildings, looking up toward the sky. Erik felt himself twitch as she did and looked up himself, finding the sky empty of even clouds.

"She can help us. But only ask what we need to know, nothing more. And do not let her touch you. They seek to change destinies with their touch." Tove pointed an angry finger up at the woman's chin. "Don't touch him, understand? I'll spill your insides if you try it again."

The woman took a step back, nodding. "Of course. But you know we cannot do what is needed here. The herbs and salts must be seen to."

The argument with the bread maker was still ongoing in spite of the noise the seidr woman had made arguing with Tove so Erik decided they may as well see to whatever divination the woman intended to show them. She showed crooked teeth behind an unnerving smile and led them through side streets and alleys.

Tove and Erik kept themselves a healthy distance behind the woman. He didn't like the way she looked around the upper parts of the buildings around them.

"Are you sure this will be fine?"

Tove hesitated. "Not entirely. People can know their destinies and know how to live within them. Why does she call you Haki?"

"It's my first name."

"But you do not use it?"

"Where I lived it would have been considered an odd

name. Erik wasn't. I've been Erik all my life to everyone but my parents, no sense in changing now."

Tove looked him over. "Haki suits you better."

"Does it?" he laughed. "I'll have to consider that. When our warband gets larger. Then you'll feel special for calling me a different name."

"That might make the others talk."

The woman came to a stop in front of them as they arrived at a small stone shop that stood on its own between the typical taller buildings of the city. Inside was a room covered with furs and carved wooden idols, a thick set of curtains separating the rear of the home from the front. The seidr woman was quick to disappear behind them, telling the pair to wait. Tove put a hand on Erik's shoulder as soon as the woman had left them alone.

"Do not give her your seed."

Erik reeled, brow furrowing in confusion. "Why would I give her my seed?"

"You shouldn't."

"I wasn't going to—"

"And if she undresses, you must resist her. Tell me immediately."

"Why would she undress?!"

The woman reappeared, still fully clothed, and called for Erik, telling Tove to remain outside. Tove dropped the pack and sat on the wooden bench at the side of the main room.

"I know how your rituals work, seidr."

Erik sat down in the chair nearest the curtain and the woman moved to the far side. She had bones laid out on the table and dried herbs smoking in bowls behind her. She kept herself standing and began slowly shifting the bones around the table. For five minutes, she slid the bones slowly into a small bowl before shifting them around and dumping them on the table. Still, she said nothing. The woman moved to the side of the room and retrieved a staff. Running her hands slowly up and down it, she began to chant nonsense. She tapped the staff on the floor once, lightly, and again, slamming it down and opening her eyes, cackling madly.

"They're here! I've done it!"

The door behind them flew open and Erik heard a horrible, familiar hiss he hadn't heard since the motel. Erik flew to his feet, flipping the table. A rage boiled in him at the woman's trick. He plunged his fist across the table, catching her in the neck, just above her collarbone. The woman crumpled backward, shrieking. A second later, before he could turn himself around, he heard Tove shout in agony.

Erik ripped the curtain open. Tove was bleeding from nearly every spot on her body, dragging a leg that was barely attached. His eyes opened wide, fixed on her as she tried to drag herself to him, crying. Between choking, pained sobs, Tove managed a few words.

"Kill them! Kill them, Erik!"

She put a hand out to drag herself to him, but it fell there and her head dropped into a gathering pool of blood as the valkyrie behind plunged the tip of a spear through her chest.

Erik flew into a rage, charging the valkyrie as fast as his legs would carry him. She barely managed to pull the spear clear and put it in front of herself to block the punch. His fist slammed against the shaft, sending a crackling ring through the weapon and sending the valkyrie stumbling back into her short-haired partner. He barely registered the stunned look on the longer-haired valkyrie's face when he charged again. She was ready this time and moved herself to the side. He saw it well enough, but couldn't change the angle of his charge. The second valkyrie slapped the flat of her glowing sword into his back, sending him tumbling through the open door.

Somehow, Erik managed to shift as he tumbled and came up facing the door he'd left through. The short-haired valkyrie was already on the charge, her sword aimed for his gut. Erik gritted his teeth, screaming. The back of his wrist slapped against the blade, driving it into the wall beside him. The valkyrie did not slow her charge and let the blade go, driving her forearm into his throat, cutting off his scream. Behind him, he heard the sound of stones and mortar crackling. The first few chunks fell to the ground around him as the wall began to collapse. A stone hit his shoulder and one cracked his skull and then, in a torrent of noise, he was buried under the weight of a building dropping onto his body.

Chapter Twelve

Erik's eyes were pulled open but a crushing pain ran over his entire body. He saw the ceiling of the inn he'd slept in the night before and was desperately confused. The pain pushed up against his brain, and though he strained against it, he let out a scream. His body wouldn't move and he could still feel weight on his chest and jagged rocks pushing into every inch of him.

He forced himself to look around the room, managing to see that it was indeed the same room he'd slept in the night before. Holding in the will to scream against the pain he heard a girl's pained screams as well. And then words.

"Let me go! Ahhhh!"

It was Tove. The sound came by the room and a second later the door opened. It was the old man, sneering.

"Other'n's back as well, jus' like I thought."

Erik battled back the pain long enough to ask, "How? There... there..." He couldn't manage anymore and screamed again from the weight. He could feel the blood flush his face.

The old man looked at him, an eyebrow crooked up. He laughed, pushing the door open as a pair of men dressed in chain armor came into the room, pulling Erik from the bed. The innkeeper's laugh was sharp and mocking. As the guards dragged him by, the old man leaned in close, hot, putrid breath pouring out into Erik's face.

"Can't die here, boy. Nowhere left to go."

The guards dragged him, wailing, through the inn's lobby and out to a small cart in the street. He saw them toss Tove into it as though she was a corpse. She jerked as she landed, screaming out, and she was clutching her chest when they brought Erik to the wagon. He was tossed in beside her in much the same way, landing hard on the boards. The landing sent fresh spirals of pain through his body, flashing at every point where a rock must have crushed some part of him. It felt as though every one of his bones were broken but he could see from looking that they were intact and there wasn't so much as a bruise on him. The horses started pulling the wagon and every bump was agony. Tove flailed against the pain, slamming her hands into the floor of the wagon and gritting her teeth, tears streaming down her bright red face.

He wanted nothing more than to pull himself to her and hold her still, but his body responded to every command with only more pain. It was a jolt-filled ride past a small pair of open gates and into a yard with no buildings that Erik could see pointing up. They were pulled from the back of the cart and Erik saw that they were in a stone courtyard, a keep in the middle. They were not being taken to the keep, but to a side building that was far less ornate. Inside was a room with a guard, who covered his ears as the pair came past him. It seemed to be nearly second nature to the man, who had only barely looked up from a plate of sausage he was eating. Stairs descended to a widening hall with a fork at the mid-section. Tove was taken to the left and Erik could see they meant to take him to the right.

"Hey! Hnn— no! No! Bring her back god— agh... bring..."

"Ho hooo, spirited one, you."

It was all the strength he had and all it had managed was a remark from one of the guards. They took him to a room with three doors and angled toward the one nearest the hallway exit. He heard a deep, rattling, nasal voice from behind the middle door.

"Who... is it? New? Someone... new? Smells! H-h-he smells!" The words came as though they were huffed out with great effort.

The guards took Erik to a plank bed in the corner and dropped him onto it. He curled up reflexively against the shock it sent through him and before he could open his eyes again, he heard the sound of the cell door shut.

Hours crawled by, the nerves in his body never once letting him have a moment's peace, often causing involuntary spasms which only stood to worsen things. There were no windows and the shifting orange light outside of his cell told him only that they'd used torches or something similar. He couldn't begin to fathom how many hours had passed when he was at least able to lie still and gather his thoughts. He remembered the valkyries vividly, and the forearm that pressed into his throat. The wall had fallen, he knew that. And he remembered the pain in his shoulder but nothing after. How long had it been before they awoke in the inn?

He was exhausted as the pain slowly faded and he fell asleep for some amount of time he wished he could estimate. It may have been night already, for all he knew. And even as hard as he tried, he couldn't remember where the sun had been in the sky when he was thrown onto the wagon. The pain was mostly gone when he woke, but his muscles still tried to cramp with the slightest move.

Erik rubbed at this neck, feeling it to be sure everything was where he expected it to be. He took a few deep breaths before standing up and walking around the cell. It was stone from side to side with only a small block missing in the corner. Erik walked over to the hole, looking down it. It went pitch black after only a foot or so, but he could hear rushing water at the bottom. He thought of the toilet in Kvernes and decided that the dark staining around the hole was most likely from whoever had used it before him.

He went back to the bed, tired from just that small bit of work. The door was obviously thick, he could see as much by the area between the bars in its window and the wood that extended to either side. It was nothing he'd be able to knock down and with rock on either side of it, he figured the walls weren't likely to give way if he slammed against it. That was the whole of the cell for him to look at. The wood under him was smooth, at least, but he couldn't call it comfortable.

A guard walked by the window of the cell, peeking in. Erik stood up and shouted at the man.

"Where is Tove?! Hey!"

He rose to his feet and pushed himself toward the door to the cell, holding onto his stomach to give himself some support against the dull pain of sudden movement. He reached the door and grabbed the bars of the window.

"Where is she?"

He saw the guard head back down the hallway, not even glancing at his door as he went. Erik took the time to look around the small room outside his cell a bit. There were a pair of torches and not much else. He dropped back down, moving back to the bed, not sure why he was in the cell to begin with. The valkyries had attacked him. Was that enough to lock him up? It would hardly be possible to lock up the agents of a god, so had they taken him instead? They had looked at him with suspicion and maybe even malice in Kvernes for the same reason. Vali had even tried to kill him in the name of saving the city. The sentiment rang true enough. They'd toppled a building onto him just to stop him breathing.

There was no more sound outside of his cell for a time, so Erik went to sleep again. He was pulled awake by the sound of scraping rock against his cell floor. He jumped to his feet to look for the source. He quickly walked the room looking at the edges of the walls from bottom to top and then scanning the rest, but there was no sign of what might have made the sound. It could have come from outside, he told himself, thinking of how everything in the stone halls echoed horribly.

Erik sat back on the wooden bed, restless. It was then that he realized that the pain had faded entirely. The realization frustrated him all the more as there was nothing he could think to do. To make it all worse, he was either being toyed with or becoming paranoid. Neither would serve him well inside the prison. There was another prisoner but the man hadn't made a sound since he'd been brought in.

The door to his cell opened and a guard came in holding a small bowl.

"Dinner."

Erik stood up.

"Hey," the guard warned, backing away. "Steady."

"Where is Tove?"

"You can take your dinner or have it thrown at you. Which is it?"

Erik sat himself back down and the guard placed the bowl on the ground before backing out and closing the door. He went to it as soon as the guard was gone, and began to eat it as fast as he could lift the spoon. It was only runny gruel but it was something, at least. He hadn't realized how hungry he was until the food hit his tongue. He made embarrassing noises as he stood, forcing spoonful after spoonful into his face.

The sound of rock scraping on rock caused Erik to spin. He dropped the bowl at the sight of a gaunt man coming toward him at inhuman speed. The man grabbed him by the face, squeezing his cheeks together. The man's grip was too strong to be called normal. Erik slapped the hand away and the man backed away from him, putting his arms out as if mocking Erik to goad him into a fight.

"A... fight. No... no need... for that here." He gave a slow wheezing laugh.

Erik looked the man up and down. He was in tattered robes and had a long black beard coming down from his face. The hair on his head had not fared as well, large patches missing and the rest wiry and thin. There was muscle under thin skin that rippled as the man slowly hopped back and forth in front him.

"Who are you?"

"A neighbor." The man's eyes turned to the cell door and widened. He licked his lips and then turned his attention to the bed. "You slept. Slept in here?"

Erik didn't answer.

The man lurched at him. "Don't—"

When Erik raised his fist, the man reeled backward, throwing his hands up.

"Didn't..." The man drew a deep, wheezing breath and continued at his terrible cadence. "Didn't mean to..." He nearly choked on the word. "Frighten."

Erik watched closely as his neighbor stepped back into the light from the cell door. There was a strange twitching in his throat. The man saw him looking and put his hands over the twitching mass.

"The brain... never forgets. Never."

Erik heard footsteps in the hall and the strange man twisted toward them for a half second before scurrying back to the hole he'd come through and disappearing back to the other cell. Erik followed him but still barely managed to catch the loosened brick in motion. It was barely wide enough for a man at the best of times, let alone at the speed the gaunt figure had pushed himself through it.

The door to his cell opened and two guards came in, one holding a short length of rope. Erik turned to them and adopted a defensive posture. The nearer of the two guards sighed.

"We're here to measure you, boy. No sense in making it difficult. Ain't nobody ever died from getting measured."

Erik didn't let his posture loosen. "Measured for what? A noose?"

The guards both laughed.

"What good'd a noose be?" The near guard turned to the other. "What about it? Want to have to sit an' listen to him scream another day away?"

"Rather not, thanks."

Erik finally loosened and took a step forward.

"Good boy," the near guard said. "Arms and legs apart."

The guard with the rope laid the rope against the inside and outside of Erik's legs and down the lengths of his arms. It was as if he was being measured for a suit, but that seemed unlikely.

"What's this for?" Erik asked.

"Impatient, ain't he?"

The rope guard chuckled at the other's quip. "He'll be cured of that before long."

The guard finished measuring him and stood up. The other looked at him. "You remember it all?"

They walked to the door, the rope guard chuckling. "Near enough."

The door was closed and the footsteps fell away down the hall and it was quiet again in his cell. They'd measured him for something and they would come back. When they did, he would be ready. If they were as slow as Tove's brother, he might be able to find a way through them. The valkyries were another problem, but they had taken a day to find him in Lofgrund and they hadn't come to find him in the cell, so there was hope.

CHAPTER THIRTEEN

HE FELT A TAPPING ON HIS FACE AND THE FIRST THOUGHT through his brain was to tell Chris to let him sleep. His mind caught up before long, remembering where he was and Erik sat up on his flat wooden bed as quickly as he could, pulling away from the hand. His eyes were still bleary with sleep when he struck his hands out at the man, who'd come back into his cell.

The man's face was close to his own, staring. Erik could see, his mind now much clearer since the pain had waned, that the man didn't really look to be much older than he was. He was maybe in his early thirties, but thin and strange in his movements, especially the constant twitching of muscles around his body.

"Slept... you must be... must be planning to stay." The man backed away a few steps, letting a breathy, ragged laugh trickle out. "Wake where you slept. A b-b-blessing," he sucked in a breath, eyes narrowing, "and a curse." He smiled, teeth yellow and black. "So... so long as you're safe, isn't it... enough? We... we can be safe h-here. They don't come down. You and Haki are... safe."

Erik stood up, taking a step away from the man. "Who are you? What do you mean 'you and Haki?'"

The man tapped his chest. "H-Haki." He nodded. "I remember... it all. That much... a-at least. They call me..." He shook his head, his neck twitching violently. "The Lost."

"Why are you here? And them? You're talking about the valkyries, right?"

Haki pulled away from him when he said the word valkyrie. He said nothing, just looked at him in terror.

"You've died, right? I had fucking... fucking rocks. They fell on me." Erik mimed the building collapsing, not sure why. The man seemed so lost in his own mind that Erik felt he needed to do as much as he could.

"Can't... die." Haki the Lost moved toward him, reaching out hands for Erik's face. "Only the hand... that made us all c-can destroy us one."

He had strained too hard to say the words and a knot formed in his neck. He pulled his hands down and away from Erik, retreating to rub on the area the knot had formed.

Erik stepped away from the bed, moving himself toward the door slightly as Haki moaned and barked angrily, pawing at the cramp in his neck.

It wasn't half a minute before it subsided and Haki looked back up at Erik with mad eyes. He walked over and pulled Erik's hands up, placing them to the twitching muscles of his neck.

"No... wound. No scar."

Erik didn't move his hands, but Haki still worked them

along the muscles. It was an unnerving feeling in every sense of the word.

"Why don't they want us to get to Valhalla? Isn't that the whole point?"

Haki threw Erik's hands down, pacing away angrily. "Know... nothing. Stupid... fool boy. Talk strange... smell... strange. There is no... honor. It's..." His eyes flared with anger. "...games. Toys, a-all of us."

Haki swiped at the air. Lost in a sort of rage, he seemed to forget that Erik was in the room for a time. Finally he calmed, staring blankly at the floor. His head turned slowly to face Erik.

"But... you have... come." Haki swallowed hard and pulled in a breath. "To stay with me. A neighbor... of my own."

"You're wrong there. I'm not staying in here."

Haki lunged at him, grabbing Erik by his ripped shirt, pushing him into the wall. Through gritted teeth he forced his threat. "No... one... leaves. They won't... let you. I... won't..."

Erik's eyes narrowed and he clenched his jaw. Haki's threat fell off and as Erik's fist rose up, a look of terror flooded the man's eyes. He scattered away, yelping.

"Not... fair. The... stench." He hacked coughs out. "I know... that smell!"

"What smell? What the fuck are you talking about, you crazy piece of shit?!"

Erik walked at him, but the sound of heavy boots and rattling coming down the hall sent Haki scurrying over to his cell. He watched the speed of it, still not convinced Haki could be human. Why had he been scared enough to run? He wanted answers and it didn't seem likely that Haki would come back to his cell anytime soon.

Erik cursed under his breath and went to sit on his bed. The guards had visited a few times, only looking into his cell, never opening the door. He wanted to keep them from suspecting that he had any plans by making them comfortable with the predictable nature of his actions. They'd see him as compliant and that would give him a chance. At least, he hoped.

He heard the sound of multiple footsteps as they came nearer. Three pairs, though one sounded to be bare feet. The echoes in the jail were terrible and as much as they told, they made specific sounds hard when there was too much going on. Had they caught someone else? Was there going to be a new prisoner for Haki to inflict his madness on?

They stopped in front of Erik's door and he stood up, not sure what to do. He wasn't ready yet. Was now the time to make a run at them? He took a few steps forward and the door came open. The guard looked into the cell without any sense of concern before quickly stepping back away. Erik stopped, confused by the motion until he saw Tove. She was shoved into the cell, and immediately dropped to her knees, falling over hard on the stone floor. Before Erik could even think of what he should do, the door swung shut again.

He ran to Tove, kneeling down beside her as she groaned in pain on the floor. She was dressed in dirty, loose shorts and something approaching a sleeveless shirt. They were made of cheap, rough linen and there was blood on them in a few places. He could see bruises all across her legs and arms.

"Tove!"

When she heard his voice, she immediately turned her head toward him, coming to her knees. She wrapped her arms around his waist.

"Erik, praise Odin." She squeezed him too tightly, burying her head into his stomach. I thought you'd been taken—"

He knelt down, pulling her away, looking at her. "What are they doing to you? Why are you covered in bruises?"

She looked at her arms. Her voice quivered a bit. "They... It's a punishment. It doesn't matter. There are worse things. We have time together, we must use it."

The sound of footsteps returning made Tove stand. Erik put himself in front of her. The door opened and guards looked at him like he was insane. They placed two plates down on the floor just inside the cell and closed the door again. They had fried sausages and boiled vegetables and bread on them, in stark contrast to the gruel he'd been given before.

"That's way better than what they gave me last time. Do you think it's poisoned?" Erik asked.

"What would it matter?"

She had a strong point, though Erik was in no hurry to relive the pain that came along with his last death. He walked to the plates, picking them both up and bringing one to Tove before moving to his wooden bed. The meat was pork, it was tough but had been seasoned with salt and herbs. Tove tore into it without a second thought.

"Did they give you anything to eat before this?"

She shook her head, too focused on the food to bother replying with words. He tore off half of his link of sausage and put it on her plate. In spite of her full mouth, Tove tried to protest. Erik stopped her.

"They're treating you worse than me. I don't know why, but you eat while you can."

Erik took a bite of his food. It wasn't as good as what they'd had at Inga's but the fact that he considered the comparison said enough about what he'd been given. It was hard to make sense of.

Tove had slowed down by the time she was through half of the plate and it seemed as good a time as any to ask questions.

"You've seen the layout of this place, right?"

Tove nodded, swallowing a bit of food. "I don't see any trick to this place. Two hallways with cells at the ends of them. The only other rooms I managed to see as they brought me were just down the hall from these cells."

"Okay. I can't remember being brought in clearly, but

I remember seeing a guard at the end of the hall. And two regularly come down here to look around."

Tove was back to her food, though she'd slowed down. She took a few more bites, saying nothing. "I think they count four in total. The two who brought me here are not two I've seen."

"So two for us, two for your side. But we don't know if they're the same as the one, maybe two at the front of the guard house." Erik forced himself to eat, though the distraction of deciding how they should get out made it hard to care about the meal.

"Six total, and armored." Tove frowned, poking at the last bits of food on her plate idly. "I don't know that I can be of help, especially if they keep… if the punishments continue. Walking is painful."

He could tell by the tone of her voice that she hadn't wanted to admit it, that she didn't want to talk about it. The anger that was becoming so familiar to him crept back into his mind. He shook it off as best he could. There was nothing to be done immediately.

"Erik?"

"Sorry… I got lost in thought for a second. Can we just go when they come back for you? Are they coming back for you?"

"I don't know." Tove looked at the door as she said it. "They've told me nothing, only come to flog me and then leave. I've been through worse, but knowing what it's like won't keep my legs working." She slammed a fist against the bed. "I won't… I cannot be useless."

"Then if they come back, we'll go."

Tove stood for the first time, on shaky legs. "This is all I can manage. If there are more than two, you'll just be stabbed and suffer for nothing. And I couldn't stand that."

There were footsteps in the hall as soon as she finished talking. Too many to begin pretending there might only be two. Erik jumped to his feet, looking at the door.

Tove put a hand on his arm. "Promise me."

He turned to look at her, his expression softening.

"And promise you'll come for me when there are few enough guards that you can kill them."

He nodded wordlessly as the guards came into the area with the door. There were at least four behind the familiar pair who were waiting just across the threshold, others no doubt waiting in the hallway beyond. He had no idea what they were there for, but stood ready in case they came in holding weapons. The door opened and the normal two came in first.

"Alright, girl. Back to the dark."

Erik took a step forward, but he felt a tug on his torn shirt. Tove walked past him quietly, looking over her shoulder with a smile.

"I will be waiting."

He nodded stiffly, trying not to scream or curse or do anything that they might take out on her when she was gone. She was led away with the door still open. Erik went back to his bed when she was out of sight, no longer caring what the commotion was about. He heard the guards outside shifting into the area outside the cells and Haki the Lost spoke up as they did.

"Ásví! I know... that sound! That... dress on... the stone. Ásví... h-have you come... to see me? To... see Haki?"

A metal rapping sounded against the cell door next to his and Haki whimpered, saying nothing more.

The guards formed a wall outside of the door, parting to the side forming a small row and putting clenched fists over their stomachs. Erik heard the quiet click of wooden shoes on stone and the light dragging of a heavy fabric across them.

A woman came into the room, deep red hair falling down over a cloak with fur shoulders and heavy silk trailing behind. She was in her mid-twenties by every estimation Erik could make, whatever that might have meant in Helheim. She unbuttoned the cloak and let it fall behind her as she stepped into his cell, walking to the center and facing him as he sat on the wooden bed.

"Clothes!"

They were the first words the woman said, and not to him. The guards gathered up her cloak and another came in holding a set of very soft looking cotton clothes, the pants brown and the rest dyed light blue.

They were placed on the bed beside Erik. He looked down at them and then back at the woman whose gaze met his.

"Well? Dress yourself."

Erik raised an eyebrow, looking to the guards and then back to her.

She sensed his hesitation. "I've seen more than one cock in my time and I mean to see yours today, else the clothes would have come before I did. Now dress."

Erik did as he was told. He could feel the eyes of the woman on him as he took off his clothes, trying his best to be naked for as little time as possible. When he was done, she gave a wry smile.

"You're better looking than was reported, I'll hand you that. But not much muscle." She lifted her chin toward the bed. "Sit."

Erik did as he was told, his eyes moving to the guards regularly. They had again formed their wall in front of the door, ready, in orderly fashion, to burst in should they be needed.

"Tell me your name."

"Erik."

"The whole of your name."

Erik looked at the wall, where his neighbor so often came through, knowing the man was listening. It made him hesitate.

"Go on, boy."

"Haki Erik Styrsson."

The woman raised her eyebrows for a moment but made

no further comment. "I am called Ásví. My husband is jarl of this city and the attendant lands but he often finds himself away pleasing himself with farm girls under the pretense of seeing to the needs of the people. As such, I am responsible for your being brought to this place."

Erik shot up from the bed and the guards started in, but Ásví raised a hand, stopping them. Erik ignored them. "Then you know why Tove is being punished. And you can stop it."

Ásví was calm. "I do. And I will not. She aided one of Odin's chosen in violation of an accord that stretches back much longer than you can imagine."

"How could she have known?!"

The woman did not so much as shrug, but delivered her answer in a flat, cool voice. "She could not have and it would have made no difference. But I have questions for you."

She walked over, leaning in to his neck. He could feel the warmth of her breath on his skin and she inhaled deeply. She pulled her face around to just in front of his and narrowed her eyes to study his. She turned away, returning to the center of the cell before facing him again.

Ásví rubbed down the fabric on the front of the heavy, deep purple silk dress she wore. "You have a smell about you. I am not so keen to them as some, but I know it well enough. But your body does not lie. You know not the first thing about battle. How is it that you made a valkyrie bring down a building to stop you? Is Thor your god, perhaps?"

Erik let out a sarcastic laugh. "Made? I couldn't make a valkyrie do anything."

Her expression turned to steely suspicion. "Is that how you see it?"

His brow shifted to show his confusion. "How else would I? The fight barely lasted twenty seconds."

There was an immediate murmur among the guards.

Ásví's face returned to the calm it had been. She smiled, almost warmly. "You don't know enough to lie, do you, Erik?"

"Why would I bother? I'm trapped in this cell, so what's

the point?"

"Trapped?" She put a hand over her mouth, covering a tiny laugh. "The doors in these cells do not lock. You are free to go as you like."

"Bullshit!"

"Have you tried them and found them locked?"

Erik's jaw fell open. He hadn't.

"Then you haven't." She laughed in spite of her attempts to maintain her demeanor. "I had thought you were wary enough not to try. But you only..." She drew in a breath, composing herself.

"What about Tove, then? You're torturing her. And you brought me watery oatmeal. And now I'm supposed to believe this isn't some trick? What do you even want from me?" His mind was racing, but he didn't have an answer for why any of it was how it was.

"I regret that we did not expect you on the first day." Ásví walked back over to him, placing a hand on his chest and letting it run down to his stomach before pulling it back up. "I will say it plain so you understand. Your girl will be punished for nine days and nine nights. Then she will be free so long as she does nothing more." She leaned in, whispering in his ear. "You will be killed by valkyries if you so much as step out the front of this place." She leaned back, pushing him down onto the bed. Her voice rose back to normal. "That is the extent of our accord with them." She put on a coy half smile. "And I will watch it each and every time."

Erik looked up at the woman. He had no idea if she was a friend or an enemy or something altogether different.

The smile faded and she turned, walking toward the door, the guards forming their passage again. "I expect to be entertained, Haki Erik Styrsson."

Chapter Fourteen

It took him hours to get to sleep after Ásví had left the room, and even then he did so sitting in the far corner of the cell from Haki's frequently used entrance.

The smile on Tove's face as she walked back to be tortured was something he couldn't manage to shake from his mind. His brain would reach out, trying to quell the guilt of what was happening to her, reminding him that she had joined herself to him in Kvernes and that he hadn't asked her to come along. No matter what excuses came, the guilt didn't go. Her constantly repeated joke that they were a warband had wormed its way into his mind and he'd started to count on it being true. She must have as well. She'd saved him from being pulled into the speed of life in Kvernes, that was something he'd had time to realize sitting on the floor of the cell for what must have been two days by now.

He couldn't help counting every waking hour since they took her from the cell, wondering what they were doing and when he could get to her. Ásví had told him the door was open, but he'd been sure it was a joke. Parts of him screamed that he should check it. It had made it all the harder to sleep, but he knew the guards would likely make their rounds as scheduled even with the important visits he was offered. And there would be food soon enough as well. They would be fuel to test the limits of what Ásví had claimed he was allowed to do.

Erik stood after a few minutes spent looking at the far wall, waiting to see if Haki would come and harass him again. He hadn't moved the stone since Ásví's visit, or more accurately since Erik raised his fist.

Without realizing it, Erik had slept with his fists balled and they'd stayed that way for however few hours it was. The tendons were slow to stretch so he walked the cell, pressing his hands open on the walls while he spent nervous energy. He had confirmation of his worries over timing when the guard pair started their rounds of the cell area. Erik put himself by the door to listen as they came by.

The sounds of boots stopped at his door. One of the guards pulled on the door as he looked in, ignoring that he couldn't see Erik at all, and continued on. The pair stopped in front of Haki's door, continuing a conversation Erik hadn't heard the beginning of.

"No real sense in her worryin', but talk of valkyries in town gets people that way, I reckon."

"That's women though, eh? Love to worry, them."

It must have been the guard who wore a longer beard that checked Haki's door, because he heard the gruff voice of the man call out.

"Ah, shit it all."

Erik heard feet stumble back away from the door, so he stood to see. The guard who'd stumbled back was holding a hand over his mouth.

"He's not gone and done it again."

"He only fucking has." The guard pulled his hand down and wiped his beard flat.

The more kempt of the two, a stout brown-haired man who looked thoroughly unfit to guard much of anything, walked to the door. "Yer turn ain't it?"

"Fuck off, it ain't."

"Gods be good, I... fine." The stout guard opened Haki's door.

From his cell, Haki started talking to them. "A... visit. How pleasant... a... pleasant visit."

"My bloody arse it is. Out"

Haki scampered out of the cell but stuck to the wall nearest. The stout guard went in, complaining, while the other moved to Haki.

"How many fuckin' times we told you? How many's it been?" Haki did not answer. "Stop shittin' in your cell! There's rooms for it, down the hall. Fresh wool, better'n I use at home. Use them if you need a shit."

"Can't... they'll come. They'll kill." Haki started a fit of hacking coughs and the taller guard gave up chastising him.

"Just push it down the fuckin' hole and let him sleep in the stink. Not like he cares. It'll dry soon enough."

The stout guard returned from the room. "What you think I was doin'?"

The guards didn't usher him back into his cell or do anything of the kind. They just started walking away, continuing their conversation.

"Maybe the new one stays inside so that's an end of it."

They walked off down the hallway. Haki followed the guards to the edge of the main area outside the cells and they didn't seem to care or pay much attention one way or another. Haki came walking over to Erik's door, looking in.

Not wanting to be seen, there was no other choice but to crouch and hope that he went away. If he was going to have another conversation with the crazy man it was going to be on his terms, and it was definitely not going to be right after guards complained about him shitting in his cell.

A metal creak from down the hall sent Haki scattering back into his room, shutting the door. Erik went back to pacing around his cell. He'd have to leave and see exactly what the truth was. It was another forty nervous trips back and forth across the stone floor before he grabbed what he thought was just a wooden handle for the door. He twisted it to the side and heard a metal latch slide open, the door swinging free.

He'd wasted time and it hit him all at once. It was time he could have spent finding out whatever he could or attempting to get to Tove. Guilt was another distraction, one he couldn't afford, so Erik pushed the thoughts out of his mind as best he could and took a step out of the cell. There was no sudden alarm, though he half expected one, and no wind of judgment came rushing down the nearby hall to greet him. Those things did very little to settle his stomach. He saw the room properly for the first time, through clear eyes. There was a small desk between Haki's cell and the third at the far end of the room. It looked as though it was kept clean but there were no real signs of wear on it. Erik ignored the things in that direction, not wanting to deal with Haki unless it was entirely necessary.

The hallway was larger than Erik remembered. He stood at the edge of the room looking down it for a few seconds before taking a step into it, not sure if Haki was speaking truth when he said the valkyries would come for him. No one did. The two doors that Tove had mentioned were there, on the left side of the hallway as he moved north toward the exit. Erik pulled on the doors and found them to be exactly as the guard had described them. There was tightly pressed, clean wool sitting next to stone seats with holes. He poked his head over one and saw that it went down more than a few feet into what sounded to be the running water that ran under his cell.

Erik came to the fork in the hallway that had always been there. Looking down the fork they'd taken Tove through, he saw two guards standing in the hall. One tapped the other and pointed a silent hand in Erik's direction. They chuckled and started a conversation that Erik was too far from to hear clearly. They didn't care. A creeping anger began to rise in him. No one had found the time to tell him any of it, but they'd made sure to beat Tove. They likely hadn't missed a session by even a few minutes. His jaw clenched and he felt his hand tighten to a fist. He could go get her now. He might make it past the two of them. But it wasn't something he could count on. He had to know what would happen if he walked out the front. There may have been a dozen guards there or worse, Haki's fear might have been based on more than a lost mind.

The small administrative room at the north end of the hallway held two guards. A younger guard with a short beard and an older guard who was one of the first clean-shaven men he'd seen in a while. He was fat and ill-suited to a face without hair on it, but the patchy spots that had grown stubble suggested that there were reasons for it. The two guards who normally did rounds weren't in the cells as far as he could tell. He made sure to remember it. They may have been part of general grounds patrols, since he was a prisoner of the valkyries more than anyone else.

The fat guard snorted as Erik came into the room. "First run, eh? Hah. Hope you've got quick legs, boy. That courtyard's made for them to cut you lot down."

The younger looking of the two said nothing, only watched Erik with a sad expression, something like pity.

Both of the guards lost interest by the time he'd made the short walk across the room to the door.

Erik placed his hand on the door handle and took in a

deep breath. He turned the handle, the hot, late-afternoon air flooded in, the men behind him groaning in annoyance. As soon as Erik's eyes told him the way across the yard was clear he started running as fast as his legs would carry him. There was a wide gate that stood open, but it was a direct shot across from him. They would either come or they wouldn't, so the only thing to be done was to run across the yard.

His eyes shot around. Guards took notice of him, pointing at the spectacle of his attempt to flee and then looking skyward. Erik ignored the sky above him, turning his focus back to the gate. He knew the sound well enough and there was nothing in the air that was of concern to him. He was nearly halfway across the yard when he heard the sound he'd been waiting for.

The hiss was directly behind him and his body tensed almost as if on instinct as soon as the sound hit his ears. He kept his eyes on the gate, waiting for the sound of their charge. The hissing noise grew and Erik stopped dead, forcing himself to shift to the side, and then screaming in his mind for his legs to carry him forward. The golden-hot spear lapped at the stone ahead of him and just to the side. A series of confused shouts came from around the yard as the guards saw what had happened. Erik ignored them, turning his eyes sideward as the valkyrie came by him. It was the short-haired valkyrie. They were twins in every other respect, and freckled. His mind shifted. How had he been able to see her freckles?

It didn't matter, he shook the thought away, knowing the distraction meant the end of him. His feet felt the change in the type of stone underneath and he felt the shadow of the gate pass over him more than he noticed it. He was in the streets of Lofgrund. Erik turned to the west and pounded his feet down on the stone, taking off as fast as he could manage. The hissing of the valkyries arched over walls around the keep's court and they were behind him again. There were people in the square ahead, they'd slow him down too much to pass through and the valkyries wouldn't care about plowing through them to get to him. He didn't much care either, but they would cause enough delay to put a weapon into his back. He wouldn't have that. Erik stamped a foot, turning himself around and squaring up to his pursuers. He'd gladly take a blade to the chest if it meant a chance to put a fist to the women who'd cut Tove to pieces.

The valkyrie with the loose braid squared up, her twin waiting back and watching. She charged like it was all she knew. Erik followed her. She moved like Haki had, only he could see all of it. He ducked, putting the blade of her short sword just above his arm but the valkyrie managed to angle it down, catching the edge of his shoulder. He spun his elbow up and over as she passed by, planting it at the base of her neck. She thundered to the ground, splitting the stone. He lifted a foot and stomped her arm, hearing a satisfying snap.

The hissing to his front grew in volume and he turned back to see the other charging him with her spear. He had nowhere to move. The spear tip plunged into his stomach and Erik let out a deep, guttural yell. He could feel the blade searing his insides, but it wasn't pain. Energy seemed to shoot through him. He swung straight for the valkyrie's face, catching her in the chin as she tried to spin away from the punch. He caught her, not cleanly, but it was enough to get her to take her hands off the weapon. Erik grabbed the staff of the spear and pulled it from his gut. His skin sizzled under the heat of it. He tossed it aside and ran toward the short-haired valkyrie, who now bled from her lip. She turned to flee as he chased and Erik reached out. His hand almost found purchase on the armor over her shoulder blade but instead it wrapped around something he hadn't seen before. A faintly shimmering thing that came through a small slit in the leather. He gripped it tightly, the hissing noise dimming for just a second before his hand flew apart, shredded by invisible wings. He stopped, his hand useless and the pain starting to flood. With one arm limp, the valkyrie he'd put to the ground plunged her sword up through his ribs and into his heart. He felt the blood bubble and the strength in his legs disappear. He dropped to the ground, dying.

His eyes opened what felt like a second later and he was in the corner of the cell. The pain came immediately after his mind returned to him. It was the same as it had been with the wall. Hours of blazing pain that faded too slowly and a hand he was convinced would never work again from the way it felt. He'd heard the guards laughing as they did their rounds, saying word was the valkyries had flattened him into the street. When he could stand again, he did but there was still the distinct feeling that the steel was still inside his body. Bending to either side dropped him to his knees, but he was beginning to understand the pain better. It wasn't manageable, but it faded soon enough and he could at least do simple things. He went to the door of his cell and opened it, walking directly to Haki's.

He pulled the handle up and the door came open. Haki was sitting on a ratty sheet, curled at the edge of a wooden bed that had been worn over every inch. The smell of his shit was still fresh, but the pain kept it from Erik's mind for the most part.

"I want answers to some questions Haki."

The broken man rocked back and forth, staring at Erik. "Went outside... didn't you? I... thought you were... a neighbor."

"I'll die out there as many times as it takes."

Haki shook his head violently. "The brain... never forgets. Never. Never forgets." He just started repeating fragments of the phrase over and over again.

"What are you fucking talking about?! Never forgets?!"

"He doesn't remember the words so well anymore."

Erik whipped around to see the younger guard from the administrative area. "Explain it to me."

The guard sighed. "Come out of there. At the very least he deserves some peace."

Erik looked back at Haki. He was clawing at the wood below him, eyes fixed on the door.

There was no reason to stay in the cell, so Erik did as he was asked. He closed the door and the guard motioned to the chair at the desk beside the cell, offering it.

"Sitting hurts. I'm out, what did he mean?"

The guard nodded. "It was something he used to say when he first came. How long did it take you to get to Lofgrund after you awoke in Helheim?"

"A week, maybe."

A look of surprise shot across his face. "Then... in Spring..."

"Nothing. I just left. They attacked me here."

"How did you die in Midgard? In battle?"

"No, valkyries came and... look, explain shit."

"Valkyries came to Midgard?" The guard shook his head. "Wh— No. It's... When Haki arrived here, he had already developed a twitch in his sword arm. Said they'd cut it off a hundred times at least. He was proud of it. He used to say, 'Even if the body mends, the brain never forgets.'"

"The damage?"

"Seems to be. No one dies like the chosen, so I didn't believe him. Every day, he walked out that door and stood in the yard, waiting for them. Hrist and Mist. After a hundred days, he could only go every week, if that. Still he stood and faced them. A hundred days became a thousand and he spent months in that bed, screaming. He started to run then. It didn't help. Eventually, he broke."

Erik looked at the door to Haki's cell. He could hear moaning weeps beyond the wood. "Even now? They won't let him go?"

The guard shook his head. "They'll never let him go. You either." He looked down the hallway, absently. "I warned you. Do what you like with it."

The guard went away, back to his post, and Erik was left alone with only the feeling of a sword in his chest and the muffled wails of a broken man.

CHAPTER FIFTEEN

ERIK RETURNED TO HIS CELL, THE STIFF PAIN IN HIS CHEST proving to be enough to dissuade him from trying anything more drastic. His hand had gone numb in the hours since he'd woken up and he was unsure if that was something he should be concerned about. Knowing how Haki came to be the man that he was, Erik couldn't help but find himself worried.

As uncomfortable as the bed was, it was the best place to sit, ignoring the chair that would no doubt mean forced interactions with the guards or with Haki if the man ever regained whatever was left of his mind. He had sat down with the intention to plan a way past the valkyries and to Tove and there seemed to be a dead end at each of them. He considered that it was possible that the guards would simply move out of his way and let him go to Tove, but that didn't seem entirely likely. He resolved to find out properly when the pain had gone down, waiting in case they reacted violently to his approach.

The real insurmountable problem was the valkyries. Time kept passing and Tove had barely been able to stand when she'd come before. He would have to carry her and he wasn't fast enough on his own to deal with them. He'd run the first time not planning to get as far as he did, but the information was valuable. They'd done more than charge when pressed. They could fight on foot and it was unlikely that they'd give him as much opportunity to find clear ground in his next attempt at leaving the yard.

No matter how many ways he tried to think around it, there was no way of taking Tove along with him and making it clear of Hrist and Mist. That resignation brought another thought to mind. Though the yard presented only a single way clear through to the city, they weren't limited in that way at all. They could wait where they pleased, attack from whatever angle they liked, and knew which direction he'd be forced to head. Whichever of the pair had crushed his throat was undeterred by walls. And if they cared about the damage he'd done during their fight in the street, they wouldn't give him the simple pleasure of being attacked in turn. They were in pairs for that reason. It was something he felt stupid for not understanding before. They'd only taken it in turns to fly at him because he posed no threat. And suddenly, he wondered if he did pose a threat. All of those were things he had to know before he could step foot in the court again. They would learn how he moved, he had no doubt of that, but he had no way of improving himself stuck in the prison alone. Haki wouldn't be of help. He was incapable of it.

Nothing viable had presented itself by the time food arrived. More sausage with vegetables, this time with a side of fresh fruits and what looked like a thick yogurt. Along with it, there were a fresh pair of clothes, the ones he'd woken in being torn and blood stained. He hadn't even thought of it until he saw the new ones. He ate before changing into the new clothes, inspecting the old ones for any sign of blood that wasn't his own. There was nothing. It made him start to wonder if he'd done any damage to them at all or if it had been some dream he'd had while lost in the pain of returning to life. Maybe that was how Haki had lost himself.

The food was good, better made than the sausage he'd been given when Tove was in. It was more smoothly ground and had less gristle than before. The fruit, as well. It was a strange addition along with the sour yogurt. Dessert for prisoners seemed like an odd thing. As much as Ásví might have pretended he wasn't a prisoner, he could still understand the walls of the cage around him.

The feeling in his hand was returning around the time he finished eating, so when the meal was done Erik stood and walked to the wall. He took a deep breath and punched the stone, not hard, but it was enough to hurt. A bit of skin peeled from his knuckles and the uncaring stone sat unblemished. There was no feeling inside him like there had been during the fight and he couldn't understand why or how he'd been able to keep pace with the valkyries. Haki may have known. He could move like them. Not as quickly, but still, it was something. The only person capable of helping him was buried deep inside a madman.

Erik opened the door to his cell, walking out into the main room. It was quiet down the hall, so he made his way to the toilets, cleaning himself up as best he could. There were buckets of clean water, and with no other place to put the wool, he tossed it down the hole in the seat. A few pads of wool gone, he didn't hear anything resembling rising water so he breathed a sigh of relief, happy not to have flooded the hall as there was a fair chance it was run down toward the cells.

He stood in the small stone closet for a minute, gathering his nerves. He'd decided that he was going to see what would happen if he walked casually down the other hallway leading from the fork. They'd brought Tove to him so it was possible he might be able to go and see her. She was being punished for helping him, but they hadn't tried to stop him from leaving.

Erik went to the fork, looking down it. The guards looked at him, not laughing as they had done the day before. They were thirty yards from him at least, but when he took a step down the hallway, they backed up, pulling their swords immediately. Yesterday they'd laughed at him. He took another step down the hall.

"You ain't allowed down here, einherjar. We'll die if we have to." The guard who spoke had a look somewhere between panic and fury.

All Erik could think, over and over, was that they'd laughed at him before. It was what he'd expected of them in a way, but the trembling of the guard's voice was odd. And it was the first time he'd been called einherjar by anyone. What had changed? Was it that he'd tried to flee? Haki must have done it dozens or hundreds of times.

He turned around and headed up the hall to the administrative area. There was only one guard sitting at the desk, a thin, tall man who jumped when Erik came into the room. The man said nothing, only watched Erik until he decided to return to his cell.

He heard the telltale signs of Ásví's procession coming down the hall before an hour had passed. Haki didn't bother rising to call out to her like he had last time. The doors opened and a guard came in, leaving a mattress sized for Erik's wooden bed on the floor before leaving. The columns formed beside the door and Ásví walked in, wearing a loose, shimmering blue dress.

She clapped and a chair was brought in behind her. She sat in it crossing her legs and the guard who had brought it scurried back out into the main room.

"Close the door."

There was hesitation at her order, but it was done and eyes peered in from the outside, watching him intently.

"Ignore them," she said, shifting her weight in the chair. "You're talking with me. And it would be rude of you to ignore a guest bearing such gifts." She waved a hand toward the mattress. "Now, before you start asking inane questions about the farm girl you dragged here, I will make my point. You've impressed me, Haki Erik Styrsson." She looked down at her dress and picked at a small piece of lint. "Or, should I admit, I had underestimated you."

She looked at him, expectant, but Erik shook his head, not understanding.

"The wall guards saw your fight." She drew in a breath and then sighed. "The rumors spread well through the keep before a formal report came to me. Parts of it I simply won't believe. They say you broke the arm of a valkyrie." She scoffed. "It's preposterous. But then, they are excitable men. But there were parts I cannot ignore. The damage to the street. The blood you drew from the mouth and nose of one you managed to strike." She leaned forward, pushing her breasts together and smiling at Erik. "I had them describe it to me. And I should thank you." She leaned back. "I've not felt so excited in as long as I can remember."

Erik stood, ready to shout, but Ásví held up a finger and he stopped though he wasn't sure why.

"I will make this clear before you begin your protests, I have no will to see Odin lack for his einherjar. The glory of the gods is the glory of us all. You understand that, I trust." She stood up, walking toward him. "I can do things for you to make the struggle to free yourself from the valkyries outside less uncomfortable. So long as you entertain me."

"And how am I supposed to entertain you? Dance?"

She laughed, grabbing the hand that had been shredded. "In a way, yes." She rubbed her thumbs around the meat of his palm and then put his hand to her face. "I want to see you struggle." She smiled, but it was a dark expression, full of malice.

Erik ripped his hand away from her. "Tove—"

She threw her hands up, spinning away, walking back to her chair. "Again with the girl. She is not yours and if she were, her punishment is not complete."

"And why does she have to be punished? Some part of your covenant?"

Ásví sat back down. "No. Those laws are my own. Those who bring comfort to the chosen are inviting destruction on my city."

"Your husband's city, you mean."

She shot up from the chair, shrieking, "My city!" She calmed herself, brushing her dress into place, and walked over to Erik. She slapped him across the face as hard as she could manage, drawing blood as an overturned ring tore across his cheek. She took a deep breath. "This does not need to be our relationship, Haki Erik Styrsson. You are einherjar. Not some simple chosen. My men have seen it and I will see it for myself soon enough. I would have my hand in your greatness. And if I cannot, I will do all that I can to make you like him." She nodded toward the wall to Haki's cell. "Enjoy your reward and think on my kindness."

She turned then, going to the door. It opened before she got to it, the men forming columns for her to pass by. A guard came in and took the chair as the rest of the procession made their way down the hall. No one bothered closing the door to his cell and they left more quickly than they came.

They left the mattress and Erik went over to it after shutting the door. He left it on the floor and pressed over the length of it, suspicious that it might contain something dangerous. He was unsure whether to be disappointed or elated when it turned out to be just a normal mattress. No part of him wanted to accept comfort from Ásví, not after her threats. Even without them, it was clear she had plans for him that weren't built around his concerns.

Another meal was brought shortly after Ásví had left. It was the closest they'd brought food in such a short span. Her threat repeated in his brain as he looked over the food. It may have been something else. Another gift so that he would consider how kind she was, maybe. He could find no reason to skip the meal if they intended to feed him. There was no strange smell or taste to it and Erik couldn't imagine Ásví was the sort to derive entertainment from poisoning him alone in his cell.

He was only a few minutes past finishing the meal when he heard the sounds of the large procession coming down the hall again. His door swung open and the familiar columns were in their place, oddly with swords drawn. And men in full plate armor came in. It was a piece of armor he hadn't seen on anyone, even when he fled across the yard.

"Ásví has sent for you." The man's voice was muffled by the heavy helmet, but Erik was sure he'd heard it properly.

He stood up and the man in full plate took a step out of the way of the door so that Erik could pass by. There were more guards in the room than came with Ásví. It was strange, but there must have been a reason. A second man in plate moved ahead of him and the columns formed to his sides. He was boxed in as they walked down the hallway toward the administrative room. Was this how they moved the prisoners? Would the valkyries ignore them?

They came to the door that led to the yard. All at once the man in heavy armor tore it open, rushing out of the way. Before Erik could grasp what was happening, the man in full plate behind him dove into his back, forcing him out of the door into the yard. The door shut behind him as he slid across the stone beneath.

He was to his feet as the hissing came into his ears. He looked up to see Hrist and Mist already charging. The longer-haired held the spear in her off hand, but it wouldn't have mattered. The searing blades plunged into his chest before he could move. The air up through his throat felt like fire. They pulled the blades out and pushed them in again, through his stomach. They were pulled free once more and Erik fell forward. He looked across the yard and saw Ásví standing in the center, staring. There was a scowl on her face like she'd never shown in the cell.

He felt the weight of a scalding hot maul land on his back. A radiant wave of pain poured through him before his body fell limp. His limbs refused to move and he knew that he would wake in agony. He clenched his jaw, using the last of his strength to look up at the valkyries who stared down at him with angry eyes. It was their revenge and they wanted him to know it. They never looked away as he bled to death on cold stone he could no longer feel.

CHAPTER SIXTEEN

PAIN WAS, FOR ONCE, SOMETHING ERIK WAS MORE THAN happy to be able to feel. It didn't stop him from screaming or tears from pooling and falling, but he knew that what the valkyries had done had been undone when he returned to the stone room.

Ásví had proven a point, that much was clear to him in the hours he was forced to lie in the bed. When his mind cleared enough that he could form thoughts, his head flooded instead with incoherent rage and plans for revenge. They didn't leave, even well after the pain subsided enough that he could once again sit himself up. He saw the rolled mattress exactly where he left it.

He chuckled, in spite of himself. "Give with one hand..."

There was an immense feeling of weight on his lower back, or at least his brain told him there was. It didn't stop him from standing, but there was no way he could manage to walk cleanly. A few weak attempts to waddle around ended with him losing his balance to one side or another and Erik decided it would be better to wait a bit longer to try and get himself around.

The futility of walking brought a bit of clarity into his head, at least. He knew he would have to escape and there was nothing to do except play against the woman who'd sent him to be slaughtered. What she must have expected was to have her actions serve as a sort of warning. "Look what I can do to you," she seemed to be saying. The more Erik thought about it the more he decided that it must have been how she considered the action. She'd seen Haki and whoever else had been in the prison die hundreds or thousands of times and likely thought nothing of having Erik killed. There was only one way forward from that if he wanted to act outside of her expectations and that was all out war. He couldn't give her any warning of it and he knew what his first move would be, but they couldn't come immediately.

He'd broken the valkyrie's arm. He knew that now. He'd seen her favor it. It meant they didn't heal immediately, even if they were some aspect of Odin. He didn't know why, but it worked well enough for his purposes. It was why the guards were terrified before. They would fight him, but how many times? If he could find the speed and strength that he had against the valkyries, he could handle any number of guards, but it was fleeting and mercurial to say the very least. It came on from nowhere and left before he'd finished the fight.

Haki was shuffling around in his cell and Erik was tired of idling. He stood up and walked himself slowly to his door. It felt for all the world like he was bruised down to the bone all across his chest. The ache was bad enough without the weight that seemed to be on his back, urging him to want to correct against a force that only the higher part of his brain knew wasn't there. He left his cell, finding no new guards had been assigned to him and that there was no extra noise in the halls. Ásví really must have expected him to take it as a warning and leave it there.

Erik dragged himself to Haki's cell door. He could feel the look on his face and knew that entering with such an expression would only scare the broken old warrior. That wasn't his intention. He needed more than Haki likely had to give and he intended to try his best to drag it out.

The handle turned and Haki was pacing around the middle of the cell in small circles. He stopped, looking at Erik with a confused face.

"Neigh... bor?"

Erik nodded. "Haki. I, uh... I came here to talk to you, o' great warrior." It wasn't a convincing first effort.

"What... what trick is this?"

He shook his head, walking slowly into the room. "It's not a trick. I want to know about you. I heard stories. I don't know how to talk about these things, but I respect you."

Haki narrowed his eyes in suspicion. "R-Respect? How? Why?"

"I heard that you..." He had no idea how to phrase it so Haki would go along. "I heard you, um, felled many men. Great warriors."

Haki's posture turned toward Erik the slightest bit. "You... you know... the stories? My stories?"

"I want to know them."

There was half of a crooked smile on Haki's face. "I ha- haven't... in ages."

"I want to be like you, Haki. Strong and manly and brave."

It was only half a lie. Erik was beginning to understand what it took to become like Haki. To rise every day and go face torture when you could sleep and eat. Somewhere he lost to it all, but he was still a man worthy of respect.

Something in Haki's eyes cleared just the least bit. "You would..." He hacked, gritting his teeth and slapping at his neck. "...be a fool... to wish it." He sucked in a breath and bored into Erik with cold, dark eyes. A second later the hazy look returned. "Stories... was it?"

Erik narrowed his eyes. "How did you learn to move so fast?"

Haki laughed his slow, ratcheting laugh. "Learned?" He coughed. "Touch of... Odin." He drew in a breath. "Makes a... a man... what he was meant... to be." He squealed low and soft, delighted by Erik's interest. "A... warrior. Great... warrior."

"But it's hard to feel, right? It slips away?"

The man slid slowly toward Erik, shaking his head slowly. "Nothing... hard... for a warrior. A firm grasp... is crucial." He wrapped bony fingers around Erik's arm, squeezing tight. His eyes cleared again. "Does it... slip from you... boy?" Haki sniffed the air. "You're... no warrior. Leave me... be." A wide, vacant grin spread across Haki's face. He slapped Erik on the arm and began a slow awkward dance around. "Killed... so many," he wheezed. "A great... warrior."

Erik left the room, closing the door. He stood outside, staring aimlessly at the walls. Behind him, Haki shuffled a dance without rhythm, singing incoherently about his prowess. Whatever Erik thought he had gone into the room for, he'd come out with nothing. The whole tiny world inside Ásví's walls was built to make a stacked game that he was forced to play. The mattress was proof of it. The gruel must have been as well. A warning before he knew there was a game to even play. And Tove.

His stomach was on fire, angry at the farce he was stuck in. Before he knew it, he was walking down the hall toward the fork. Without so much as a second's hesitation, he rounded the corner. The guards' eyes widened as he closed on them. They scrambled back, drawing their swords. It was slow, but Erik knew there was more in him. Where was it?

He wanted to scream.

"Stop right there, einherjar! You can't—"

The guard was drowned out by the battle cry of the other, who charged at Erik, sword overhead. He slashed down, Erik moving to the side and the sword clanging against the stone beneath, throwing the man off balance. Erik planted a fist into the side of the man's chain armor. A muffled crackle sounded somewhere beneath his fist and the attacking guard rolled away under the power in the punch.

The battle cry became screams of pain and the other guard decided there would be no more discussion. He charged at Erik. It was slow at first, but the feeling in his mind slipped away and the blade suddenly came speeding toward him. It caught the edge of Erik's arm, pulling a chunk of meat off just above his elbow. The pain flared and the man slowed again. Erik sunk a fist into the man's chest, collapsing it and sending the guard off his feet and a dozen yards through the air. There was no sound from him other than the clatter of his body on the stones.

The pain from the cut on his arm was enough to make him forget the pain of walking, so he was thankful to the guard for that in some way. As he passed the silent guard, he saw that his body was dissolving toward the ground. It dissipated as it went, taking anything touching his skin along with him. A chain vest, boots, and a belt remained when the body was gone. Erik looked at them, realizing he'd never seen the other side of death in Helheim. He lifted the chain vest. It was too large for him, but he pulled it over his head, jogging now toward the end of the hall.

There were only six rooms in the cells at the end of the hall and of those only one remained shut. It was latched with a wooden bar. Erik flipped the bar up out of the way and worked the handle, swinging it open. The cell was small and smelled awful. He couldn't see Tove, so he took a step in.

She was in a corner, braced against the wall, staring with terrified eyes at him as he came in. "You'll never get a sound out of my—" When she realized it was Erik she stopped. He heard her whimper. "Erik!" She began to cry as he came over to her.

"Can you walk?"

"It hurt, Erik. It hurt so much."

As he reached down to put his arms under her to lift her she grabbed at him.

"You're bleeding."

Erik nodded. "I killed them. One of them. We're not done."

She smiled for a second, wincing when he lifted her up.

"You okay?"

She nodded, wiping her face. "I'll kill the others if you hand me something to stick 'em with."

"Good, because I'm pretty sure my arm is fucked."

He started toward the door, jogging as best he could. Tove was gritting her teeth and trying to hold herself as still as she could by bracing against him. He'd have walked if he could. Back in the hall, there was still no one new to bother him.

"He's takin' the girl!" He groaned. "Someone put steel in this bastard! Hey!"

Erik put a foot in his ribs on the way by, not stopping to bother with anything else. The man yelped and curled up but stopped his yelling. There were men coming by the time he got to the fork, more than a few and some dressed in full plate. He rounded the corner, never having intended to do anything else, and ran as fast as he could manage back to the cell.

He could hear the clatter of armor behind him as he dropped Tove on the stone.

"Sorry, no time!"

He spun, whipping the door shut. He gripped the handle as tightly as he could, leaning himself against the stone wall beside it, crouching down so as not to be in the way of anything they might try to stick through the bars. The first set of guards arrived and tried the handle twice.

"He's got it held shut!"

"Move!" Another in heavier armor stepped up, yanking on the handle, but he was forced to pull it up to open the door and Erik had the better leverage. He yanked for half a minute before giving up and sticking his head to the bars. "If you don't let us in—"

"Go fuck yourselves, morons! No one's coming in here." Erik was breathing heavy, terrified and ecstatic and completely without a plan for what to do next.

He hoped their side of the handle would break first if it came to that, but they might overpower him eventually. Whatever gave him strength had no interest in his holding the handle. He looked over at Tove, a smile on his face as the guards outside decided what to do. She was looking with deep concern between him and the barred window in the door.

"Hey!"

She turned her focus to him.

Erik nodded toward the mattress. "Get some rest on that."

Tove's eyes moved over to the mattress and then immediately back to him, astonished at the suggestion.

"What? I got this. Just, you know, quick nap."

She laughed, regretting it immediately, and then crawled her way over to the mattress. They started pulling at the handle again as she laid it out. It was in the far corner, well away from any of the trouble at the door.

Having failed to pull the handle open, they started in with the swords, poking their blades through, coming nowhere near him. A spear would be too steep an angle, they all agreed before cursing whoever had decided that the doors should swing out from the cells.

The numbers on the guards began to drop after the first few minutes, several staying behind. They had discussed things and decided that Ásví needed to give them instructions on what they should do. They'd given up trying to pull on the handle but hadn't left the cell alone just yet.

"Don't reckon she'll let them valkyries down, do you?" There was fear in the guard's voice.

The other of the remaining two guards was unconcerned. "Nah, they ain't allowed down these parts. 'Sides, why'd she put valkyries in here just to pull open a door? He can waste in there all I care."

They pulled a few more times, absently, but Erik held the door shut. Another guard returned, calling the remaining guards over. He couldn't hear the conversation well, but all three took their leave of the main area. He was unwilling to believe they'd gone for the first half hour, but eventually Erik risked standing. He looked into the main area and saw no one there. After allowing himself a small stretch, he sat back down beside the door and put his hands back on the handle.

Tove was sleeping peacefully on the mattress. He watched her for a while, glad to have her in the cell for his sake almost as much as her own. He hadn't realized how unbearable the time had been until he looked at her. There was no warmth, nothing worth smiling over or enjoying. He blamed himself for waiting.

The regular rounds came by as normal and the guards spent a few minutes yanking on the door. They left after, seemingly unconcerned that they'd failed to get in and do whatever Ásví wanted them to. They were likely counting on him sleeping and Erik had no good way around it. He hadn't intended on working around it at all, only on buying enough time that Tove might be able to walk on her own. He could manage that much, he knew it.

A second round of guards came through an hour or two later, pulling at the handle in turns. It wasn't easy on Erik's arms, especially not with the pain of the bit that had been cut off. The wound had stopped bleeding, at least, but it did him no favors. They waited around for far less time after failing to pull the door free, leaving him time to rest his arms. They had sent only men in armor to try the door. It made sense, considering what he'd done to the guards, but it gave him more than enough warning.

Another group came, this time louder than the last. They were shouting, riled up. When they came close enough Erik could tell they were drunk.

"A'right! Firs' one gets 'im outta that shitbox, gets a look at Ásví's tits."

The men all laughed and then cheered.

"So hoos up firs'?"

"Aye!" a man shouted.

Erik couldn't see any of them and he had no intention of looking, especially not now. The noise had woken Tove up and she stood up, shakily, moving herself over to him. The first man began to yank as Erik noticed her.

"You can walk? Great."

She angled her head around him, looking up at the door. "How many are there?"

Erik focused on keeping his grip tight against the pull of the handle. "Dunno. I think they turned me into a drinking game. Could be at this for a while."

The man yanking the door gave up and all the men laughed at him.

"I'll not hear a laugh at me! Le's see you fucks pull it open then! He's a bear's strength, I swear it!"

They booed him and the next man came to try. It went on in turn for longer than Erik was happy about. They began playing other games, only pulling at the door when they were bored. The noise grew, though, rather than died. More men joined.

It had been nearly three hours and Erik's hands were red, worn raw from the wood dragging against his skin. The men had just finished a song and were about to begin another when Erik heard a strange noise.

It was a horn. A warning, loud, deep, and close. The men

all hushed, before a panic set in among them. He heard them go rushing out of the room in complete disorder. The room outside was quiet, only the sound of mail jangling down the hall. He called for Tove to check the door. She did.

"Empty. They've all gone."

Erik stood up, looking out the door himself. The sound of the clattering armor had faded and the horn winded. In the space between one sound of warning and the next, a noise flooded into the room. A noise Erik had heard before, only briefly.

It was the booming sound of stone collapsing onto stone.

CHAPTER SEVENTEEN

THE NOISE WAS TOO FAR AWAY TO HAVE COME FROM THE far end of the tunnel and there likely would have been dust. Erik kept his eyes locked on the room through the bars in the door. There were a few swords that had been left behind. He was still not entirely convinced that this wasn't some plan by Ásví to trick him. The horn sounded again, this time cut short. A half second after it stopped, another boom roared into the cells. There was no reason to wait, he decided, so he turned to Tove.

"I'll be right back."

He turned the handle and pushed the door open, running as quickly as he could to the two nearest swords, throwing them into the cell. He stood up to return to the cell when he heard screams. Not shouts of battle, but the sounds of dying men. They were coming from the end of the hall. The distinctive shift of chain mail sounded, beating a feverish rhythm toward them. Erik didn't wait to see what the man was fleeing, but he had a guess. He made it back into the cell as he heard the man scream, begging for his life. The door closed and he latched it, grabbing a sword and kicking the other to Tove before spinning to face the door. There was no point in holding it shut, not now.

The hall went silent again and he heard something he hadn't expected. It was Haki. He was making a sort of high squeal. Erik heard the door to Haki's cell open and the man walked out.

"She's... come back... for me! Finally!" He wheezed, his voice elated. "To see... see me to... Valhalla! Heeee!" The noise was inhuman, an uneven, manic screech forced through an unruly throat. "Come back... for Haki!"

Erik ran to the door, looking out the bars. Haki started what must have been the nearest thing to a run he could manage, and Erik followed him over to see Göll come from the hallway. His mouth dropped open. Her armor was torn and she was bleeding from her arms and from a deep cut above her eye. They were sealing visibly in just the short time he'd seen her.

Haki ran to her and she slapped him away, forcing the broken man against the far wall. It would have killed anyone else, but Haki climbed to his knees, he said nothing but Erik could see on the twitching face that his world was shattering all over again.

Göll looked at him for a moment, not sure what exactly to make of the man. Erik could see a wave of recognition slowly come across her face which was replaced by a look of pity.

Erik wasted no time opening the door when she turned to face it. He kept his sword in hand, unsure if she had come to see him out or to join her sisters in their slaughter.

"Been a while."

Göll nodded. "We have little time."

Erik looked at Tove who stood against the wall nearest the door, sword ready to ambush whoever was fool enough to come into the cell. Erik wasn't convinced.

"Why are you here?"

The answer was the same as it had ever been. "I have come to guide you to Valhalla."

He looked at Tove and nodded. She came to stand beside him in the cell and Göll's eyes opened. There was a flash of confusion.

"What is that?"

It wasn't the most polite way to phrase things. "Tove. She's..." He lacked for a better way of saying it. "We're a warband."

Göll shook her head firmly. "No. You should not have a warband. You are sworn to Odin. She cannot accompany us."

"I'm sworn to exactly fucking nobody, Göll. And she's coming with us."

"Odin will—"

"Odin will go suck a dick, for all I care. He's had his sky cunts cutting holes in me—"

Tove punched him weakly in the arm, though her face suggested she'd meant it seriously. "Do not speak ill of the Allfather! Show respect."

Erik was confused that she chose that point in time to argue with him, considering that the discussion was over whether she would rot in a sadist woman's prison.

"She's coming."

Erik said nothing else and walked out of the cell. Tove followed him, keeping close. She kept herself behind him, but it did little to stop Göll from staring at her. When Erik spoke the valkyrie returned her attention to him.

"We leaving or what?"

Göll nodded stiffly and turned, starting down the hallway. There was no limp or hesitation in her walk, but she had clearly been in a fight with Hrist and Mist. There were pieces of remaining chain mail in the hallway where she had cut down the men who attempted to flee from her and Erik tensed. He could remember their talks in the motel, how she'd seemed almost human underneath her stern manner. Now it was hard to see much beyond a valkyrie.

Tove stumbled behind him, interrupting his attempts to figure out exactly what Göll was to him. He turned.

"I'm carrying you."

She frowned. "I can walk."

"And if we need to run?" She looked away. "That's what I thought."

He picked her up, something which Tove was happy to huff about in spite of her body not having healed itself in the few short hours since he'd managed to rescue her. If it could be called a rescue. He was being rescued by Göll more than he'd rescued Tove or himself.

The administrative hall had a half dozen pieces of plate and chain strewn around it. There was blood on nearly every surface in the room. It was as much of a horrific scene as Erik had witnessed, until Göll pushed open the door. It swung open on one lazy hinge, revealing a yard full of spilled blood and limbs and chunks of flesh. He wondered why they hadn't dissipated until he properly looked around. Many of those who'd been dismembered or disemboweled were still alive, lying in heaps. Every building in the yard had been destroyed, along with large spans of the walls. There were large fires in several of the collapsed areas and he swore he could hear screaming from under the rocks. It dawned on him that they'd likely slept there.

"Nowhere left to go," he mumbled. "Jesus."

Göll scanned the yard and increased her speed to a jog. Erik kept pace with her, awkward as it was with Tove in his arms, and they exited to the street. Massive crowds had gathered since the noise had stopped but none of them moved into the yard. The people parted as quickly as they could when Göll moved toward the square, some clamoring in a panic to do so.

The valkyrie didn't even seem to notice them as she walked past. Near the statue in the center of the town square was a cart pulled by two impressively large horses. It was far from the only horse-drawn thing trapped in the square, just the one nearest the line that Göll was taking through the crowds. Erik realized she may have been moving for the cart intentionally. Even as the crowd began screaming, the horses at the head kept their calm and, in fact, seemed almost entirely uninterested in the goings on around them. The driver saw her approaching and, rather than signal the horses, he abandoned the cart. Göll climbed up into the driver's seat and turned to Erik. She didn't say anything, just watched him carefully as he loaded Tove into the back of the cart.

When he'd loaded her in, Erik came to the front and took a seat beside Göll. She snapped the reins on the horses and they started moving slowly through the steadily parting crowd. The screams and shouts died and turned to quiet staring, at least in the area near to their cart. Even as slow as they'd been walking, he hadn't felt nervous until he was perched on the cart, slowly pacing through the crowd at the behest of the horses.

"Is this safe? Aren't we a little exposed?"

"We have time. This will be faster soon enough."

Göll scanned the sky, which made believing what she'd said just the slightest bit harder to do. They cleared the crowd and picked up speed through the main streets. People heard them coming well enough in advance to be out of the way by the time the cart thundered past. The wind across his face filled him with excitement even as the threat of the other valkyries coming weighed on his mind. They would be clear of the city soon, and he couldn't be more elated. It had started out as such a pleasant place.

They were at the edge of town, Göll showing no intention of slowing down as guards turned to look. For a moment, it seemed as though they might try to stop the horses, but the men parted, perhaps deciding that if trouble was leaving the city it was not worth stopping. Or it may have been recognition of Göll's armor. Whatever the reason, they were outside of Lofgrund. He felt Tove's hand on his back for a brief moment. He turned and saw her sitting with her back to him, the city walls shrinking slowly. He put a hand on her head and felt her shaking beneath it. She buried her head in her knees, crying too quiet for him to hear over the sound of the horses.

He turned to Göll who looked at him out of the corner of her eye.

"So, why'd you come back?"

Göll frowned, not with any sense of malice or anger. "I cannot pass so easily from one realm to another as a human who's died. It is natural for you to come to Helheim. You are welcome here."

"So you never left me behind."

She nodded, turning to look at him. There was regret in her expression. "I meant to prepare you. I knew you would be alone for a time. I worried when you died," she looked back at the road, "that Vár's influence would have tainted you. But when I arrived back in Helheim, I could still feel you." She put a hand over her heart. "Somehow I felt you even more strongly. It's... strange. You must have lived well in your time here."

"That's strange?"

She narrowed her eyes. "No. There... I have chosen before you. The others, no matter how they lived, there was no change."

Erik thought of Haki, but couldn't bring himself to mention the man or ask her about him. Had he been one of her chosen? Had she abandoned him? There was a way of asking that she might answer.

"What if I had dishonored myself, or whatever you'd call it?"

"You would be unfit for Valhalla and the unworthy..." She paused. "There is no need for them."

It was unsatisfying, like so many answers he'd received, but Erik was not interested in pressing the issue. To his surprise, even though he had intended on riding quietly for a while, Göll spoke to him.

"Why have you taken on a follower?"

"Sorry? Follower?"

"The girl. She cannot enter Valhalla. She cannot accompany you to the feast or to battle."

"Why would she need to do that?"

Göll looked at him, perplexed. "You said you were a warband. And you lead it?"

"Yeah, I lead it, sure."

"She has agreed to that?"

"Maybe? It was her idea. Why should I argue?"

Göll slowed the horses to a stop and stood. She turned to Tove. "Stand, girl."

Tove spun around, terrified, and crawled away. "Why? What is this? Erik?"

Erik put an arm out in front of Göll who slapped it away.

"I have questions for this human. Why did you form a warband with him? Surely you know the meaning."

Tove backed herself up against the far edge of the cart. "I did. What of it? He is no slave." Her voice shook, betraying the nerves underneath the front she was putting on.

Erik was losing his temper. "One of you explain this, seriously."

Göll's jaw clenched, her eyes boring into Tove with intense focus.

Tove looked at him, her expression softening, asking for pity. "A warband is an ancient thing. It is as much a family as one of blood."

Erik could not understand the look on her face or her

repentant tone. He looked to Göll who was seething.

"And?"

Göll spoke. "They cannot be broken." She took a step toward the rear of the cart, Erik stopping her. "Tell me girl, who is your god?"

Tove found her voice for the first time. "Odin, the Allfather."

Göll spit at the side of the cart. "Then you knew."

"I knew!"

Erik shouted, stopping them both. "One of you tell me what the fuck is going on."

Göll properly turned her attention to him for the first time since they'd stopped. "She has attached herself to you that she might come to Valhalla unchosen."

He understood enough to know that was something complicated. And that he was likely to be held responsible for it. Tove stood up.

"I knew, Erik. I'm sorry. Odin protected me in life and I wish to serve him!"

Göll barked, as angry as he'd ever seen her. "You do not choose how you serve the Allfather!"

Tove curled away from Göll's words defensively, but said nothing else. Erik was lost for how he was meant to feel. He couldn't know the gravity of things, but they were not nearly far enough from Lofgrund for him to feel comfortable sitting in the middle of the road any longer.

"Is this something we can solve here, Göll?"

He watched her swallow her frustration and return to her seat, taking up the reins. He turned and sat without another word and Göll snapped at the horses. They started their trot and Erik settled into the seat. The things he didn't know were beginning to be so much more than an inconvenience. They'd ridden for a few hours before he could no longer hold the question.

"What will happen if she comes to Valhalla?"

Göll didn't answer for several minutes. "If…" She did not

seem to want to say it. "If she is found worthy as your follower, she will be allowed in."

"And if not?"

"She will be destroyed."

The word choice was one Erik couldn't imagine was flippant. She had meant the word as it sounded. There was no more talking as the heat of the early evening dipped into the balm of a humid night. The plains gave way to hills and empty land to forests. The night passed, Erik finding only an hour of rest. The sun rose again and in the afternoon the air began to dry and the temperature drifted slowly down. They stopped only briefly, the horses showing no real sign of tiring in spite of their near constant work.

Tove came to him while they were stopped, nervous to say anything. "I am sorry."

Erik held in a breath, unsure what he was supposed to feel. He let it go all at once. "I don't know what to say, Tove. I don't know what any of it means. She said you'd be destroyed."

She nodded. "And likely, you will be mocked for having tried to bring someone unwilling." She perked up, forcing a smile. "But I intend on being worthy!"

"And if you're not?"

The thought of it seemed to rush over her, replaced by the same forced smile. "I have you. You are amazing, Erik. You seem to know innately what you must do, even Göll has admitted it. She said she felt you more strongly. It's proof! I will follow you and work to live as you do."

Erik weakly worked out an exhausted laugh. "I know what to do, right. That's pure fantasy. I just do whatever stupid thing flies into my brain."

She punched him, more firmly than she had before. "Do not talk ill of my warchief."

He smiled and Tove did as well, a genuine smile. She returned to the cart ahead of him, sinking back into the rear, a look of worry settling on her face. Göll said nothing when he came back to his seat. She had heard the entire conversation, he knew that much, but she only slapped the reins and let the horses begin to do their work.

As evening came on, the leaves had begun to turn to yellow and light green. It was perhaps a few hours before dark when Göll pulled the horses to a stop.

She stood and stepped down to the road below, looking up at him. "We are near enough to walk."

Chapter Eighteen

THEY HAD WALKED TWO HOURS AWAY FROM THE ROAD when Tove couldn't walk well enough to continue. She was surprised when Erik offered to pick her up and carry her as long as he could manage. It was nearly dawn when his legs started to falter underneath him. The forest was thicker by far where they were than it had been by the road.

He stopped, putting Tove down near a tree. She leaned against it and Erik went to Göll who was watching the woods with cautious eyes. The terrain had turned to large hills and it was no longer a matter of simply walking along flat ground.

"Is there a reason we can't rest?"

"No." She answered without pulling her eyes away from the trees. "There should be no problem with a short rest."

"What about food and water?"

She shrugged. "There is none."

Erik took a breath, trying to maintain his patience. He'd talked to Tove for the bulk of the trip and that had done little to improve Göll's mood, it seemed. She hadn't said anything specific about where they were headed. "Somewhere safe" was all she had managed to offer up. It wasn't exactly the sort of answer he wanted, but what could he do about it? Starting a fight with her would be pointless. Tove didn't know the area, so it wasn't as though they could abandon her either and Erik didn't want to. Whatever Göll was, she was another sword that would be pointed at any valkyries who showed up.

"Why don't you tell me anything?"

She kept scanning the woods, letting the question hang in the air.

He wasn't willing to let it lie. "Seriously, why can't I know this shit? If you'd said something at the motel, I might have known that I was supposed to stay in the room. And now we're talking somewhere, who the fuck knows where, and I'm back to the same state. I don't know shit and maybe I'm walking toward getting my chest split open again." He slapped at his chest. "Again! Is that how this works? Are you even on my side?"

She spun around when the question hit her ears, her eyes locked to his. His face dropped and the anger fell out of his body when he saw her. She looked like she was holding back the weight of a mountain and that it was killing her.

"You are one of Odin's chosen." She choked the words through gritted teeth, her eyes crying out that they weren't the words she wanted to say. "I have come to guide you to Valhalla."

Erik frowned for a half second before forcing his face to straighten. He put a hand on her shoulder and the tension fell out of her muscles. The normal stoic air returned around her and she nodded at him.

"I'm sorry." She said the words casually.

He understood well enough to guess what had happened. "I won't ask again."

She turned her eyes back to the woods. He started back toward Tove when she spoke, more softly than he'd ever heard. "Haki Erik Styrsson... thank you."

He nodded without turning back and sat himself by the tree next to Tove. She looked at him.

"Why did you forgive me?"

Erik laughed for the first time in what felt like forever. "You're not even going to lead in with anything? Just straight to that?"

She furrowed her brow. "Why are you laughing? I need to know! I've wronged you."

He gave an exaggerated sigh. "When I was a kid, there was this set of cards. You were supposed to collect them, for a game. They had little pictures and I managed to collect all of them. It was the first thing I ever felt like I'd ever accomplished in my life. My mom..." He paused, not having thought of his mother in longer than he realized. "She..." He shook his head. "She threw them out one summer because she said I was spending too much time with them. They were my whole world and I hated her for it." He looked at Tove. "She wronged me." He smiled and looked away. "But there are worse things than being wronged."

He was quiet for a while. Tove made no attempt to speak, only watched him. He wanted to sleep, even as the sun rose up over them. The day was cool and pleasant and the sound of the wind in the trees was too much.

He was woken up by Tove shaking his shoulders some hours later. It almost startled him how peaceful the world was. Seeing Tove's face looking down at him only made Erik more confused.

"What happened?"

She stifled a laugh. "You slept."

He'd oriented himself about the time he asked the question and how he felt a bit stupid. "That doesn't seem like something I'd do."

She motioned to the sky. "The sun seems to set earlier here. We should go."

Erik looked up through the orange and red trees. They'd passed into Fall sometime during the night and he hadn't been paying attention to the trees when there was enough light out. Thinking back on it he remembered that there were leaves they'd been trudging through in the night but not that morning. He assumed they were just moving across the line into Fall but it was something else.

"Were the trees…"

"Green?"

"Yeah…"

Tove nodded as Erik pulled himself up off the ground. The leaves were starting to fall already. Göll was looking impatient, but she hadn't bothered to wake him up. He couldn't imagine a world where she'd spoken to Tove willingly, so he ruled that out.

"Well, let's pretend I didn't accidentally fall asleep and get going."

Göll started walking without the need for any further prompting. Erik fell in behind her and Tove behind him. She was walking steadily, but he couldn't help feeling that he'd prefer she walked ahead of him just in case. Göll might have complained though so Erik filled the space between them with his body to keep any awkward conversations from forming.

The sun set earlier than Erik had expected. Spring and Summer had been close enough except for their temperature that he hadn't thought much of it, passing from one to the next. They must have been trekking north through the woods nearly as much as they had over road. It was growing colder during the evening than it had the night before. Night fell and they walked on for nearly another two hours before the trees suddenly cleared, revealing a dimly lit house in the middle of what had been dense forest.

They'd barely stepped a few feet into the clearing when a man came out of the house. He was tall and broad, with a barrel chest and a thick beard. He was too far away to see much more, other than that the man was holding a hammer and a sword which flared with bright white light at its tip.

He walked a few steps out of the small house, holding the sword aloft, pointing its light toward them.

"Who's come to my home? And at night! If I'm not pleased at your faces, I'll—" He lowered the sword, cocking his head to the side. "Göll?"

The light dimmed and the man walked toward them. Göll took a step forward. It was the first time Erik had seen her willingly walk toward another person.

"Völundr, I apologize."

He walked past her, ignoring the valkyrie as casually as if she were a post stuck in the ground. Völundr walked up to Erik and leaned in close to him. The man's hammer came up under Erik's chin, pushing his face up.

Völundr said nothing, giving only a minor glance at Tove before turning around. He slapped Göll on the back as he walked by.

"Come on, then. You'll want to eat my food. Might as well get it over with."

Völundr walked back to his house and walked through the open door. Erik came up beside Göll with Tove in tow.

"Who is that?"

"A blacksmith."

She started toward the house and Erik kept pace beside her. He could tell he wouldn't get much more out of her but it felt strange walking into a man's house without knowing anything at all about him. They'd been invited at least, which put Erik's mind at ease a bit.

Tove pulled Erik back and whispered in excited tones.

"Did you see? The sword was magic." She was practically bouncing.

The house was warm inside, lit with a large fire in a pot-belly stove. There were some simple chairs a short distance from the fire. At the far end of the main room, there was a kitchen with a small table that might hold six if people sat close enough. There were a few doors along the far wall that were most likely bedrooms and one at the back. There were other buildings that Erik could just see the outline of when they were in the clearing.

Völundr was at a small wood stove. He pulled a few pans down from the racks above it and placed them on the steel cook top. He set to cooking up some meat and eggs and almost as an afterthought, tossed in some vegetables. It was ten minutes at least before he noticed that they had been awkwardly standing in his main living area and told them to sit. Erik sat at one end of the table, Göll and Tove flanking him leaving the opposite seat open for Völundr.

"What's your name, boy?"

"Erik."

Völundr sighed. "The whole name."

It was a theme Erik had failed to realize the importance of. "Haki Erik Styrsson."

"Hm, a good name."

Völundr tossed the food in the pan. It was a visible mess, Erik could tell that even from his seat. It was finished cooking and put onto plates and brought to the table.

"Thanks. For the food." Erik said it as the plate was placed in front of him.

"Hooo, I like that." Völundr took his plate and went to the seat they'd left open at the table. His attention turned to Göll. "It's been some time since you've ventured out of your little world, Göll. And now you come along with friends."

Erik wasn't intent on waiting to ask whatever he could. "Her little world?"

Völundr dug into his food, heaping a forkful into his

mouth. Erik noticed the utensils as he did. They were expertly made, not the awkward things he'd seen through the rest of Helheim.

"Göll is an ale-bearer." The blacksmith chewed loudly, pointing his fork at Göll. "Something like a thrall among valkyries." He laughed. "She's weak and scared, as so many of her status are. But I can't bring myself to dislike her. She's unlike her sisters."

"A thrall? Like a slave?"

Völundr scrunched up his face, waving his fork around. "No, no. Not so much a slave as the least of her kind."

Göll stared straight down at her plate as Völundr spoke. She was ashamed of every word the man spoke, a fact Völundr noticed.

"And look how it weighs on her." He laughed. "She does not know her own worth. Ah, it's pitiable." He smiled at Erik. "You've begun to see it already, haven't you Haki?"

Erik's jaw clenched instinctively when Völundr's gaze focused on him.

Völundr's smile widened. "Those are good eyes. I wonder if she even bothered to look in them." He poked at Göll absently with his fork. "Have you, Göll?" She ignored the question and he came back to Erik. "So Haki, how have you found Helheim? Welcoming to your sort, isn't it?"

There was nothing to be gained in being stiff with a man like Völundr, Erik could tell that much, so he smiled and laughed.

"Too welcoming. Hard to get a moment's peace, you know?"

Völundr slapped the table. "Isn't it?! You understand, I can see it. They all want something, whatever it might be. But you can't give it to them or—"

"Or they'll lock you in a stone box."

"Haaahaha!" Völundr roared with laughter, pushing another forkful of food into his mouth. "You've met Ásví!"

Erik laughed. "Oh yeah. We met."

Völundr leaned over the table. "Did she touch it?" He eyed down toward Erik's crotch. "She does that. She's a sick one."

"I thought she was going to!" Erik pointed at him, finally taking a bite of the food Völundr had cooked. It was awful. "This is awful!"

Völundr laughed again, slapping the table repeatedly. "It is! I'm useless as a cook!" He stood up from the table holding a hand out across it. "I'm Völundr. I like you, Erik."

Erik stood and clapped his hand around Völundr's forearm. The blacksmith's grip felt like it could easily snap Erik's arm. They sat back down and went back to their food.

"Who's the girl?" Völundr nodded sideways at Tove.

"Tove. She's the second in my warband."

"Said with confidence." He eyed Göll who had at least come as far as looking between them as they talked. "You're a bold one, Erik. I can't hate you. In fact, I welcome you to my home. Stay as long as you like, and your warband." He looked at Tove and smiled. "Oh, but she's a troublesome one, this girl." He finished his plate and stood. "Can't have you sleeping with her. No doubt Göll wants you here for work." He slapped a hand onto Göll's shoulder. "Am I wrong?"

Göll spoke, "I have brought him here to train, yes."

Völundr patted her shoulder and walked off, tossing the plate onto a counter top. "It's safe here, Erik. So long as you can ignore that small beauty, you'll have the time you need. I doubt it will be much from the smell of you."

Erik looked at Tove. She was flushed beet red, staring down at her food. Erik kicked her foot and she yelped, looking over at him then immediately back down to her food.

Völundr came back to the table but didn't sit down. "I've decided on a condition, if you don't mind."

Erik leaned back in his chair. "I might mind."

"I can't imagine you will, not if I understand you as I hope I do. I'll have you apprentice for me while you're here. Even as short a time as you'll be here, a warchief should understand steel."

"I can't argue with that. I'd love to learn."

"The right answer." Völundr walked away from the table. "It's time I slept. You'll be in my room, Erik. I won't tell a man when he should sleep, but we'll wake early. And you'll be worked hard."

"Thanks for your concern."

Völundr waved his hand, pushing open the door to his bedroom. It shut and Erik looked at Göll.

"Are you okay?"

Göll looked at him. "I'm fine. He told no lies about me. They are my own failings."

"I'll believe you." He looked to the other side of the table. "You?"

Tove nodded. "He's strange, but..." She considered her words for a second. "I'm happy to be here."

"Great." Erik stood up. "I guess tomorrow I'm going to get my ass kicked and learn to hammer on metal. Exciting."

CHAPTER NINETEEN

VÖLUNDR WAS SNORING LOUDLY AND ERIK ALMOST MIS-
took the sound of Göll opening the door for another noise
from the blacksmith. It was the movement in the bottom of
his vision that caused him to sit up. The sight of Göll in her
armor wasn't comforting, especially when only half-seen
in a haze of sleep. The only times he'd seen the distinctive
gold-trimmed leather in Helheim were not pleasant ones.

He sat up, ready to be attacked but Göll only wordlessly
waved for him to follow her. If she'd noticed or cared about
the emotion behind his reaction, she hadn't shown it. Erik
dragged himself out of what had passed for a bed, a linen
sheet over a stack of cow hides. He hadn't slept well, but

that was something he was beginning to grow accustomed to. Völundr didn't so much as break the rhythm of his snoring between Göll's entrance and Erik's exit from the room. It was hard not to find it annoying that the man slept so well.

Göll was waiting in the main room of the house, standing near the back door. She looked him over.

"You should wash."

"Now?"

"No. We have too much work and too little time."

"So you were just saying I smell like shit?"

She turned and opened the door to the yard behind them and walked out of it without answering the question.

"Hey!" Erik followed her. "You can't just…" He gave up, slumping in defeat as he went through the door.

Outside, Göll walked across the yard toward a stone building with several stacks coming out of the roof. Having called Völundr a blacksmith, Erik could imagine what the building was for. The valkyrie disappeared around the side and came back with her hands loaded with swords of varying lengths and shapes. She dropped most of them, letting them clang against each other and fall to the ground. There were two shorter swords left in her hands. It was only when he saw her flip one of the swords over and grab it by the handle that he realized that her own weapon was nowhere around.

"Where's your fancy one?"

She walked to him, offering the other sword she'd brought with her. "It is a part of me. And useless for our purposes here."

He started to ask why she'd used it back in the empty lot before realizing that swords were not easily had in the average city back home. He took the offered blade, looking it over. It was dull and looked as though it was made to be. He flailed the sword around a bit in what he imagined was a sort of pattern to test it. Really, he had no clue what it should feel like and likely came off as an idiot, but he could think of nothing else to do.

Göll took her place halfway across the small clearing.

"You have not been here long, but I wish to see if anything has changed." She let the short sword hang casually by her leg. "I will warn you. I cannot withhold any of my power for your own sake."

A knot formed in his stomach, but Erik nodded and readied the sword. He did his best to remember how she'd shown him to hold it, but was not convinced he'd gotten it right.

Göll charged. He could see her move, but only barely. It was an improvement, considering he could not feel whatever power helped him to see the others. She only came into sharp focus when she stopped beside him, her sword already angled up to pierce his ribs. He tried to move the sword over to block or to strike her or to do anything at all. It was far too slow and she jabbed the blunt edge of the sword into his ribs. He felt his skin pull before popping past the rounded tip of Göll's weapon, the metal clacking off of half of his ribs before she pulled it back.

She stood fully when Erik grabbed at his side, taking a few steps away from him. It was a dull, throbbing pain, unhelped by Göll's disappointed expression.

"Again." She started back across the yard.

Erik was rubbing his ribs. "How can you move so fast?"

"Because I must." She spun when she returned to her previous spot. "Ready your sword."

He did so, slowly. "To fight the others? Like at Lofgrund."

Göll frowned. "Luck was with me there. Somehow Mist was injured."

She'd barely finished the sentence when she became a blur crossing the yard. Erik could see the direction she was moving, but little else. He tried to flip his sword over, but it did not find purchase. Göll's did, the edge bludgeoning his stomach. She came around behind him, stopping and planting an elbow in his lower back. He'd already started to curl forward over the pain of the first strike when the second pulled him back the other way. There was no way to remain standing and his knees gave. He squawked in pain and put his arm over his stomach. He was still holding the sword, he knew, something that Erik decided to take some amount of pride in. It was all that kept him from tipping over onto the ground.

Göll came around to the front of him and cast her imposing shadow down over his suffering.

"You could hit me softer, right? If you wanted?"

"Yes." She looked at her own sword. "Your speed has improved a bit. But you would still die."

Erik pushed down on the sword, hoping it would help him stand. Instead, it dug into the soft soil and he fell over, barely catching himself before his face hit the ground. He pushed himself up, standing with a groan filled with both annoyance and pain.

"I'm going to remember you said yes even though you changed the subject." He leaned the top half of his body from side to side, trying to coax his stomach into dimming the ache of Göll's sword blow. "So, how do I get faster? How do I not die?"

"Dying cannot be avoided."

Erik rolled his eyes. "How do I die less?"

"You must learn to see." She tapped his sword with her own. "And you hold a sword like it means to bite you."

He turned the sword over, looking at his grip on it. "It might."

Göll was unimpressed by his joke and turned around, walking back to her place. She repeated her attacks, changing them each time. The drop in his stomach every time she ran at him made Erik swear he could just feel the edges of the power inside his body. It must have been what she meant by learning to see.

Somewhere in the mid-morning hours, Tove came and sat in the grass beside the door to Völundr's house, watching them quietly. Göll seemed as though she wanted to protest, but she hadn't ever found the will to do so if Tove's presence bothered her.

It was around noon when Völundr finally appeared in his own doorway. He watched them for a moment but quickly grew bored. He cooked another terrible lunch, saying that Erik would come and work after the meal.

"The dishes are yours to see to, Göll." He stood, laughing, when the meal was done. "Erik, with me."

They left, Tove looking depressed for a lack of anything to do. As the two men walked across the yard, Völundr looked Erik over.

"Never swung a hammer, have you?"

Erik shrugged. "At nails, maybe. Not much call for blacksmithing anymore." A firm hand clapped him on the shoulder.

"Then you'll be useless to me?" Völundr laughed. "A true apprentice."

The door to the stone building was made of steel, engraved with the picture of a long-haired valkyrie with large, feathered wings. She held a runed broadsword. Völundr swung the door open without commenting on it and Erik was concerned enough about being terrible at the work that he didn't bother to ask.

Inside the stone-walled shop were tongs and hammers and bars of steel of every size. In the center of the room was a large stone, polished flat on the top with a thick plate of steel laid on top of it, the edges rounded down to hold it in place. There was a brickwork forge at the far corner, the stack rising out of the roof. Völundr pointed to a wooden crate of rough balls of dark rock, at least they looked like it to Erik.

"Place those by the anvil. And an empty one next to them."

He lifted the box up, looking at the balls. They were knobby and full of tiny holes. The shifting of the chunks as he walked gave off the distinctive clank of metal.

"Got to start with the basics for a man like you or I'll lose the whole day explaining things." Völundr was at the forge, lighting a bit of kindling on a lip near the mouth of it. The kindling lit and he squatted to see to the charcoal beneath. "Well, you've missed the dirty work, though." He chuckled. "I'm disappointed. Wanted to see you waste a day panning in a river. You'll be dirty enough by the end."

Erik placed the crate onto the floor and ran back over to grab an empty one. Völundr had managed to get the fire established. He stood up and walked to the far wall, pulling down a hammer, some tongs, and a soft bunch of leather. He laid the hammer on the anvil along with the leather and held up the tongs.

"You'll be doing the work today, Erik." He handed over the tongs. "Do what I say and I won't have to beat you." Völundr laughed and grabbed the leather, tossing it at Erik and then moving to the far side of the anvil. He picked up the hammer and leaned against the steel. "And I won't have you being surprised at my change in mood. This is my meaning. If you work my forge, you'll take it as serious as I do."

"I intend to."

"You say that before you've even let a bead of sweat drop." Völundr pointed at a sizable bellows attached to the forge. "Let's start. Stoke that fire."

Erik leaned the tongs against the anvil rock and put the leather over his shoulder before moving to the bellows. It was operated by a chain coming from the ceiling. He pulled on it, nerves turning his stomach to knots. He let the chain go and the air forced its way into the forge. A deep roar answered from the guts of the brick furnace and flame licked out from the mouth.

"Again! Until I tell you to stop!"

Erik worked the bellows a few dozen times, his arms already burning from the effort when Völundr shouted his next order.

"Have those tongs and stick one of those blooms in!"

The blooms must have been the bits of rough metal in the boxes. Erik ran to the tongs, pushing them awkwardly into the box. He missed a few times before finally grabbing one.

"About time!" Völundr laughed at him derisively. "If it was a country girl, you'd have picked it up without being asked, wouldn't you?"

Erik shoved the metal into the fire. Calling the heat uncomfortable would have been a gross understatement. He held it in the fire until it was glowing hot and, without being able to see it, Völundr called for him to pull it.

"On the anvil! Now!"

Erik ran over, placing it on the anvil and pulling the tongs.

"Hold it! Don't be stupid!" Völundr swung the hammer at Erik's head but he was much too far away for it to have struck him.

Erik put the tongs back around the bloom and Völundr started hammering the metal. His strikes were thunderous, sending chunks of dark debris off of the metal and onto the wide surface of the anvil.

"Flip!"

Erik did, and Völundr hammered the other side flat.

"Wipe it." Erik hesitated for a half second and Völundr lost his patience again. "The anvil!"

Remembering the leather on his shoulder, Erik pulled it down, moving the tongs to the side with his other hand. He wiped debris off the anvil and put the metal back.

"Too cold! Back on the fire. And work the bellows."

Erik put the bloom back in the fire and went to the bellows, doing as he was told until Völundr told him to move. The bloom was reheated, brought back for hammering, and the process repeated until the rough, dirty ball was turned into something resembling a steel bar.

Völundr didn't slow. He barked for Erik to drop the bar and pull a new bloom. With the process in his mind now,

Erik had more confidence. His speed wasn't to Völundr's standards on most things, but he worked through two-thirds of the box with no more than a few screams and swipes at his head. Most of those were from new steps being added without Erik expecting them. More charcoal, sweeping the floor while steel heated, that sort of thing. It was the heat that began to slow Erik down with the last few boxes. He could see that Völundr had barely broken a sweat and didn't want to complain.

"Don't like the heat, do you boy?" Völundr's tone had softened as the day went on, surprisingly. He mocked Erik now as a piece of steel heated. "Afraid to take your shirt off? What sort of embarrassing torso are you hiding under that filthy rag?" He laughed.

"I'm not the one who built a fucking forge inside of a small box of rocks."

"I like the heat! Reminds me to keep breathing."

"How the hell does it do that?" Erik pulled the steel without being told and ran it to the anvil where Völundr started working it.

"Couldn't say!" He laughed as the hammer powered down onto the steel. "It just sounds good!"

They finished working the metal into bars. It was dusk by the time the door of the smithy opened for them to leave. There was plenty of cleaning to be done, even with Völundr helping. Tove ran up to Erik as soon as he was out in the yard.

"Erik! Have you made anything exciting?"

He huffed a laugh. "Mostly rectangles of metal. Nothing that cuts anything."

Völundr came walking past them, chuckling at the sight. "He'll not make anything. They're my hammers, girl."

She didn't respond to the statement, simply followed Erik as he walked by. Völundr pointed off toward the setting sun before they reached the house.

"Hot spring off that direction. Should be good enough for a bath. I'd rather smell my own terrible cooking than your stink, Erik."

Erik stopped dead. "A hot bath? You're fucking with me, aren't you?"

Völundr stopped, turning to look at Erik. "No, you earned the right. And with a girl cooing after you so bad, I'd feel awful if I let you go on smelling so terrible. Not much I can do for your clothes. Doubt you'd fit into mine."

"I wouldn't ask for anything else. Oh, man... Völundr, you know how to end a day of work."

"Go."

Erik didn't wait to be told twice. He immediately set off toward the west, finding a small trail that had been cleared away. It was only a few hundred yards to the spring. Tove had followed him along and Göll was coming down the path as well. Erik chose to ignore them, stripping off his clothes and tossing them into the spring. He followed them in, sinking into the water with a loud, long moan. Tove snickered behind him.

"I'm not going to look back there and have your mockery ruin my bath."

He waded over to his clothes, rubbing them together to get some of the dirt off of them. The dirt came away, clouding the water but the muck flowed away toward a crack in the rocks. Völundr most likely built it, if the flat slate along the bottom was anything to go by.

"Today was terribly boring." Tove spoke up when he'd ignored her for too long.

"What can I do about that, exactly?" He turned around.

Tove shrugged. "Nothing, yourself. But I want to train."

Göll had been standing quietly until she said she wanted to be trained. "No. I refuse."

Erik sunk down into the warm water. His muscles felt as if they could melt away in the heat of the pool. "Why?"

"I have no responsibility to this girl who has attempted to steal what belongs to you."

"Fair enough," Erik held up a finger to stop Tove's immediate move to complain. "But you know I don't plan on leaving her, so what good will it do us if she can't fight?"

"It is not my responsibility," Göll repeated with an annoyed look. "And I'd likely kill her, even with a dull blade."

"I don't care about dying." Tove was insistent. "I want to learn. It's not as though I am helpless with a sword."

"That you think it's a question only of skill shows you as the silly girl you look to be."

Tove puffed up, annoyed. Before the argument took off, Erik pulled in a deep breath and submerged himself in the spring. There was only the sound of a trickle of water through the rocks. It was calming, something he knew couldn't last forever. There would be pain, the valkyries would find them or be waiting for them. All the more reason to enjoy what was in front of him.

When he came back to the surface, Göll and Tove were still arguing. They'd completely forgotten he was there from the looks of it. Erik watched them, drawing their attention when he could no longer hold in a small laugh. They both turned to him at the sound.

Tove pointed a hand at Göll. "Tell her to train me!"

Göll scoffed. "And why would I listen?" She looked at Erik in the spring. It was the most emotion he'd ever seen from her. With complete sincerity, she said, "Tell her I'll never train her!"

He could feel a stupid grin spread across his face and without saying a word to either of them, he took another breath and disappeared back under the warm water.

CHAPTER TWENTY

THE BOOT CONNECTED WITH HIS RIBS SQUARE AND ERIK doubled over, gasping for air. He'd managed to get to sleep easily enough after the relaxing bath, even though he'd been forced to sleep without his clothes while they dried.

He looked up to see Völundr's dark face staring at the door. It was a very different expression than he'd had at dinner when he was mocking Erik for walking around wrapped in a sheet.

"Come. Assist me."

Erik nodded, standing himself up, the pain in his ribs dulled but still present enough to tell him the kick was not simply something meant to wake him up. He pulled on damp clothes and Völundr led him out to the main room. Göll was standing there and watched as they went by. She started to follow but Völundr turned to her.

"You stay here valkyrie." The blacksmith's voice was grave and Erik could smell liquor wafting out of his mouth. "You swore I'd have an apprentice so long as you stayed here."

Göll stayed in her place, looking at Erik with just the slightest hint of concern in her barely furrowed brow.

Völundr led him out the back and, to Erik's relief, opened the door to the workshop. Inside, the smith began rifling angrily through stacks of metal bars and ores, pulling open drawers, emptying their contents onto the floor. He spun, looking at Erik with wild eyes.

"Clean after me! What do you think I've brought you for?!"

Erik rushed to the metal and began stacking it as quickly as he could, returning the ores to their places while Völundr found a piece of metal that suited his needs. The bars that had been tossed aside were returned to wooden boxes as Völundr began to hammer at the dull yellow metal. Erik moved on replacing the contents of the drawers that had been dashed out onto the floor. The drawers were labeled with specific rune carvings. While he could read the labels, knowing what some of the things on the floor were turned out to be a matter of guesswork. There were small chunks of more precious metals, things Erik had no experience with. As much as he thought Völundr was paying no attention to him, any piece of metal placed into the wrong drawer drew a shout.

The last drawer hadn't yet been filled and put back into place when Völundr called for a forming hammer and a dowel. Erik held his hand by various sizes of hammer and wooden rod until he didn't receive a barked insult and laid them on the anvil where Völundr had split the gold and made it roughly round and thin enough. Erik watched as the smith's hands became a blur, working the gold around the dowel and forming it down, hammering it smooth with tools he was sure weren't meant to be used to do such detailed work.

It wasn't ten minutes before Völundr called for more tools. A small chisel and a burnisher. The chisel Erik managed on the first try, but not knowing that the burnisher was a small crooked piece, failed at it enough times that Völundr was forced to point to get him to the right part of the wall of tools. Erik watched again as the metal was worked with the new implements. The detail was like nothing Erik had ever seen put into a piece of jewelry. It was detailed and precise to a degree that he hadn't imagined someone could work with only old tools and their hands.

Völundr took the ring to a few small boxes full of sand, polishing it in places and rubbing it rough in others. He spent an hour on the work, bringing the finished product to Erik and holding it up to him, eyes red and tortured.

"What do you see?"

Erik looked at the ring, knowing there was some trick to the answer he was meant to give but knowing he would never guess the trick before Völundr lost his temper. "A ring. A beautiful ring."

Völundr spun around, whipping the ring against the far wall. "Beautiful! Of course it is! But it's not... right!" He nearly howled the words, half crying, and went back to the bench, starting on the other piece of gold. His breathing was labored and he seemed more aware of Erik's presence. "They're never right, Erik."

Even as unfocused and unsteady as he seemed in the chair, Völundr did his expert work again, this time faster than the first. He finished the ring and put it on the anvil, frowning down at it. He picked up his hammer and smashed the ring flat, sliding everything off the table. From under his shirt, Völundr produced a simple leather chain holding a ring in the same design that had been on the two discarded rings. Only... it wasn't. The depths between the grooves cut into the ring seemed to go miles deep and the gold shone almost unnaturally in the light.

"Is it magic?"

Völundr stared into the ring. "No." He scoffed, eyes heavy with drink and lack of sleep. "It is only metal. A token of love to mock me until the end of all things." He looked across at Erik, stowing the ring. "What do you know of magic?"

"Nothing."

"I'd call you a liar, but you might agree." Völundr walked to the back corner of the shop and pulled a blade with no handle from a pile. He came and laid it on the anvil. There were runes chiseled into it and angled lines snaking up the length of the blade. "Magic is all around us."

Erik laughed. "In the rivers and the trees or some shit?"

Völundr pointed at him. "You mock but it's true. As much here as in Midgard. A river..." He leaned back. "What is a river spread over land? Something with no depth. Useless, barely something a man would notice. But give it direction..." Völundr slapped the sword against the anvil and electricity arced out from it, crackling in the air before dissipating.

In spite of the risk of electrocution, Erik held his hand out.

"Boo!"

Erik jumped back, immediately wishing he hadn't. "Oh, you're an asshole." He exhaled, relieved in spite of Völundr's mocking laughter.

"I was worried you'd confused it for a pert breast, the way you were looking at the damn thing." He laughed for too long and entirely too hard from Erik's perspective. Eventually he regained his composure. "Tell me, have you been in battles? Not Göll's playfights."

It was all Erik could do not to tense up just thinking about it. "Yeah. A few."

"With the valkyries?"

"Yeah, a few."

Völundr smiled and leaned forward. "Get any good licks in?"

Erik chuckled at his enthusiasm. "A few."

"Oh?" He seemed genuinely surprised. "You wouldn't lie to a man fool enough to bang on metal, I hope."

"Hey! I don't lie!" Erik's mouth turned to a mock-smug smile. "Well, sometimes I lie." He feigned reassurance. "But never about fights! Haha, I think I even broke one's arm. Mist maybe."

The easy smile faded and Völundr's brow came down, not believing what he'd heard. "You what?"

"Yeah, she was flying at me, so I sort of caught her with my elbow and then I stomped on her arm. Some sort of einherjar power, maybe." Erik chuckled, wanting the expression on Völundr's face to go back to something more relaxed. Instead, his face only became more serious.

"You've seen their backs then? Describe it."

Erik let go of his pretense of casual conversation, realizing there might be information he could get from the smith. "The shimmering wings, right? I couldn't see them very well. Tried to grab them. Split my hand into a thousand pieces, give or take."

"You were bare-handed?" Völundr stood suddenly.

"Yeah, I—"

The smith's rough hands grabbed Erik's arms, feeling them and checking the fingers one by one. He did the same to Erik's neck and face, looking intently at his eyes for longer than he'd inspected the rest. Völundr turned around, pacing the room.

"Is that weird? There was this guy, Haki, he—"

"Go sleep."

Erik was confused, taken aback by the sudden command. "Are you not coming?"

Völundr walked over to him, smiling. His eyes were almost twinkling when he placed thick hands onto Erik's face "Go. Sleep." Völundr pulled Erik up and walked him out the door. "Tell Göll not to bother me. And not to leave until I come out."

"What should I do?"

Völundr laughed. "Keep playfighting with your valkyrie."

The door to the shop closed and Erik heard the rattle of metal inside. As he was walking across the yard, smoke started coming out from the stacks. Erik showed himself back inside, not nearly as tired as he had been when Völundr had woken him up. Göll came walking to him as he made it back into the house.

"What did he want?"

Erik looked over his shoulder before closing the door. "Help with some rings."

Göll shook her head. "Still, that ring." Her eyes scanned over his face. "That was all?"

"Yeah, we talked a bit. About magic swords. That sort of thing. He told me to go sleep."

Göll nodded her agreement with the last statement. "You should. We will be training in the morning."

"We?"

"You."

He put a hand on her shoulder as he walked by, not thinking anything of it. She twitched when his hand landed on her. Erik realized it was the first time they'd touched that didn't involve a weapon.

"Good night, Göll."

She hesitated, not responding until he was near the door to the bedroom. He barely heard her. "Good night, Erik."

The morning came and Erik rose to the sound of an argument in the main room. He left Völundr's bedroom and found Tove and Göll having a heated discussion. Tove was holding a practice sword.

"I'm better than him with a blade and you know as much!"

Göll noticed Erik before she could manage a response to Tove.

"Outside, Erik. It's time we got to work."

Erik groaned, the girls' meaningless fight resulting in another morning with no breakfast. Völundr hadn't returned to sleep the night before, so it was just as well.

When they entered the yard, Tove was sticking close to Erik's back. Wisps of smoke were floating out of the stacks in the shop. He could hear the sound of a hammer working metal. Tove left Erik's back and stood beside the house with her training sword. Göll retrieved the two from the previous morning and handed Erik his. The training began with Tove watching as Göll began her charges. For the bulk of the morning, it was just watching but before long Tove was mock guarding against the valkyrie's attacks on Erik.

A few hours passed before Göll lost her patience with it.

"You're not meant to be practicing! Stop what you're doing!"

Tove pointed the sword at Göll. "No! I'll learn it however I can and you won't stop me!"

"I won't have you waving around cheap mockeries of the things I instruct Erik to do."

"Instruct, hah! You barely tell him a thing. Just abuse him constantly."

"His body will learn faster than his mind!"

Erik was happy for the break, but the arguments weren't relaxing ambiance. "Both of you lighten up."

"Perhaps you should take things less lightly," Göll snapped. "The girl is better than you with a sword by far."

"Well, maybe you should train her then." He wanted to laugh, but he was fairly certain Göll would push the blunt sword through his face if he did.

Göll huffed and took her place in the yard. Erik readied himself and the training went on, Tove continuing to fight with shadows. Lunch came and went with no break except for water. It was punishment, Erik was sure of that but he wouldn't complain. It was a frustrating bunch of work. The edge of that power in his mind was no closer to his reach no matter how many times she ran at him. His eyes were slowly getting used to her movement and he was starting to catch up. He'd even caught the edge of Göll's sword a time or two, but there was nothing behind it, not like when he'd fought Hrist and Mist. It was worrying, enough that he wanted to ask how long it might take until he reached whatever was inside, but the arguments had left Göll in a sour mood.

Dusk came and Göll finally called an end to the practice, heading inside without saying anything to either of them. Tove walked over to Erik, sweating profusely. She pulled on her shirt, fanning herself in the cool air.

"She said I was better with a sword than you."

Erik frowned, tossing the practice sword into the grass a few feet away. "Well, you cheated."

"How have I managed that?"

"You're older than me."

She shoved him, smiling, and trotted into the house. Erik followed her in. Göll was waiting in the kitchen with Tove at the table.

Erik looked at them both and then over to the workshop. "Wonder how long he's going to work. I'm starving." He looked at Tove. "Why don't you cook us something?"

Tove scoffed. "I'm no housewife."

"Hey! You cooked in the woods!"

"That was different."

"How?"

"No house."

Erik rolled his eyes hard enough that he nearly pulled something. It was a point he couldn't argue. The smug satisfaction Tove was beaming in his direction made him frustrated at his lack of a response.

"Well, I burn things. That's all I know how to do."

Göll's voice unexpectedly entered the conversation. "I will cook."

Erik was sure he'd misheard. "You'll…"

"Cook," Göll repeated. "I have been in the kitchens of Valhalla. I have seen Andhrímnir do his work."

"Well, that's... good? I'll eat whatever you make. Happily." He smiled at Göll and she nodded, turning to start her work.

Erik joined Tove at the table. "I'm bathing first after dinner."

"I think the better swordsman should bathe first." Tove was still beaming.

"If you keep up like that, I'll challenge you to a duel."

"And I'll accept. So be careful."

Erik leaned back in his chair. "The thanks I get for rescuing people."

Göll set to work cooking, finding pork and vegetables. She cooked the food simply, preparing a sauce out of various herbs that she went to gather from the edge of the clearing and wine and the juices in the pan. Tove shouted at the valkyrie when they ate it, accusing her of using magic. It was easily the best food Erik had eaten in Helheim.

"I am not nearly as capable as Andhrímnir." Göll was modest, but he could see her hide a tiny smile when she turned back to clean a pan she'd used in a bucket of water. He wondered how she'd done so well with the food considering she never ate.

"Why don't you eat?"

The thought was on his mind so he said it aloud.

"I have no need to."

"Yeah, but you can eat, right? Why don't you just eat for the taste? Food tastes good. Some food."

"I have no need to."

He recognized the pattern and a flush of anger ran through him but he let it pass and finished the last piece of food on his plate. "Well, thank you for the meal."

Tove stood up, taking her plate. "Agreed. It was delicious. Whatever you may think of me, Göll, I appreciate you." She placed her plate down and reached for Göll's back. The valkyrie leaned away from Tove's hand.

Erik leaned his chair back and let it come back down, clacking against the floor. "Guess you've still got a ways to go Tove."

She looked at him, letting the awkwardness wash away, replacing it with a smile. "I do." She darted toward the door. "The spring will fill up if I don't hurry." She ran off, leaving the door open. Erik could hear her laughter fade off into the distance.

CHAPTER TWENTY-ONE

IT WAS MORNING AGAIN AND VÖLUNDR HADN'T REAP-
peared in his room when Erik rose. It was just barely light
out and Göll hadn't come to drag him to training just yet.
It was a welcome change from the rough morning's reverie
he'd received of late.

Opening the bedroom door, he found Göll standing in
her usual place, looking through the open shutters of a window at the front side of the house. She looked over at Erik
and then back out the window before finally deciding to
walk over to him.

"We will train again today."

"I had sort of guessed that." Erik yawned, stretching out.

"Tove still sleeping?"

"It's no business of mine where she is or what she's doing."

"So, sleeping?"

Erik headed to the table in the kitchen. There was still some food left from the night before sitting in a dish on it. It had been meant for Völundr but the man hadn't returned from his work. Curious, Erik opened the door. The smoke from the shop had stopped, but he could still hear the occasional ping of a hammer against metal. That made the food fair game as far as Erik was concerned.

He came back to the table, looking at the dish and giving a conflicted sigh. "Alright, I'll be fair."

Göll followed him as he went to the door where Tove had been sleeping. He cracked the door open to find a much nicer room than he'd been sleeping in, with a pair of plush beds only one of which was in use.

Tove was spread out across the entire bed in which she slept. It was a far cry from the way she'd slept in the bedrolls, and an interesting sight to say the least. The bed frames weren't high off the ground, so Erik crouched beside Tove. She was sleeping in loosely wrapped linen that barely still clung to the areas she'd used them to cover.

Erik poked at her face, mashing in the meat of her cheek. Tove didn't so much as break the rhythm of her breathing.

"Tove, get up. Breakfast."

He hadn't said the words quietly, but it still brought no response from the sleeping girl.

"Alright. Well, I tried."

He flattened his hand out over her forehead and snapped his wrist down. The satisfying noise of a well-executed slap rang out and Tove's hands swung up toward the spot he'd hit.

"Ah! What?" She opened her eyes and saw Erik squatting beside the bed and Göll standing in the door. "What is this? Is something happening?"

Erik stood up. "Breakfast." His eyes rolled down over

her and he looked away. "And get dressed."

Tove looked down at herself and yanked the covers up over her body. "There's nothing wrong with my current state!"

He shrugged as he walked out of the room. "Hey, *you* covered it up."

He could hear her shift toward the table beside the bed. There were things on the table. Not wanting one of those things to collide with the back of his head, Erik shuffled out of the room, ducking and laughing. Göll followed him back to the kitchen where he sat at the table and started eating from the dish. Tove came and joined them, fully dressed. She sat down in a bit of a mood and began picking at the food with a sour look on her face.

"It's hardly right to sneak into a room while someone sleeps."

"Sneak? I thought we were a warband? Don't warbands share everything?"

"Hmph!" She popped a piece of carrot into her mouth and said nothing more on the matter.

Erik was more interested in what Göll had planned for the day anyway. The afternoon before she had begun teaching him more about how to move the sword and the things he was doing wrong rather than simply rushing at him.

"So today, I get to learn how to swing the sword, right?"

Göll ignored the half-sincere question, but Tove did not.

"What would you do, swinging the sword at something you cannot hit?"

"I feel like you two are ganging up on me."

"Finish your food," Göll said, flatly.

Erik gave a mocking grimace to the command and finished eating. He stood up and motioned toward the door. "Alright, let's go have another day full of bruised rib meat."

"At least you are prepared for it."

It was as close as Göll ever got to a joke, and Erik enjoyed them. He could hardly stand the seriousness of most of the things involved in his being dragged to Helheim, so the small bits of humanity were important to him. Whatever Göll thought of him, he couldn't bring himself to dislike her presence. Maybe he'd read into things more than made sense, but he would swear there was more to her than the stern face she was forced to put on. Völundr seemed to agree with him and it had only made Erik's interest in her grow.

She handed him the sword and Erik felt that he might want to retract his wistful thoughts if the look on her face was anything to go by. The day started up much like it had every time she set out to train him. She charged across at him bullishly and he struggled to keep up. Something was different about today though. She was more vicious in her strikes, and the normal look in her eyes was not there when she walked back across the yard. It was something harder and less like her. It had been an hour and a few dozen charges when the skin on Erik's flank finally broke open, trickling blood.

Tove dropped her practice sword when she saw him place a hand over his shirt and draw back blood. "What are you doing?!" She was shouting at Göll as she walked to Erik's side.

"Back to your place, girl!"

Göll's voice was unmistakably angry and it proved enough to at least stop Tove in her tracks. Erik looked over, nodding to Tove.

"It's okay. I'm fine." He put on a sideways smile.

He wasn't. It hurt, horribly, but for the first time since they'd come to Völundr's little plot in the woods, he could feel the energy inside him slip closer. It wasn't by much and Erik couldn't quite understand why, but he was determined to see how close he could come to grasping at the only thing he had to use against the valkyries who actually wanted him dead.

Göll didn't wait for Tove to clear before she charged again. Erik struggled to keep pace with things and again her dull blade dug into his side. In spite of willing himself to stand, Erik fell to one knee, doubled over by the pain. Tove began immediately running toward him. Göll spun, facing the girl.

"Stay back!"

Tove ignored the order and Erik saw Göll rear back the blunt sword. He came up, back toward Göll and the training sword dug hard into his shoulder blade. The metal hit bone along his shoulders and ribs. He stumbled forward, saved only by Göll's last minute decision to soften the blow. Tove caught him awkwardly, and they both fell to the ground. She had meant to kill with the swing. It hadn't been square on his spine and he was thankful for that at least.

"You could have killed him!" Tove screamed.

Erik heard the sword drop before he was able to turn himself over. When he managed it, he saw Göll rushing toward the edge of the forest. He rolled himself off of Tove's legs and sat on the dirt. Tove stood up, moving to his back.

"Are you alright? Was anything broken?"

Erik laughed, but it hurt more than he was excepting and he ended up groaning more than anything else. "Yeah, I'm fine." He pulled himself to his feet. "I should probably go talk to her."

"Talk?!" Tove was incensed by the suggestion. "She nearly just split you in half. And she meant to kill me."

All he could do was sigh. "I know." He did his best to show her a reassuring smile. "But I don't think she meant it."

"You can only be so naive!"

He laughed. "That sounds like a challenge." He paused, thinking about what to do exactly. "Look, can you, eh…" He hesitated to ask. "Can you cook something? I'm pretty hungry and I have a feeling I should eat before afternoon training."

"Why would you train with her again?"

The picture of Tove pulling her dying body across the floor of the shop in Lofgrund flashed through his mind. He shook it away. "I have to. You're just mad right now, but you know I'm right so... just... lunch. Please."

She nodded, frustrated, and walked toward the house. "If she kills you, I'm not sitting by your bedside."

"Well, I'm sleeping on the floor so you won't have to."

She didn't laugh, but Erik chuckled at it anyway. When she was inside Völundr's house, he turned and started limping toward the edge of the woods. He'd made it only a few feet in when Göll came rushing up to him.

"Why would you leave? It's dangerous here."

He had to laugh. "So, you ran off not expecting to be followed?"

She turned her head away. "I've done something unforgivable to you. To... To Tove." There was true sadness in the way Göll carried herself. It was subtle, but Erik was convinced he wasn't wrong.

"I don't think she's the one who got hit with the sword."

"But it was meant for her."

Erik sighed, failing to lighten the situation, knowing he shouldn't have tried. "Why did you swing at her?"

Göll looked at him, a hint of desperation in her voice. "We have little time. They..." She strained, but did not finish the thought. "We have little time." She frowned at him, her eyes begging him to understand.

"I know. I had that feeling without you saying anything." He chuckled, putting a hand on her arm. "I mean, I'm a dim guy, but I get the general idea. Plus, I like Völundr so I'd hate to see anyone come wreck his place up." He turned around. "I'm going to go eat lunch. It'd be weird if you weren't there staring at me." He looked back. "You coming?"

She followed Erik out of the woods and back to the house without saying anything further. Tove left the food on the cook top when Erik came back, rushing over to him and throwing an angry glance at Göll.

"Are you sure nothing was broken?" Tove pulled up his shirt and Erik moved to pull it back down, but just squawked in pain.

"Nothing's broken, Jesus. Stop trying to check out my sweet body."

"Your bird chest, you mean." Tove mussed his thickening beard. "At least you look something like a man elsewhere." She let his shirt drop and walked back to her cooking. "Fine."

"I am sorry for what I've done." Göll's words were directed at Tove. A fact which caught the girl entirely off guard.

"W-what? You're talking to me?"

"I am."

Tove looked to Erik. He just offered her a half-hearted shrug.

"I... accept your apology."

Göll turned away from Tove, going back to her normal stance, more or less facing Erik at all times when he wasn't sleeping. Tove finished cooking in silence as well. It was hard not to be amused at the awkward silence that a moment's consideration had brought into the room.

Erik's wounds had healed enough by the time he was done eating lunch that continuing would be easy enough, even if Göll kept up her abuse. They returned to the yard, Tove back to the side of the house with a sword to mimic the training.

Göll came to him before beginning. "I cannot be easy on you."

"Hey, just don't panic. And tell me whatever you can. It's not like I want to be on the other end of a sword again. I can take it." He put on a cocky grin. "And besides, pretty soon, I'll figure it out and you'll be the one in trouble."

She shook her head dismissively and walked to her spot, charging again. The sword slapped against him and Erik grunted. As much as he prepared himself, it wasn't something he could call enjoyable. It was only six or seven rounds of attacks later that the door to Völundr's workshop opened and he came out, complaining.

"Constant noise from you insufferable bunch." He tossed

some pieces of metal held at the ends by long leather straps. "You'll bother me the better part of a decade trying to teach him to use that sword, Göll." Völundr pointed at the things he'd left on the ground as he walked past them. "Try those. They'll suit him better." Völundr yawned. "I'll be having a shit, a meal, and a long nap. Try to keep your noise mindful of my delicate needs." He chuckled and disappeared into the house.

Erik walked to the straps, picking them up. Göll stayed in the spot she always began from. He held them up toward her. "These are mine?"

"They seem to be." She narrowed her eyes at the strange items. "It is rare for him to forge something for someone, though I've never seen its like."

Erik turned the pieces over in his hand. The leather was wide but thin, with a steel buckle at one end that looked to be angled wrong. The main portion was a flat piece of steel, etched as the magic sword had been. There were small curved protrusions spaced along it. He rolled it over in his hand and the steel landed flat against his palm, the protrusions fitting perfectly between his fingers. It was a steel grip and leather wraps to hold it to him. He sat down with them, working the first wrap around his hand. It buckled at an angle, the leather forming a point at the bottom, mid-way up his arm. He put the other on and stood up.

"What good is a bit of metal on the *inside* of my hand?" Erik walked back to his place on the opposite side of the clearing from Göll. "I'm not supposed to use the sword, right? Just my fists?"

He balled his fists around the metal for the first time and immediately felt the power that had been so long at the edge of his mind flow in like the rush of a broken dam. His eyes widened and found Göll across the yard. He was smiling in amazement.

"It's some kind of—"

Göll's expression changed to one of terror and confusion. She dropped the practice sword and a familiar hot glow grew out of her hand. The spear sizzled in the air and Tove screamed for him to run. It was too late, Göll was bearing down on him, her eyes fixed on his face.

Erik tensed, the sound of her hissing wings catching in his ears. But she was clear to him, not a blur. He could see the dirt fly from where she took off as if it was stuck in the air. He took a deep breath and stepped to the side as the tip of the spear came by him. He planted his fist in her ribs and Göll whipped away from him, crumpling under the force of the blow. He hadn't thought he'd swung very hard, but her tumbling body told him otherwise.

The valkyrie crashed through two barrels of collected rainwater, just missing the edge of Völundr's workshop. She stopped against a third and sat there a moment, motionless. Erik started toward her until he saw her jaw clenched. She stood, looking at him in disbelief. A single word came out of her mouth, almost an accusation.

"Berserker."

CHAPTER TWENTY-TWO

GÖLL BACKED AWAY FROM HIM, SHAKING HER HEAD IN disbelief. "No, no. It cannot be."

Erik took a step toward her. "I'm really sorry, I didn't... I didn't mean to hit you that hard. Are you okay?"

Göll turned, still shaking her head, and a hiss let out from her back as she flew off toward the north. She was gone before he could even start to run after her. Erik turned back to Tove.

"Tell Völundr what happened. I'm—"

The door to the house opened with Völundr standing in the frame. "No sense going after her."

"But—"

"Come eat. I'll tell you something good if you do. Time someone did, anyway."

Erik looked back toward the direction Göll had flown off.

Völundr clapped his hands to pull Erik's attention back to the house. "She won't go anywhere too far off. Trust me on that, at least. Now," Völundr turned, "come eat."

Tove came over to him as Erik was unbuckling the wraps to remove them from his hands. She looked at the work Völundr had made.

"Are you sure you don't wish to follow her?"

Erik answered her without looking, focused on removing the wraps. "I want to." He sighed. "But Völundr knows things, and I'd better know them too, if I'm planning to go talk to Göll."

Tove followed him back to the house and Erik entered, taking a seat facing the door, leaving it open. If she came back to the yard he wanted to see. He laid the grips across his legs, keeping a nervous hand on them. Völundr looked briefly at the open door, shrugged, and then sat plates in front of the two already at his table before preparing a plate for himself. He sat down, casually, immediately taking a large bite of the mess he'd cooked.

He chewed noisily, Erik staring at him intently the whole time. As much as screaming questions at Völundr might have been what felt important, waiting was the only real option.

Völundr swallowed hard, coughing. "I really ought to find a new wife." He chuckled. "Even a comely boy who can cook. Wouldn't be so much different from her." A nod at Tove brought on immediate complaints.

"I am not—! I am a full-grown woman."

He ignored the complaint and looked over at Erik. "She can cook, can she?"

Erik smiled, in spite of himself. "She's not a housewife."

"I'm not! At least one of you knows proper respect."

Völundr laughed. "Good. I was worried Göll's tantrum would sour the mood. I've had enough of sullen faces in my time." He took a deep breath and let it out slowly. "Hand me the grips."

Erik pulled them up and tossed them across the table. Völundr caught them, turning them over in his hands.

"Held up well enough." He leaned in to inspect them more closely. "What do you know of valkyries, Erik?"

"Not much. They pick who goes to Valhalla. And apparently, the others try to kill whoever gets picked."

Völundr nodded, moving his attention to the second grip. "That's the barest part of it. Do you know the reason why they attack?"

"No. Göll wasn't very forthcoming."

Völundr huffed in amusement. "She wouldn't be. Not her fault, that sort of thing." He tossed the grips onto the middle of the table. "You've put a lot of strain on those already. Should hold well enough, but you'll want a smith who understands what I've done." He ate another forkful of food. "The trial, the path from death to Valhalla, you might be thinking of it as a sort of test for the chosen."

Erik nodded. "I had been."

"Most do. But you aren't the only one being tested. A valkyrie's place in Odin's eyes is built from how useful she can be to him and little else. The weakest, they bring ale to the slain or other menial tasks. Servants, mocked by the others, you understand."

"They called her that on Earth... Midgard, I mean. Alebearer."

"And so she is," Völundr said through a mouth full with food. "Most of the rest have made themselves happy in their low status and take no chosen. Göll... she's never given up."

Erik took the grips, putting them back in his lap. "Great, but why would she run away from me?"

"I was getting there, impatient prick." Völundr laughed. "I like you. Still, understand that to understand this. The ale-bearers are mocked, toyed with. And you are a berserker. And you shouldn't be here. And she knows it."

Erik's eyes narrowed. "Shouldn't be here? A berserker just... they lose their minds in battle. Punch really hard?"

"Maybe the Saxons said as much, but as most things, they misunderstood." Völundr rose from his seat. "But I've lost interest. Ask your valkyrie, she should be able to say that much. I'll sleep now."

Erik shot up but Völundr held up a finger before he could say a word.

"So long as my good will is in your hand and in your belly, I'd tell you not to ask too much." Völundr smiled. "It's only polite."

The smith wandered off to his bedroom, shutting the door. Erik turned to Tove.

"Why shouldn't I be here?"

Tove looked as confused as he had. "I have never met a berserker. Only one warrior came through Kvernes, and my town in life was small and not given to fighting."

Erik clicked his tongue, annoyed, though not sure at who, exactly. He picked up the grips and began wrapping them around his fists.

"I'm going to find her."

"I'll go as well."

Erik nodded. "Of course, we're a warband."

She pushed the plate of food away and ran outside ahead of him. When Erik went out, he found her looking through the barrel for any swords that would be sharp enough to do anything with. She found one, though it was nearly too large for her.

"You sure you'll be alright with that?"

She looked at the sword as she came closer. "Better than nothing."

"Can't argue with that. Hopefully we're not going far. She came to me earlier."

Erik started jogging toward the north, exiting the

clearing with Tove just behind him. The woods were thick and there were only a few hours of sun left. Erik genuinely started to worry when Göll did not immediately come to him like she had before. Were there reasons behind it? Had she decided to abandon him? What would that mean for him? Maybe she would come and attack him. It was a bitter thought but not one that he could let leave his mind. Erik cursed Völundr for leaving him with so little information. There was no way of knowing what being a berserker meant here, not unless Göll would tell him. The smith had seemed unconcerned that they would go after her. Maybe he had lost interest in Erik remaining alive now that the grips were completed. His thoughts were dark and he had no reason to question any of them.

They had walked what felt like nearly a mile when small trees along the rough trail ahead of them were felled. Erik looked at the stumps as he stepped over the first of them. It had been sheared off smoothly and the top was singed black.

"Well, she was definitely through this way." Tove looked at the stumps. "I'm not sure how I feel seeing this, Erik."

"Me either." There were scratches on the trees deeper into the forest, deep cuts burned into the wood. "I hope she's calmed down by the time we find her."

The felled trees eventually stopped, replaced by divots in the ground, cut by the same weapon. There were large squares pounded around them.

"Why's she so pissed off?" Erik mumbled the words to himself, marveling at the destruction.

The signs of violence disappeared and they were still making their way slowly along the same trail. Erik began to worry she'd flown up and out of the forest entirely. There was still time to turn back and make it to Völundr's by nightfall and they were well away from safety in the woods, if Göll had given him the truth before. He was at the edge of convincing himself to turn back when he heard a distant, rhythmic thundering. It stopped for a few seconds and then came on again.

Erik started running toward it, making sure not to let Tove fall behind. He wanted to squeeze the grips and run as fast as the power would let him, but he couldn't. If Göll was fighting other valkyries as she'd done before, Tove would definitely suffer in his absence. He heard the sound of splashing water and saw a small lake through the trees, a waterfall along the north edge of it. He waited in the trees until he saw that only Göll was there, striking the ground with her fists, sending the earth under them shaking with each blow.

"Wait here." Erik held a hand up to Tove as he started off forward.

He came into the clearing, his fists lightly wrapped around the grips, not sure if he would need them.

She stood up, looking at him and screamed, her face in anguish. "What are you? Who? Are you another of their tricks?" She stomped the ground, sending dirt flying. "Have you come to laugh? To mock me?"

Erik held his hands up. "I don't know what you're talking about, Göll. I'm just... you saw how I lived."

She grabbed at her blonde hair with her hands, pacing back and forth. "Then there is some mockery. They... they have some plan. They will all laugh again. 'Oh, a berserker? You should have known, silly Göll. And yet you brought him here. No doubt he is unworthy.'" She screamed at the sky. "I can hear them now! Come out, all of you! I'm on to your tricks."

Erik walked closer to her. "Göll, look at me. I don't understand."

She looked at him, her eyes narrowing and her lips tightening. "A berserker cannot be. Not in Helheim." She went back to pacing.

"Why not?"

She walked up to him, looking into his eyes, her voice serious and her breath heavy. "A berserker is blessed by his god. The power flows only when their god wills it."

"So... my power..."

She gritted her teeth, calming herself as much as she could. "A god has granted you their boon. And surely, Odin will not allow one with such a boon into his hall. On a power not earned?!"

"You say surely..."

Göll turned away from him and then back. "There... there has never been a berserker in this place. Hel would not allow it." A look of realization. "Or it could be one of her schemes! How had I not suspected it?" She went back to pacing. "I should have run at her the moment I saw her."

He went to Göll, grabbing her by the shoulders and turning her around. "Calm down and let's think through some things. You said something about feeling me? Right? Like, you can track me?"

She looked at him as if she'd had an epiphany that wasn't altogether reassuring. "Yes, it is... I can feel you still. Stronger than I've ever known." She put a hand over her heart. "It's... why?"

Erik dropped his head, letting out a relieved sigh. "Okay." He looked back up at her, taking his hands off her shoulders. "Maybe it's not so bad. Maybe I can still prove myself."

She smiled. A real, complete, toothy smile. "I... It could be possible." She looked at him. "I have never— all my chosen until now— I have never made it so far."

She hugged him suddenly and Erik almost screamed, not having expected it. The hug was too tight and too long. She realized, pulling herself back and straightening back to her stoic norm, swallowing hard. It seemed almost mechanical, the smile disappearing from her face.

"I apologize for my outburst, chosen."

He felt the metal in his palm twitch as she said the words, but bit his tongue, sure she would say nothing of value about her sudden change in demeanor.

"Don't worry about it. We've got a long walk back."

Göll nodded stiffly. "It is dangerous in these woods. We should return immediately."

Erik agreed, heading back to the tree line to find Tove waiting where he'd left her. Göll walked along ahead of them and Tove turned with Erik as he passed, keeping her place beside him.

"It seemed to go well."

Erik watched Göll's back as she walked. "It went well, yeah."

Tove watched his face, her own growing concerned. "Is something wrong?"

He gave a sideways smile, unsure what to say or whether to bother. "Nothing I can do anything about. I'll tell you if that changes."

They rejoined the trail, Göll walking farther in front than she normally did. He moved up to stand beside her.

"So what's our plan?"

The valkyrie looked over at him, her face having softened a bit since leaving the lake. "We will leave in the morning, if there is nothing else you feel you need here."

"Nope, I'm good."

He looked at her, watching for any changes he could see, unsure what he even expected. Erik walked along beside Göll quietly for a short time. There was so much he wanted to say, but so little that he could.

"I'll become worthy, Göll. I'll do what I can."

She looked at him, face impassive, and then returned her attention to the trail ahead of them.

"Good."

CHAPTER TWENTY-THREE

THE MORNING CAME AROUND AFTER A DEPRESSINGLY QUIet night. Neither Tove nor Göll made much conversation and Völundr slept through the whole of it. It wasn't so much that Erik wanted revelry around their exit from the blacksmith's sanctuary. More, he wanted something to pull his mind away from the concerns of moving on. If Odin could destroy Tove utterly, the same could happen to him.

It wasn't a welcome thought. For the first time, there was some weight in his position as one of the chosen.

Völundr rose well after the sun and woke Erik, urging him to come and eat breakfast. Göll was waiting outside the room and Tove woke up as the sound of clanging in the kitchen brought life into the small house.

"Leaving today, are you?" he asked as he lit the stove.

Erik put himself into a chair at the table in the kitchen, stretching his arms over his head. "Seems like it."

Tove came and joined him at the table, looking much rougher than she normally did. She yawned absently, looking at nothing in particular with bleary eyes.

The ingredients went into the cold pan that Völundr had placed on the cook top. "Headed north?"

Göll left her place by the window and came to the table as the conversation picked up. "We will."

Erik yawned, deciding in his boredom to push on Tove's arm. "I guess it's gonna get colder."

"A silly question, maybe, but I don't notice much in the way of warm clothing on you."

"No, we had a pack," Erik looked at Tove who shook her head. "Yeah, they took that in Lofgrund. So it's just what we're wearing."

Völundr began to crush black pepper into the food, smelling his hand when he was done. He reeled back, a fit of sneezes coming out, one after another.

Erik doubled over laughing. "What did you think was going to happen?"

The smith stood, wiping his nose. "I enjoy the smell!"

"Hahaha! No wonder you live out here alone."

Völundr stirred the food in the pan and served it onto plates. "The thanks I get for letting people into my home. Come out here, judge my cooking rituals. Used to be there was respect for a man..." He sat the plates down, took a seat, and looked across at Erik. "I've no more help to offer, berserker. I keep myself away from the cold anymore and there's only enough furs for myself."

Erik took a bite of the food, coughing almost immediately and then sneezing from the pepper. "Good god, how much pepper did you put in there?"

The smith laughed. "As much as I like!"

Tove coughed and sneezed as well. "It's terrible!"

The complaints only made Völundr laugh all the more. He took a bite, coughing himself after he did. "There's— kuh— a..." He sucked in a breath. "I may have overdone it a bit." He grimaced, straightening himself up. "There's a town to the north and the west. Göll may know it." She nodded in affirmation. "They'll have supplies."

"But we have no money." Tove looked at Erik.

Völundr stood up immediately.

"Your food'll get cold," Erik said, mockingly.

"If that makes it taste better, I'll be glad to have it cold."

Völundr went into his room, coming back with a small pouch, tossing it on the table. A half-dozen silver coins spilled out, the bag not nearly empty. Tove pulled the purse over, beginning a count of them.

Erik protested. "We can't take that, man."

Völundr returned to his seat, looking woefully at the food. He waved Erik's complaint away without looking up. "I've no need for silver shaped into coins. And besides, no apprentice of mine goes unpaid."

"But—"

Völundr turned his eyes up to Erik. "Enough modesty. A man takes his rewards, graciously or not."

They talked and joked and finished the terrible breakfast. Erik was happy to have such a morning be the last one there. It was nearing mid-morning when they finally took their leave, following the trail toward the north. Völundr had gone back into his workshop rather than see them off with any sort of fanfare.

The grips were comfortable enough to wear through the day, to Erik's surprise. He'd put them on just before leaving and almost forgot they were there within a few minutes of having done so. They moved north through the forest, passing the places where Göll had destroyed the trees, finding them all replenished. It was only midday when they came to the road that Völundr had mentioned. It trended toward the west for a time and then to the north, but the way was easy and well-worn. Erik could not imagine there were people moving down the road so often, but the trees had remade themselves so it was hardly something he could call himself entirely surprised by. The leaves began to disappear from the trees and the temperature dropped somewhat drastically over the ensuing hours. There was no mistaking that they'd come to the edge of Winter.

The sun had already dipped low in the sky by the time they came to a town larger than Erik had expected along the road. It was perhaps twice the size of Kvernes, though the construction wasn't nearly so advanced. There were earthen-walled longhouses scattered through the area, with wooden buildings and longhouses mixed in and no pattern to them at all. The buildings along the main road through the center of town formed a rough square around the widened road. It was the only stonework to be seen in the whole of the city as far as Erik could tell.

The buildings had signs at least, one labeled "Supplies" in utilitarian fashion with no ornamentation like many of the others. Erik pointed to it.

"Supplies. That's definitely the first stop."

"I agree," Tove said, her voice edging toward annoyance. "This cold is unbearable."

Erik started toward the door to the shop. "I doubt it gets better."

Inside was a sallow-faced old man, sitting on a stool in the corner of a simple shop. The goods were all laid across tables. There was not much on offer but it was all clearly meant for people moving north. Just from the door Erik could see a selection of furs, bedrolls, crude picks and shovels, and packs. There were more things buried, no doubt, and items were placed under the tables as well.

Tove immediately set about grabbing a fur cloak and wrapping it around herself. Erik decided to go and talk to the old man, who looked at him bitterly as he approached.

"Headed north, are ye?" The man rolled his jaw as if he were chewing something. "No sense in it." His eyes rolled over to Göll. "'Spec you got no choice in the matter though." He snorted and then hacked phlegm clear of his throat. "What'll ye be botherin' me for?"

"I..." Erik felt awkward trying to ask anything considering the man's attitude. "Is there anything we need? Anything you'd recommend."

The codger hacked out a sarcastic laugh. "Recommend ye don't go. Nothin' good ever come from up that way. But since ye'll have none of that, take whatever firewood ye can carry. No trees once yer deep enough."

"Thanks." Erik turned, grabbing a cloak as well before beginning to look through the rest of the store.

There were thicker clothes, some lined with fur. They were priced heavily, a silver each, but there was no sense in saving money if the man's advice was true. Erik wondered about it.

"Göll, is there... how much do you know about Winter?"

"Very little. I've never had cause to go. There are no cities that I know of."

"Aye, no cities." The man joined in. "Only warbands and fools chasing death."

That was good enough for Erik. Völundr had given them nearly thirty silver pieces and they spent all but eight on supplies. Both Erik and Tove were wearing packs, most of the goods in his so they could fill the other with food. They left, having changed clothes in the corner of the shop with the grudging approval of the owner.

A few doors down from the supply shop was a sign with two words on it, "Butcher" and "Eatery." Erik pointed it out and Tove was happy to see it.

"Anything to be done with Völundr's cooking." She trotted off toward the building, pulling the door open well ahead of Göll and Erik arriving.

The shop was clean and well-lit, in spite of the lack of

windows. It wasn't nearly as humid inside as the supply shop had been either. A woman was already talking to Tove when Erik came in.

"The warband, is it?" The woman chuckled to herself as if not taking the idea seriously. She saw Göll and her expression shifted to something more grave if only for a brief second. "I see you're headed north, then. Drop your packs, and have a seat." She motioned them toward one of the three tables in the restaurant. "I know what it is you'll need heading north."

She followed them to the table where Erik and Tove dropped their packs. They took their seats, except Göll, and the woman looked to Erik.

"How much have you got?"

It was an odd question he thought, but not an unreasonable one. "Eight coins."

"Silver?"

"Yeah."

She smiled politely. "And you mean to use it all on food, drink, and a meal? With the three of you—"

"Only two."

Her eyes flicked to Göll, who stood behind Erik, and then back. "Then you'll have nearly a week's worth."

"Is that enough?"

"I couldn't say. No one's come back from Winter."

Erik sighed, Göll offering nothing in the way of a confirmation. "Then we'll hope it is. We'll take whatever seems best."

The woman smiled, standing. "I'll bring the meal before we settle the payment."

She disappeared into the back for a few minutes before returning with a thick stew of lamb and potatoes. It wasn't particularly flavorful, but Erik couldn't bring himself to complain after the breakfast he'd had to very literally choke down. Tove produced the coin and paid the woman. She brought them large mugs full of strong ale.

"This will be what you'll have in the casks. It's strong, but slower to freeze and warms the body."

A large man with a full red beard brought out two small casks of the ale and nodded at them wordlessly before strapping the tiny wooden barrels to the sides of the packs. He said nothing and returned to the back room. The woman who had served them came back when they were nearly done with the meal and placed a number of wrapped cloth packs on the table, opening them up. There were root vegetables in three and two full of fresh meat. The last of the packs was filled with dried and cured meats.

"Are those all to your satisfaction? We take great pride in what we sell. I won't have anyone head north with useless goods and our name attached to the sale." The woman looked at him, her smile gone and an air of genuine concern in its place.

Tove stood and looked over the products on the table. "They're as good as any I've seen grown, even in Spring." She sounded amazed by her own assessment. "These are grown here?"

The woman gave a proud nod. "By the hands of people around. We share in the rewards of our effort."

Erik looked over the meat himself. It was deeply colored. "What's the meat?"

"Venison. The land is hard to work and there is little to sustain more than a few sheep. Most are used for wool, except those that come up lame or who grow too old." She motioned a hand toward a plate of food. "The misfortune of a lamb is what allowed for the stew you eat now."

"Lucky us."

She nodded, smiling. "Very lucky indeed. Frigg must be watching over your journey to her husband's great hall."

He let out a sarcastic laugh. "I hope."

The woman excused herself back to the rear of the shop and they finished their food. Tove filled her pack and they put them back on. The woman appeared to clear their plates.

"I hope Winter is not too harsh for you. And that the things you've bought here sustain you."

Erik thanked her and they left back out into the street. The sky was shifting toward a darker blue.

"How much light left do you think?"

Tove looked up at the sky. "It seems to change the farther north we are. And we'll be walking north again."

"Well, not like we can just sleep in the road."

They went back to walking, Tove complaining shortly after they'd passed the edge of town.

"How can they stand to live in such a place? This cold, always? At least winter passed in Midgard."

"Hey, at least it's not windy." He half expected wind to start as soon as the words left his mouth, but thankfully none did. "It'll get worse either way, so complain all you can while you're still warm enough to do it."

"I will!" She kicked at the dirt in the road. "Perfectly good land where the cold doesn't bite at you and they choose to live where they'll near starve without constant effort."

"Seems dumb to me too, but then I'm walking through what I guess is an icy wasteland just so I can spend forever fighting, or whatever happens."

"Serving Odin will bring you glory," Tove protested.

"Yeah, yeah. It doesn't seem so bad, really. I guess on some level I like the idea, even. I'm just saying that it's hard for me to call them stupid from where I'm standing."

She let the subject go, still grumbling about the cold as they walked. There had been maybe an hour of viable light left and before long they were talking in nearly pitch black, except for the moon. An overcast rolled in, draining the last of the light from the world as the clouds thickened in front of the moon. Erik felt his way to the trees at the edge of the road and called for Tove and Göll. Tove worked her way to him, grabbing onto his arm when she found him and not letting go.

"What the fuck is this about? How can it be this dark?"

He heard Göll's voice from the dark, not far from his side. "There is not light in Winter except the sun and the moon."

"Information that would have been useful before the clouds showed up." Erik sighed. "Göll, can you make a fire?"

"I can."

He heard steps move away into the woods, so he made his way around the tree he'd managed to lean himself against and looked off into the dark, unable to see anything else. Tove's grip on his arm tightened as the minutes passed.

"It's fine, we'll be fine." He didn't believe it and the noise of Göll's work gathering things to build a fire only made him convinced that the valkyries would be on them, not even needing to make a noise. They could see him, and he could do nothing. He suddenly remembered they hadn't slept since Völundr's and that the packs would be left for the valkyries to destroy or someone to collect come the day.

The quick shuffling of wood against wood was calming somewhat and when a light sparked in the distance, Erik started toward it, keeping Tove's hand in his. Göll was only a few dozen yards away, but the fire was well-established by the time they got to her. The wood seemed to burn nearly of its own will and it didn't char nearly as quickly as Erik expected.

"Why does it burn like that?"

Göll looked at the wood. "Fire is crucial to humans in Winter."

It was all she said before turning her eyes to the woods and away from them. Tove dropped her pack and pulled her bedroll, Erik doing the same in short order. Small flakes had started to fall from the sky, but they dissipated as soon as they touched the ground. They seemed to be like the leaves in Fall, giving way to the nature of the world rather than any common sense. The ground was certainly cold enough for them to stick without melting. It was a fact that made

Erik's choice to put some distance between himself and the fire one he regretted, immediately moving his bedroll as close as he could manage. Tove had done the same already. It barely helped.

Erik stared off into the black beyond Tove and the fire. There was no joy in the wonder of a black world for him. As strange as it might have been, he couldn't bring himself to feel wonder, only fear. The valkyries were out there, he knew it. He couldn't be sure where, but he swore he could feel them watching. There was some small comfort in closing his hands around the cool steel in his palm, but sleep was the only thing that mattered now. He forced his eyes shut and hoped his mind would quiet enough that he could rest.

CHAPTER TWENTY-FOUR

THE SMALL AMOUNT OF WOOD THEY HAD USED WAS STILL burning when the dim light of morning told Erik he'd be fine to get out of the bedroll. It was still cold and he'd only removed the topmost layer of the clothes he'd bought from the old man. He was quick to put them on, not getting too far from the fire while he did. He nudged Tove awake and went immediately to Göll who was still standing her vigilant watch over the woods around them, spear in hand. He could see the road not far away, and in between the little sleep he got he hadn't heard anything. Göll was quick to disabuse him of any feelings of comfort that might have made their way in as the sun came up over the ridgeline far to their north.

"There was movement in the night."

It was the last thing he'd wanted to hear that morning, but made him sure, at least, that the feelings he'd had weren't simple imaginings.

"What sort of movement? People? Animals? Valkyries?"

She kept her eyes moving around the trees as Tove dressed by the fire. "They didn't come close enough for me to be sure of anything."

Erik worked his arms in a circle, trying to get the cold to stay out of them at least until he'd eaten something. "We'll eat and get walking."

He expected she'd say nothing, so Erik turned away from Göll to see Tove readying some meat, finding it hardened not quite to freezing.

"This place is terrible, Erik. The air is cold, the ground is cold, the meat's gone frozen. What are we even meant to do with frozen meat?"

Erik walked to the pan Tove had prepared and picked it up, holding it out to her. He shook it when she didn't put the meat in, prompting her to do so. Erik then held out his hand for the knife she was holding and retreated to the far side of the fire. He sat and cut the meat into the thinnest strips he could manage and put it on the fire.

"Pour some of that ale in there."

Tove did as he requested and the pan let off a massive plume of steam. He leaned back away from it instinctively, but kept the knife in the pan working things around.

"We had this thing back home that was sort of like this. They called it barbecue, but I don't see how pushing stuff around on a big rock is any kind of barbecue."

All he received for his attempt at sharing a detail from his life was a blank stare from Tove. He had her cut some carrots thin as well and throw them in and they ate when it was done a few minutes later.

"It's not awful," she said, chewing the meat.

"Yeah, well, we don't have soy sauce or anything."

"Soy sauce?"

"It's a thing made from fermented soy beans. Really salty, great with meat."

"Sounds disgusting."

"That's the correct reaction to about ninety percent of the things I eat when you just describe them. It's all in the taste."

"Well, it sounds as though it tastes disgusting."

Erik shrugged off her entirely uninformed thoughts on soy sauce and they finished eating, packing afterward. There was a log in the still-burning pile that had barely been scorched and they stood in front of it considering what to do.

"Well, we can't just pour the ale on it. We need that," Erik said. "And I'm not going to look for a stream. So... leave it?"

Tove was quick to nod. "I agree. But," she hesitated, "what if the trees catch?"

Erik looked up above the fire and around them. "Well the snow didn't stick. Maybe it's fine."

"And if it is not?"

"We can out-walk a forest fire, probably."

"Do you have experience doing something like that?"

"No, why would I?"

Tove's sigh was decidedly annoyed. She picked up her pack. "We should begin walking. There is only so much light in a day up here."

Erik grabbed his pack as well and they returned to the road with Göll keeping a short distance in front of them. The grips were surprisingly comfortable in spite of sleeping in them and his arms didn't seem concerned with having leather next to the skin for so long. There wasn't much chance of sweating in Winter and having to find the grips in a situation where a fight might come from nowhere would just end him up dead. It was likely something Völundr had considered when he'd made them.

They had been walking for only fifteen minutes at the

most when Göll came to a stop, looking into the woods. A few seconds later, Erik heard the footsteps that had brought her to a halt in the road.

"Wait! Wait, you in the road! Stop, I beg of you!"

A thin-haired man came stumbling out of the woods in heavy furs, carrying a small pack. He nearly lost his footing but caught himself and stayed there catching his breath for a moment. He stood himself up, looking Göll over before looking around her.

"I am called Jari. I have been lost in this wood for weeks. Tell me—"

"You look well-fed to me, Jari." Tove spoke up before the man could continue.

Jari's expression soured for a moment. "I said lost, girl, not without provisions." He turned to Erik, his face returning to the pleading look it had been before, but he kept his distance. "I know how it must seem, but I was separated from my party. I don't know where they have gone, nor where I am and—"

Göll charged the man, pulling her blade across his stomach. The guts spilled out, Jari screaming and falling to his knees. His hands went wet and red as he tried to gather them up in a mindless panic.

"No! No! Not again, not again! Get... get back in..."

The blood was draining quickly and his strength faded along with it. He fell over, clawing toward Göll's feet as he hit the ground. Tove ran to the man, pulling open his pack.

"Stones!" She shouted the word, kicking the man in the ribs before turning to Erik. "There must be more!"

Jari still croaked slow breaths on the ground as Tove and Erik went over him, gathering around Göll. The valkyrie scanned the woods slowly with intense focus. Erik could hear the breath behind him grow staggered and fail. He turned his eyes back, seeing all but the pack dissipate into the ground. He'd been wearing only a single layer of clothing if Erik understood the way of things. Göll stood quiet for a few more minutes before giving her report.

"There is nothing. No one comes to avenge him, if they were near enough to do it."

There was no screaming, so whatever camp he'd been a part of wasn't nearby. It wasn't worth sitting and waiting for someone else to come for them, so they returned to their trek along the road north.

As the hills grew more aggressive the road came to an abrupt end, giving way to only a dense forest of evergreens and steep walks up hills. The climb began and Erik became increasingly concerned about how near the trees were to one another in some places. There were plenty of places to hide any number of people, or valkyries for that matter. As hard as it was to see from behind the clouds, the sun was past the halfway point in the sky. It was when flakes began falling that Erik moved up beside Göll, putting a hand on her shoulder to stop her walking.

"We've got to eat now. And then we can't stop walking until the edge of this forest. Is it clear?"

Tove came up to join them and Göll scanned the woods.

"I cannot see anyone. If they move quietly enough, the snow will cover them at a distance."

Erik pulled his pack. "That's good enough." He pulled a single piece of wood and sat it on the ground. "Someone light that up. We're doing this fast."

The pan came out as did the venison and Göll lit the fire. Tove watched him slice it thin again as she prepared potatoes in the same way she'd prepared the carrots that morning.

"We could eat dried meat if you mean to keep us moving."

Erik looked around. "No, I want to save that for when we're out of other things. And I want them to get less if they manage to kill us. These are the things they'll be after, most likely."

Erik cooked the food as quickly as he could manage. The potatoes may have gone a bit better with the food, but he could hardly bring himself to enjoy the meal. His nerves were beginning to get to him and having to gut a man who meant to trick them was doing very little to calm them.

They returned to their walk, Erik urging Göll to move a bit faster than the pace she normally kept. Tove kept pace, though not without some effort, but she didn't offer any complaint as they worked northward through the woods. It was late afternoon, or at least late for Winter, when the clouds gave way and the world was bathed in orange light. It made checking the woods to the west nearly impossible and, worse, the shadows moving across his face made for a constant distraction.

It was the least he'd spoken to Tove since they'd met, but neither of them could bring themselves to carry on casually after Jari had showed himself. The heavy air made Erik hate the forest even though it was truly a beautiful place to be. The sun was nearly down and the world had dimmed, but ahead of them was a clearing. He could not see how wide it was from behind Göll, but it appeared to be at least wide enough to keep them safe.

As they came to the edge of the trees, Erik could see what it was. A wide, flat valley stretching out for several miles below them. There were mountains to the north side of it and all of it was devoid of trees. It was all stone and snow.

"Perfect."

Tove came up beside him. "Perfect? Won't we be exposed?"

Erik shook his head. "If there are more of them, we want them to have to come to us. And we want as much warning as we can get."

"And if they have bows and arrows?"

He tapped Göll. "Hey, could you stop an arrow?"

"An arrow could not pierce this armor."

"There you go. Besides, it's pretty much our only option." Erik was satisfied, though Tove didn't seem to share his confidence.

They started down the treeless hill into the valley and walked across it. The sun disappeared and the light of the moon took its place. The stark white of the snow did its job reflecting the light above them, making it easy to see off in all directions well enough to be sure that any movement was not simply shadow shifting on shadow.

Erik figured they'd come close enough to the center of the featureless valley when he decided they would set up camp. Göll saw to the fire again, making quick work of it as the bedrolls came out. There were occasional freezing gusts of wind from the north. Not wanting to spend the night dealing with wind destroying his nose, Erik made a small arched covering out of some spare clothes and a few sticks from his firewood bundle. Tove did the same and pulled out the food. They could spend a bit more time preparing it so Erik took the pan, gathering up some snow. The divots he made started filling themselves in slowly from the bottom up.

He put the pan over the fire, watching the snow idly replace itself as the minutes passed. It had just barely started to steam when he put cubes of meat into it to thaw before relaxing, letting the fire warm him.

"This is at least less nerve wracking than the forest."

Tove looked around. "The view's better. I would still gladly trade the weather for any warmer sort."

"Even in Summer? Ugh, sweat. I don't need it. I mean, this is too much, sure, but I'm not one for sweating. These furs won't be soaked and disgusting tomorrow morning."

"You like convenience, is your problem." She waved a dismissive hand. "Sweat is good for you. The cold is no good for anyone."

"And how could you enjoy a good fire if it's hot all the time?"

"A Spring night is plenty cool enough," Tove scoffed.

"No way, not for enjoying a fire properly. You have to be that kind of desperate cold where your fingers are starting to hurt."

"My fingers *are* starting to hurt."

"See? And isn't the fire nice?"

"Not even near nice enough. And what about a mug of cold drink? Useless here."

"But warm soup!"

"Bah!" She waved a hand at him, putting the last of her cubed potatoes into the pan.

There was a bit of dried meat around the cured pig belly that Tove cut away and tossed into the pan. It rendered down and they began cooking the vegetables. Erik looked at Göll. Her back was to them but she was only a few steps away.

"Do you get cold, Göll?"

"I can feel the cold."

He tilted his head. "I don't know if that's the same thing. Tove, is that the same thing?"

"Seems close enough."

"What about the heat? Does that leather armor ever get unbearable?"

"I cannot remove the armor, only change its shape."

"Sounds rough. I guess I'm probably stuck wearing these grips for a while. Taking them off seems stupid."

Tove shook the pan, stirring the contents. "Are they uncomfortable?"

"No, not really." Erik looked down at the grips. "I just hope they work when I need them." He remembered the meat and put it in the pot.

Dinner was the best of the meals they'd had and, when it was done, they decided to bed down for the night. Erik couldn't manage to sleep, no matter how hard he tried and eventually gave up. He came out of his covered bedroll to find Tove had not shared in his trouble. She was sleeping soundly, mouth open and nose bright red.

He walked to Göll. She was standing silently, as ever.

"Thanks for watching over us. I've never said it before, so it felt like I should."

She looked at him for a moment, her eyes lingering as though she wanted to say something, but she didn't, not until she looked away. "You should sleep."

"Don't I know it. If you know how to make me, let me know." He took in a deep breath and let it out again, the cold air not bothering him even without the thick overcoat. "I've been uneasy since we got here. To Winter, I mean."

"I have felt it as well, your unease." She looked at the ground for a moment. "It is... strange."

"Strange how? Are you not supposed to feel stuff I feel?"

She rubbed her fingers lightly over her chest. "I do not know. I have never..." She looked back up and across the field, leaving the sentence to hang in the air.

Erik chuckled. Looking at her, he couldn't help but smile. "I get it. There are a lot of new things for me, too." He looked out over the snowy valley floor. "Can't say I hate them, though."

The cold had finally worked its way through to his skin and so Erik went to sit in front of the fire for a while. The night was quiet except for the occasional snort or shift out of Tove. His eyes had almost grown heavy enough to convince him to retire to his bedroll when a sudden fog began to roll in. The heavy air moved in quickly and it was warm, unnaturally so. Erik stood, moving to Göll.

"What is this? Is this—"

Göll was shaking visibly, her eyes locked to the sky, scanning in a panic.

"No..."

The humid air was all around them, thick and unnatural. Erik turned his eyes to the sky, but found it empty. It was the sound that told him why Göll shook as she did. His body clenched and his hands wrapped tight around the grips.

Not just from one, but from every side of them, there came a shallow hiss circling in the fog.

CHAPTER TWENTY-FIVE

THEY HADN'T YET CHARGED FOR WHATEVER REASON, BUT one of the valkyries had begun to talk to the others. He couldn't make out the words, but it was strange enough as it stood. They rarely talked. He slapped Göll on the back to draw her attention, holding up a hand when she looked to show the grips.

"We'll be okay."

"You haven't slept," she said, more plainly than he'd have liked.

His heart sank when he realized she was right. If they managed to kill him, they would likely also get to him long before Göll could hope to. He'd never survived an encounter with the valkyries.

"Tove! Get up!"

He heard a groan from the other side of the fire that cut itself short as Tove realized why she'd been interrupted. Erik took a deep breath and balled his fists tight around the grips.

The fog seemed to roll back and he could hear the voice of the valkyrie hidden in it clearly now.

"Seems his warband has readied itself. Go!"

The hissing flared around them all at once. Three of the four made for him, the fourth stayed behind. Göll moved to his front to intercept the nearest of them and he spun to address the other two, coming in at angles from the edge of the camp.

They were both wielding short swords. The first had blonde hair braided tight. She charged ahead of her brown-haired sister. The blonde showed no signs of slowing and Erik knew what they meant to do, the first would swipe and the second would stab at him. He had no intention of playing into their game. He charged himself, causing the trailing attacker to slow, surprised by his speed. The blonde kept her sword aimed at his chest. She moved more quickly than Göll, but it was nothing he wasn't prepared for. He slapped the sword to the side and swung upward, catching her in the chest and sending her spiraling skyward. She recovered and flew away.

Tove had grabbed the knives they'd bought, leaping quietly at the brown-haired valkyrie and nearly managing to plant the knives into the leather armor, but just missing. Erik watched the scene, amazed at Tove's speed. She'd never shown anything like it before. More, she was quiet, unbelievably so. The valkyrie swiped at her, recoiling away, but the swing was shallow and Tove found her footing, moving toward Erik.

"How many?"

"Four, at least!"

The blonde was rounding for another charge when the

fourth swooped above them. She was far faster than the other three. "Göll, your chosen outfights you! How much shame can you bring upon yourself? I've dirtied myself with the air in Helheim, and this is all you have for me?" She flew off, cackling.

Göll was in something of a stalemate with the other valkyrie, but she was keeping one of their number busy, at least. As Erik turned his eyes to the fourth, the brown-haired valkyrie charged him. Erik shifted toward Tove, not having his balance quickly enough to do anything more than dodge.

"Hlökk, you are as embarrassing as Göll! At least put a cut to the boy."

A thundering crack sounded from behind and Göll slid back toward them, her feet dragging snow as she barely kept upright.

"Why have you come, Róta?! This is not your place!" Göll barked the words up, but did not wait for an answer, readying her spear and flying toward the valkyrie she'd been in combat with.

The valkyrie above was no longer talkative, as Hlökk and the blonde came again for Erik, this time stopping short to drive their blades at him from the ground. Erik slapped the spear tip away from his stomach and charged. As he ran up the length of it, the blade followed him back, forming into a short sword. He was forced to reverse course. Behind he heard another thundering blow. He could not turn to see it as the blonde slid in to his side. He had barely dodged the blades aimed at his gut when he saw Tove move out of the corner of his eye. She ran behind him. He heard a hissing at his back as soon as she'd started toward him and spun to see Göll on the ground and the third valkyrie charging. Tove planted herself in front of his body and before the space of a blink, a glowing white blade punched through her chest. It was ripped away again, pulling Tove forward onto the ground, where she fell, motionless.

Erik let out a vicious scream, turning back to the

valkyries who were readying their blades against him. His eyes met Hlökk's and he saw panic flush over her. She moved to flee but he grabbed the neck of her leather armor. He could feel it trying to shift its shape underneath his hands, but he refused to let it and the armor obeyed him. Hlökk screamed in terror and Erik swung, his knuckles crashing against her face, pressure blowing her hair aside before the impact. She crashed across the ground, tumbling away into the fog, her body limp and still. He screamed again, hearing Tove's screams as she reincorporated, and rushed at the blonde who fled outright.

He'd almost caught her when Róta dropped between them, jabbing a sword into his side before he could change course to avoid it. Without thinking, he swung, catching Róta's shoulder. She was pulled back by the blow and the sword was pulled free, leaving a gushing wound.

From the fog, he heard shouting and a loud crack split the air around them. At least a dozen human men and women pounded into the camp, swords pointed toward the valkyries. He fell to his knees as Róta called for a retreat. The fog faded away entirely and Erik rolled forward, bleeding freely from his stomach. He put a hand over the wound, desperate to hold in whatever he could. They would find him alone in the woods. He rolled over onto the ground, staring up at the moon at the far edge of the dark sky. A man with long, wild hair and a full, braided beard came over to him, crouching down and smiling.

"We won't let you die, einherjar." He laughed. "The walk would be too long to find you again."

Erik's strength faded and the world went black around him. When his mind returned to him the first time, he realized it felt like far too much time had passed for him to have died. The pain came shortly after, but he swore he saw a woman pressing the area with something and an awful smell.

He woke again, the cold wind blistering against his face

as the light of day had started to fade in. He heard Tove's screams from somewhere not far off and, though the sound made him wish to rise and do whatever he could for her, his body would not listen and sleep took him again.

The sun was on his face when he felt a dried crust get pulled away from his skin. His eyes shot open, but an attempt to move failed him almost immediately. A woman with high cheeks and pale, freckled skin leaned over him, putting a cool hand on his head.

"You're wounded, einherjar. You should sleep."

Her soft voice was kind and convincing. Erik closed his eyes again as another warm, terrible smelling paste was applied to his wound. It was calming, aside from the smell.

It was dusk when he finally woke with enough strength in his body to fight sleep back. He was lying on top of his bedroll, covered with sheepskin blankets. There was a large fire burning and at least a half dozen men sitting around it. There were two women as well, one cooking and the other tending to Tove. Her screams had turned to pained moans, at least.

Erik stood himself up, groaning through the hurt as he did. Behind him, he heard the shifting of familiar leather. He turned to see Göll standing quietly behind him. The wound had closed, but not enough to allow him easy movement. The noise had drawn the attention of everyone in the camp. As surprising as it might have been, Erik's grips were still on his wrists and he began to ball his fists when the men reached for the hilts of their swords. The wild-haired man from before stood facing Erik and holding a hand up to the others.

"Don't be so eager to die, you lot." He smiled at Erik, blue eyes running over the patched wound and back up. "Come, berserker. Sit and eat."

Erik watched them for a second, not moving. The men had pulled their hands from their swords but it wasn't entirely convincing. The women still tended to Tove and one even stood as if she were waiting to tend to him as well.

"Who are you?"

The man pulled a hand across his beard, smoothing it. "I am Flosi. And those here are my warband. Some of it, at least. I will explain, but we must dine. And Asfrid should see to your wound."

There wasn't much reason left to be concerned about them, though his brain wouldn't allow him to calm down. Being stabbed left him antsy, but they had kept him alive and Flosi showed no signs of ill-will. Erik walked to the fire and sat on the ground beside Flosi who had already taken his seat. The other men sat down after Erik had and Flosi went back to cooking meat over the fire. Asfrid came over, lifting Erik's shirt to tend to the ball of mashed herbs that was laid over the wound on his side. Erik noticed a heavy stone hammer carved with runes beside Flosi.

"You are a warband as well, are you not?" Flosi shook his head in disbelief. "Why else would an einherjar travel with a girl."

Erik looked over at Tove. "We are."

"And you are the chief? Surely the valkyrie has not joined your band as well."

"I guess I'm the chief. And I don't know what constitutes joining, so much. She hasn't sworn anything to me or whatever."

Flosi poked at the meat in the fire. "Still, a berserker and chosen, walking as a warband." He huffed a laugh. "You are an impressive and very curious creature." He waved a hand over the others at the camp. "These are a third of my band. The rest are guarding and tending the risen in the woods where we slept. They will be there days, yet."

"Days?" It sounded as though Flosi had meant to see to the wounded, but the pain had never lasted more than a few hours for Erik. He remembered that the guard had said something similarly curious about Haki.

"Truly you have not been here long," Flosi said, turning

an eye toward Erik. "Could be you are blessed. Certainly, you heal faster than most from even a grave wound. But the pain worsens and fades more slowly each time you feel it. Death is no blessing in this place." He nodded toward Tove as he spun the meat on the fire. "The girl knows well enough. She must have known death dozens of times now the way she screamed."

Erik looked at Tove. "She... she lived in Spring. In a town with no fighting or anything." Asfrid finished removing the herbs from him, running her fingers across the wound and stood up to go. "Thanks, sorry. I appreciate it." Erik turned his head back to Flosi.

"There are horrors, even in such peaceful towns full of smiling people." Flosi waved one of his men over to remove the meat from the fire. "A place where every man only smiles makes it impossible to see what lies behind it." The warchief turned his full attention to Erik. "But I am uninterested in that girl or her life in some town full of soft, unmanly things. I am interested in you, berserker."

"Why?"

The men all laughed and Flosi gave a wry smile. "I think you have an answer for that without asking it." His lips curled in consideration as he looked Erik over. "I have seen many berserkers in Midgard. Fought them. They were devout men, touched by the rage of the gods as blessing for their life lived in glorious battle. In Helheim, I have never seen their like. Not in my thousands upon thousands of battles. So..." Flosi's eyes narrowed. "I'd like to fight you."

"No thanks."

Flosi broke out into laughter and the others followed him, a few pointing at Erik. "I'd thought you might say that."

Plates of meat were brought. There were no vegetables, just slabs of elk or deer.

"I have a proposition..." Flosi stopped a moment. "I've not asked your name."

"Erik."

"Is that all?"

He wanted to sigh, but held it in. "Haki Erik Styrsson."

"Hm." Flosi seemed to consider his name, taking a large bite of meat and chewing it thoroughly before speaking again. "Then Erik, as I said, I have a proposition."

"Sure."

"I assume you make for Gjallarbrú."

Erik's expression went blank. It wasn't a place he'd heard of. He turned to Göll who stepped toward the fire for the first time. "We do."

"Of course," Flosi said, tearing off another bite of meat with his teeth, chewing it loudly. "We will guide you to Gjallarbrú as payment for a chance to test ourselves against the valkyries. They fled, but it was a glorious battle for what time it lasted."

"We can't really sit here for a few days." Erik looked toward the woods to the south.

Flosi followed his gaze. "Oh, they will stay. We will travel with those who are here, so soon as the girl is well enough for the trip."

"How will the others find you?"

"Does the girl not see to the runes? Is she not your wife?"

"Tove? No, she's... we're just a warband."

Flosi chuckled. "You are a strange man. Then I will put your mind at ease. The runes will guide my wife to me. That is her work to do and she does it well."

"Then, I'll take you up on your offer."

Ale was brought and they drank a toast to the agreement, sealing it according to Flosi. Erik felt out of place among the warband. They were familiar with one another and only Flosi seemed to react to him with anything approaching civility. The meal had passed and the men sat talking when Jari approached, limping. He was welcomed without a second thought, most making fun of him for having had his guts split. The man's angry eyes followed Erik for a time before he was handed a mug of ale and his attention was drawn away.

Erik motioned for Göll to follow, taking her toward Tove, who slept fitfully. The women gave him space and he used it to talk privately, so much as he could in the small camp.

"You recognize that face, don't you?" He talked in as low a whisper as he could, keeping his eyes on Tove and running a hand over her hair, smoothing it.

Göll nodded silently.

"We need their help through the mountains but I don't like this. I didn't like it before. If they do anything, *anything*, I want you to cut them down as fast as you can."

He sat the rest of the night with Tove, Göll at his side. They all stared at him but none more than Jari. The uncomfortable night wore on and Tove was finally able to sit toward midnight. Not long after Flosi called for the camp to be broken down. It was time they started their march to the north.

CHAPTER
TWENTY-SIX

ONE OF FLOSI'S MEN CAME OVER AND QUIETLY LAID A sword on the ground in front of Tove. The sheath looked to be expertly made. Tove picked it up and pulled the blade free from its housing. It was no cheap, cast-off sword that they had in spare from the look of it. It was well-cleaned, well-kept, and thoroughly sharp. She sheathed it and stood slowly.

"It will be better than the knives, at least." She winced as she swung the belt around to fasten it to her waist. "Maybe I'll even manage to cut one of them if they return." Tove looked around the camp. "Who are these people? They helped us, so I assume they mean us no harm." She spotted

Jari. "Though…"

Erik grabbed Tove's pack, holding it up for her to put on. "They're a warband. They'll guide us to Gjallarbrú."

"The great bridge?" She flushed with excitement. "How far?"

Erik turned his eyes to Göll and got no answer. He shrugged. "No idea. And… it's a bridge?"

"It was in the old tales. The great golden bridge that Hermód crossed to retrieve Baldr from Hel's side and return him to Asgard."

"So Hel's land started on the other side of that bridge?"

Tove looked around the camp. "I believe so. I cannot know for sure. Though only the dead may pass the bridge. It's said to be guarded by a giantess."

"Well, great. So, warband, valkyries, giantess. That's a reassuring list."

Erik rubbed his hand across the wound at his side. It itched even though it had mostly healed. He'd not survived such a wide wound before, so it was possible there was nothing odd about the lingering discomfort.

The warband was packed, and Erik picked up his supplies, joining Tove and Göll as the lot of them got underway. The flat of the valley was crossed simply and they made good pace to the foothills of the mountains that towered above them. It was a winding path that only occasionally went north so much as it moved up into the hills. They'd traveled for only half a day, but the sun was already nearly below the horizon, and worse they had topped a hill and were moving into a narrow valley. Mountains rose up sharply on either side of it and as they descended into their shadow, Erik realized that the sun had not risen above where the mountains now towered above them.

The cold deepened and the shadows were thick around them, the light fading quickly. Still, the warband ahead of them seemed not to notice the difference. They laughed and carried on. It wasn't rare for them to turn and stare at Erik from time to time. Tove watched them, annoyed.

"I'll bet they're mocking you. Saying you're skinny and have no muscles. I hate it."

Erik laughed. "Aren't you the one saying I'm skinny and have no muscles?"

She looked up at him. "Of course I am, but I am allowed. They are not our warband and they should watch their tongues."

He let his amusement fizzle away, leaving a half-smile. "Are those the only complaints you have?"

Tove scoffed. "We haven't the time for me to list my complaints."

"Sounds like you picked a terrible warchief all on your own then." He turned to Göll, enjoying the atmosphere more than the serious walk they'd been on so far. "And what about you? Anything you want to get out?"

"It would do well for you to learn to fight," Göll said flatly.

Erik laughed again and one of the men from the warband slowed to come back toward them. "It's good you're enjoying yourself so much, *berserker*." The words were not meant in good nature, that much was obvious from his tone. "Refusing a duel and carrying on among women. It's some wonder the gods would bless you." The man looked at Erik, sneering. "Or maybe they haven't. All I saw was a man stuck like a pig and crying."

"Shut your mouth, oaf! If it's a fight you want, I'll gladly send you back to your bed!"

The man spun, a mocking smile on his face and the laugh to match about to leave his mouth. Tove charged him, putting her leg behind his and pulling him down. She planted a boot firmly in his ribs and jumped back as he swung for her foot. Tove pulled her sword as a roar of laughter rang out from the warband ahead of them. The man rose, incensed, drawing his sword.

He was easily twice her size in every meaningful way. Tove was ready for him, though. The man charged and Tove side-stepped, letting his falling blade glance off of her own. She wasn't nearly as fast as the night before, but she moved better than she had in Völundr's yard. The man charged again and she parried him, slapping the flat of the blade against the back of his leg. He shouted in frustration and Erik saw a faint glow in the man's hands as he spun to come at her again.

Göll became a blur, appearing in front of Tove as the sword came down. A spear of blue energy shot off of the end of the sword as it struck against her unmoving shoulder. The magic misted harmlessly in the air and the man scrambled back away from Göll, his rage turning to fear with each step. When he saw that the valkyrie was not moving to harm him, he started back forward, shouting complaints.

"You would let the girl provoke a fight and then interfere?!"

"You provoked a fight, oaf!" Tove screamed from behind Göll. "And you should not have stopped it, Göll!"

Göll spun, taking Tove by the shoulder. The girl froze, it was the first time Erik had seen Göll touch anyone other than him. "If you wish to fight, then learn to!"

"Why don't you teach me then!"

"I intend to!"

Tove stood dumbstruck by Göll's proclamation and the man shouted, annoyed at having been ignored. Göll turned her head toward him, her face showing that she did not intend to hear his voice any longer. The warband saw what Erik had, at least, and was quick to come and lock arms under the raging fighter, pulling him away from Göll as Flosi came forward. He yelled at the man.

"If you want a fight, pick one properly."

"He—"

Flosi immediately struck the man on the jaw with full force, knocking him unconscious. The rest let him fall to the ground. The warchief turned to Erik, walking at him, hammer on his shoulder. "I'll apologize for my man. If he wanted a fight, he ought to have said it outright."

Erik looked at the man, slowly working his way back up on unsteady legs. "It's fine. I have no intention of fighting any of your people."

"I've told them as much, but you understand how fighters are."

"I know the type, sure."

Flosi turned and ordered the warband to begin their march again, the light having faded nearly entirely. The moon was much the same as the sun had been, keeping itself low in the sky. It provided nearly no light. Ahead of him, he saw dim green lights come out. Flosi kept beside him when they returned to their walk.

"I've noticed you watching Jari."

Erik was on edge after the fight and he kept an eye on Flosi's hammer. "That's all you're going to say?"

Flosi held up a hand. "We sent him, I know. But he was not told to lie to you."

"I'm gonna call bullshit on that, Flosi. He had a pack full of fucking rocks."

The man sighed. "Fair, then. We meant to attack you before we knew you were a berserker."

"And now you don't intend to attack me?"

"Not unless we must. I have given my word and unless you mean to malign my good name, I will keep it. You allowed my men to taste battle with valkyries and showed the face of a berserker to those who have not seen it. There is more value in those than I think you know. We followed you meaning to take those things and you gave them to us and more. That is a debt we've made for ourselves and I'll repay it."

Flosi walked away with that and went to the front of the warband. He was given a glowing green stone and the pace of the warband increased to a speed beyond what they'd managed during the day. It was a slavish march through a too-long night. Erik's legs had not failed him in the days of walking, but whatever kept wounds healing did little for him when the work had been so constant with so little rest. There was no room for a complaint from either himself or Tove about the speed or the awkward terrain of the dark valley with the warband leading them through. They were in strange territory, now without light for the bulk of their waking hours and only dim shadow for the rest.

Even with the fur over him, the pain in his side was there, a constant feeling of needles jabbing into him. It was dimming slowly, but Erik figured sleep would be the only way past it. His feet had gone numb hours before he realized that the warband had no intention of stopping in the dark. They had gone quiet, all of them staring down in silence as they walked along with their strange glowing stones. It wasn't until the sky showed the first signs of light that they slowed. Erik watched them as they seemed to come out of a trance, the stones dimming and showing themselves to be simple rocks carved on every face with runic shapes. He was near enough that he could see them, but they didn't form anything resembling words that he knew.

They stopped as soon as they found enough level ground to form a camp, a trio of fires being set up immediately, one that seemed to be for Erik and his group. He laid out bedrolls beside it, wanting to sleep immediately, though he knew he'd be too hungry to manage it. Once the camps were prepared, Flosi came to them as Erik rubbed on the wound in his stomach.

"It will clear completely if you die."

Erik frowned down at the red line on his stomach. "I'll pass, thanks."

Flosi waved Asfrid over and she brought heavy ale for them. She went away, promising to bring back meat when it was prepared. The ale had been warmed in spite of the fact that they'd just stopped. Erik looked over to the meat and found it wasn't frozen either.

"How'd you keep this stuff liquid?"

Flosi smiled. "The runestones." He took a massive swig and let out a satisfied breath after it had gone down. "They have been forgotten by most. Takes tens of years to learn to carve them so they do anything at all. Like most things, the younger ones think they are just old stories, but Odin gave us the runes and he would not give us a boon so powerless." Flosi took another drink, shaking his head. "You've distracted me. I wanted to come and understand you and hope that you would understand me. You seem to have taken offense at our plan to attack you. A warband fights, Erik."

"Is that a law?" He did not want to provoke the man, but Erik was growing tired of being told what his actions were meant to mean.

"There is no such law. Only the word of a warchief."

The man wanted to continue but Erik was tired of listening. "And if I told you how to run your warband, what would you say to me?"

Flosi stopped, any politeness fading from his face for a moment before it returned. "You've made your point well. I have not respected you. But why call yourself a warchief and those who follow you a warband?"

"I have a war." Erik's eyes turned reflexively to the sky, scanning it.

Flosi followed his eyes up and realization grabbed the warchief. "I cannot argue with that. I find myself wishing that it were mine after the battle I saw."

"Agree to disagree," Erik said, shaking his head at what sounded to him like a madman's wish.

The meat was brought and Flosi asked Erik about his time in Helheim. He recounted the story, Flosi insisting on details of every minute of his time in Lofgrund and jealous that he'd met with Völundr.

"I have looked for his place in—"

Göll stood as Tove finished her meal. "You will train, Tove."

Tove leapt to her feet, not wasting a moment. "Good."

Erik called after her, "What about sleep?"

"I'll sleep when I can no longer move!" Tove didn't bother looking back. A few cheers rang from the far side of the camp.

"She is another thing I'm jealous of."

"Tove?"

Flosi laughed. "Yes. There are few I've seen who would defend their warchief so readily. Twice no less. A death is not something that passes so easily as in Midgard."

Erik looked off at Tove as Göll began showing her how she ought to hold her sword. He hadn't given much thought to her act when the valkyries had attacked. He hadn't thought much of death at all, even as her pained screams from the night before tore at him. Flosi had put a different view of it in his head.

"Flosi, would you go to Valhalla if you were chosen?"

He seemed caught off guard by the question. "Would I..." Flosi's brow furrowed under the weight of the question and he looked into the flames of the fire. "Of course... An honor like that, you could not hope to ask for more in life."

"Even if it meant leaving your warband? Or seeing them destroyed for being unworthy?"

Flosi's eyes did not look away from the fire, his voice was soft, unsure. "You ask strange and difficult questions, Erik."

That was all he said. They finished their meat in silence, Flosi leaving when the meal was done. Asfrid came to collect the flat plates and mugs and returned to check his wounds.

"I've not seen Flosi so talkative in many, many years." She smiled up at him. "We are all thankful for you for that, even those who do not show it well." She poked at the wound and Erik jumped. She giggled, standing. "Sleep will do you good. There is only so much sun here." She bowed her head and walked away.

Erik stood, rubbing his hand over the still aching place Asfrid had touched. He walked to the edge of the area where Göll was practicing with Tove. The valkyrie was pulling her punches, but only barely. Tove was soaked with sweat and had stripped off her overcoat even though it had only been a few minutes. He wanted to smile, but found himself, instead, worried. Tove had died for him, suffered willingly, and she would be destroyed if she was not found worthy. Göll helping was a step toward saving her, but there was only so much time before they would find themselves at Valhalla. The valkyries would not allow them the time Tove might need.

He returned to his bedroll, lost for what to do, but knowing there was nothing he could do about it then and there. He would sleep. It was all he could do in the valley. He would have to leave the rest to Göll for now.

CHAPTER
TWENTY-SEVEN

ERIK LAY HALF-ASLEEP IN HIS BEDROLL WHEN A SUDDEN wave of freezing cold water came rushing over him. He shot up, looking around, ready for a fight but found only Jari standing with a bucket, laughing.

"Ha! Warm in your bed, berserker?"

Erik rushed over to the fire, pulling off the wet overcoat as he went and counting himself lucky that the clothes beneath were still more or less dry. The cold of the mountain pass had forced him to wear as much as he could to get a decent sleep, even as tired as he'd been. It was night again and the world beyond the fires was pitch black the way the forest had been.

Jari followed him over to the fire, satisfied with having ruined Erik's morning. He tossed the bucket onto the ground casually, taking a seat well out of arm's reach from Erik.

"You been real comfortable since you got to Helheim, ain't ya?" He talked entirely different than he had during his stint pretending to be a lost traveler. "How'd one soft as you end up so blessed?"

Erik scoffed, rubbing his arms, trying to will the fire to warm him more quickly. "Blessed? That what we're calling it?"

"How'd you count it, berserker? Such a terrible life being chosen, folk who'd die for you, able to stand alone against a valkyrie? The things of legend and you'd even question it?"

"Not everyone wants to be a legend. I'd trade your jealousy for not having a burning spear jammed through my chest."

Jari stood up, disgusted at the suggestion. "Might as well you spit in the mouth ah the gods!" He took a step toward Erik. "And we're on some fool walk by your account. Nothing to fight in here, nothing to kill!"

Erik wrapped his hands around his grips and as Jari noticed the movement he took a step back, calming himself.

"Could be I was hasty in my words..." He paused for a moment, considering what to say next. "But I'd not waste such gifts, not near the way you do."

Jari walked off and Erik went back to watching the fire. When he was warm enough he went to retrieve his coat, laying it by the fire to dry. It had not absorbed as much water as he'd worried it might. He could hear the sound of Tove and Göll practicing not far from the fires, but he wasn't able to see anything more than the occasional flash of dull orange through Göll's blade. There was a consistent sound of metal on metal, which told enough about Tove's progress. Erik went to their packs and retrieved some of the thoroughly frozen meat. He began slicing it thin, returning to the pack to see to the ale casks, finding them to be filled with half-frozen slush. He filled a pot with ale and took it to the fire. The meat cooked slowly, the cold in the air pulling much of the excess warmth away nearly as fast as the fire put it in. Tove and Göll returned to the fire as the food was nearly done. There were cuts all along Tove's arms and a few across her sides and back. They were shallow and the blood had already frozen, stopping the bleeding, if any of the wounds even still remained open.

Tove sat down and, without a word, set to eating the meager meal that Erik had prepared. She focused intensely on the food, turning between bites to snap off small lumps of frozen blood.

"Did you get any sleep?" Erik asked.

Tove looked over at him, smiling. "An hour, maybe. I couldn't stand being in the bedroll, so I had Göll make good on her word."

Göll came over to Erik's side, watching the other men in the camp. She looked as composed as she always did. Erik spoke to her, keeping his face aimed at the fire and trying to keep the cold out of his mind.

"So, she's not terrible, Göll?"

"Her way with a sword is passable. But she moves faster than she ought to be able."

Erik raised an eyebrow looking over his shoulder at Göll. "How can you tell?"

"I have observed humans in Helheim many, many times. She moves as though she was touched by Odin, handed the gifts of the chosen."

He perked up at that. "So maybe she's worthy?"

Göll shook her head. "I cannot say. I do not feel her. If she was chosen, she is not mine."

Erik turned to Tove. "Do you feel anything? Any... like... magic?"

Tove shook her head. "Nothing. I've felt less tired as we've continued on, but nothing more than that. Even when I fight, I feel as I always have. Only..." She thought of how to say it. "The world seems to move more reasonably."

Erik thought of how Haki moved in the cell in Lofgrund, almost as though his speed were second nature. There had been nothing special about him to the people in the prison. But who would have chosen her?

"Göll, if she's in a warband with me, she could still be chosen?"

Göll nodded. "Nothing prevents it. But, normally..." She hesitated.

"Normally, what?"

"It is common to be able to feel the chosen for all valkyries. It..." Her words caught in her throat and Göll straightened. He could see a strain in her neck and she fell silent.

Erik stomped the dirt, his jaw clenching in annoyance. Something kept Göll from speaking, and he suspected it did not do so gently. Whatever his existence was, hers was as bad, at least, and tied to stronger, crueler bonds.

The food was done and they packed. The fires were extinguished with buckets of melted snow and the usable wood was reclaimed and stowed. The speed of their march was as punishing as it had been the day before. Shortly after they began the pace slowed and Flosi came to the rear, sidling up to Erik with a pleasant smile.

"A beautiful night," Flosi said sarcastically, laughing at his own jest.

"Yeah, hard to keep myself from enjoying the view."

"At least your spirits are high. You'll need them." Flosi gave a satisfied exhale after sucking in the cold air. "We are a day and a bit more from Gjallarbrú. I intend not to stop until we're in sight of it."

"Works for me. I'm not really interested in an ice-cold alarm clock."

Flosi didn't seem to understand him, but laughed after a moment's awkward look. He returned to the head of the warband and the speed picked up again.

The dark seemed to move in on them, pulling even the

scattered lights of the runestones closer to their sources. The wind picked up, bringing flecks of ice with it. Erik struggled to keep his eyes open as much of the time as he wanted, the ice making it nearly impossible. The blister of the wind and its debris were beginning to numb his face as well. He trudged on through it, feeling Tove regularly grab at his coat to be sure she was still near him.

The wind began to let up, even as the terrain worsened. The light did not return to the runestones, somehow still dimmed by the oppressive night around them. Suddenly, as they reached a plateau, the line ahead of him halted. He narrowed his eyes, closing on the lights at the rear. He heard the unsheathing of weapons and wrapped his hands tentatively around the grips. A torch was lit at the front end of the plateau and it was then that Erik realized what had stopped them.

There was a dense fog forming around the warband. More torches were lit, revealing the area as best as they were able. Erik felt the warmth of the fog as its edge rolled over him. He balled his fists around the grips.

"Tove, sword."

Göll had pulled hers already, the spear glowing dim in the night. Erik marched through the warband, their eyes locked to the edges of the light of the torches.

He hadn't made it to Flosi when the first hiss swooped overhead. Erik could not see it, even with the vision afforded to him by his power. He rushed for the front and found Flosi holding his hammer at the ready. At the back, where Erik had been, the first sounds of clashing steel came, along with pained screams.

"They've come Erik!" He laughed, running over. The warchief pressed a runestone into his hand, a leather loop run through a stone to allow it to be worn on the wrist. "Here. It will pull you toward Gjallarbrú. Trust in it and leave this battle to us."

"I can't just—"

Hlökk swooped over, striking down at Erik. It was Flosi who struck out at her, swinging his hammer with incredible speed. It was not enough to catch the valkyrie. The man's face was glowing with excitement.

"Go, berserker! I led you along hoping for this fight! Do not take it from me!" Erik nodded and Flosi turned. "My thanks! I'll repay you at Ragnarok!"

The warchief charged off, the runes in his stone hammer glowing a deep black-purple. He let out a thundering cry and slammed the weapon against the ground. Ice flew into the air and the fog blew back, revealing the valkyries in the sky. Spears flew at them immediately and they swarmed away, then back at the attackers below. Tove pulled Erik's shoulder and he spun, taking the chance to flee.

They were in a dead run for as much of a mile as the terrain allowed, the sounds of the fight fading away from them. The runestone had tugged gently on his wrist the whole of it, pulling him back on course as he veered in the dark. Tove pulled on his coat again and he slowed, turning around.

Göll came to him. "They will not follow."

"Why not?"

"A valkyrie cannot refuse a fight. And the other warband struck at them. Flosi was not the only among their number with a magic weapon. They may fight well."

"So how long do we have?"

"A... day." She struggled even to get those words out and they came from a much more natural voice.

"Doubt I can ask why." He paused to collect his thoughts. "A day, okay. We can make it to this bridge if we keep going like Flosi planned."

"I have no complaint," Tove offered.

"Good. So let's go."

So they did. Erik had hardly caught his breath from the running, but it was a drive now to see their way through to the end of the valley and out the other side before the valkyries could return. At least if they were to be mired in darkness, he wanted a place where the three of them could move well enough to stand something approaching a chance.

Their path through the mountains began to climb and the hours passed by. The temperature became unbearably cold, Erik barely managing to keep his wits in the temperature at the front of the line. Göll kept herself at the back and Erik couldn't think of a good reason for her not to. The valkyries would likely come from that direction if they meant to attack as soon as possible.

The ridge finally flattened and the light began to stream back into the world. Erik breathed a sigh of relief that there was at least something to allow them to see beyond a few steps ahead. It had made the steady pace he tried to keep all the more difficult. He couldn't help but feel impressed by the effortlessness with which Flosi's band had moved through such similar terrain.

Above them, the mountains began to trend slowly downward, as did the curve of the valley. The temperature began to rise even. When it would have been dark among the mountains, the sun still had hours left in the sky and Erik was even considering removing the furs he wore. He began to grow nervous, worrying they'd been sent south without him realizing. Calming, he took stock of things. The sun was still on the correct side of the sky and the stone had not changed its direction.

A few sharp declines brought them to the edge of a snowy forest, the stone urging them through it. They followed, the sun seeming to slow in the sky the deeper into the wood they went. Finally, they came out the far side.

Below was a lush valley and at its far end, the glittering gold roof over a massive bridge stretching across a gorge. The north end was fed by a waterfall. Around the end of the bridge on their side of the gorge was a large city, twice the size of Lofgrund, at least, and an enormous stone keep sat at the entrance to the bridge itself. Even outside the walls proper, there was a small city of what looked like wooden homes and shops, smoke coming from many of the chimneys.

The temperature rose rapidly as they descended, warming to near how he remembered the air in Kvernes being. He stripped off the overcoat, turning to Göll. "Will we need this from here?"

Göll shook her head and Erik tossed it aside. Tove did the same. Before long they made it to flat land and started toward Gjallarbrú. It was still dusk when they came to the outskirts of the city outside the walls, though the light was fading. Gas lamps were nearly everywhere along the main street, however, even out this far. There were cobbled streets and, even with dozens of people around, plenty of room for them to move. There was a deep comfort for Erik in being around people again. Tove seemed to share his feeling, coming up beside him.

Tove sniffed at the air. "There's food."

"I know. I can smell it." He sighed. "We got any coin?"

Tove looked up at him, pouting as though she'd just remembered. "Please, Erik. We cannot eat that frozen meat again."

"So we go rob someone?"

She looked around. "There may be someone willing—"

"You! You three!" A guard was running toward them wearing heavy armor. He trotted to a stop, catching his breath. "Modgudr sends her regards. She has been expecting your arrival and welcomes you to Gjallarbrú." He turned around, looking over his shoulder. "If you would follow me, she has requested your presence at the Grand Keep."

CHAPTER
TWENTY-EIGHT

THE GUARD WALKED STIFFLY AHEAD OF THEM. IT LOOKED to Erik that he was trying his best to do a parade march by himself. People along the street stopped and watched as he went by with the curious trio behind him. Mostly, they stared at Göll, not bothering to pay much attention to Erik or Tove.

They approached the gate, finding it guarded by a half dozen men who snickered at the guard who was escorting them. That was the end of the parade march, their escort slinking away as a larger man with a full beard approached from behind the line of guards.

"Welcome, chosen. Or, if you've made it so far, it makes

only good sense to call you einherjar." A chuckle rolled out like lazy thunder. "We have been expecting you. And," his eyes narrowed as he looked Göll over, "your valkyrie. I apologize, I do not recognize her face." He laughed again. "Though I have manned this wall for ages and it has been so long since any have been chosen." He scanned over Tove bringing his attention back to Erik. "I am called Wilhelm Haftorson, lead guard of this south gate. We are pleased to have you among us. Might I ask for introductions?"

"Sure. I'm Haki Erik Styrsson." He pointed a thumb at Göll, "Göll," and a thumb at Tove, "Tove."

Wilhelm nodded, looking them over. "A fine name for a fine man. You are welcomed to Gjallarbrú. Men!"

Erik tensed until he realized the men were issuing a salute to him. Wilhelm spun on his heel after they'd saluted.

"This way."

They followed, the men watching him as he walked by. They looked at him with eyes he hadn't seen on anyone since he'd arrived in Helheim, especially not anyone who was aware he was one of the chosen. They whispered about him, but with tones of reverence and nods of admiration. Wilhelm led them through a door beside the main gates and into the guardhouse inside of the wall. The interior was stone, lit with oil lamps, and simply adorned. The quality of the furniture was nicer than he'd seen in Lofgrund by a good measure. They did not stop in the room, being led up a few flights of stairs and ushered into a room that Erik had not expected existed in all of Helheim. It was a plush room with polished marble floors and velvet-lined furniture. The walls were still stone, but they were polished flat and adorned with pieces of art. There were even glass windows along the wall facing south.

Wilhelm entered, moving to the side of the door and putting an arm out to signal that they should enter. "I hope it is of great comfort to you after your journey."

The line was clearly not one of his own, some rehearsed

thing he was meant to say to important people. Erik entered first with Göll and Tove close behind him. Göll was expectedly quiet, but Tove was as well, uncharacteristically so.

Wilhelm straightened up, standing in the door frame. "Someone will be along shortly with things to eat. I apologize that it will only be something meant to tide you, but a custodian should be along soon. If you need anything, please do not hesitate to call for one of my men. And if they cannot satisfy you, call for me." Wilhelm's face turned serious and the air of rehearsed formality fell away. "Haki, I am done a great honor that you are in my care, for however short a time. And I have heard tales of the journey north. No harm will come to you here, on my honor as a man."

Erik was taken aback by the sincerity of the man across from him. "Thanks. I'll put my trust in you, then."

"You honor me." Wilhelm bowed his head and turned, pulling the door shut as he went.

Erik couldn't help but listen to see if it had been locked and a few seconds after, he went to try the handle. It was open and swung freely. No one guarded them in the hall. He came back into the room, Tove taking a tentative step toward him.

"Is this some trick?"

"It doesn't really seem like one," he said. "If it is, I'm not sure why they'd bother putting us in a room with windows and a valkyrie."

Erik went to one of the four couches in the room, taking a seat and telling himself it was possibly fine to relax. His mind was not listening to the suggestion. Tove began exploring the room. There were tables with runners along them and drawers, none of which contained anything. A writing desk in the far corner was stocked with paper, a quill, and ink. She held them up.

"What are these?"

Erik turned, laughing when he saw what she was holding. "They're for writing."

She looked at the implements in her hand, unconvinced. "How?"

He stood up from the couch and walked over, placing the paper on the table. "Now, I don't really know how to use this kind of pen..." He opened the ink, dipping the quill in. He dragged it as gently as he could across the paper and wrote his name. It was the first thing not written in runes he'd seen in what felt like forever.

"What are those shapes?"

Erik cocked his head to the side, making sure he'd written it properly. Whatever let him read runes and understand Göll didn't seem to work the other way. "They're letters. Not runic ones." He held the paper up, pointing it at Göll. "Göll, hey! Can you read this?"

She looked at the paper for a moment. "I know the letters of Midgard's southmen. It is your name."

He turned back to Tove who looked at the paper with intense curiosity. She dipped the pen and was about to put it on the paper when Erik stopped her.

"Okay, be gentle. If we break it, they might stop being so nice."

Tove nodded, pulling the rough shape of runes across the paper, spelling her own name. She smiled, pleased with herself. "Why do they not have this in Kvernes? Fools, I told you. Idiots." She shook her head, growing annoyed with the people she'd left behind. "All they've done is sit there drinking their ale and growing fat and worthless." She held up the paper. "This... this is amazing." She looked at Erik, smiling. "I was right to choose you, as Göll did."

He laughed. "Is that what happened? You chose me?"

She nodded, hugging the paper to her body. "I did. And you should praise me for choosing so well."

"Ha! Good work, then. Seeing my enormous inherent value."

Tove went back to scratching runes on the paper and Erik returned to the couch. "Will you teach me your letters one day, Erik?"

"Sure. I can probably remember all of them."

A knock came at the door and Tove dropped the pen, putting her hand to her sword. Erik closed his hands lightly around the grips.

"Come in."

The door opened revealing a young-looking guard. He came in holding a small tray and took it to the nearest table. He stood stark upright, placing a fist at a right angle across his stomach as the men in Lofgrund had done. It made Erik tense, but the guard started talking.

"I have a selection of things for you to enjoy. They are-are-are on the plate. A kth—" He bit his tongue. The boy winced, doing everything he could to avoid eye contact with anyone in the room. He took a deep breath. "I will return with a selection of wine shortly I apologize for my mistakes please do not look poorly on our guard as a result."

He had said it all as one long sentence and quickly turned, fleeing the room. Outside the door, he heard the snickering of what must have been a few other guards. Erik rose, walking to the tray. Tove had run to it more than walked and arrived at nearly the same time as he did, pushing him out of the way. She stopped, staring down at the food on the plate.

"What is it?"

Erik looked over her shoulder. It was foie gras, seared and put on tiny crusts of bread. They were hors d'oeuvres, there were no two ways about it.

"It's duck liver, sort of."

She picked it up, leaving the tiny crust of bread behind. "It doesn't look like any liver I've seen." She popped it into her mouth, her eyes widening. "What is this? It is not liver! It... it's... some kind of meat... butter."

"Haha, yeah. That's pretty much right." He picked one up and ate it. It was well-cooked and smooth.

Tove slapped at his arm, as if remembering something. "And the lights on the streets. Were they oil lamps? All of them?"

Erik had heard the gas hissing into them and knew they must have been fed by pipes. He tried explaining it to Tove but the ideas were far too foreign for such a cursory explanation. He couldn't offer answers for some of the deeper aspects anyway, so he was happy that she forgot the conversation to busy herself with food. The wine came and before they had a chance to drink any of it, there was another knock on the door. It opened and a small man with a square face came in.

"Greetings, einherjar." The man bowed at the waist, arm across his stomach as others had done. It occurred to Erik that it was how one might hold a shield. "Which of your names would you prefer you were called?"

"Erik's fine."

"Then, Erik the Chosen, if you would follow me."

The sudden addition of a title was odd, but Erik decided not to question it. He followed along and the man led them out of the room inside the gatehouse and toward the north.

"So where are we going? What should I call you?"

"I am a custodian. You may call me Custodian as a name would be beyond my station. Please keep close."

He hadn't answered the first question and his answer to the second wasn't one he had expected. The man leading them was well-dressed and moved with distinct purpose. His pace wasn't too fast, but it was brisk.

"This is the residential district. Mostly homes, you see. There is no crime among our people and very few leave."

"Uh, great?"

"Modgudr takes their needs into account and sees to the problems as they arise. Hel, glorious though her name is to hear, cares little for things which occur here. That is why she has given Modgudr the unenviable task of seeing to those who chose to spend their time here." They were out of the residential area and the man held an arm out to the right side of the street. "This area is replete with shops, carrying every good a body could desire at reasonable prices."

This was odd. There was no other way to see it. Erik felt as if he was going to be sold a small home in the city or invited to join the local government.

"I guess the shops don't have any crime either?"

The custodian ignored the statement, continuing on.

"This is the first of our four squares." He motioned to the left. "The statue is of Hel in her glory. She looks as splendid as marble is able to capture." They passed the square and another hand came out. "The entertainment district. Brothels and alehouses and games of chance. All the spices of life kept in a convenient area."

They passed through the district again, into an enormous square with a statue of Hel twice as large as the other. She was flanked by what Erik swore was a statue of Vár and a third statue, larger than Vár.

"And finally, the Grand Square. Home to the Grand Keep and all the various festivals that Modgudr provides that the people might know their blessings."

Across the square was a set of stone doors that could have easily fit ten men through abreast. It was guarded by dozens of armed guards. They were arrayed around the square and the custodian was walking toward them.

"And those giant doors?"

The question was again ignored and they walked between the first row of guards, into the center of the square. Erik would have been pensive, but for the smiles and nods from the men he passed by. The custodian took a sharp left turn, heading to the western edge of the courtyard. A pair of guards pulled open the doors as they approached.

They followed the custodian inside to a hall with polished wood floors, wainscoting and painted walls. Tove was unable to stifle a noise of amazement at the refinement of it. The ceilings were high and chandeliers lit it all fairly well.

"This way," the custodian said after a moment's silence. He'd been allowing them to take in the surroundings and be awed by them, at least that was Erik's assessment of the watchful pause inside the door.

The keep was a winding place of unfailingly beautiful decor. They passed dozens of rooms before being led into and across a grand hall lined with armor, all of it dented and pieced and torn from battle. Wide doors were pushed open and inside sat an enormous woman, muscled with a large axe leaned against the chair she sat in. She was easily seven feet tall. Erik could tell even with the woman in her seat as she was.

"Erik the Chosen, his valkyrie, Göll, and his assembled warband are hereby presented to her glory Modgudr, Keeper of Gjallarbrú."

Modgudr waved the man away. "Sit, eat."

The table was full of food, more than any person could hope to eat in a year's time. Tove did not wait to be invited a second time, rushing to a seat. Servants appeared and prepared a heaping plate for her. While they did their work, Erik moved to the seat at the far end of the table, looking down at Modgudr with Göll at his side.

"Come, Erik, let's not have looks on our faces. You've brought a new face before me, one I did not expect to see. And she eats from my plates and I have sworn your protection, haven't I? Or... I ought to have. Wilhelm saw to it, did he not?"

"He did. You can understand my hesitance."

She laughed. "I can. For rumors to have flown to me, is no small thing, berserker. But still, the way must not have been so simple." She ripped the meat from the leg of a turkey and chewed it smiling. "After Lofgrund, there are few who don't know your name. Ásví has made many wary of anyone who lives in a stone home. The woman is obsessed with elf-hood, you understand. But she will not ascend to dine with the Alfr. She has a sickness in her mind." Modgudr tossed the bone away.

"You won't hear an argument from me."

One of the servants laid a plate of food in front of Erik and he looked down at it. It was simpler fare than he expected, arranged neatly, though, in spite of the amount. He ate, keeping his eyes on Modgudr. The giantess turned her attention to Göll.

"It is your first time in my hall, is it not Göll?"

Göll did not offer an answer. The words felt almost like a provocation, even to Erik.

"I am glad to see you here, in spite of your silence. Hearing that you felled both Hrist and Mist, putting a castle atop Ásví. We've spoken of it for weeks." Modgudr leaned forward. "But I've heard a rumor about that as well. Erik the Chosen…" She wore a sly smile, her eyes looking him over. "Most have dismissed the idea as madness, but it is said you snapped the bone of one of Odin's pets. Mist, if I recall. And now you sit at my table with the work of Völundr strapped to your arms. Is all of it true?"

Erik looked up from his plate, mouth half full of food. "Sure, sounds right to me."

She frowned for just a moment. "I'd expected something different, but I do not dislike what you are. I will say it plain. I control those who pass across the Great Bridge Gjallarbrú. I require payment before I will allow you to cross."

Erik let his fork fall to the table. "That's about par for the course. What do you want from me?"

She held up a hand. "There is equitable trade. You help me uphold justice in my city and perhaps turn Odin's eye toward you as you near his hall. I have a chance to deal with a man who has worn my patience thin."

"So, you want me to catch some guy and bring him here?"

"I do," Modgudr took another turkey leg and bit into it. "A man called Ljunge. He's stolen from me, a piece of armor taken as a prize from one of the many who have tested me. The armor means little to me, but Ljunge has been a problem for quite some time. He knows this, yet he persists. I will pull off his skin for the trouble." Her voice was entirely casual, considering her promise to flay the man. She looked at the leg with a bored expression and tossed it away. "He stays at the Calf's Head Inn. It is in the entertainment district. Your custodian likely showed you the place."

"He did. But if you know where this guy is, why don't you just have your men go get him?"

Modgudr shrugged, leaning back and pushing on the handle of her axe. "I have decided that you will do it, and I need no more reason than that." She stood, taking her axe. "Eat your fill and you will be taken to the rooms I've prepared for you." With that, the giantess left.

They finished eating, Tove taking several of the buttered rolls with her. The custodian entered and showed them to their rooms, stopping by the first.

"Your room, Erik the Chosen."

Tove started in behind Erik and Göll and the custodian spoke up.

"A separate room has been prepared for Honored Guest Tove."

Tove turned. "I won't be sleeping away from Erik."

The custodian made a face but did not insist, only bowed and left after closing the door. Erik made a noise in casual surprise.

"I half expected him to complain."

The room was expansive. Ceilings as high as the rest of the room with a bed that no pair of normal person could fill. There were several writing tables, a vanity, a couch, and half a dozen chairs, all in brilliant green with silver trim around the dark wood. The room itself was similarly colored, large fur rugs on the floor being the only brightly colored things in the room. Tove went to the bed and hopped onto it.

"It's soft!" She nearly shouted the words. "How is it so soft?!"

Erik walked to the bed, pressing on it. It was down, most likely. "Feathers."

"Feathers?! It makes so much sense!" Tove rolled around

on the bed. She came to a stop, looking up at Erik. "What should we do about Ljunge?"

An annoyed sigh pulled its way out of him and he sat on the bed. "I doubt we'll have much choice there. We'll find this guy and drag him back here." Erik looked at Göll. "Are we safe here?"

She looked around the room, finding no windows, contented herself by moving to the end of the bed. "Modgudr is known to Hel. Attacking would anger Hel."

"Well," Erik said, stretching. "We'll sleep then. And figure out the rest tomorrow."

CHAPTER TWENTY-NINE

THE MORNING CAME AND GÖLL SHOOK ERIK AWAKE. HE'D asked her to the night before, not wanting to be woken up by whoever Modgudr might send. There was enough stone between their bed and the outside that Erik had been willing to remove the grips for the first time. His skin under the leather wasn't near as raw as he'd expected it to be and by the morning it had healed.

He put the wraps back around his wrists. The grips had come to fit even more smoothly into his hand after the fight with the valkyries. He hadn't even noticed that they were still on until he thought to remove them to sleep. Even though a night had passed his hands still felt odd without the leather wraps in place. There was something comforting about the constricting feel over his forearms, a stability to it.

Clothes were a secondary thought and in the time he spent making sure the grips were well-secured onto his arms, a knock came at the door. He went to answer it, only wearing his pants and the grips. It was the custodian, carrying two sets of clothes.

"Modgudr has seen it fit to offer you fine clothes."

Erik took the clothes and as he began to close the door the custodian cleared his throat with clear intention. Erik stopped.

"An addition to your task that Modgudr regrets she could not mention at your meal together. The valkyrie can offer you no assistance in your task. If she does, you will be disallowed passage if she takes active part." He finished his sentence and before Erik could begin a complaint, left.

Erik shut the door, walked the garments across the room to the bed, and tossed them down. He eyed Göll.

"You heard him?"

"I did."

He returned his attention to the clothes, choosing to ignore the annoyance he felt at the added condition. There were two sets of clothes, one obviously smaller than the other. Both had pants, though the smaller pair were much looser through the legs. They were made of cotton from the feel of them. He removed his pants enthusiastically before remembering Göll was present. The valkyrie was watching him as ever. It wasn't the first time she'd seen him naked, but it wasn't entirely comfortable even now. Her icy blue eyes always seemed to take in more than her stoic face let on. He changed quickly, pulling on the light, navy-blue coat that had come along with it. It seemed to be tailored to him specifically. He looked down at himself, dressed far more formally than he preferred, and sighed.

"Tove, get up."

Tove had slept on the far edge of the bed, falling asleep

well before Erik was able to. She sat up slowly, wearing the loose linen wrap of the sort she'd worn at Völundr's. She was slow to cover up the parts that were visible from the fabric slipping, Erik turning his eyes away. She didn't seem much to care that he was there, coming around in the wraps to look at the clothes at the edge of the bed.

"These are for us?" She began dressing. "Turn around so I can see yours."

He turned and she was still dressing, her breasts exposed. Erik looked up, trying to avoid staring. He could see her glance down at her own naked chest and then back at his clothes.

"They're nice... soft." She pulled at the coat and ran her hand across the fabric, doing the same with the side of his pants. "Can you move in them?"

"I haven't tried. I woke you up. And now I'm being held hostage."

She looked down again. "You are." She laughed. "And by such a simple thing. If the valkyries thought to fight naked, we'd never have made it out of Lofgrund."

"You're doing this on purpose?"

She nodded. "I am doing this on purpose."

Erik turned his back to her, letting out an exasperated sigh, and Tove began to dress herself. She put her sword belt around the clothes and adjusted it, checking that the weapon came clean of the sheath easily and joined Erik at the head of the bed.

"So we'll go and find a thief today?" She was smiling, still pleased with herself.

"Seems like it." He started toward the door. "I have to imagine he'd be stupid to stay considering it sounded like Modgudr knows exactly who he is."

Erik opened the door and let out a frightened bark, jumping back when he saw the custodian standing in front of him. He exhaled, the surprise fading as his brain realized there was no threat.

"Jesus fucking... What?"

The tiny man looked at him with no discernible expression which only served to annoy Erik all the more.

"I have come to guide you through the many, winding halls of the Grand Keep, that you may find the courtyard in good time."

The custodian began walking without any prompting or a suggestion that they follow and his pace was far more brisk than it had been the night before. They were shown through to the courtyard and pointed in the vague direction of the entertainment district. The doors were then promptly shut behind them.

"I have no idea if I feel welcome or not."

Tove looked at the doors and then to Erik, giving a half-shrug. "Does it matter so much?"

Erik started across the court, guards looking at all three of them as they passed. "I guess not. I'd like to avoid a fight if at all possible and knowing where you stand is pretty important in that kind of thing."

The looks from the guards were as awed and welcoming as they had been the night before, a few of the men even going so far as to offer the shield salute that he'd seen given only to Ásví prior to his arrival in Gjallarbrú. Modgudr had been well-informed and spoken of rumors circulating about him. It wasn't something Erik had expected and even though the rumors had been positive in general, there was a discomfort in having strangers know things you hadn't told them.

The edge of the entertainment district granted him some level of anonymity, at least. The clothes seemed to draw looks and the ready cooing of women in windowed stalls at brothels. They must have been fine clothing for the city as he'd seen only a few other people wearing the style. Most still ignored him, either because he walked with women already or because they recognized Göll's armor as belonging to a valkyrie. Even here, where he was welcomed as a chosen, the expressions of men changed when their eyes first landed on Göll.

There seemed to be no meaning in the layout to the district that Erik could discern. Blocky streets with no structure in the way businesses were clustered. They'd wandered the streets for a half hour when Erik finally grew bored of the aimless search and stopped a man walking by.

"Where's the, uh..." He'd forgotten the name of the inn.

Tove spoke up. "Calf's Head Inn."

The man scoffed. "There's nicer places for a bed, mister."

"I'm looking for someone."

The man laughed. "Ljunge, is it?"

Erik cocked his head to the side. "Yeah, he a popular guy?"

"That's a word for it." The man pointed back down the street he'd come from. "Five, six streets down, take a left. You'll see it. Sign like a calf's head, if you can believe. Should be able to see it from either side."

Erik looked down the street. "Thanks."

The man nodded in response and left them there. The walk was a short one and the inn was where the man had described it being, though the signs were more run down than Erik had expected. They hadn't been recently cleaned or repainted like many of the others in the district around them. There were windows around most of the bottom of the inn, dirty like the sign. Glass was no longer a rarity, it seemed, though the stuff in most windows was thick, wavy, and usually contained at least a single bubble of air.

Erik pushed the door open and found himself in a small tavern that matched the exterior in its disrepair. Old tables, rickety chairs, and a dearth of lighting meant the unclean windows had to do the bulk of the work. Tove and Göll followed him in and the smile the tavernkeep had given him quickly faded when he saw that a valkyrie was in his establishment.

The man did not move from behind the bar, looking

over at Erik, scowling. "What d'you want then? I know t'ain't drink so be savin' me time and come out with it."

It was an honest reaction, at least, and Erik couldn't fault him for that.

"I'm looking for a man called—"

"Never 'eard of 'im. Leave."

That was a bit too honest for Erik's liking. "Look, this doesn't have to be weird. You can just tell me where Ljunge is and I can just go."

"I said—"

"Alvar!" A smooth voice called down the stairs and the sound of footsteps followed it. "I've told you there's no sense in covering for me. I welcome all guests!"

A man with medium-length brown hair, held back in a tie, looked over to Erik as he came down the stairs. He had a few days' stubble and wore a wide, toothy smile.

"Especially a guest who's come with some beautiful women." He finished the short descent and walked toward them, coming to a stop a few feet away.

"You're Ljunge?"

"I am." His eyes were on Tove entirely even as he answered Erik's question. "Who are these lovely women? And why have you come seeking a visit with me? A man of your fine status, I can imagine only a few reasons."

He pointed at Tove and Göll in turn. "Tove, Göll."

"Göll, a... name... it seems familiar to me. No matter, carry on."

"Sure. I don't really have any interest in dragging this out. Modgudr told me to bring you in."

Ljunge nodded, putting a hand under his chin. "Hm, right. Modgudr..." He turned and ran.

"God damnit!"

Erik started after the fleeing man, but he was through the door and had slammed it shut by the time Erik got to the far side of the inn. The latch shuddered, taking him a second to pull it open. When he'd managed it Ljunge was down nearly a block and preparing to turn. He was fast, though not fast enough to convince Erik to pull magic through the grips. If Göll wasn't allowed to help, Erik worried that using his own power might cause Modgudr to claim they were the same. Even then, Ljunge was just a thief and Erik had no good reason to give the man a reason to draw the daggers he kept high on either leg.

Tove kept pace in spite of her size, even with Erik at a full sprint. Ahead of them, Ljunge went around a corner, working his way east in fits and starts. He knew the city well and they were essentially at his mercy. Göll followed behind at a wider distance than she normally kept even when he slept. Erik wanted for all the world to have her fly up into the air and at least keep track of the man, but he was sure it would be counted as assistance. He never escaped their view, all the while drawing them toward the east, until they came to a massive paved lot with a fountain and rails at the far edge. Looking to the sides, Erik could see that it was an outcropping, set out over the river below. Ljunge, reaching the far side, turned and smiled. He held up two hands.

"Alright, let's stop there, shall we? I have a proposition." Ljunge looked at Erik with one eyebrow raised.

"I'm listening."

"Don't take me to Modgudr."

Erik recoiled, a confused look on his face. "And?"

"That is the whole proposition."

"How is that a proposition?"

"So, no?"

"You're not offering anything!"

Ljunge shrugged and flung himself off of the railing. Erik ran over, watching the man fall down the cliff side, tumbling as his body slapped against the rocks.

Erik turned, running as his mind realized that there was a very different meaning to that act in Helheim. He blasted past Tove who watched him with a curious expression.

"He'll come back! Someone will hide him!"

A wave of realization came over Tove's face and she rushed to catch up with Erik. He struggled to remember the path that Ljunge had taken to get there and wondered exactly how long it took to return to the bed. He'd never known exactly, but it could not have been long. It'd taken the guard in Lofgrund the best part of thirty seconds to dissipate. They'd run for nearly two minutes following him and the tavernkeep would likely be awaiting his return. Erik couldn't understand how anyone could so casually invite that pain. They returned to the Calf's Head and tore in. The tavernkeep was standing casually at the bar, something Erik hadn't expected. Had he already hidden Ljunge? He thundered upstairs, pointing at a door and telling Tove to check it. There were two others and Erik picked the one he knew overlooked a side street, kicking it open when he found it locked.

He stood in the room, mouth open in pure confusion. Ljunge was climbing out the window, still dressed in exactly the clothes he'd leapt in.

"Tove, downstairs! He's running!"

She joined him on the stairs, disbelief in her voice. "He's what?!"

"Running, I don't know. It doesn't make sense!"

They flew across the floor of the tavern, coming out the other side, Ljunge this time well ahead of them. It was clear immediately that he had led them to the cliff edge.

"Tove, go ahead and make sure he doesn't go east!"

She did, sprinting over an aisle and running on ahead. She'd become fast without the need for any sort of magic and she'd done so faster than Erik imagined possible. He had gained some speed himself, but she'd surpassed him easily. Ljunge caught sight of Tove at the next intersection and cut west. Erik did the same, Tove crossing a block up, now behind both of them. He ran into the main road, a convoy of heavy horses pulling carts. Erik watched as Ljunge leaned down, pulling a small knife from his boot. He reared back and threw it, the blade spiraling toward the lead horse. It stuck deep into the animal's flesh, sending it rearing and neighing in pain. It bolted, a dozen others following suit. Ljunge, without a second's hesitation, flung himself under the wheels. Before the horses had finished pressing the spilled entrails flat, Erik whipped around, running toward the edge of the entertainment district.

"He's going back!"

Göll stayed well behind, with Tove leading Erik but not leaving him behind. He would have to send her up first.

"Go, Tove! Get upstairs. I'll wait under the window."

She did not hesitate through the door of the inn and Erik stopped under the window. It was still open and Ljunge appeared a few seconds later. He looked over his shoulder, a triumphant smile on his face. It wasn't until he'd leapt that he looked down, seeing Erik there. A panic ran over Ljunge's face as he tried to change the direction of his descent, but it only resulted in an awkward landing on the stone street. He rolled his ankle, but still tried to come up and stand on it. The leg gave and Ljunge tumbled to the ground. He rolled over to face Erik, no pain showing on his face.

"I have another proposition."

"No! And how are you fine?"

Ljunge looked down at his body. "After having died, you mean? I haven't an idea, but listen—"

Tove came back down in a rush, stopping when she saw him on the ground. Ljunge looked at her, a smile creeping onto his face. Tove covered herself up with crossed arms and moved to Erik's side.

The man shook off the distraction. "My proposition—"

"It doesn't hurt when you come back? How about your leg now?"

Ljunge shook his head. "Neither."

"Then why do you care if Modgudr skins you?"

"I don't like the way she does it."

Erik sighed. "Alright, what's your proposition?"

"Take me with you. Göll, the tall one. Well, I like both of your women, but I've remembered her especially. She's a valkyrie, is she not? They are beautiful…" He trailed off, eyes turning to Göll. "That would make you einherjar. Women love you, clearly… I would join to your cause and share in that in exchange for my willing return to Modgudr."

Erik rubbed his temples, not sure exactly what was happening. "You… want to join me… so you can get laid?"

"Laid?" Ljunge furrowed his brow. "Does that mean sex?"

"Yes."

He smiled. "Then, yes. Precisely. Sex and money. Both."

Erik crouched in front of Ljunge, studying his empty expression. "How many times have you died?"

"In Helheim? Hundreds, at least." He laughed. "Oh! But I should say, I'm terrible with a sword. Or dagger. Or with fighting."

Erik's face found his palm. "And why would that convince me to take you anywhere?"

"Ah! See, you've missed the crucial part. I can fail as many times as I need to."

As stupid as Ljunge's grin might have been, the point was a good one. "Alright, fair enough."

"Fantastic! I've wanted to see Helborgen for ages." Ljunge rolled over, starting to drag himself up on his good leg.

"Helborgen?"

"Hel's city. I hear it's better even than Gjallarbrú, with wonders no one could dream of. Are you not going there?"

Erik looked at Göll and she nodded. "Seems we are."

"I'd thought so. Valhalla is there, after all." He began walking forward, dragging the leg with the ruined ankle. "But it'll be Helborgen for me. The women there…" Ljunge gave a low whistle. "The food as well, I've heard. Incomparable, they say."

He carried on about food and women until they came to the courtyard where the custodian came and received them.

There was a scar on the man's face that Erik hadn't noticed before. It was small, just below his chin. Erik was sure it hadn't been there before.

"Modgudr awaits you in her hall. She will see the criminal Ljunge for herself."

Göll put a hand on Tove's shoulder as they started away, keeping her back. Realizing they were not following, Erik turned to see what the problem was.

"We will train," Göll said plainly.

"Alright. I'll come back when I'm done."

Göll took Tove to the center of the yard, the guards turning to watch as curiosity got the better of them.

Inside Erik and Ljunge were led to Modgudr's hall and presented to the giantess. She stood casually on a raised platform at the far end of the hall.

"Ljunge, I'm disappointed. You were caught so quickly this time."

Ljunge smiled. "He's not so stupid as the ones you normally send, it pains me to say. Ah!" He held a finger up. "But I've made a deal. I'll go with him to Helborgen."

Modgudr laughed. "And steal from Hel? You have a taste for pain, Ljunge. The berserker has agreed to this?"

"Berserker?" Ljunge gave Erik a look. "He is?"

Modgudr nodded.

"He has agreed, yes..." Ljunge's eyes went back to Erik.

"I agreed."

Modgudr seemed satisfied with that. "Then I shall return him to his bed by the morning that you may cross my bridge. Our deal is done."

Guards came in to take Ljunge who was still looking at Erik. When their hands clasped around his arms, the man seemed to remember he was being taken away.

"In the morning, einherjar! I will meet you in the square with my things!" He was laughing, suddenly stopping and wrenching away from the guards to turn back to Erik. "Oh! And I have not asked your name!"

"Erik."

"Then, Erik, I look forward to traveling together!"

Chapter Thirty

A crowd had gathered to watch Göll and Tove training in the yard. There were cheers every time Tove managed to parry a blow. It seemed to make her all the more capable, which spurred Göll on. The display was impressive from both of them, though Erik could see that Göll was holding back. Strikes that would have landed fully were glancing blows, leaving nicks and cuts in Tove's arms. Tove seemed as aware of it as Erik, pushing herself to make full contact with Göll's spear.

The training ended abruptly when Tove shouted in frustration. Her concentration must have hit its limits and Göll planted a fist squarely in Tove's chest, sending her tumbling backwards. The crowd sent up a disappointed moan and dispersed when Göll dissipated her weapon.

Erik met them as they walked back toward the keep. Tove looked at him, screwing up her face. She punched him in the arm.

"Why would you agree to bring that man along? He's clearly a letch."

"A letch? Like lecherous?"

"Exactly that."

"Maybe I'm a letch."

She punched him again. "Well then you're terrible at it. And what if he means to do us harm? What if he attacks me?"

"I mean, you can fight Göll pretty okay, so you'll probably be fine. Why, do you want me to protect you?"

She scoffed. "Shouldn't you? You're a man, aren't you?"

"So you want me to then?"

She scoffed again and walked off. Erik followed her at a distance with Göll beside him.

"She's getting better, right? I saw you putting some effort in out there."

Göll looked at him. "At least you can see that much."

"Hey! What is this? I had to catch that guy."

"He caught himself as much as you did anything."

Erik tossed his head back and forth. "Yeah, okay. But I... you know... I showed up." He kicked at the ground absently. "That's something."

The doors opened and they entered, Tove happy to keep pace in front of him, still upset.

"What do you think about the guy?" Erik glanced over at Göll. "Ljunge."

"He is pathetic." Göll kept her eyes forward, a small crook at the side of her mouth was the only change in her expression as she cast the insult out. "But he is no more a threat than any of the guards. He is likely better with those daggers than he admits." She paused. "Would you not protect Tove?"

He huffed a laugh, surprised at the question. "Of course I would. I'd protect you too, if I could."

Göll stopped, staring at him. Ahead the custodian showed Tove back into the room.

"You would protect me? Why?"

Erik's brow furrowed. "Why wouldn't I?"

"Why?" She repeated the question, her eyes shifting across the features of his face.

Erik suddenly felt awkward. It was not as serious a statement as she seemed to be making it. "You're... I don't know... I like you. There's things I want to know about you that I guess maybe I never will." He chuckled. "Maybe I like underdogs or something."

"Erik the Chosen, if you would see yourself to your room we will send attendants to see to your clothes."

Erik turned his attention to the custodian. "Yeah, sure." He looked back to Göll who still seemed confused that he didn't hate her. "You coming?"

He walked off to the room, Göll lagging behind him. They were closed back in the room and food was brought. A servant took Tove's shirt, replacing it with another. Later, sleep clothes were brought and another set for the morning. Their packs were taken away with promises that they would be filled when they woke. Erik was hesitant, but come the morning, the packs were waiting with the custodian to see them off. There were changes of clothes inside each of the packs, but no food. An oversight Erik was intending to ask about until the custodian explained.

"It is a half-day's walk to Helborgen. Snacks have been prepared and since you took breakfast in your room, I expect that you should have no trouble making your way to a suitable establishment in time." He stopped in front of the doors to the square. "I should say that it is rare to see Modgudr in such good spirits that she rewards someone so handsomely. I thought it prudent that you be made aware of her kindness and her greatness."

"Yeah, thanks." The custodian opened the door, ignoring Erik's comments. "Listen, I have a question," he said, walking through the open doors. "Do you have like a twin or something?"

"I have many." The custodian closed the door.

Erik spun, pointing at Tove. "I fucking knew it! There's a bunch of 'em!"

Tove shook her head. "What? Why does it matter?"

"It doesn't! But I fucking knew it!"

Tove turned, walking toward the gates at the center of the far end of the square. Erik followed, excited that he'd been right about the scar. Ljunge was waiting by the attendant guards. He ended a conversation when he noticed Erik coming and turned, waving excitedly.

"Good morning!" Unable to contain himself he came running toward them. "Good morning, new friends!"

He stopped in front of them and Tove walked past. Göll stopped with Erik to talk to Ljunge.

"Listen, Tove thinks you're a creepy pervert and she wants you to die."

Ljunge frowned. "How horrible, to want me to die. Flat-chested little demon girl." Erik stifled a laugh. "But it's no concern! I will remove myself from your list of worries when we arrive in Helborgen."

"Whatever works."

The guards were organizing around the gates as Erik came to join Tove at the center. Loud mechanical clanking inside the wall gave way to movement of the doors themselves. The guards took places in columns as a small crack opened in the door.

"Why are they doing that?"

Ljunge had a bored expression on. "There are those who try to return, not liking Helborgen for one reason or another."

"Why would anyone want to leave?"

"I haven't a clue." Ljunge yawned. "All those in Helborgen are allowed in by Hel herself. I've never spoken to one who fled, but I've heard stories of the unwelcome passing through. I can't say what happens to those who are caught, but Modgudr has lost her temper more than once after such an event. I saw her cast a guard into the north mountains after banishing him from the city."

The columns parted when it was clear there was no one and a guard waved them through. Göll took the lead with Tove just behind her. Erik found himself curious at Ljunge's cavalier attitude when he was clearly not among the invited. He had not joined Erik's warband formally and any protection that might have offered Tove in no way extended to him.

"You're not worried about being found out?"

Ljunge shrugged. "There's no sense in carrying on about it if I do. At the very least, I'll try to have a fine meal and bed a fine woman before I'm thrown out."

They passed through onto the bridge. The structure was even larger than the gates that had seen them out to it. Tove slowed, coming to his side.

"The scale of things has changed."

Erik had noticed it as well. There had been no doors so large as those in Gjallarbrú and no bridge the size of the one they crossed. As they came to the end of it, the land before them was perfectly flat, covered in green, lush grass. There was a different air about the world beyond the bridge.

"It definitely feels… yeah… not the same."

It struck him after a few minutes of walking. This was a place no longer concerned with the appearances that humans found comfortable. Humans could surely use the bridge and walk the path, but they were sized for other things, grander things. There was a tingling in his stomach that had started when they'd passed through the doors and it had yet to settle.

It was two and a half hours of flat land before a wall appeared in the distance. It was massive and, even though he could see it, seemed to be as far away from them now as they had walked from the bridge. He was proven right by what was an uneventful walk. One he was happy of, even though the constant blue of the sky made him uncomfortable in ways he couldn't express. Tove watched the skies as well, not having forgotten what open sky meant for them. Göll, curiously, did not. Noticing that she was unconcerned with the space above them made Erik feel somewhat silly for being so concerned himself. She'd said they wouldn't attack but he couldn't believe it. His body wouldn't allow him to.

As they neared the walls around Helborgen, flowers appeared in the seemingly endless field to either side of the road. Butterflies flew and the smell of nectar hung in the air. It was strange, and even after so many hours the feeling in the pit of his stomach had not gone. He was nervous, though that was something he expected would have passed. He shook the concern away and looked ahead to a pair of doors. They were made of dark wood with the image of a dog on each, teeth bared and eyes watching the road.

Ljunge stepped ahead of them. "The doors are open." He started toward them, stopping when no one followed him.

Erik watched Göll, who paid the gates little mind, looking to the west instead.

"Göll, I'm guessing those gates are no good?"

Göll shook her head. "It is one of Hel's tricks. There is another way."

"I'll let you lead then." Erik swung an arm to the west. "After you."

They were off again, Tove beside Erik and Ljunge behind, still watching the doors he'd almost gone through.

"He is stupid, Erik. He will cause problems."

Ljunge was quick to run forward and defend himself. "I am only as stupid... as..." He stopped, eyes turned upward in deep thought. "I am not stupid. And neither a fool! And I'll only be your problem a while longer at that!"

Tove sneered at him. "I'll believe that when you're gone. You're the sort to follow anyone who'll stand you."

"A rat recognizing a rat, aren't you?" Ljunge scoffed. "You don't talk as he does. Come, where'd you meet? When did he ask you to come along on his journey?"

Tove crossed her arms and looked away, refusing to continue the conversation. Erik couldn't help but laugh.

"You two are going to be in love before long, aren't you?"

Tove looked back. "A vile man like him? I'd sooner choke!"

"She's fine to call me vile. I'll take no insult from a girl with the chest of a boy."

She turned bright red and rushed at Ljunge, swinging at him. The man ducked the punch deftly, something that drew Erik's attention. He had ducked a second attempt when Erik spoke.

"Hey! Fight when we're somewhere I won't have to drag either of your unconscious bodies away from."

A final sneer from each of them was the end of their conversation and the walk became a quiet one. It was a short walk to a portion of wall that had collapsed awkwardly, forming a sort of arch with a path through it. It was meant to look disused, but the path through was too clear for him to believe that it was accidental. They stood at it, considering the entrance.

"I should probably go last. You know, chosen one or whatever. Less likely a magic barrier or something will lock you two out."

Ljunge was quick to move to the entrance. "I'll not argue with good logic. Through I go."

He went through with no problem, Tove followed and then Erik did the same, Göll motioning for him to go ahead of her.

There was immediate noise around them as they came into a lush park. It was a city, properly a city, bustling with life. There were trees in the parks and people walking them, unconcerned with the appearance of four people through the hole in the wall. They moved across the park, Tove and

Ljunge marveling as they approached the street.

"Those lamps! There are no flames! How..." Tove's question trailed as a streetcar rolled silently by. "What was that? There were people in it! Where does it go?!"

She returned to Erik, pulling at his shirt. He was lost in the curious view of it all himself. There were electric lights and the streetcar had been electric as well. It was something from old pictures of New York, maybe. The clothes had not changed and what Modgudr had given them still looked very much the same, though everyone wore them. Erik ignored Tove's questions for the moment, holding up a hand and jogging up to a woman who stood reading a leaflet written entirely in runes.

"Excuse me, ma'am. Hey."

She turned to him, raising an eyebrow. "Do I know you?"

"I mean... ma'am would sort of imply..." He dropped it. "Is there a restaurant around here that's good? Maybe a hotel?"

"Hotel?" She puzzled for a minute. "Oh, you must be one of those." The woman's speech was more modern than anyone he had met. "You mean an inn. Sure, there's a place down that way." She pointed up a street to the north. "Restaurant and 'hotel' all in one." She chuckled at the word and went back to her leaflet.

"Yeah... thanks."

Erik turned around, nodding to the others who had kept their distance. They came to him and he started toward an intersection, crossing north. There were paved streets but most of the traffic was people on foot. He could see no cars, only streetcars from time to time.

"There's a hotel up this way. Inn. Sorry."

None of the buildings that Erik could see were much taller than ten floors or so. They seemed to be constructed of the same sort of things modern buildings were, certainly skyscrapers could be possible. He turned his head to Göll.

"Do you know why the buildings aren't any taller than

they are?"

"Hel does not allow buildings which would be taller than her hall." Göll looked up at the buildings. "She has many strange rules."

"Not that I'm in a rush to head there, but how do we get to Valhalla from here?"

"There are gates. They are at the far eastern edge of the city. You should not delay. Hel or her minions may come and make trouble for us. Odin will be displeased."

Göll's voice was harsh. He knew it was not her own, but the edge to it was more than it had ever been. Whether it was truly Hel that put her ill at ease, or something else, he did not wish to see her that way longer than need be.

"We'll go." Erik realized Ljunge was still walking with them. He turned to the man. "I thought you were leaving."

Ljunge shrugged. "I only know the way to one place I can eat and sleep. And that way is to follow you." He smiled. "Besides, we should dine together at least. Toast to new friendships. I will buy the food, even!"

Erik couldn't bring himself to be bothered if Göll was unconcerned. There was no good reason in turning Ljunge away, and a friend was better than a stranger or an enemy if the pervert was honest.

"Sure. I'll take free food."

"Then it's settled! I'll even treat the flat-chested demon!"

Tove swung, connecting hard with Ljunge's arm. He gave no reaction which only served to further Tove's anger. She pouted again, moving to Erik's side and keeping close to him until they reached the lobby of the hotel.

It was easily the nicest hotel lobby Erik had ever seen the inside of. Fine wood carvings, with statues of gods and goddesses all around, all lacquered and shined. Off the lobby was a restaurant and there was polished wood and marble on nearly every surface. The clerk at the front desk looked up from his counter and, when he saw Göll, immediately pulled up a bell, ringing it enthusiastically.

Erik stopped. He couldn't be sure exactly the meaning of the bell, but he didn't want to seem to be a threat if burly men came from the sides of the room. None did, and the clerk waved him over.

"Oh, honored einherjar, you are most, most welcome. Please, we will take your packs."

Bellhops in bright green uniforms came out, relieving all three of the group of their packs and taking them to the side of the lobby where they waited attentively.

"It is a fine choice you've made, coming to our establishment. Might I have your name?"

Erik looked around, not sure how to feel. "Uh, sure. Haki Erik Styrsson."

"Ooh." The clerk raised his eyebrows, impressed, and wrote the name down. "Well, Haki, is that the name you prefer?"

"Erik."

"Very good. I must say, you are most welcome and, of course, as you've graced our fine inn with the presence of one chosen by Odin we are happy to extend to you our three finest rooms, free of charge, and any meals you may need." The man smiled.

Erik knit his brow. "Why?"

The man seemed more confused than Erik was. "I'm sorry?"

"Why give me the rooms?"

The man laughed. "Oh, I do apologize. It has been so long since there has been an einherjar among us here that I simply forgot how arduous your travels can be." The man came around. "I will explain and show you to your rooms." He led them toward an elevator. Ljunge and Tove both looked at it curiously, only Göll followed Eric in immediately. "I see you know of elevators, Sir Erik. An impressive man."

"Yeah, they're not new."

"Very, very good." The man was genuinely pleased for whatever reason. He waved Tove and Ljunge in, following and pressing a button. "The presence of an einherjar does us a service, of course. The brutes beyond the bridge cannot understand the glory you bring to all humankind by serving Odin. We—"

"Ah!" Tove shouted as the elevator started moving. "What's happening? This box closet is moving."

"It goes up… just calm down, okay? It's normal." She clung to his arm and Erik motioned for the man to continue.

"We all among Helborgen understand the value of the einherjar. You will make us all proud come Ragnarok. They are concerns far from the minds of those simple farmers. No offense intended to present company, of course."

They rode to the top floor, exiting. There were no windows in the hall and only four rooms at all in the area. The clerk pulled three keys from his pocket and moved to the rooms.

"We only need two," Tove said, her arm still latched to Erik's. "One would do, as Ljunge's not with us."

The clerk looked surprised. "Is he not? I'm sorry if—"

"No, it's fine. A room for him. Sorry. Just two, though."

"Very good." He opened the first door, handing the key to Erik. "Then I will leave you your privacy and show Sir Ljunge to his room."

Erik walked into the room first. As soon as Göll had closed the door, Tove lost the ability to control herself. She immediately ran to the windows, looking out over a park.

"It's beautiful! There is so much here that makes no sense! Is it all magic? The gods have magic, it must be the same for Hel. She is a goddess, is she not?"

Göll scoffed at the statement, something Tove didn't seem to care about. Erik explored the room, finding a bathroom complete with tub, shower, and toilet.

"Indoor plumbing!" He'd said the words louder than he intended to and Tove came running.

"What is it?"

"Toilets!"

Tove looked around the bathroom, not sure what exactly he was referring to. "The white chair!"

"How is it a toilet?" She walked over to it, Erik behind her, nearly prancing in his excitement.

"Look, you just use it like normal. And then..." He pulled the cord above the toilet and it flushed. He rolled his head back. "Ahhh, it makes... it's so good. Tove, you don't understand. And you wipe with this paper. Or," he looked around, pointing to a second bowl, "you use that thing. It's called a bidet."

She nodded for a moment. "You told me about the paper. I remember that." She turned around. "What is this closet?"

Erik walked to it, opening the glass door and turning on the water.

"Water!" She walked over, putting her hand in it. "Hot water!" She licked her hand. "Clean water!" Tove turned, pushing him toward the bathroom door. "You need to go. I have to use this..."

"Shower."

"Shower, yes. I need it." She shut the door behind him and he heard her giggling on the other side.

Erik went to sit in one of the half dozen chairs scattered around the room. The lights were electric but there were no more modern items. No radio, phone, or television.

"It's weird."

Göll came over by the chair. "What is?"

"It's like... old time Earth. Midgard, I guess I should call it. But there are things that should be here that aren't."

"All of it is wrong. This luxury is what Hel uses to keep the people here weak. To make them forget the glory of the other gods. She abuses her power over the dead in this way."

Erik stretched out in the chair. "I guess..." He yawned, looking out the window at the park. "She said she'd help, but all I seem to remember is getting stabbed and freezing my ass off."

"I told you a deal with her would come to nothing."

"Yeah, you did. That's fine. We'll see what happens at Valhalla, I guess."

"Good." Göll's voice was curiously flat, almost hollow. "I will guide you to Valhalla."

CHAPTER THIRTY-ONE

LJUNGE HADN'T JOINED THEM THAT MORNING FOR BREAK-
fast, something Erik had almost expected him to do. There
was more variety in the food, roasted potatoes, fish, and
more modern fare like eggs and toast. Tove ordered well
more than she could ever eat, knowing that it was free. She
seemed especially enamored of the sweeter items, waffles
and French toast.

Mouth full, she pointed a fork at her food. "You mean to
say people eat this daily in Midgard now?"

"Not daily, no. Well... some people do. They're, uh... usually pretty fat."

"It's no wonder." She shoved another fork of syrup-covered bread into her mouth. "It borders on obscene."

When the food was done, they left, Erik wanting to get a lay of the city. Göll had been even more quiet than she normally was. It was after Erik had asked for directions to a shopping area that she finally spoke.

"How long do you intend to dawdle?"

Her voice was flat again and her eyes had been dark since the night before. It had been enough to convince Erik to sleep with his arms still wrapped.

"Dawdle? Woof. Strong words there, Göll." He was growing tired of the odd air around her. "What's your deal right now?"

She looked at him, icy eyes sharp. "I have come to guide you to Valhalla. You should not waste time."

Erik shrugged. "Well, I'm gonna waste time. A lot of it. How's that?" He turned, nearly shouting at her. "I'm going to buy a fucking house here and live in this city. Sound good? You going to put your spear through me if I do that?"

She said nothing, only stopped and stared, her expression unchanged.

He looked at Tove and motioned a hand at Göll. "You see it too, right? She's being fucking weird."

Tove seemed nervous being brought into the conversation. "I do not feel I should take part in this..." She trailed off and Erik felt a pang of regret at having lost his temper.

He forced a calming sigh and they carried on in the direction of the shopping center. His mood was more than soured and Tove understood that well enough. She kept close to him even as they arrived in the shopping district. It was a street, less wide than the main thoroughfares, lined with shops from one end to another.

In spite of having come half for Tove's sake, she kept her eyes locked forward, still feeling awkward. Erik put a hand on Tove's shoulder.

"Hey, if Göll wants to be weird, let her. And maybe she doesn't want to. No reason her deal needs to ruin the day, right?" He noticed a shop that looked to be selling chocolates. "You ever heard of chocolate?"

"Chah..." She'd heard the word but it was foreign to her.

"Jesus, Kvernes is like a horror show when I think about it. Anyway, you'll like it, I think, considering what you did to your breakfast."

He started toward the shop. Modgudr had given them some money and he figured that would be as good a place as any to spend it. Tove came behind him, complaining.

"It's not my fault I ate so much! Who wouldn't? You're the odd one for not eating it, I say."

"Yeah, yeah."

They came into the shop and the woman behind the counter was quick to hold up a welcoming hand.

"Welcome in! I've got candies and chocolates, as you can—"

Göll came in and the woman stopped.

"Oh, you..." She looked from Göll to Erik. "You are einherjar?"

Erik laughed awkwardly. "Look, I guess. I'm happy to pay for things. It's weird for me if I don't."

The woman shook her head. "Oh no, I couldn't allow that. Have as much as you like. It's my honor."

She came over, suddenly much more attentive to them than she had been. There were others in the shop who stared at Erik and Göll, smiling and talking excitedly. It felt undeserved in so many ways and even if it weren't, it was off-putting. He tried his best to ignore it, pointing Tove toward some truffles.

"These are usually pretty good."

The woman behind the counter grabbed a pair and handed them over the counter. Erik bit into his immediately while Tove looked it over. The chocolate was expertly made, something he hadn't expected.

"What is it? It looks like droppings."

Erik smiled, trying not to laugh. "It's a... candy. A treat.

It's sweet."

"Like the breakfast?"

"Yeah, more or less."

Tove took a bite of the truffle and chewed it once before spitting it out onto the floor. Everyone stopped, looking at Erik as he burst into laughter, doubling over.

He held up a hand at the woman who ran the store. "Haaa, oh god." He blinked back tears. "Oh man, I didn't know she'd do that. I'm sorry." He was still laughing.

Tove blushed bright red, shoving him to the side. "Why must you laugh so hard? It tastes odd! I don't trust it!" She crossed her arms. "You people have terrible habits in food. All of this is strange!"

She stormed out. The owner waved him after her, smiling, and Erik apologized again before running off to catch her. He came out laughing and Tove turned to him.

"You're picking fun at me, I know it."

He held his hands up. "How could I know you'd hate it?"

She pointed past him into the store. "It looks like an owl pellet is how! And tastes like a honeyed one! Bitter and odd and sweet and... and... mushy."

"Some of us would call that smooth."

"Well, some of you are touched with some mental sickness, then!"

Erik was laughing again, Tove's face turning red. "Alright, I'll get you something you like."

"Two things."

He rolled his eyes. "Sure, two things. One has to be food."

She huffed. "I don't see why it is you want to feed me so often."

"I don't see why you never refuse."

She kicked at him, her foot missing shallow as Erik hopped away from it. They carried on, to a shop selling ground beef on French rolls. They weren't quite hamburgers, though they were definitely something similar. The meat was spiced and there was some sort of jam on the bread and they were sat out. He mentioned the word hamburger to the man assembling the sandwiches and received only a blank look followed by an apology. Erik ordered a couple when Tove said she liked the sound of them and the lukewarm sandwiches were wrapped in paper and handed over. They weren't exactly what Erik had hoped, but Tove liked hers well enough, so it satisfied a part of his debt for having tricked her into eating the chocolate.

They'd made their way past half the shops on the street when Tove spotted a curious one. It sold weapons from the looks of it, very much in the style of the world on the other side of the bridge. She went into the shop with glee, Erik following her, somewhat surprised when he realized that the bulk of the items available were jewelry. Tove took little notice of the smaller baubles, her attention focused squarely on the weapons and shields that adorned the walls and stands.

"Welcome, einherjar. I hope the day finds you well." The difference in speech was immediately apparent. "I'll gladly supply you with whatever it is you need. And I'll not hear a word about co—" He noticed the leather wraps on Erik's hands. "Beg pardon. Those are finely made. Nothing here I could offer to be of aid. And that's no word of modesty."

Erik looked down at his own hands and then back at the man. "Don't worry about it." He nodded down toward the boxes that lined the wooden counters. They had glass windows and contained rings and necklaces and the like. "I'll look at this stuff. While she finds something she likes." He nodded at Tove and the man followed his look.

"As you'd have it, einherjar." The man turned his attention to Tove. "Then, little miss. What'll it be?"

Tove looked at the man as if it was the first she'd noticed him. Without answering she pulled her sword. It was dented deeply from her training with Göll. The man winced to look at it and picked it up.

"What's happened to you, poor dear?" He spoke to the sword, turning it over. "A pity, but at least it served you." He laid the sword down, eyes returning to Tove. "I've a few this size in the back. A moment."

He disappeared into the back and Erik turned his eyes to the jewelry in the cases in front of him. The designs were meticulous, beautiful. He recognized Thor's hammer among them, but there were others as well. A bow and arrow. He vaguely remembered hearing about a god named Ullr whom it might symbolize. There were ravens and spears and dozens of other designs, most seemed connected to gods in some way.

The shopkeep returned holding a pair of swords. He pulled them, showing impressive blades, though neither had runes of any sort. Tove smiled wide when she picked up the first, swinging it freely. It was plain to see it was light and the grip was near perfect for her hand.

"This one."

The man laughed. "You don't wish to try the other?"

Tove shook her head. "No, this is the one." She poked at the air a few times. "I'm sure." Tove removed the sheath she wore and put it on the counter, replacing it with the new one.

The shopkeep smiled. "It suits you." He turned to Erik as Tove continued busying herself with the sword. "You've eyed those pieces for a time. My apprentice makes them. She's deft with a hammer, whether striking a blade or tapping fine jewelry." He chuckled, half sighing. "I swear the girl surpassed me years ago but insists on learning still."

Erik nodded. "I'll take another piece, only if you let me pay for it."

The man came around to Erik, a conflicted look on his face. "I couldn't charge a man who brings glory to Odin."

"What if I insist? Call it a gift or something, I don't know."

"I... I apologize, einherjar."

Erik sighed, looking down at the case. "These are silver?"

The shopkeep opened the case. "Platinum. Finer than silver and not given to tarnish."

There was a silver shield with a thick chain. Erik lifted it from the case. The circular shield bore a pattern turned and repeated in each quarter.

"That one? A beautiful shield, if I say so myself. The pattern gives protection, through the ancient magics, or so my own master told me so long ago. I'd not trust it over armor," the man laughed. "But there are strange old ways even the gods have forgotten, or so the tales go."

"I'll take it."

"With my blessing, at that. I hope it finds you well at Ragnarok."

The man bowed and Erik started to the door, seeing that Tove already had. She was outside inspecting her sword in the light of day. As the shopkeep saw the second sword back into the back room, Erik stopped at the edge of the shop, quietly putting two gold coins Modgudr had given him onto the counter.

When he was outside he turned to Göll, her face still serious. He pulled up her hand, and she watched him, impassive. He placed the shield into it.

"I'm sorry I yelled. And I'm no good at this sort of shit. But I want you to have this. That's why I had to pay for it. At least I can pretend I earned that gold, whether it's true or not." He smiled. "You don't have to wear it. Just... I wanted to give you something."

Göll's eyes seemed to shift, light coming back into them somehow. She looked down at the chain, a soft, confused frown on her face.

"Haki Erik Styrsson!"

The voice was one he hadn't heard since the first time a sword plunged into his body. He turned to see Vár walking toward him down the street. Tove was confused and solved the issue by coming closer to Erik.

"Vár, what an entirely unpleasant surprise."

"As much a surprise as your ready progress in coming to Helborgen."

"Yeah, about that, I thought Hel was supposed to help

me? I'm already here."

Vár scoffed in annoyance. "Do you believe the world is so simple as that? Or that your journey is through?" She shrugged. "I suppose that depends upon you, but still... my goddess offered you help, true. And said to come and find her. Failing your own end of a bargain does not mean the other has as well."

"So why are you bothering me now?"

"A strange way to see it," Vár said, looking over Tove. "And I've heard of your warband. Hel was pleased to hear you'd done such a thing."

Göll took a step forward at the mention of Hel but Erik held an arm out to stop her.

"Okay, so what is it you want?"

Vár put on a wry smile. "I've come only to welcome you to Hel's beautiful city. And to remind you of her outstanding offer of aid, should you choose to accept it." Vár's gaze shifted to Göll and the smile faded. "We have good reason to believe you should need it."

"Sure, great. Tell her if I hate Valhalla, I'll take her up on it."

Göll's hand appeared on Erik's shoulder, gripping it hard. He turned his head half to her when he saw Vár give a disbelieving smile.

"A deal well struck."

"Wait, what? No, no. I was—"

Hel's agent laughed. "I will make sure you are well looked after, then."

Göll pulled Erik back and rushed at Vár who fled before the valkyrie could do anything. Göll turned on her spot.

"What have you done?!" Göll shouted the words, her voice ragged, as if she'd not used it in days. "You must not—" Göll stood bolt upright, her eyes darkening. The words choked off, locked in her lungs.

From behind, Erik felt the tip of a sword push into his ribs. It was a familiar sting, he even knew the shape of the blade. Tove screamed, drawing her sword, but it was too late. The blade had hit his heart.

His chest spasmed as Tove tore through the crowd after the valkyrie who stabbed him. He hadn't even seen her and didn't now. His eyes were locked on Göll. She fell to her knees, muscles in her face twitching, a tear running down her face. She still held the necklace in her hands. Erik smiled and the world went black. He prepared himself for the pain to come.

His eyes tore open, and he was again unable to move. He felt his arms being pulled, and blades run through the meat of his forearms. His eyes cleared for a half second of the tears the pain forced from him. There were three valkyries in the room. One to either side. They were working their blades through the leather of his grips, whipping his only weapon away. The third picked them up, snapping the metal clean in half. As a scream worked its way out of him, a hot blade laid across his neck. The valkyrie pulled, a look of pure rage on her face. Blood poured into the hole she opened, choking him as he writhed on the bed. They all watched as he died again.

He came back in the same bed, immediately wet with his own blood. The blade came toward his neck as soon as his mind returned to him. He felt the power come but it was too late. He managed to slam a fist into the table at his side, destroying it.

He rose a third time to the sound of the door to his room crashing open. Ljunge surveyed the room, delaying two of the valkyries. The one who had cut his throat did so again as the other two put holes in Ljunge.

Erik returned, the power was somewhere deep beneath the pain coursing through his body. He could feel it there, but he could not find it. His bleary eyes saw Ljunge charge into the room again, shouting and bearing a pair of daggers toward the valkyrie who stood guard. He fell as the blade came across Erik's neck again.

The valkyries took his life once more, Ljunge coming as they fled out the window, taking much of the wall of Erik's room with them. Erik could see nothing. His throat throbbed and twitched violently. He could hardly pull a breath, gasping every ounce down through an unwilling throat. The air was not enough and the world slowly faded only to come roaring back, the pain seeming to multiply each time he lost his battle to breath.

The images of the time after that were sporadic. Ljunge was there, panicked. Tove came. A picture of his body being carried lived somewhere in his mind. All he could wonder was where Göll had gone. He could not calm himself, desperate to force an image of her into his mind. He did not know how long it had been or where he was when he felt a cool hand on his forehead and soft breath in his ear. It was Göll, her true voice, soft and kind.

"Sleep now, Erik. You are safe."

Chapter Thirty-Two

It was more than a day before Erik could stand the pain enough to open his eyes. There was no mistaking how Haki ended up in the state Erik witnessed. Looking around, Erik saw that he was propped up in a bed, unable to speak. The walls were all intact but he was still in the same hotel he had been in before. Göll was watching the windows. She turned when he stirred, the first to notice he had come back to his senses.

Tove, seeing Göll move to the bed took notice, slapping at Ljunge's shoulder. She was the first to speak.

"Erik, I'm sorry we..." Tove paused, looking down at her feet. "I ran back as fast as I could manage when I realized."

"It's fine." Erik's voice was broken and the words came only with great effort. "Göll, is that normal? What they did?"

Göll's expression was not the strange one she'd worn for the days before, but something softer. "The tactic, yes. But… to attack in Helborgen. It is unheard of. Hel refuses to have her city disrupted."

Erik rolled his head back against the pillow behind him, the pain flaring. When it subsided, he looked at the windows. It was night. "So, what do we do?"

Göll shook her head. "It is strange. I can only think Odin has some plan for you."

"And why do you think that?"

The moment she went to speak, Göll's throat seized, violently, her face locking to an intimidating scowl. The darkness flashed back to her eyes. She put a hand to her neck, touching a familiar chain, and her throat released its tension all at once. She inhaled sharply and turned to the window.

Anger ran through Erik, the flutter in the pit of his stomach making itself known again, worsening even. It hadn't left since they'd passed into the plains outside Hel's city.

Tove stepped forward. "You should go. Einherjar belong at Odin's side. He must be… upset somehow. Perhaps that you took aid from Völundr. We found his work, broken." Her eyes moved toward the table beside the bed and Erik saw the tattered remains of the grips there.

"Göll, can you still feel my presence?"

Göll nodded her affirmation. "More strongly than I have ever heard it described."

She quickly stopped the sentence, returning to her silence, though Erik could not sense any tension in her neck. She may have been trying to avoid it occurring at all. Erik rubbed his own throat. The skin was smooth and the muscles were calm beneath. How many times must Haki have experienced that pain? Tove shifted her weight, drawing Erik's attention.

"We… We should…"

Ljunge stepped past Tove. "She cried near the entire time. Shame she wasn't here to do anything. Not like me." She swung at him and he dodged it, laughing. "It's not often I see a man brutalized like that. Can't say as I have a taste for it. Still, couldn't lay blade to any of them. That's rare by me."

Tove looked at him. "Should it come as a surprise? You said yourself you're no good in a fight."

"And I've not lied to anyone before today." He snorted mockingly, looking back to Erik. "Life is made easy when a person assumes they know a man's reasons. I adventured for longer than I stole and I found myself bored in Gjallarbrú with no means to cross." Ljunge looked serious for the first time since they'd met. "I would join your warband, if you'd have me. Ah!" His face brightened as he extended an arm. "I do enjoy sex and coin, though. That was true."

Erik studied him for a moment. "You'd bind yourself to me? Odin may destroy you if you are found unworthy."

Ljunge shrugged. "What better way could a man hope to end?"

Erik clasped Ljunge's arm and shook. "Welcome aboard, then. And good luck."

Ljunge stepped back, looking at his own hand as if it had grown just then. "You…" He turned his hand over, considering the back of it. "I cannot say as I have ever formed a warband with an einherjar, but I was not expecting that."

"What?"

"A… feeling. I feel lighter." He shook his head. "In my head, maybe. I've joined no warbands in Helheim. I simply didn't expect any strange effects."

"Information hasn't been particularly high on the list of things I've been given down here." Erik pulled himself to the edge of the bed. He stood himself up, finding that he had been changed into sleep clothes. "I'll change, then we can go see if Valhalla is all it's cracked up to be."

Ljunge left the room, saying he did not want to see Erik

naked again. He dressed and they left the hotel. The clerk was decidedly nervous as their party moved through the main lobby. The courteous bows were all still in place, but they were well aware of what had happened to him. If he had any reason to doubt Göll's claim that valkyries did not attack in Helborgen, the looks on the faces in the hotel lobby would have removed it.

Out on the street, Erik kept his eyes narrow. It was dark and he could not watch the sky, but the attack had not come from there. An attack meant to avoid notice by Hel's own hounds. Vár could keep pace with the valkyries in Midgard and with Göll just before he was stabbed. There must have been others.

He found a map of the streetcars for the city near a group of waiting people. They watched Göll nervously, not paying much mind to Erik. It was possible that news of the attack had spread. They were only a few blocks from the hotel and at least their region of the city would have talked about such an event. They were nearly six blocks from what was a main road that ran through the whole of Helborgen to the east.

"Valhalla is to the east?"

His raspy voice drew more stares. Göll nodded without a word, but still the people slid away from their group.

Ljunge chuckled. "It seems they'd rather not accompany us."

Erik gave a strained smile. "Their loss, right?"

They left the stop, walking toward the main road. The streets were bustling and as they moved out of the area where he had been attacked, the stares faded, replaced by people hurrying from one place to another. Erik welcomed the disinterest in him, at the very least he could feel for a moment as though he was not marching toward his own undoing. It was a possibility he could not ignore. He hardly knew Ljunge, but had no reason to refuse the man. If nothing else, he would provide a distraction for Erik to use so that he could escape with Tove. There was a question then of how much sanctuary Hel could provide, if any. And what would become of Göll. It was too much to consider, but he had no other course. At least, he would see Valhalla before seeking Hel.

The wait for the streetcar was a short one, but there were others with them. It arrived, half full, and Erik's paltry warband entered the front of the car, standing near exits and windows on Erik's suggestion so that they could see themselves clear if a fight came for them.

There were not stops, as such. The car simply slowed near the exits and people left or entered. There was a constant flow of people, something which troubled Erik. There were many valkyries, he knew that much, but he did not know their faces. The others were on edge as well, Ljunge with his hands at a new pair of daggers he'd bought and Tove ready to pull her sword.

Erik only stood, staring blankly out the windows, watching every face he could manage and thinking of what he should do. They had crossed half the city by streetcar when Vár called to Erik from the back of the car. He had not seen her enter and she was walking toward him. Göll turned, readying herself for a fight.

"How did you like it, Haki Erik Styrsson? The cruelty of the valkyries is worthy of legend, is it not?" She smiled at him in anticipation of his answer but did not wait for one. "Göll has taken her part in such cruelty, of course." Vár feigned a frown. "Though it seems she lost a taste for it."

"What do you want, Vár?"

"I've only come to watch you cross the city. Hel is pleased with the simple conditions of your agreement to see her aid you." Vár looked at Göll and tilted her head to the side. "Should you need it, of course. I'd hate to offend."

Ljunge looked Vár over. "She works for Hel? I like her spunk." He extended an arm in greeting.

Vár slapped him across the face. "Like it at a distance." She turned her eyes back to Erik. "Hel recommends that you should see her rather than make this voyage to Valhalla."

Göll snapped at that. "She would! Stop muddling his mind with your tricks!"

Vár ignored the shout, keeping her eyes locked to Erik. "Well?"

His voice was still raspy and speaking still hurt, but he managed to say it. "I'll go see Valhalla. Be a real waste of a trip if I didn't at least take a look."

A disappointed frown came at his response. "You are free to choose what you wish." She stepped to the edge of the car. "Good luck." With that she stepped off.

Erik had forced it down, but the churn in his stomach was getting worse the closer they came to the eastern edge of the city. The track circled at the end of the line and Erik's group took their leave when it did.

Erik shook his head. "I think I'm hungry or something. I... let's eat some food, okay? Valhalla will still be there." He forced a grating laugh, coughing halfway through it. "Besides," he croaked, "Ljunge still owes me a meal."

Ljunge laughed. "Have a girl slap me and then have me pay for a meal. I'm beginning to wonder if I've misjudged you Erik."

Erik smiled at the thought. "Hey, if people know your intentions, or whatever."

Ljunge shrugged and headed off toward the side of the road. The eastern part of the city was much the same as the other end, though there seemed to be more in the way of residential shops in the section they'd ended up. Tove kept close to Erik, as did Göll. They watched the world around him closely. Erik had given up on it, the odd feeling in his stomach turning to something approaching a burning. It was neither debilitating nor painful, but it distracted him. He only thought of it and scanned the buildings across from them. He left it to Ljunge to pick the place and they ended up in a quiet little restaurant that had simple tables and chairs. It was run by a husband and wife who welcomed them enthusiastically. They saw Göll and offered to give things for free, Ljunge immediately turning them down, cheerily saying that he was paying for the meal and that he would not allow them to keep him from repaying his debt. That was enough for the couple and Ljunge took his seat with them at the table.

"You were better at that than me."

Ljunge smiled. "A man's honor is not something to be refused."

Food was ordered and Erik, hoping to distract himself, turned his thoughts to Ljunge.

"What did you used to be? Before landing in Gjallarbrú, I mean." He'd never been offered many discussions about people's lives before Helheim and it seemed to him that it may have been something they wanted to avoid.

"Ah, yes." Ljunge leaned back in his chair, thinking over the question. "Many things. A man can be what he wishes in Helheim, at least to a point. I led something of a boring life once and decided I'd rather not. There's a risk in this place of becoming quite insane if you keep your mind in your head." He took a hesitant breath. "For a time, I played the bandit. Robbing travelers and small villages if I could manage it. I met men who made it their purpose in life to do such things and no longer found fun in it after seeing them do their work. Lately, I steal." He chuckled. "You're aware of that, I suppose. No one is truly poor in Helheim. Not as they were. But still, those with less react in a way I found unexciting. The powerful, though... they never fail to make theft exciting or interesting."

"By tearing your skin off?"

Ljunge smiled, pointing. "Exactly! You understand!"

"I really don't," Erik said, chuckling. "I don't think getting skinned is my thing."

"Bah, it's fine once you've gotten used to it."

"You know other people feel things, right?"

Ljunge laughed at that. "They keep saying. Seems a terrible way to go through life."

The food came. It was good, not that Erik could eat much of it. Tove watched him with concern in her eyes. Ljunge paid, agreeing to half-price after a minor argument with the owners of the shop. They thanked Erik repeatedly for choosing their restaurant. It didn't seem worth explaining that he hadn't done anything of the sort.

Erik had Göll lead them when they left the restaurant. She walked ahead of Tove, who kept herself next to Erik. Ljunge lingered at the back, idly watching women as they passed. If he had a concern anywhere in his mind, Erik couldn't see it in the way the man acted. Perhaps he was truly sick of death. Or maybe he couldn't care what happened in any case.

The ball grew in Erik's stomach as they neared towering stone walls. The gates and inlaid carvings on the wall were lined in gold. The images were very different from the gates Hel had placed at the entrance to her city. These were of valkyries and Yggdrasil and swords crossing over shields. The gates ahead were open a crack and people flooded into it. People making for the gate passed by him, all of them revelrous. They talked with excitement about the battle.

"There are spectators?" Erik gritted his teeth as he looked up at the gates. The feeling in his stomach suddenly twitched, causing him to stumble forward.

Tove ran to him, forcing his eyes to meet hers. "What is it?"

Erik shook his head. "Just... nerves maybe. I've got a weird feeling in my gut."

She looked ahead at the crowd flowing through the doors. "If..." She stopped. "Odin is great and wise. But if you believe... if..." She struggled with the sentence, conflicted. "If you believe you should go... elsewhere, then I will follow."

Ljunge came to his side. "I am with the demon. I joined meaning to follow you."

Göll turned, a concerned expression on her face, her

fingers tracing the chain of the necklace he'd given her.

Erik smiled, trying to force the odd feeling in his stomach down. He let out a slow breath, looking over at the gates with narrow eyes. His lips turned down at the sides as he steeled his resolve, trying his best to sound casual.

"No." He closed his hands into empty fists. "I mean, we already came this far."

CHAPTER THIRTY-THREE

THEY WALKED TOWARD THE GATE, GÖLL IN THE FRONT with Erik beside her and Tove near behind. Ljunge kept his casual distance, not seeming bothered by anything around them.

The gate rose up above them as they approached. The turning in his stomach had become nearly unbearable. He felt as though his abdomen would burst and worms would fall out. Still, he followed Göll to the back of the crowd. They filtered in, hardly noticed by the people around who all buzzed excitedly at the prospect of their trip beyond the golden wall to see the einherjar battle.

A few of the more boisterous men and women cheered at

Göll when they saw her armor, though the valkyrie showed no sign of caring if she did at all. Her eyes seemed to be focused somewhere beyond the cracked gate. The light from beyond it was blinding, though it seemed to die before ever traveling past the stone threshold. No light spilled over the wall either. It wasn't so strange considering that a winged murderess stood beside him, but somehow Erik was awed by it more than anything he'd seen in Helheim.

The awe fell away, replaced by a sense of dread as the ball in his stomach seemed to crystallize. He winced, leaning forward, pressing his stomach but finding nothing there. Tove put a hand on his back and Erik forced himself back up straight. He turned and gave her a reassuring smile even as the feeling streamed out into his chest, pushing through him with each step he took. Erik gritted his teeth and pushed forward, ahead of the rest, wanting whatever he felt to be done or to kill him if it was going to. He shoved people out of the way, most of them hardly stopping to notice or care.

In the final steps before the threshold the light began to change. The sky turned a bright blue with the sun high within it. As he slammed his foot across the stone and found himself beyond the wall to Valhalla, the winding tendrils inside him faded, as if whatever it had been smoothed out into his body. It didn't disappear. More, the feeling became suddenly normal.

He looked around as Göll and the others caught up to him. Tove rushed to his side.

"Are you alright? Why would you run ahead like that?"

Erik looked down at his hands, feeling as though he could move them more freely somehow. "I don't know... there was this... feeling." He looked at Göll. "I should have said something maybe. Is that normal?"

Göll looked at him for only a brief moment, a hint of concern on her face. "I have never heard it spoken of."

"Has it gone now?" Tove looked down at his hands.

"Yeah, it's… I feel better."

She gave him a look, not believing what he'd said.

"Really. No joke."

For the first time, Erik looked around. They were in a wide stone square, statues of Odin and Thor and others placed all around and people gathered around them, chatting happily. To their left, there was a large, open field, an enormous tree in the center of it and a forest at the near end. At the far end of the field was what must have been Valhalla. It easily dwarfed any building Erik had seen in Helheim. It stood twenty storeys tall and ran the length of the field, hundreds of yards in each direction. The unnatural sun shone off the golden roof, patches of which were covered in grass. Another great tree was growing through the top of the hall itself and even so far from it, Erik could see a pair of immense animals walking idly around, grazing from the grasses and the tree as they liked. Doors ran the length of Valhalla, each with gold inlayed with the shape of some symbol of Odin. There were a pair of ravens on one, a pair of wolves on another, the steed Sleipnir in the center. On and on they went.

The sight of the building somehow brought him no joy and before he'd made a thorough accounting of what it was he wanted to do, Göll started toward it.

"Hey, Göll."

She did not stop so he trotted to catch up with her. Her face was stern, solemn, and her eyes were fixed on Odin's great hall.

"Hey!"

He grabbed her arm and Göll whipped around, seeming to snap out of her trance.

"We must go to Valhalla." She said the words almost as if there was panic hidden somewhere beneath her placid exterior.

"Why? Why right now?"

A murmur came over the crowd and Göll's eyes shot to

the sky. There was terror in them. Erik followed her gaze up and saw six valkyries hovering, a pair each with eyes locked on a chosen member of his warband. Panic flushed through him and he felt his body tense. They did not move, only watched.

"What is this, Göll? Why are they watching us?"

Göll shook her head, her hand raising to the chain on her neck. "I... I do not know."

Erik's expression turned sour and he looked up at the valkyries. Rage started to bubble in his stomach and the power he'd had so much trouble finding rose in him immediately, more readily than it ever had.

"Tove! Ljunge! Draw weapons!"

They did, both lowering their stances. The valkyries looked to each other for a moment and then back to Erik. He could hear the hissing and it stirred something terrible inside him. He felt pure hate.

The moment the first of the valkyries twitched to fly at them, Erik slammed his fist down into the ground below, sending stone and dirt flying up into the air.

"Go! The tree line!"

Neither Tove nor Ljunge waited to be told again. They fled at speed, keeping pace with Erik even as the power coursed through him. The valkyries followed, though not Göll. She still stood in the clearing, dumbstruck as people screamed around her, fleeing the fight.

Erik kept himself behind Tove and Ljunge, watching as the valkyries slowly closed the gap. As his warband cleared into the woods, Erik spun.

"Göll! Come on!"

He saw her snap out of her haze and he pulled a fist back, burying it in the arm of the first valkyrie to reach him. Four flooded past him, only the partner of the one he'd struck remaining behind. He ignored the other, turning to move into the woods. Göll was well on her way to the trees, flying over the crowd toward them.

315

Erik sped through the small forest, catching up with the valkyries who had split Tove and Ljunge. His warband were handling themselves well, keeping pace ahead of their pursuers and striking if they got too close. Erik closed on Tove first, reasoning that Ljunge could handle any damage he sustained. He stopped in front of a thin tree, plunging a hand through it, and before it fell, dragged it down in the path of a charging valkyrie. She stopped, looking at him for a moment and then returning to her pursuit of Tove.

It was all the support he could manage, as the pair who meant to attack him had found him among the trees. He spun to meet them. Their pace was quick, but seemed to slow as seconds passed. He slapped away the first blade, putting a square fist into the nearest valkyrie's ribs. She was pushed away, her body snapping trees with a disturbing lack of resistance. The other drove at him, Erik forcing the short sword she held away, pounding her down into the ground where she formed a divot. He left the valkyrie there and returned his efforts to finding Tove. From the corner of his eye, he could see Göll moving through the forest parallel to him. A look of determination on her face gave him hope that whatever pulled at her resided for the time. He did not want to fight her, not ever.

Erik saw Tove rushing toward Ljunge. They came together and stopped, valkyries circling them. He could do nothing at his distance, but he rushed at them with all the speed he could manage. He was yards away when the sound of a deep, bellowing horn pierced the air around him.

Their attackers stood bolt upright, eyes turning toward Valhalla. He felt panic at the sight and turned to find Göll. She had dropped to her knees, screaming in pain. The two who had attacked him were at her already. They grabbed Göll, dragging her into the sky.

"No! Hey!"

He rushed after them, stopping hard at the edge of the forest. There was only open field between them and Valhalla and the valkyries were well across it and in the air at that.

Tove and Ljunge were quick to come to his side.

"Why would they leave? Why did they attack?" Tove was breathless, looking at the glimmering hall.

"I don't know. They took Göll."

Ljunge crouched after sheathing his daggers. "I don't get the impression that was something we ought to have expected." He looked up at Erik. "What will you do?"

"We have to go, right? They took Göll."

"Took her to her home, you mean."

Erik snapped at Ljunge. "And who goes to their home screaming? Huh?"

The horn blew again. Erik stood, pensive, watching the hall for anything that might leave. Instead, cheers came from the square and wide doors along the length of the hall opened. Thousands of men and women began to file out into the field. The procession was slow and seemed to be endless, the first out finally coming to a stop only a few dozen yards from the tree line where Erik watched. He could see them well enough. They were dead-eyed and listless, shuffling in place. They had spread fairly evenly across the entire field and all of them watched the hall with a sort of cold detachment.

Ljunge leaned to Erik. "The battle."

Erik nodded. "Should we join? We should, right? Maybe we can get to Göll."

Tove nodded. "You are einherjar. It is your place to join them."

"Sure, and maybe..." His eyes rolled across the slack-shouldered fighters. "Maybe it will help you two get in. To prove you deserve it."

Tove nodded, though not enthusiastically. He knew she had seen the look on those in the field. It bore none of the glory Erik had been sold. One more thing that was not what he believed. One more thing he could have been told.

Expressions of horror grew on the faces of the einherjar

in the field. Some even pleading with their eyes. The horn came again, and he could see the will inside some of them break as they pulled their swords and axes.

Erik watched a moment as the battles began. They were fierce, desperate. Each fighter finding another and screaming as though there was nothing they could hope for but to survive the day. A woman plunged an axe into a lethargic man's leg. He fell, screaming.

"No! No, not again!" He wept as he bled out into the grass.

Ljunge stood, watching with a knit brow. "This is... What glory is there in this?"

Erik gritted his teeth, sucking in a breath. "What can we do?"

They had to fight, he knew that. Göll was taken. There would be no answers or meaning if they fled. He charged out onto the field, finding it hard to look behind and see if Tove and Ljunge had followed.

He met the axe-wielding woman and she gave a shout, swinging. She was slow. The einherjar all were, glacially so. He could not afford to be kind. He punched the woman's face and her skull caved under his hand, skin splitting and she wrenched away under the force of the hit. Her body dragged and then rolled across the ground. Erik looked to his side and saw that Tove and Ljunge had joined him. They faced as little resistance as he did, putting blades through their first opponents as though the men were made of hay with bones of sticks.

Another charged him and Erik reeled back, again putting his fist through bones as if they weren't there. It was the second attacker that drew attention to him. Others stood away, not wanting to engage him, one fleeing to another side of the field. He marched forward, Tove and Ljunge off to his left, tearing through all those who came at him.

He had neared the tree in the center of the field when a large man showed himself, bearing a pair of axes and covered in blood. He did not look nearly so lost as the others had, and pointed the end of his axe at Erik without a word. An open-mouthed smile showed that the man had no tongue. Others circled them to watch the fight. The man charged but to Erik he may as well have been walking. A pang of guilt rolled through him, until he thought of Göll's screams and the world came crashing back to him. The warrior swung his first axe and it came down wide of Erik's arm. Erik reached a hand out, swatting the man with the back of it. He disappeared in an instant from Erik's view, his limp body clipping three or four others as it went. The gathered men fled, getting as far away as they could manage, some running themselves into the path of Ljunge and Tove and finding blades put through them in spite of any effort to remain alive.

As he neared Valhalla, Erik saw that the valkyries were gathered along a balcony that ran along the space above the doors. They stood, watching the battle with little interest. Even as they worked their way across the field, felling any that came near them, the warband drew no particular concern from the valkyries. The field had nearly been cleared of fighters when Erik realized he could neither see nor hear the crowd and hadn't since he entered the field. It only seemed to stretch on toward nothing in either direction. Even the forest had disappeared.

His warband came together with only a dozen men left on the field. Ljunge's shirt had been torn by cuts. Erik could see his body was covered in scars below the neck. Ljunge looked down as he came close, realizing what Erik was looking at.

He laughed. "Scars are a man's pride. But never on the face."

The remaining dozen closed on them, forming a loose group. Erik sighed. "I thought it was supposed to be one on one combat."

Tove's breath was heavy from the work of moving across the field. "They seem not to have heard that."

The men broke into groups of four, each squaring in front of one of Erik's band. Tove and Ljunge moved away, immediately putting distance between themselves and the groups. The men gave chase while Erik stood his ground facing down the ones who'd chosen him. Three enormous men and a woman sized to match. They moved out, circling around him.

They charged at once, Erik putting swift blows to the first two, ending them instantly. He spun, striking the woman beside the head. It was the fourth who caught him. He felt the familiar metallic press of steel against his side. Erik braced for the piercing pain but it never came. The man grunted, throwing his weight into the stab. The sword bent and snapped, the tip spinning into the air and falling harmlessly onto the ground beside the dissipating corpses. Erik turned, planting a foot in the man's chest. The man pulled up his hands to catch Erik's kick, but the force of it dug him into the ground where he wrenched over backward when the dirt no longer gave way.

Erik watched as Ljunge and Tove cut down the einherjar who chased after them with no real trouble. A few errant swipes of the blade came close to Tove, but she seemed to use the strikes to draw her attackers in close.

When the last of them were cut down, they rejoined Erik and a deafening horn sounded. The valkyries turned their eyes to Erik all at once and he felt his blood run cold. He readied himself, Tove and Ljunge taking his lead and preparing for a fight even as they were exhausted from the one before.

A single pair of doors just in front of him opened and a woman with long, golden-brown hair walked from them. She was dressed in flowing white and stopped as the doors closed behind her. She smiled at Erik.

CHAPTER THIRTY-FOUR

SHE SEEMED TO HOVER UNDER THE WHITE, FLOWING GOWN, almost radiant in the midday sun. Her face was gentle and her smile was calm. Erik found it hard to pull his eyes away from the woman, beautiful as she was. He did, looking up to the balcony. The valkyries had returned to Valhalla, leaving him in the yard with only the woman, Ljunge, and Tove. It did little to calm him, only raised more questions.

The woman came to a stop just outside arm's reach, smiling politely.

"Welcome, Haki Erik Styrsson, to Valhalla."

She gave a small bow, large breasts swaying under the thin cloth she wore. Behind him, Erik heard Tove punch

Ljunge. For a moment, he relaxed.

"It wasn't a very warm welcome."

"You must have many concerns." It was all she did to address his statement. "I am called Eir and I am the highest of valkyries currently at Valhalla, so I have been sent to see to you." She looked him over, at no point so much as sparing a glance for Tove or Ljunge. "If you are wounded, I will care for you."

"I'm fine." Noticing her focus so completely on him pulled the reality of where he stood back into his mind. "What's the game here? Are you going to kill me? Where's Göll?"

She kept her pleasant smile, seeming for all the world like she could not feel any other emotion. "I have come to see you inside. You are…" She paused, her smile not fading. "You are a unique presence. Göll has been prepared to stand with you as you face Odin. He has called to have you brought before him."

Erik's eyes narrowed, the sense of a threat rolled through him. Her phrasing was something he could not rightly ignore. Facing Odin could mean many things and he doubted the valkyrie would explain herself even if pressed on the matter.

She turned, looking over a shoulder with the same smile. "If you would follow me, I will show you to Valhalla and your destiny."

Göll was inside. There was no other place to go. He could neither see the square nor the forest. Erik had locked them into whatever awaited them inside the moment he set foot on the battlefield. He stood in his place, Eir walking a ways away and turning to wait for him, no sense of impatience about her.

He turned to his companions. "Look, whatever this is, if things go bad, run."

Tove shook her head. "Why would we leave you? We are a warband."

Ljunge shrugged. "As simple as she is most times, the

girl says some good things. Go and see what waits for us in Valhalla."

Erik pulled a breath and shut his eyes, letting it out. Tove put a hand on his arm, smiling up at him when he opened his eyes again. She spun him around and pushed him toward Eir.

The valkyrie resumed leading them into the open doors when Erik walked toward her. Inside the doors was a narrow room with a dozen smaller openings that led into winding, single-file hallways. Light seemed to fill every inch of the space, though it came from nowhere. Exquisite gold-trimmed, stone statues of warring men and stoic gods were placed throughout. Runes praising Odin were carved into every wall along where the stone met the gold ceiling, the shields that formed it glimmering above them. Even the walls held paintings and tapestries showing great battles of both men and gods. They bled from one to another. Views of the Aesir and the Vanir clashing gave way to scenes of long dead kings of men where valkyries watched. Eir led them through the winding cathedral, built in honor of glorious death, until they came to a door. She pushed it open and Erik followed her out into a towering hall. It was empty of any furniture and the walls were lined with horns and weapons and more statues. Beams of light shone down impossibly from each side of the room. Erik could smell the faint lingering odor of ale.

Eir walked them all to the center of the floor and back toward a large door with torches to either side. The door was on flat ground, while another at the far end of the hall sat up a few stairs at the far edge of a landing.

Their guide turned to them, smiling. "You will await your audience here, in this spot." She nodded before turning and starting across the hall. As she moved down the carpet, the doors at the far end of the hall opened and Erik heard the familiar hiss of valkyrie wings in the air.

They poured in, four at a time, flying up and lining the

walls of the hall, the hiss quieting as they stood themselves on small outcroppings. There were dozens, they all stared at him with empty eyes. Göll was brought in, escorted by two more of her kind. Her head was down and she barely put any strength into her steps as she walked across the room. She was brought to his side and left there, the valkyries taking their places along the wall. She did not look up at him, only kept her eyes toward the ground. The necklace he'd given her was still around her neck.

"Göll. Hey. Hey!"

He reached out for her, but before his hand came to her arm, Eir cleared her throat.

"You will now have your audience with the Allfather."

Eir walked to the side, stopping just past the edge of the door. It came open and the feel in the air changed immediately. Erik's head began to spin, as if he were under a wave, being dragged across the bottom of the sea. An enormous man, old and without a hint of joy in his face entered the room. He wore armor made of leather and plate and on his back was a spear that seemed to repulse Erik's eyes from even attempting to look at the tip. It was unmistakably Odin, King of the Gods and Wanderer and so many other things. Erik felt the power rise inside of him, his hands trembling in terror just from the presence of the Aesir before him. He stood in the presence of a god and his body knew it more honestly than he could fathom.

"You." The word from Odin's lips seemed to ring on forever, lost down a well with no bottom. "You dare to come to this place. After all my warnings." The mighty king snarled, lips curling in anger. "And one of my own would bring you. Your influence has pulled her from my control. But no longer." Odin shook his head, fire burning behind disappointed eyes. "You have come to bring ruin, Haki Erik Styrsson. To us all. And for it, I will see you destroyed, along with all those who would aid you. Even my own."

Anger rose behind the fear, Erik willing his body to

move, his mouth to speak.

"What would you say for yourself? A creature such as you, born of mistakes? Do you regret the crimes you would commit against us all?"

Erik shook free of the oppressive air around him. "I don't know what the fuck you're talking about. I haven't done anything."

Odin's face changed, flashing what Erik swore was fear for only a moment before settling to an impressed calm. "You bark, baring your teeth to claim innocence. And yet you stand in my hall with a warband. Corrupting my very precious daughters, wounding them." His voice flared, the power of it pushing Erik backward. "That you would so besmirch my good will! That you would ignore my attempts to hand you salvation! You must be destroyed!"

"Fuck you, old man!" The rage in him flared, pulling him free of the grip of Odin's power fully. "You want to kill me? Huh?! Haven't your valkyries done it enough?"

Odin clenched his jaw, the hate in his eyes was pure and powerful. "You have forced my hand, Haki Erik Styrsson. Göll will be destroyed and you will see my pain. Then you will be undone."

"You won't fucking touch her!" Erik's voice rose to a roar, the windows shaking as he screamed the words. "Understand me?!"

Odin's eyes opened wide. The fear was there, Erik saw it. The Allfather's eyebrows twitched. "You... you! I will not let Skuld's words come to pass!" His voice was paranoid, nervous, not at all the godly thunder it had been. "Gunnr!" A valkyrie flew down to his side instantly. "Destroy Göll!"

He laid a hand on the valkyrie and the color of her spear shifted to a deep purple, almost black at the center of the blade. Göll did not move or even look as Gunnr charged. Erik felt his body push through the air as he rushed in front of Göll, the spear nearly at him already. He balled his fist and swung at the weapon. It shattered in the valkyrie's hand, but she did not stop. Erik had counted on it.

His other fist came up, elbow cocked. He put all the energy he could find inside his body into the blow, turning his body to put his weight behind it. He struck squarely on Gunnr's face, her cheek crackling under his fist. He let out a guttural yell that shook the very walls of Valhalla and pushed through any resistance he felt. The valkyrie came to pieces, her blood and skin splitting. The pieces turned to shimmering rubies and scattered across the hall. Gunnr was gone.

Erik stood and let another yell ring out.

Odin bristled, his rage growing to match Erik's own. "Kill them!" The valkyries hesitated. Madness flashed again in Odin's eyes, quickly subsumed by the rage. "Now!" His voice shattered the windows of the hall and the valkyries took to the air. Göll dropped to her knees, screaming. She fell over to her side, wrapping her arms tight around her chest. Erik saw Odin take a step, knowing he could not turn to face his warband. Behind he heard the sounds of battle. Ljunge gasped first and then came a scream from Tove. They were lost behind him. The valkyries did not set upon Göll, only turned.

Odin came to the first step of his landing, his foot coming down. Fire in his eyes, he drew Gungnir from his back. Erik's body screamed in rebellion, begging him to flee but he would not take himself from Göll's side.

Behind he heard the valkyries scatter and the doors to Valhalla flew open, a hot wind carried behind them. Göll's pained screams stopped and she lay still on the floor. Erik did not pull his eyes from Odin, only listened. Odin's eyes left Erik and the rage became indignance.

"Why do you defile my hall, giantess?"

Erik turned, his eyes finding Hel standing in the doorway, Vár at her side. She was taller than Modgudr in spite of her appearance in Midgard and now wore a flowing dress that seemed to shift from red to black as the light hit it.

"Oh don't look at me like that, Odin." She sighed. "I'm

only here to keep up my end of a bargain."

"You would interfere in this?"

"I would." She chuckled, waving Vár toward Erik. "Is there any reason I shouldn't?"

Odin lifted his head, looking down at Hel, still holding Gungnir in his hands. He pointed the spear at Erik. "You know what he is. And yet you would stop me? Is that what you wish on us all?"

Hel laughed mockingly. "Of course I know. Why would I bother with him if I didn't?" She smiled coyly. "But a bargain is still a bargain."

"And why should I not be rid of him? What do I care for your bargains?"

Hel's face darkened but the smile remained, daring Odin to defy her. "You can destroy him. Go ahead. But you know I'll have you return what's mine if you do... all of it." Her tone changed to one that was almost chipper. "Or, you can let him walk out of this wonderful hall and return to my wonderful city. I mean, either one works for me, but since I came all the way here, I don't feel like leaving without a gift."

Odin seethed, his teeth grinding. Without a word, he put Gungnir back in its place and stormed out of the hall. The valkyries left with him and the hall stood empty again, except for Erik, Göll, Hel, and Vár. Hel immediately turned and took her leave.

"Just in case I need to say it myself... Come see me, Erik. We have a lot to discuss."

With that she was gone, Vár still at his side. He ignored her, crouching beside Göll. She was breathing, but exhausted. Erik lifted her, struggling to hold her up with exhaustion coursing through his body. The blow that killed Gunnr had been nearly all the strength in him. He walked from the hall with Vár beside him. She kept close to him as they walked into the square. It was empty now, quiet.

Erik looked at Vár. "Why are you here?"

"Seems I'm not allowed to watch you from a distance

anymore. Hardly my own choice." She looked him over. "Though, you are certainly more interesting than Hel had said. Saving a murderess and standing against the Allfather." She laughed. "Very interesting."

They returned to the streetcar, Erik eager to return to the hotel and make sure that Tove and Ljunge were still alive. There was no way of knowing if they were. Vár offered no help, saying she'd not had the pleasure of dying in Odin's hall of doomed men.

He reached the hotel, carrying Göll upstairs. She had shown no sign of waking during their trip and her breath was still shallow. It was stable enough, though. The clerk seemed surprised to see him return but came to Erik anyway when he entered.

"Y-y-you have... returned? From Valhalla?"

Erik walked past the man, who turned, following him. "Yeah. Seems like it."

"That is... very..." The clerk cleared his throat. "Of course, you are still welcome. Your party has returned... they... the girl seems worse for the wear but the man— such a charming man— he said it would be alright." The clerk entered the elevator and pressed the button for the top floor. "They are in the same room."

Erik thanked the clerk, carrying Göll to the door. He could hear Tove screaming from the far side. Vár opened it and Ljunge stood, hands going to the empty sheaths at his sides.

"Erik." He calmed seeing Erik. "And the valkyrie." He chuckled. "I hadn't expected either of you, if I'm honest." Ljunge smiled, giving an exaggerated bow to Vár who scoffed and went to find a chair.

Erik took Göll to the bed, laying her beside Tove before collapsing onto a couch and giving a heavy sigh.

"I'm hungry."

"Punching a valkyrie hard enough to turn her to gemstones likely does that to a man. Not that I'd know." Ljunge was looking at Vár. "Why is Hel's seductress here?"

Vár looked at Ljunge. "You would do well to mind how you speak of me."

Ljunge looked at Erik, eyes wide. "I like her, Erik."

As much as the comfort of Ljunge's carefree nature was welcome, Erik could not stop himself worrying about Göll. He would have to go and see Hel and have some answers to his questions. He sat up on the couch.

"Ljunge. Go order some food. I'll explain everything that happened in Valhalla." He paused. "Well, all the parts I understand." Erik looked at Göll lying motionless on the bed. "I'll be asking Hel about the rest."

CHAPTER
THIRTY-FIVE

LJUNGE BROUGHT FOOD, INCLUDING SOME FOR TOVE, IN case she made it past her pain, and some for Vár, likely in case she would like him better for having done so. She ate the food but showed no real appreciation for Ljunge's effort. Though Tove had stopped her screaming, she was still incapable of moving for the most part.

When the meal was done, Ljunge sat himself unnecessarily close to Vár and acted as though it was incidental, turning the attention to Erik.

"What plans do you have?"

Erik sighed, unsure exactly what it was he intended to do. "Assuming Hel has no intention of carrying on, I plan on finding out what we're supposed to do now." Erik buried his head in his hands in frustration for a moment. Without moving his hands, he continued. "It seems pretty obvious that *fucking Odin* wants to kill me. That's a pretty new piece of information to deal with."

Ljunge crossed his legs, leaning toward Vár. "Well, what have you done to him?"

"Nothing. I didn't even believe in him until I ended up getting stabbed in the lung by flying crazies. Maybe a few hours before, actually, but that's not really important."

"You did not believe in Odin?" Ljunge gave a disbelieving laugh. "Who do you imagine made humans?"

Erik held up a hand. "That's really going to take a long time to explain. I was wrong. I'm okay with that. It doesn't matter. The point is I didn't do anything. I was just... I lived in an apartment, not that you know what that is, but I wasn't important."

Vár drank from a cup of tea Ljunge had brought. "He speaks the truth. He was wholly unimportant in Midgard. Pathetic by most measures. And weak. Not even a hair on his chin." Erik started to complain but Vár finished her thought. "He's come a long way."

He was taken aback by the comment. "I don't like that you're being nice to me."

"Honesty is neither kind nor rude." Vár sighed and swatted Ljunge who'd gotten too close. The swipe drew blood from a fine cut. He did not lean away. "I am growing very weary of being in a room with this man."

Ljunge leaned back. "Yes, but he leads the warband so it falls to us to put up with him." He shook his head mournfully. "A pity I wasn't picked. You can admit that you feel as much, Vár."

Vár stood. "How long do you intend on sitting in this room, Haki Erik Styrsson?"

Erik rubbed his temples. "Until Tove can walk. And then we'll go to Hel's... keep? Castle? Her whatever."

She walked to Erik's place on the couch, grabbing his arm and pulling him up. "Your clothes are a mess. I won't have you see my mistress in them and I will not sit in a room with a living mistake of personal judgement for any longer." She turned. "Pervert, you will watch the two that remain here, do you understand me?"

Ljunge gave a wide smile. "I will do anything that pleases you, Vár."

She shivered, pulling Erik toward the door. Erik pulled back stopping short.

"What about an attack? Won't they come for Göll?"

Vár pulled the door open, shaking her head. "Odin would not risk his precious einherjar for an ale-bearer. A norn, perhaps. Likely he has already fled to Asgard and is waiting to see what it is that you do." She turned, walking into the hall. "If you are satisfied then follow me. We will return for them when you are well-dressed."

Erik followed Vár out into the elevator and down through the lobby. When they were out on the sidewalk, she slowed her brisk pace, falling back to Erik's side. She looked at him quietly as they walked toward the street full of shops he'd been to only a few days before.

"What?"

"You are strange to me."

"I can imagine. Mind if I ask some questions?"

"I will answer what I can."

"How long have you served Hel?"

She thought on it for a moment. "Hm. More than a thousand years, if I were to guess. The days fall together after so long."

"And you remember all of them? People don't go crazy? I'd probably lose it after farming for a few hundred years."

"They remember enough. My mistress is subtle and lifting the weight of the ages is not something simply done. She understands their minds well enough."

"Magic, then."

"Crassly put, but if it will move you on to a more interesting question..."

"Why serve her?"

"Hel is the only sane creature in the nine worlds." Vár turned to him, her eyes serious. "You would do well to keep that in mind. And to respect it. That is all I will say. You may ask her questions about herself."

Erik laughed absently, looking around the street. "So you're upset I didn't ask more things about you in particular? Like what's your favorite meal."

"I felt no such thing. And I enjoy fried things."

He smiled, not letting Vár see. It was possible she wasn't as bad as she seemed. "Thanks, by the way."

She looked at him out of the corner of her eye. "For?"

"Mystery swords. Standing between me and a valkyrie. Stabbing me in the lung."

It was meant half as a joke, the stabbing bit. She'd helped in ways he hadn't understood at the time and, in truth, he wanted some reaction beyond what she normally gave.

She said nothing, the rest of the walk being a quiet one. They arrived at a store selling clothing. Vár went in first and the clerk there seemed shocked to see her.

"Madame Vár! I was not aware you were nearby. I apologize for... for... being... slack?" An apology that made no sense. "Of course, whatever you need will be supplied."

"Didn't realize you were famous."

Vár ignored the clerk, answering Erik. "I am known." She turned her attention then to the panicking girl. "Dress this one. He's seeing Hel. And bring a dress, one smaller than mine. Sized... nearly for a child. Or a girl who looks like a child. Like mine but more colorful. It should please the farm girl, yes?" She asked the question to Erik, not expecting an answer and turned back to the clerk. "And an outfit a fool might wear."

"Yes, at once."

It was clear from the girl's face that she hadn't understood for a moment what it was that Vár had meant by the last part, but she set about her work, measuring Erik. When she was done, she turned to Vár.

"Is... is the fool... is he roughly the same size as this man?"

"It does not matter. A potato sack would do, so long as it is clean."

The girl nodded, nervous to the point of terror, and went into the back. She returned with a dark pair of pants for Erik, alongside a button up shirt, waistcoat, and an overcoat. He was sent to a changing room. It was finer than what he'd been given by Modgudr, but it fit awkwardly.

The clerk seemed pleased with it. "I will make adjustments, it shouldn't take a moment."

He returned to his old clothes and stood waiting with Vár. People who passed the shop saw her and continued on.

"Are people scared of you?"

Vár looked over her shoulder out the door. "Most people are scared of me, yes. It saves me a great deal of trouble."

"Don't you get lonely?"

Vár sighed, immediately annoyed at the question. "You are not so stupid as to ask such a question, Erik. I am not fooled by your amiable face and easy nature. I've seen you in thought. But since you asked, I will answer. I do not consider the unwelcome praise of simple people to be companionship. I am not lonely, and if I were, that would hardly remedy it."

"Well, if you want a friend, you can just tell me." He held back a laugh. "You don't have to act so tough around me."

"This is where you expect me to laugh and give you a playful hit on your arm, isn't it? I am not your farm girl." She looked at him. "I find you interesting. Hel has not told me what it is you are, but even I see there is something."

The clerk came back and Erik tried on the clothes again. They were a perfect fit. His old clothes were wrapped into a cloth bundle and the clothes Vár had ordered into another and they were sent on their way.

Ljunge stood when they returned to the room, Vár throwing the bundle at him. Tove was sitting in the bed, Erik went to her as Ljunge began to unwrap the bundle in his excitement.

"Are you alright?"

Tove looked down at her legs. "I am... I... thought you would not return from Valhalla."

Erik chuckled. "That's a solid guess. Hel came."

"Ljunge told me all that you told him. We will go and see her now?" Tove's hands were trembling, there was fear in her voice. "Has Odin forsaken us?"

It meant more to her than he could have known. There was no answer he could give to the question that would help her, not really.

"We're going to talk to Hel. I'll find out what I can."

She gripped the covers to at least try to stop herself shaking with worry. She nodded quietly, tears forming in her eyes.

Erik could not imagine how it must have felt to be hated by one's god. It was meaningless to him and Odin was only a legend who wanted him to be destroyed. For Tove it was not that way. Perhaps for Göll as well. Ljunge seemed unperturbed by the ire of a god and more interested in harassing Vár. He'd quickly changed clothes into a lemon-yellow outfit that Erik had just now seen.

Ljunge smiled at Erik when he laughed at the sight.

"It suits me well, does it not?"

Vár was visibly annoyed that Ljunge was so pleased with the outfit. Even Tove laughed at the sight, in spite of herself.

Erik turned back to her. "We're going whenever you're ready."

She gave a determined nod. "I am ready." She moved to the edge of the bed and stood, wincing.

Ljunge threw Tove the dress and she looked it over.

"How will I fight in this if we are attacked?"

Vár scoffed. "The same as you fight in anything else. Or

would an enemy seeing your crotch render you unable to fight?"

Tove's expression went immediately angry. She walked into the bathroom in a huff and changed there. The dress fit her well enough. It was well-made with fine fabrics. Thick blue and tan cotton with intricate silk designs between the cotton pieces. She offered no complaints after having put it on and, if Erik wasn't wrong, seemed somewhat pleased to be wearing it.

Erik lifted Göll from the bed and they left, taking a streetcar to the center of the city. They went to the north, through a portion of the city that saw much more variety in the building design and the colors present. It was the closest to a difference in affluence among the people in Helborgen that Erik had seen. Some of the things there looked nearly modern. It reminded him that there had been no telephones or radios, but that the kitchens seemed fairly modern among other oddities.

"Vár, why are there no phones or radios or anything?"

Ljunge and Tove looked at him as though he'd spoke another language but Vár just kept walking.

"Too much comfort makes people boring."

It was all she said. Hel's keep came into view past the end of the northern part of the city. It was set across a sprawling, nearly empty lot, paved flat. The only features in the lot proper were a pair of hulking, obsidian dog statues. They seemed to follow Erik. They were only a dozen yards from walking between the twenty-foot statues when Erik realized they *were* following him. The necks had turned ever so slightly.

They continued past them and Erik could swear he heard them growl as he came to the stairs that led up to the main entrance. It was a simple staircase, if very large. It again reminded him that he was among things he could not understand. At the top landing, steel doors stood in front of them. They were thick, attached to heavy frames set into what looked like solid slabs of stone. There were intricate carvings along them. Erik recognized some of the figures as gods and goddesses, all of them bowing before Hel or falling before her in one way or another.

The doors opened without Vár having to make their arrival known and they walked through, the doors shutting behind without anyone in attendance. Servants came immediately moving in parallel to them without saying a word. Both were women dressed in black and gold. The outfits, in their color at least, bore a resemblance to what Vár often wore, though she favored red over gold in what Erik had seen at least.

They came to a stop at a waiting room off the main hallway. It looked much the same as the hotel lobby, though dressed in far more red and with more even lighting. Food was waiting there and Vár stopped at the door.

"Your warband will wait here."

Tove protested immediately. "And why should we do that?!"

Vár looked at her, no hint of hesitation in the answer. "What Hel has to say to the leader of your warband is not for you to hear. I can return you to your bed if you wish."

Tove's nose wrinkled, not liking the explanation but unable to argue against it. She turned to Erik instead. "Be wary."

Erik nodded. "Yeah, I will."

Ljunge and Tove went into the room and Vár continued showing him through the keep to wherever it was Hel was waiting.

"There is no cause for concern, Erik. If Hel meant you harm, she would not bother coming herself. Or having you brought here."

"I'm not sure where you learned to reassure people, but you're awful at it."

"I did not mean to reassure you."

Erik rolled his eyes. He had been carrying Göll for some time and even with whatever had snapped in him the day before, she was beginning to grow heavy. The power in him was not entirely constant, it seemed. Though he was far stronger than he had been.

The turns began to involve descending stairs and lights turned to torches. He was not brought to a grand hall, but to a blocky stone room with a stone table in the middle of it. Fire lit the place and Hel awaited him on the far end of the table. Vár saw him in, staying by the door. Hel looked past Erik.

"You can go, Vár." She nodded and was off. Hel patted a hand on the table. "Put her down here."

Erik gave Hel a deadpan stare. "You know how this looks, right?"

She shrugged casually, a gesture that seemed out of place considering the elegant dress she wore. "There are things I can't change, Erik. No need to be so stiff."

He sighed and, lacking for other options, placed Göll on the stone table, not stepping back from it.

Hel smiled at him mischievously. "Did you see the carvings? Out front?" She chuckled to herself. "They hate it so much." She sighed. "Oh, but you'll get all upset again if I carry on too long." She clapped her hands on the stone, taking a step back. "I should start at the beginning. Don't worry, I'll be quick. Humans, that's you, were created by Odin, Vili, and Ve. So, Odin has a very tenuous grasp on you even at the best of times. It upsets him, you see. Valkyries, they are not afforded that luxury." Hel pointed at Göll, knitting her brow when there was no movement. "Ah right. Of course. I figured you wouldn't be able to stand the noise."

Göll stretched out immediately, her muscles all taught and knotted. She let out a horrible scream, tears pouring from her eyes.

Hel laughed, raising her voice to shout over the screams. "You see, Odin can do as he likes with her. And this is what he likes."

"What are you doing?! Help her! You did it before, right?"

Erik put his hands on Göll, but she showed no sign of realizing it.

"I only made her quiet, you see. She has been in this pain since Valhalla. Odd you decided to keep her away so long."

Erik slammed his fist into the table. "Why are you telling me this? Just get to the fucking point!"

"So stubborn."

Göll went quiet again.

"She's still in pain, isn't she?"

"She is, and will be until you listen." Hel's face went grim. "Odin has... ways. Urges. Or did. Now he is a broken, paranoid fool. Ever since putting his eye down that well." Hel shrugged. "It's his fate."

"The point!"

"Calm down, Erik. I'll arrive there when I want to. For a man who has spent his time in my world frustrated by knowing so little, you've grown very impatient suddenly."

Erik snapped his mouth shut, looking down at Göll, trying to hold in his anger.

"Done? Good. So, Odin had a baby. Plenty, in fact. And very, very few of those babies had babies."

Erik's eyes turned up to Hel.

"I see you get where this is going. Odin is something of a very literal father figure for you. Or should be." She chuckled. "And now for the beginning of the interesting parts. He saw that all the others were chosen by valkyries and that they died in battle and on and on. But the woman who bore your ancestors? She married a coward. They fled to a farm on a tiny island and Odin simply forgot. No prowess in battle, no notice from an increasingly mad old god. It's good, right?" She laughed.

"Why does he want me dead?"

"No, no. There's an order to these things. You're upset that Göll is in pain, remember?"

Erik looked away, stomping his foot. "Yes. Fuck. Tell me something useful."

339

Hel pouted. "Not useful that you've got the blood of the Allfather? I mean, that's just being unreasonable, Erik." She sighed. "But I've promised you help and a story is hardly that." Hel returned to the table and Göll's limbs wrenched out, screams returning again. "Man can never steal from a god, Erik. Not really. But there aren't any men here— not exactly— so stealing a little valkyrie..." Hel eyed down at Göll.

"How?!"

She smiled. "Will yourself into the place that Odin sits. She is a piece of him. You must make her a piece of you."

Erik shook his head. "I don't..."

Hel shot him a coy smile. "The kiss of life."

"No, this... this is weird. You're fucking around."

Hel shrugged and Göll sucked in a breath, another scream erupting as soon as she had the air for it.

"How am I supposed to..."

Göll quieted.

Erik rolled his head back. "Okay, fine."

He leaned over her, his hand at her cheek. Her eyes opened, clear and icy blue. "Erik?"

He raised an eyebrow. "Sorry."

He put his lips to hers and felt Göll's chin press toward him. He could feel the very life flowing from him. The world became hazy as her cold lips flushed with warmth and she rose from the table, sitting, her hand on his chest.

He pulled back as Göll opened her eyes again. She looked down at him, realizing what had happened and shoved him away.

"What... what?!" She spun, seeing Hel. "No... Erik, what deal have you made? I..." She put a hand to her chest and looked back at Erik. "You... But you are human."

Erik stood up, holding his hands up. "She told me it was the only way to help you. And... I mean, it was nice." His knees went weak and he fell onto them. The hard stone was unforgiving. His vision blurred and returned, thoughts swirled in his head.

Hel snapped and his mind cleared. "That's better. Now, I think, since I got to witness such a beautiful scene, that Göll should share her secrets."

Erik stood, looking at Göll with curious eyes. She looked at Hel and back to Erik, desperation plain on her face.

Göll shook her head. "I have no secrets."

Hel rolled her head in annoyance. "Come on. Tell him why you are the only ale-bearer who still finds chosen? All of them with a particular name."

"...Haki." Erik whispered the name.

Göll came to him. "It was not... A seeress told me. She said that I would one day deliver to Valhalla a great warrior. One who would be remembered above all others ever brought to Odin's hall."

"Me? It can't be."

Göll would not meet his eyes. There was something she knew that Erik did not, that much was clear. He looked to Hel.

She raised her silver eyebrows in surprise. "Oh, me? Fine, if Göll wants to be bashful around the man who literally gave her a second chance at life." Hel came to the front of the stone table. Erik looked up at her, waiting. "There is a story. It says that when Odin tossed his eye down a well, he gained more than wisdom." She continued past, waving for them to follow. "He remembered all of the ages. Every Ragnarok. And he came to fear them." They climbed the stairs, Hel happy to let her story sit until she was back at the surface. She continued as they moved down a hallway. "The other gods, they have come to fear Ragnarok as well, hearing Odin's stories of the horror that awaits them. He wishes to break the unerring cycle of time."

They came into a grand hall, filled with light. Vár stood in the middle of it, looking at them silently. Hel walked to her and turned.

"He gathers power to himself, desperate to avoid his fate."

Hel smiled. "Let's tell another story, Vár."

Vár nodded. "It's time he knew."

"Another story, then. One Göll hasn't heard either. Odin came to the norns when he had chained mighty Fenrir. And he said 'What is there left? What could bring me to ruin?'" Hel smiled. "'A son by your own seed,' they said. 'A boy called Haki will bring Ragnarok.'"

Erik's eyes widened and Hel began to laugh.

"No... it can't be me."

Hel's laugh became an insane cackle. She drew a deep breath, satisfied with herself. She smiled down at Erik.

"Oh, it is." She placed a hand on his shoulder. "And you will need help."

THANKS FOR READING.

MORE AT
RPFBOOKS.COM

46034106R00197

Made in the USA
San Bernardino, CA
23 February 2017